TROPICAL

Heatwave

Dean Alleyne

Tropical Heatwave
Copyright © 2019 by Dean Alleyne

Library of Congress Control Number:	2019936769
ISBN-13: Paperback:	978-1-64151-773-7
PDF:	978-1-64151-774-4
ePub:	978-1-64151-775-1
Kindle:	978-1-64151-776-8

All rights reserved. No part of this publication may be reproduced, distributed, or transmitted in any form or by any means, including photocopying, recording, or other electronic or mechanical methods, without the prior written permission of the publisher or author, except in the case of brief quotations embodied in critical reviews and certain other noncommercial uses permitted by copyright law.

Although every precaution has been taken to verify the accuracy of the information contained herein, the author and publisher assume no responsibility for any errors or omissions. No liability is assumed for damages that may result from the use of information contained within.

Printed in the United States of America

LitFire LLC
1-800-511-9787
www.litfirepublishing.com
order@litfirepublishing.com

ACKNOWLEDGEMENTS

I would like to thank those friends without whose support and encouragement this novel might not have come about. I am especially indebted to John Prince of London UK, a friend and fellow head-teacher, for his inspiration and literary guidance; to Len and Marion Ray of Watford UK for their unfailing encouragement; to Carol McClary of Alberta, Canada, for her objective opinion and advice as I wrote each chapter. Finally, a special thanks to Angela and Kathie and all the staff at Airdrie Public Library, Alberta, Canada, for their assistance.

1

A cool afternoon breeze ruffled the curtains of an open window in a large two-gabled chattel house in suburban Bridgetown, bringing welcome relief to those inside suffering under the intense heat of a mid-afternoon Caribbean sun. The full-length veranda at the front, suggested the occupants were not working class though not quite middle-class. In Barbados, like some other Caribbean islands, the design of a house said a lot about its occupants. For instance, a single gabbled house with no veranda suggested a lower standard of living than a two-gabbled house with a veranda. The window design was also significant. Those with shutters only generally suggested a living standard lower than those with sash windows and glass panes. The 'grandfather's clock' in the corner struck three. The cat, curled up on the floor having a siesta, jumped through the nearest open window. In the corner opposite, was an indoor palm which reflected the rays of mid-afternoon sun falling softly on its green elongated leaves wafting gently in the incoming breeze.

Dennis, dressed in a dark-grey suit, crisp white shirt and mottled tie, all supported by a pair of shining black shoes, emerged from one bedroom accompanied by a tall man in black, whose expression bordered on a painful grin. He had sat quietly in one corner of the bedroom, as Dennis clambered into an outfit without any knowledge of how it got there. He was sure he did not buy the outfit. *'Am I in a dream, it can't be, can it?"* he pondered, his body beginning to stiffen with fear. Marriage was not the thing he wanted, and, like the cat, he felt like bolting, but there was no hiding place from what was about to happen. Dennis was trapped in a social system grounded in religion which scorned having children out of wedlock in general and among teachers in particular. The refusal to marry a girl whom, as a teacher you had made pregnant, could result in immediate dismissal by any presiding vicar in Anglican Church schools of which they were quite a few at that time. And as the Church was closely associated with the state, it meant no further employment in any other government department. This made life extremely difficult for the unfortunate person for, not only did you make a dive in social status, it also became very difficult to get another job in an island with so small an economic base. Dennis was just about to be saved from falling into such an abyss.

After a long wordless moment, Susan emerged wearing a modest white dress with a shoulder length veil and escorted by another man in a dark suit. This jolted Dennis into realising it was not something from *Alice in Wonderland* but a live scene in which he was about to play a major role. Susan was the eldest of three children and, being the first, often found herself having to look after her younger siblings from a very early age due to the occasional but prolonged illness of her mother. She also found herself having to assist in a small two-door shop owned by her parents, particularly when her father would return to Trinidad after a short break to work as an engineer in the oil field. Sadly, as a result, she was denied a secondary education.

On the other hand, Dennis had received the Rolls Royce of education Barbados had to offer and had just entered the teaching service with high hopes of one day becoming an academic and reaching the top of his profession. He saw himself as the flagship of the family, for no one in his or previous generations of his family had ever attended a secondary school. He had always done very well at primary school and was considered by his parents and grand-parents as having what it took to do well at secondary level. It was a view supported by a private tutor who prepared him for the entrance examination to his first secondary school. The tutor saw him as dedicated and with a burning desire to do well.

Dennis and Susan met in the sitting-room to be married by the head of the Pentecostal Church in Barbados, a short, burly character who found it difficult to break a smile across a face that seemed as rigid as if set in a mould. He was the kind of man whose looks alone drove fear through the veins of many people and was known to run the Pentecostal churches with a rod of iron. Dennis had seen him visit the Pentecostal church in his village on many occasions but, until now, he was at a safe distance. The sitting room was modestly furnished with one double cane-bottomed mahogany chair and three singles all adorned with white laced doilies and, for this occasion, a small vase of flowers had been added. In the middle was a small table with a book opened at what Dennis supposed was the marriage ceremony. Apart from Eunice, Susan's mother, a woman of about fifty, bespectacled and neatly dressed, the only others present were these two men in dark suits - witnesses Dennis later found out - whom he had never seen before. It was as though they were plucked from the air or hurriedly dragged in from the street. Eunice knew that, with a good secondary education, Susan's two younger sisters would have a very good chance of finding desirable husbands, but that since Susan was unfortunate not to have attended secondary school, her chances of doing so would be less. She was therefore not about to allow this opportunity for getting Susan married to a young teacher slip by. Dennis cleared his throat and the man standing beside Dennis gave him a side glance.

"I think you better mop your brow," he suggested, where upon Dennis nervously retrieved a white hanky from his inside pocket and did so. The intense heat of the afternoon, plus a feeling of anxiety and utter helplessness, set his sweat glands into overdrive causing beads of perspiration to pop out all over his face, sometimes forming what looked like miniature rivulets flowing down his face onto the front of his white shirt. So intense was the heat, that Eunice had no alternative but to open the street door to allow more air to flow in. Standing there, listening to and following the instructions of the pastor, Dennis kept thinking, '*Who are these men and where did they come from, and who seem ready to plunge me into the depth of the unknown?*' It was a carefully choreographed scene but one for which he had no chance to rehearse. Yes, it was a shot-gun wedding.

Susan was eighteen. Dennis was nineteen. But even at this stage there was no inner voice whispering to them that they loved each other. Yet in less than thirty minutes they were husband and wife and in another hour, they had started their honeymoon in a small self-catering house in Bathsheba on east coast Barbados. It was one of ten timber-framed beach-houses, all painted grey and white, each with its veranda looking out to non-stop white crested breakers barrelling in and crashing onto submerged flat rock before making their way up a sandy beach. A scattering of casuarina and coconut trees set within luscious tropical vegetation, formed the backdrop to the line of houses enhancing the natural beauty of the crescent-shaped bay. Only a narrow tarmac road separated the houses from the beach which formed part of the sprawling crescent-shaped bay of Bathsheba.

What should have been a happy moment was already beginning to cause Dennis much mental turmoil for he had no control over the unfolding drama even though he was a key player. A pang of restless worry seized him. *'Who bought my suit? How did they know my size? And who were those two men? Where did they suddenly appear from? And who is it that arranged this wedding, this honeymoon and beach-house?'* There seemed no end to the questions and certainly no answers as he found himself swept along in a current from which he had no escape. It was like a canoeist who, having lost his oars, finds himself speedily swept along to a ragging waterfall.

It was mid-morning the next day and the azure blue of the sky was only momentarily broken by the occasional wisp of a high cirrus cloud. A couple of humming birds darted here and there between crotons and hibiscus at the front of the house. Dennis sat in the veranda with his feet on the bannister and crossed at the ankles. He was focussing on the foam crested waves rolling non-stop to the shore as he tried desperately to bring some kind of meaning to what had happened. The entire episode had taken place even without the knowledge of his parents, brothers or any family. There was no festivity, no three-tier cake, no roast goat, and no rum and coconut water. So deep in concentration was he that, were it not for a fruit vendor seeking his custom, he would not have heard footsteps from behind. It was the resident housekeeper, a woman of about forty-five, bringing him a glass of coconut water for, even at ten o'clock, it was already scorching, forcing Dennis to contemplate an early dip. With a duster in her hand, she leaned against the bannister facing him with her back to the sea, the breeze gently flapping her collar. She looked at him painfully for everything about him screamed regret. Nothing was said for a few moments, but Dennis was eloquent in his silence.

"What's the matter Dennis, you don't look very happy?" she remarked, looking somewhat concerned. He took three sips of the coconut water and slowly replaced the glass on the small table next to him. An incoming wave crashed against a large rock just off the shore, sending white foam five meters into the air and momentarily catching his attention before he glanced at her with a look of despair. Betty the housekeeper, was a woman who was clearly one of vast experience and a good insight into how most mothers with girls would tend to think.

"I wish I could tell you," he muttered with his hands clasped behind his head. In this pensive mood, he was reliving some of the wonderful moments he enjoyed with girls both while at school and after, the picnics, the beach parties and the young women whom he thought would have been more in-tuned with his roadmap for the future. But he also knew that Susan would find it very difficult to play a significant part in his game plan and it was with regret that he realised they were mere visitors in each other's world.

"Don't worry, I think I gleaned certain things from a conversation I had with your mother-in-law," she said quietly, looking around to make sure that nobody was in hearing distance. Dennis returned the chair to its upright position and gave her his undivided attention. "You see Dennis, you were trapped," she exclaimed, and Dennis eyes immediately grew fifty per cent larger. "Susan's mother saw you as a good catch. After all, you are a young teacher while her daughter did not even go to secondary school and, from what I can see, the marriage was well planned. You were not to know what was going on because they knew that you would have told your parents who would have objected." Dennis took a large bite of a mango he had bought from the vendor and then refocused his attention. "They also knew that, in your position as a teacher, you would not have been allowed to continue teaching in a church school without marrying the girl whom you had made pregnant, especially since your mother-in-law and the village vicar are such close friends."

"How did you get her to tell you this?" asked Dennis, now looking somewhat perplexed. The housekeeper cleared her throat and whispered, leaning forward as though she expected to hear footsteps on the wooden floor at any moment.

"Listen to me young fellow, Eunice didn't just volunteer to tell me. It was merely because I observed that, when you arrived yesterday evening, there was nothing about you to say you were just married. I have been around long enough to know these things. For the entire evening, you seemed to be always in a quiet mood, saying hardly anything but always thinking. When you went to bed, I started a conversation that would force her to come out with bits of information related to the wedding." Dennis narrowed his eyes. "This marriage is nothing you did, it was something done for you, and someone else was involved, a man but I didn't get his name although she did mention the word *uncle* at one time. You were simply a pawn on their chessboard," she added. Dennis looked at her in sheer amazement. "But I know what you want right now," she said, before disappearing quickly to return with another glass of coconut water only this time, laced with rum. But such information triggered a number of thoughts in his mind as the housekeeper went about her business of dusting.

****

Susan and Dennis had stumbled into each other less than three months before on a west coast beach where he often did a morning jog. The tropical orb was already making its presence felt as Dennis did his usual run on an almost deserted sandy beach, pausing only momentarily to maximize his intake of sea air infused with the raw smell of seaweed. Small fishing boats that were at sea all night, were already making their way to a small fishing village further along the coast. It attracted his attention until, in the distance and fast approaching, was another jogger: short, with large brown eyes. As the gap between them narrowed, her slender body grew larger revealing a shape accentuated by a tight-fitting swimsuit that responded colourfully in the sunshine falling gently on her wet ebony skin. They crossed each other with a quick hello carried on an inviting look. Within ten seconds, the splashing sound of jogging feet on damp sand suddenly stopped. Dennis pulled up, turned and gazed steadfastly at the moving figure disappearing in the distance. He gathered a few pebbles in his hand and commenced throwing them out to sea. *'I wonder who is she and where is she from? I have never seen her on this beach before. Perhaps, if I time it well, I might see her here again tomorrow'*, he pondered. Next day the beach was again almost deserted, but Dennis was rewarded with a scene in which they were the only two players for there she was on her run. Fired up with imagination, he asked, and was allowed to join her.

"Are you from around these parts?" he asked, his voice now jerking with every stride. "No, I am from St. George, but I am here spending some time with my aunt. I am sure you know that St. George is one of the two parishes in Barbados without any sea, and I love the sea." She seemed as anxious as Dennis to strike up a chat, but it soon became apparent that, for conversation to run smoothly, they would have to stop jogging. Lying facing each other on the sand, they allowed the ebb and flow of gentle waves to envelop them. Conversation was now flowing as smoothly as the saline ripples caressing their bodies. They made figures in the soft sand with their fingers only to see them repeatedly washed away by receding ripples. Now caught up with infatuation, little did they know that their lives were about to take a turn and that a new chapter was about to be written.

They met on a few occasions after that but soon realized that, to allow themselves to fall in love, would do neither of them any good. Family background and deeply entrenched social customs meant it would be better to end this episode as quickly as it had started but, in the excitement generated by two young and inexperienced people, Susan became pregnant. They both knew they were not in love but Eunice, Susan's mother, had other ideas. In her eyes, Dennis was a catch not to be missed. He hardly knew Susan but, there he was, now caught between a rock and a hard cliff.

Dennis finished the rum and coconut water and asked the housekeeper for a cold beer. He drank half and tilted the chair on its hind legs again, this time allowing his head to rest on the window shutter behind him. The large rock less than 100 meters standing majestically out of the water like a giant mushroom, due to long-standing marine and wind erosion over many years, again caught his attention. It was a rock frequently displayed in brochures on tourism in Barbados and had become internationally known. Gazing at this majestic work of nature, he recalled the days when he and his friends as small boys would walk quite a distance along the beach from Belleplaine to reach this rock. It was the very rock from which they would spend much time jumping into the breakers which would take them to shore. He had hoped that these reflections would help him cope with the agony he was experiencing but, instead, they served to bring his current thoughts into sharp focus.

'*What have I done? What am I doing here? What am I even doing married? How did this all happen? Okay, I know she is pregnant, but how could I be that stupid as to get married and without my parents knowing? I am not even in love with her. My friends are still free to do what they like and here am I, a married man.*' It was as though he had just emerged from a bad dream. Dennis needed more than a sea-breeze or the lapping of waves on a sandy beach to cool a brain now running hot. While in this heated mood, Susan joined him, carrying a bottle of lemonade which she poured into a glass with ice and, like the housekeeper before her, she propped up against the bannister directly opposite Dennis. A quick glance at his expressionless face made her's tightened. She felt his thoughts were not encouraging. He allowed the two front legs of the chair to return firmly on the floor and then finished the beer. Holding his head in his hands, he leaned forward allowing his chin to rest on the bannister and then closed his eyes for a moment to slow down the flow of emotions this hasty marriage had set in motion. It was a drawn-out stillness not typical of newly-weds on their honeymoon.

"I was just here thinking that we really don't know much about each other and here we are married," with a screwed-up face and sounded unhappy. Just at that moment, a small flock of blackbirds foraging among sea-grape trees for ripe fruit, took to flight. They were obviously disturbed by a group of five lads coming up the beach, stopping momentarily to pluck winkles from partly submerged flat rock and who themselves wanted to share the succulent fruit. With his brain now in re-wind mode, Dennis recalled how he and his friends as small boys did a similar thing after a game of beach cricket. Popping up on his mental screen too were the many days during the summer holidays when they would walk for miles across harvested cane-fields or go mango and cashew-scrumping in the hills outside the village, or the fun they had sharing jokes about each other particularly on moonlit nights. Now here he was thrust into a role for which he was not prepared. To him, that freedom now seemed light years away from his current situation. It was the kind of morning that impelled Eunice and the housekeeper to have a splash in a rock pool, a relatively safe place near the shore for non-swimmers. Susan placed her lemonade on the small side table and looked at Dennis with a half grin and an angled head.

"What? Are you scared? Are you suddenly thinking I am not good enough for you? Perhaps you are thinking you should have waited and married one of your girlfriends from school, you know, one of those educated ones. It isn't my fault I didn't go to secondary school. I didn't have a chance because my mother was often sick for long periods of time leaving me as the oldest to look after my two younger sisters. Not everybody was as lucky as you." She railed at him. He looked at her with no idea what to say for he knew that much of what she said was the truth. He merely shrugged his shoulders and returned his focus to the large rock, wishing he could put back the hands of the clock. In a strange way, he felt she had hit the nail on the head for he thought a great injustice had been done to both of them by a woman whose sole intent was to get her daughter married off at all costs. For her, it was too good an opportunity to be missed. Like other young men, Dennis found pleasure in dating a variety of girls until it was truncated when Susan became pregnant, a situation that would change the course of his life, for while he had no alternative but to accept fatherhood, he certainly did not feel quite ready to embrace marriage.

After the honeymoon, he made a point of paying a daily visit to his parents in the village where he was always greeted by them in a manner as though nothing had happened. But on one occasion, his dad asked him to join him in a drink of rum and coke and then took up his usual position in his rocking chair by the window before gazing at Dennis with a shallow smile. "We heard what happened and

I think we know why it did. You were having some fun like I did as a young man, but unfortunately for you, Susan became pregnant. And we know that as a teacher in a church school, you would be expected to marry Susan. To do otherwise would have meant sacrificing your job and limiting your chances of getting on. Take it from me my son, you are not the first to get into this situation nor will you be the last. The long and short of it is that the vicar can hire and fire," he explained, and his mother took a long audible intake of breath. He could see in their faces that they regretted what had happened and especially not being able to make a contribution to their son's wedding. But, in spite of this, they were making a fairly good job of masking their hurt.

"Don't worry my son, things have a habit of working out, although not always in the way we expect them to," exclaimed his mother with an anxious glance. Dennis moved slowly to the east window where he stood gazing at the breadfruit tree in the back and thought of the days when he would sit on a suitable branch and do some of his homework, and of the pasture not far away where he and his younger brother would take the goats and sheep to graze. Such memories provided a kind of temporary escape from his current mental turmoil.

"Would you like some coconut water, Dennis?" asked his mum with a heavy heart. He turned and placed his hands on her shoulders.

"Yes, thank you, mum, but I want to say how sorry I am about what happened. Things moved so quickly within the last thirty-six hours leading up to the marriage that it was difficult to tell anyone. Everything seemed to be planned without my knowledge," he declared in a heightened state of emotion for, at that time, a real fear of the future gripped his heart. His dad stood up and shook his hand.

"Should things not work out, do remember you always have a home here," he said quietly. "We wish you good luck, my son," added his mother as they embraced each other. Dennis did not love Susan and, from what he had seen and heard, he saw themselves as mere pawns in a game played out by her mother and her uncle who had got wind that Dennis was after his daughter and was determined to put a stop to it at all costs. It was in his interest therefore to support a plan made easier by a code of practice supported by his sister. But for Dennis, acceptance of the overwhelming reality of marriage, was difficult.

2

The tide of emigration sweeping the Caribbean during the late fifties and early sixties had reached Barbados from where many young men and women were leaving to start a new life in the UK or Canada. Young men were drawn to the UK to work particularly in the transport system: the buses, trains and light manufacturing, while many young women entered hospitals to do nursing or to work in restaurants and also light manufacturing. It was at a time when Britain was still rebuilding after the Second World War and was short of workforce. It was during this too, time that Susan's father and a sister left for England as part of the migrant work force and they seemed to be doing well. It was against this background that Dennis hatched a plan which he thought would be beneficial for Susan and himself. *'What if I could persuade her to join them in England, she could then attend evening classes to obtain basic qualifications to improve her life chances? I could then join my brother in Montreal and enter McGill University to do a degree,'* he pondered. In his naivety, he was hoping that the distance between them would eventually lead to a collapse of the marriage, allowing them to pursue their own interests.

Susan did eventually join her father and sister in the UK after much cajoling but, unfortunately for Dennis, his side of the plan to get to Canada fell through, leaving him no alternative but to join her later in the UK much to his regret. But the move to England had only served to widen the gap by emphasizing the incompatibility between them in values and expectations. It was such that it wasn't long before any attempt at sensible conversation often saw her becoming verbally aggressive, all of which triggered certain thoughts in his mind. '*Why is she always so aggressive. Is she unhappy with me and can't say it? Seems as though it is the only way she can express herself and we are now unable to carry on a conversation,*' he often thought. They were on divergent paths and quietly they both wanted to break free. The marriage was now heading for the rocks within two years of arriving in England.

It was a damp evening in Autumn when Dennis went to his local pub to have a drink and think things over. He was about to finish his drink when his good friend Delbert entered and was approaching the bar when he spotted Dennis.

"What are you drinking, Dennis?"

"I'll have another whiskey," he replied. They were quietly chatting about experiences they were having in their different work-places when Delbert rested his glass on the table and gave Dennis a squinted look.

"Is everything okay with you Dennis, you seem to have something on your mind." He knew Dennis well enough to spot his moods. Dennis relayed the story and Delbert gave the matter some thought before taking another sip of whiskey.

"Perhaps Susan is thinking that it would have been better had she been married to the kind of man prepared to do a day's work, go home, eat and settle down to the TV until bedtime. Or she might be suddenly realising that she is out of her depth being married to you. How long were you all together?"

"Just about two years, half of which we spent apart because she was in England about nine months before I arrived," explained Dennis.

"Perhaps, there is your answer. Neither of you have had enough time together to know each other. I am sure you are both now learning things about each other which are causing concern. For instance, does she know you are the kind of man prepared to do all it takes to realize your goal which is, to gain graduate status and re-enter the teaching profession, and that attending Birkbeck College on evening, is an essential sacrifice you have to make to achieve your goal? And did you know that she was not too interested in moving up the social ladder, preferring to have a working-class man instead?"

TROPICAL HEATWAVE

"Probably, because I don't think she ever understands what I am doing even though I try to explain over and over again," replied Dennis, sounding very dejected.

"It seems as though you are now poles apart and nothing short of a miracle will close that gap," exclaimed Delbert. By then physical gratification in the bedroom had slumped to an almighty low. They were together but without togetherness. Conversation of which there was very little had almost dried up giving way to the occasional grunt. She wanted out as much as he did but neither of them had the courage to say so. Instead, Susan in her frustration thought, *'I must find a way of showing him he is no better than me.'* She was in search of an equalizer.

It was a hot summer day in late July with temperatures exceeding 28°C. Dennis had used a week of his summer break to attend a one-week course in salesmanship held at a hotel in Birmingham. He firmly believed that, as a part-time insurance representative, he could augment his income substantially. On the course, he was given the fundamentals of motivation and salesmanship in preparation for a part-time job with a well-known Insurance Brokerage in the City of London. The course ended at 2pm that Friday and Dennis signalled his enthusiasm and intention by closing three substantial sales on his way home.

The late July afternoon sunshine was making its way forcefully through the west window on the first floor into the small box room of his house which was his study. On one side were shelves filled with books drawn from the world of geography and insurance. On another and just over his desk, was a large map of the world on which he had drawn a circle around Barbados to make it more visible. Sitting with his back to the door compiling a summary of the course, he would occasionally raise his head to glance at the dark green elm on the pavement now reaching pass the first-floor window. He often spent much time gazing at its leaves displaying flickering shades of green in the sunlight while listening to the chatter and laughter of small children riding their bikes up and down on the pavement below. Sometimes he would even gaze at that speck on the map (Barbados) and relive his journey from there to London.

But that afternoon a side glance at the mirror near the wall chart revealed Susan approaching. He turned and there she was standing in the doorway, her hands extended upward against both posts. Their eyes met with blank expressions. There was no *'how did the course go.'* Instead, she made her way with a sense of purpose across the room and parked herself on the corner of his desk.

'That's odd. She has never done this before, I wonder what has brought this on?' he thought to himself. It drew some concern from him, but he remained quiet knowing not what to anticipate. Susan took a deep breath and folded her arms. At first, he thought she was bringing him a cup of tea for the kettle was whistling just five minutes before her arrival, but perhaps, in the light of current circumstances at the time, it was naïve of him to expect such.

"I have something to say to you that you might not want to hear." It was her monotone voice which suggested she had to muster the necessary courage to say what she was about to say. He pushed his chair from the table and positioned himself where he could see her face clearly.

"Oh, that sounds ominous," squinting short-sightedly into her face, anxiety beginning to creep in with every breath he took. She gazed through the window in an effort to avoid his eyes.

"I was picked up by the police for causing a disturbance in a shop and I have to appear in a magistrate court next week." It was blunt and cold. The words came out terse and dry, falling on his brain like bricks falling on a galvanized roof. She was expressionless. He either pretended he didn't hear or didn't want to hear. The pen dropped from his fingers for he was too shocked to feel either regret or grief or even pain. He pushed the papers on which he was working toward the back of the desk and blinked several times in a second before clearing his throat. The room temperature suddenly shot up causing him to break out in severe sweating.

"What did you say?" he asked quietly, and in a composed manner. Having come to grips with what she said, he felt as though he had walked into a nightmare. It was a few days before his return from his a one-week stay in Birmingham that Susan was in a nearby supermarket when, by shere coincidence, she met a young woman with whom

Susan was convinced Dennis was having an affair. They happened to be selecting items from the same shelf at the same time when Susan challenged her, all of which quickly moved from a verbal explosion to a physical skirmish forcing the manager to summon the police.

"You heard me. I said I was picked up for causing a public disturbance in a shop," she blurted with a chiselled face but this time louder, and for some reason, with the expectation he would respond with aggression. Instead, Dennis gritted his teeth. His blood began to boil but, with every sinew in his body, he remained perfectly calm and looked at her firmly with a furrowed brow.

"What on earth made you do such a thing?" he replied quietly but anxiously awaiting her response. Susan left the corner of the table and made her way to the door where she made a half turn with her hand still on the door knob. It was a face now impregnated with an extra supply of blood when she bellowed,

"What made me do such a thing? What do you think? You are the educated one. Can't you work it out?" she shouted, her voice reaching an extra decibel or two. Temperatures within the room were now similar to those outside for it was as though the room had suddenly become a combustion engine in motion. Susan had for a long time felt that Dennis was paying her less and less attention and more and more to the woman she met in the grocery shop. Although she couldn't prove it, she was of the opinion that Dennis was flirting with this twenty-six year old Jamaican woman who had occasionally called him on the phone.

"Work out what?" he asked in a state of total disbelief. He simply did not want to accept what his ears were telling him.

"You see Dennis, you never thought I was good enough for you. I don't even know why we ever got married. I could have brought up my child on my own," she snapped, with eyes like steel.

"You know as well as I do why we got married," was his short retort, as he tried to remain calm.

"Why? Was it because if you didn't, the vicar would have thrown you out of his school? Maybe I felt something at first even although I always knew you didn't love me. It didn't take me long to realise you preferred one of those more educated girls like my cousin." A series of furrows and small droplets suddenly appeared on Dennis' forehead and he gave her a scathing look. "Since we came to England, things have got worse and, to tell you the truth, I don't even recognize you as my husband any more. What's the use being married to you?" She now loathed everything he was and did. Dennis straightened himself in his chair and, with narrowed eyes under a deep frown, shot her a look of astonishment.

"Yes, I want you to know how it feels to be just an ordinary person leading an ordinary life like me. Yes, like me. Who knows, if you now lose your job because of what I did, you might even get a job on the buses or on the trains, you will then know that not everything is in a book. You pay more attention to books than to me. Well, 'Mr. High and Mighty Book-man,' what are you going to say to your friends now? One of us had to do something but, strange enough, you couldn't find the answer, could you?" He looked at her blankly knowing not what to say. Words failed him. She laughed. It was dry, empty and menacing. "You see, the answer is not in the book. It's not in the book. It's not in the book," she shouted, pounding her way down the stairs.

Susan had made a statement about her frustrations of living with a '*book-man*' as she described him. Dennis was dumbfounded. She had driven a dagger right to the core of his pride and had succeeded in shaking him. Fleeting images popped up on his mental screen among which was the crashing of his career before his very eyes. He grappled with thoughts like: '*What would happen if my employers got hold of this? Where would I stand? Here am I once again looking down the barrel at the demise of my career.*' He returned to his former position at his desk and tried to straighten his mind. Children playing on the pavement below the window had all gone in for their tea. Little voices were now replaced by workers' footsteps making their way home. The sun in the west lay hidden behind terraced houses on the opposite side of the road as Dennis pondered, '*this is the kind of stupidity that makes me more determined to get out of this loveless marriage.*' The writing was now clearly on the wall.

3

The smell of freshly cut grass in the nearby park permeated his entire body, stimulating every blood cell. Blackbirds high up in the beach and elm, and sparrows, chaffinches and blue tits darting around in hedges below, contributed with a chorus of song. It was the kind of theatre Dennis needed to wipe away the Monday morning blues as he made his way to join the morning rush pounding its way down the escalator to board the Piccadilly Line train at Turnpike Lane underground station. He had done this walk several times before, pass the small junior school, the four small convenience shops, the news agent, the butcher shop with his display of prime cut meat, the 'fish and chips' shop, the launderette, filled with steam brought on by early users, the betting shop, and even the window cleaner doing his bit to get the public house (pub) ready for the day's customers. He would usually find time to say a quick hello to the occasional friend waiting at the bus stop but, that morning, nothing interested him as he made his way to the station. His mind was pre-occupied with finding reasons for what had happened and how it would affect his career if it got out, but most of all, what to do about it. Dennis now saw himself as needing the love of a woman who could complete him as hungrily as he sought the essence of life itself.

Within thirty minutes he had arrived on the platform at Kings Cross station, a major interchange for London Underground Train, and certainly no place for the feint-hearted during the rush hour. To new arrivals, it can seem quite daunting to see hundreds moving in different directions, all seemingly at the same 100 paces to the minute and all supposedly knowing where they are going. That morning, Dennis appeared to be on automatic mode. He was mindless of the crowd around him, a kind of suspended animation. He alighted from the carriage, which resembled a container into which smoke had been pumped, and navigated his way through the bustling crowd to arrive on another platform. Here, he would await the Northern Line train to Bank Station not far from the Bank of England where he now worked in the finance branch of the post office in Cannon Street in the City of London. He had joined the ranks of civil servants and financiers in this financial hub of UK where, except for Dennis, the dark pin-striped suit combined with a bowler hat, a briefcase and a brolly were the norm, and all iconic symbols of a London city worker. But of course, Dennis stopped short of the bowler hat.

Standing shoulder to shoulder, he could feel the pressure increase with every wave of commuters that surged on to the platform and yet, the masses of people dashing around him, did nothing to reduce his loneliness. He felt cocooned within his own world until a light tap on his shoulder caused him to jerk his head around sharply.

"Oh, hello Lawry, I didn't know you used this line as well," slipped jerkily from his mouth as he held on to an overhanging strap in an effort to maintain his balance during a slight bend in the tract. Lawry was one of Dennis' work-colleagues. Lawry folded his paper and put it into his briefcase.

"I use the Northern line occasionally," replied Lawry, "but sometimes this platform can become so densely packed, that the only direction in which you can look is straight ahead at posters on the far side of the tract, and perhaps, that is why you didn't see me approaching." But it was this colourful display of goods and services on such posters on which Dennis was able to focus, that usually provided him with a momentary escape from his mental torture, as he waited for the next train.

"The only saving grace is that, provided there is no hold-up further on the line, the waiting time is only a few minutes, about three, to be more precise," exclaimed Dennis before slipping into one of his usual thoughts. At that time any loud conversations were frowned on while travelling on the underground. Most passengers would usually be reading a paper or a book or just sitting quietly. *'What would happen if this train was stuck in the tunnel for a long time? Here we would be, like all the others, filling our lungs with smoke, while at the same time wondering when we would be on our way again.'* Of course, such a thought was often quickly dismissed on arrival at the next station when the opening doors allowed a welcomed breath of air to enter the stuffy carriage.

As he boarded the train over the following weeks, his mind was always occupied with a matter far more pressing: one that had to be attended to if he was to realize the goals he had set himself. But he felt trapped. He had found himself in a marriage which neither of them wanted. He wanted to break free and move on, for he could feel frustration creeping into his life. He was now desperate and felt he had to do something about it. So closely were passengers stacked that it often reminded him of matches standing on end in a box. Some men had even developed the skill of holding on to an overhead strap with one hand for balance and holding a brief-case and 'brolly' in another while reading a newspaper folded in such a way as to make reading possible.

It was on such a morning that Dennis boarded the train at Kings Cross and took up his position like a smoked herring hanging from a hook while trying to read a novel folded back-to-back. Experience had told him it was hopeless even to try getting a seat, so he never tried but that morning a very heavy bounce from another commuter in a wave joining the train, jerked his head upward allowing his eyes to fall on a young attractive woman in a seat less than three meters from where he was standing. He had seen her on a few of occasions before usually sitting in the same seat, but he had never rustled up enough courage to approach her. The young woman was conspicuous for she was often the only black person, apart from Dennis, in that carriage. Dennis judged her to be no more than twenty-six but, that morning, looking at this attractive young woman as she worked her way through a cross-word puzzle, tugged at the very core of his heart and set him thinking: *'I wonder if someone like her would have been my partner but for the folly of my youth and the domineering traditions of a society that threw me into a loveless marriage.'*

It is easy to make excuses for one's poor decisions in life and even harder to face up to their consequences but perhaps it was probably the boredom of rural Barbados or the frustration at not moving on to the next step in academia that a grammar school education had promised, that led to his life-shattering stupidity. It was more likely the latter reinforced by his over-active hormones that, in the physical gratification which he momentarily secured, he made a girl pregnant and found himself shackled and dispatched on life's highway in the straightjacket of a loveless marriage with a woman where the only points of contact were within the confines of whatever was physical and not mental or emotional.

Now here he was looking at the most desirable female he had ever seen since arriving in England, while thinking of the mess his life was in and the hopelessness of his future. What could he offer this Venus who would occasionally raise her brown eyes and send him a soft smile!

For a few moments, he was lost in thought but, looking in the direction of his Venus once more as he disembarked from the train at Bank Station, he was able to flash her a smile in return. Pam was just about to settle at her desk when a colleague made her observations known.

"My word Pam, you look a bit bright and breezy this morning, I haven't seen you like that for quite some time. What has brought this on?" uttered Charlene with a mischievous look and looking for any recent gossip.

"Oh Charlene, you wouldn't believe it," she replied with a deep sigh.

"Wouldn't believe what, Pam?"

"Well," replied Pam, dwelling on the word for a moment, "I met this nice-looking guy on the train this morning. I have been quietly eyeing him for the last two weeks and I believe he was doing a similar thing. Every time I look at him standing and reading his novel, my heart would give a slight tug." As she said that, her entire body quivered. The excitement generated between Pam and Charlene caught the attention of Liz, another colleague, who was just having a cup of tea but paused for a moment to join them. It was normal to have a cup of tea and have a chat before starting work but that morning, the topic was very different. Charlene and Liz knew the harsh treatment Pam was experiencing with her husband and often wondered why she was putting up with it. It therefore did not surprise them to learn that she was at last attracted to someone with whom she seemed to have fallen in love at first sight. They both wished her good luck.

That morning, as Dennis made his way along Cannon Street, he had time to reminisce over the tragedy of his life which triggered a number of thoughts. *'I wonder if she could be that special woman for whom I am searching. This time, I will really get to know her, especially since she looks like someone who exercises her mind and she seems to have a certain gravitational pull on me.'* He thrilled at the thought of the enjoyment, at the thought of finding out who this woman was and what it would be like loving her and with her loving him in a relationship of total fulfilment. Over a period of three weeks, hemmed in as he usually was in a crowded carriage, he was still able to quietly observe her doing her crossword. She would always be comfortably seated while he would often be hanging from a strap or pressed against a closed door. But there was something about her that demanded his attention and created a need to gravitate towards her.

Pam always sat in the same carriage which Dennis made sure he joined every morning and covertly gaze at her. Not only was he spurred on by her beauty but also by the recurring thought of never having seen a black woman traveling this way before to that square mile known as the City. During the early and mid-1960's, it was most unusual to see blacks working in the city centre and he had the notion that it was not yet ready for a wave of blacks and he even considered himself a break-through and a novelty. *'What is she doing here? Where does she work? If she works in the City, she must be well qualified.'* These were some of the thoughts which drove him to want to satisfy his burning curiosity.

It was the era of the mini-skirt, a period in the 60's when young women wore skirts short enough to excite onlookers and yet long enough to cover the essentials. Young women joining the train made sure you had something to remember, something to set the mind racing for the rest of the day and, among this brigade, was the young Venus sitting not far away. So strong was this attraction that men, while seemingly reading a newspaper, sitting or standing, would have an extra eye covertly focused on these beautiful specimens of nature. It was a pageantry which was sure to bring an inner joy and excitement to many a commuter, a pageantry only momentarily broken by the train pulling in to a station for a change of actresses. The *Square Mile* welcomed this mini-skirt invasion. It added a certain flavour to a city gent's ploughman's lunch (a roll or sandwich and a pint of beer or bitter) and brought a new dimension to lunch-time conversation in pubs. Dennis was among the audience who enjoyed the daily theatre in which he considered the girl sitting less than two meters away to be playing a leading role.

It was within such a setting that Dennis would gaze every morning at this young woman while making sure she did not see him although he had the feeling that something was quietly nudging her to say to herself, *'I think he is looking at me.'* He could sense that, out of the corner of her eye, she could see him do a slow appraisal of her, the kind men do when they are wondering what a woman looks like without the clothes. It was the moment when Cupid was just about to draw back his bow and let his arrow flow. It was a gaze only occasionally interrupted by the intermixing of out-going and in-coming passengers every time the train stopped at a station. This jockeying by passengers to find a place to sit or stand would often find him pressed embarrassingly against another woman in such a manner that would make it difficult to move or sometimes see her.

Dennis was blessed with the skill to perceive or read a situation with reasonable accuracy. *'How can I be certain she is not having similar thoughts?'* he pondered, and felt she was feigning a smile masking something deeper, something that was hurting. To him, she seemed to be running away from something. Little did he know that the moment was not too far away when he could put his feelings and perceptions to the test. He was about to board the train that morning and take up his usual position when their eyes met and held for a moment. It was as though they were programmed to do so at that particular moment. Hers was carried on a look as soothing as the gentle ripples created when a small pebble is dropped into the calm waters of a quiet pond. There was a sparkle in her eyes as they looked at each other for a brief silent moment, enough to say, 'hello' with their eyes rather than with their lips. Words hung in the air above a silence that was still sufficiently eloquent to trigger something in him. *'Could this be my lucky day? Could she really be the one? Has Cupid's winged arrow found its target?'*

4

Pam and Dennis were each caught up in an unpleasant marriage and were now on a secret mission to find someone, to find their ideal partner. Two days later when the train pulled into Kings Cross station there she was again sitting in the same carriage and in what seemed to be the same seat. As usual, Dennis had made sure he was standing in the right position on the platform to board that carriage. Like she had done many times before, she raised her head from the crossword and, peering through a window that seemed opaque from the dust whipped up as the train rattled along, she saw him about to board the train. As he entered, full of the usual excitement and satisfaction that there she was again, she quickly beckoned to him that the seat next to her was empty. He made a quick dash for it, speed being the essence if he was to secure that special seat. He knew that any vacant seat was targeted by passengers who, like vultures, would descend upon it with great rapidity. One only had a split second to gain occupancy. *'Could this really be my day? Could this be the moment I am waiting for? Could she be the one?'* In fact, he could hear himself say these words in a voice that sounded almost operatic. Although there were some whites who would consciously avoid sitting next to a black person, there was no way that this would occur in Pam's case for she was very attractive.

Now settled snugly beside the one who had captured his attention over the last three weeks, he placed his briefcase horizontally on his knees and cast a beseeching look at the woman who, with every passing day, had filled his mind. But he also knew he had to seize the moment before arriving at Bank station where he would leave the train. Sitting beside her, he could feel the warmth from her thigh radiating through his body.

"Halloo," he said, letting his voice flow over the word carried on a casual smile, "I am Dennis and thanks for saving the seat for me. I usually have to stand all the way to Bank station." One of Dennis' strengths was his ability to start a conversation even with a stranger, although in this case, one could hardly consider Pam a stranger, for how could a woman who had occupied every corner of his mind for the last three weeks be still considered a stranger!

"That's okay, I am Pam," she replied affectionately, breaking into a gentle chuckle and revealing a set of white teeth just barely visible between a pair of beautifully curled lips. He cleared his throat. Two passengers standing nearest to them in the aisle seemed to sense what was going on and sent them an encouraging smile which they acknowledged by sending one back.

"Can I ask you where you are from?" He knew she was from the Caribbean but wanted to know what island, for they had not yet conversed enough for him to detect her accent. This was essential, there being a degree of prejudice between and within some of the Caribbean islands.

"Barbados," she replied proudly, the word leaving her lips with a certain panache. It was a trait often observed by two of her work colleagues Liz and Charlene during chats about the islands. She often took the opportunity to highlight the development of Barbados focusing on education and making a point that its literacy rate was 99.7%. It was on this that her pride was founded for she, like most Barbadians, was proud to be a part of such an island. "My mother is Barbadian, but my father is from Guyana," she added, still focused on the crossword but pausing momentarily to answer any questions.

"And you?" she asked, now spending a little more time to observe him more closely as she folded her paper away. Dennis was now so overwhelmed with his initial success that it almost slipped his mind he had to reply until a jolt by the train caused him to look up and see her eyes searching for his.

"Oh, ah, ah, yes, I am also from Barbados, St. Andrew to be more precise," he said hastily but tentatively for he was aware that people from St. Andrew were considered backward by those from other parishes. After all, it was the only parish with very few tarmac roads and certainly no street lights. One of its greatest assets however, is that it was considered one of the largest bread-baskets in the island, providing most of the fresh or home grown-food that would help to feed the people throughout the island. There was nothing unusual about their opening lines. This was the normal way by which migrants from the Caribbean in the sixties broke the ice when meeting for the first time.

On discovering that they were both from the same island, there was an immediate undercurrent of mutual satisfaction. Neither of them had been in England sufficiently long to acquire the English accent but with the ice now broken, they were happy to drop their guards and open up a bit. Conversion was slightly louder than normal for the noise of the train rattling along had made it almost impossible for them to hear each other. Standing passengers would covertly stare at them in sheer curiosity for it was not customary to see blacks travelling on a city bound train at that time of the morning. Little did such curious onlookers know that they were privileged to be witnessing the opening scene of a love drama.

"And where in Barbados are you from?" he asked in an appealing voice.

"St. Martin's, a small village in St. Phillip near the sea on the east coast. If you know St. Martin's church, I lived just around the corner from there," she explained, her eyes sparkling with expectation.

"Yes, I have passed that way on a number of occasions while on excursions to the Crane Beach. You are lucky to have such a breathtakingly beautiful beach with its vast expanse of white to pinkish sands on your door step," he exclaimed, and her eyes lit up as she acknowledged the compliment.

"Yes, I know," she replied, anxiously awaiting the next question for she too realized they had limited time to sound out any inter-parochial prejudices before reaching the station. "I have seen you for

TROPICAL HEATWAVE

some time on the train and I wondered where in the city you worked because you always got off at Bank station," she added.

"I work in Cannon Street in the Finance Branch of the Post Office." He was now feeling more confident. His answer spurred her on to look more closely at the dark grey suit he was wearing and the brown leather briefcase he was carrying. Like him, she too thought it most unusual in the mid-sixties to see a black man so attired and working in the city centre. She sighed quietly for, in her eyes, Dennis was coming up trumps.

"What about you?" he asked politely, for this was the moment he would have his curiosity satisfied. Pam, the Venus that had captured his undivided attention for more than three weeks, smiled softly.

"Oh, I work for the Ministry of Transport at St. Christopher House just over the river not far from you?" she whispered.

"Where is that?" he asked with an inquisitive look under a furrowed brow and in the hope that she would give the answer he wanted.

"Very near London Bridge," she replied. A glow of excitement crept slowly over his face as though to say, *'That's a bit of luck because we are not far from each other.'* Seeing the train fast approaching Bank station, they quickly exchanged workplace telephone numbers and arranged to meet the next morning for coffee at a small cafe in lower Cannon Street. As he emerged from Bank underground station and strolled along Cannon Street to work that morning, his mind was fully occupied with the events of the last week in general, and of that morning in particular. He liked what he had seen and heard but still felt she was feigning a calmness designed to conceal an underlying feeling of fear. *'What agony of despair is she going through?'* he pondered, *'and could she be really working at St. Christopher House, in the Ministry of Transport, in an office so near to the City of London?'* But, before he could work out the answer, he was in the lift going up to the second floor to sign on in an office in which walls, once cream in colour, were now heavily dingy from the daily emission of smoke from pipes, cigarettes and cigars not to mention diesel and other fumes from the street below.

Dennis' desk was one of twelve occupying the entire third floor offering an excellent view of Cannon Street below with its daily hustle and bustle of city gents and girls who, dressed in their mini-skirts, became a daily reminder of his Venus. His colleague Lawry, sitting at the desk directly opposite and who was equally as perceptive, noticed that he appeared in a pensive mood that morning and concluded there was something different about him. What he didn't know was that Dennis was about to be drawn into the vortex of a romance and that he had made contact with his Venus. At tea break that morning, they both strolled over to the large third-floor window as usual to imbibe in the scene below. Lawry was not just a work colleague, he had also become a friend who, like most of the others, smoked heavily. It was not uncommon to see the occasional cigarette flying through the air like a guided missile aimed at another desk where someone would interrupt its flight and say "thanks" to the sender. Unlike most of the other male members of staff, Lawry usually wore a half suit, a combination of brown and light brown with a leather patch sewn into the elbows of his jacket. It was clear to Dennis from the many conversations they had together that, among other things, he liked gardening and one of his other pastimes was studying Russian, snippets of which he would demonstrate in the office from time to time. But the most significant thing however was that he was also responsible for teaching Dennis his job. The conversation that morning was curtailed when a phone rang.

"I think it is yours Dennis," uttered Lawry.

"Thanks Lawry," replied Dennis who asked for an excuse and made a quick dash to answer the caller. This mad dash did not go unnoticed by the two clerical assistants who took turns to take a large teapot around to staff at tea-break but who would always find time to send Dennis a soft smile and sometimes to have a quick chat with the new boy on the block. He was never sure whether it was curiosity or a desire to become friendly until after tea that day when Maureen, the shorter and more attractive of the two, crept up stealthily behind him like a panther and briskly rubbed her hands in his hair causing him to turn around swiftly and look up to be greeted with two blue eyes breaking through a broad smile.

"I'm sorry Dennis, but I long wanted to find out what black hair felt like, especially the short curly type like yours. I hope you don't mind." As she spoke, the excitement in her face, having reached a peak, started to dwindle away like the slow flow of ripples returning to the sea from the shore. She was obviously very satisfied with her experience.

"No, I don't mind," now looking somewhat surprised. He was unaware that he was the first black person to be employed in that office and that perhaps, Maureen might not have come so close to a black man before. She was the more talkative of the two girls and was probably trying to show her affection, but Dennis knew that society was not yet ready to accept black and white couples and that, to go against that, would be to court danger. Episode over, Dennis returned to his pensive mood while getting on with his work which again drew the attention of Lawry sitting opposite.

"You okay Dennis? Only…ah, you seem to be in deep thought this morning." he inquired in a searching voice while releasing smoke rings from a freshly lit cigarette not unlike those released by Indians in a Western movie. Every puff of smoke, mixed with the beams of sunlight, made its way into every nook and cranny of the office. Varied shaped pipes would join the cigarette and cigar brigade to ensure you left the office at the end of the day, smoker or not, well drugged up with nicotine and smelling like a smoke den.

"Yes, I am okay," Dennis replied with a quiet chuckle as he commenced to pull out a couple of drawers in search of a document to do with a matter on which he was working.

5

Pam had an unusual upbringing, one that saw her spending six months in Guyana and six in Barbados during her childhood and early adolescence. It was a situation brought about because her father was from Guyana and her mother from Barbados and they had agreed on this. But it was in Guyana that she acquired certain values and skills, though at a cost. Her father was married to a Guyanese woman and had a daughter about eight years younger than Pam. This half-sister enjoyed a middle-class life: a nice home, attended the best private secondary school and was surrounded by all the necessary things you would expect a young adolescent girl to have. It was a far cry from what Pam experienced in Barbados with her mother who had barely enough to keep her and her younger siblings clothed and fed. To make matters worse, as soon as she was ten, her annual six-month period in Guyana was that of a maid carrying out domestic chores as well as catering to the needs of her younger half-sister. Her step-mother therefore saw no reason to send her to secondary school even though she showed all the signs that she was capable of doing well at secondary level. It was a kind of *'upstairs, downstairs'* model where the maid and other servants were not permitted upstairs except when asked to do so. There were two different worlds and her half-sister never allowed her to forget her place in the household.

But, during her annual six-monthly stay in Guyana, Pam was able to observe some significant aspects of their lifestyle and values: the kind of friends they entertained and how they did it, their taste in food and furniture, the places of interest they visited, the comfort in which her sister was brought up and much more. These were some of the experiences that helped to shape her values and define her goals. Her dream was to one day achieve a similar lifestyle. Each period spent in Guyana saw her become more and more obsessed with the desire to prove to her step-mother, her father and half-sister that she would one day achieve the 'good life' as she saw it, despite being denied a secondary education. She was determined to overturn those negative perceptions of her held by them. It became not just a goal, but a burning desire to reach a level that would enable her to help her mother in Barbados who had to work long hours in a hotel to bring up her two younger siblings. For Pam, it was a matter of some urgency, which is why she welcomed the opportunity later given by a relative to pursue her goal.

It was 1956 and she was on her usual stay in Barbados when Oswald, her uncle, observed how well she catered for the family and felt she could do a lot better, given the chance. "What would you really like to do Pam?" he asked with narrowed eyes, as she was preparing the evening meal.

"I would really like to be a nurse, but I didn't get the chance to go to secondary school, so I have no school certificates," she replied, looking at him with beseeching eyes and hoping he would help. He himself had spent some time in Guyana and knew what life for her was like and what she was expected to do whenever she was there, but he also knew that, at that time, there were not many options opened to girls without a secondary education. The main options were: working as attendants in small shops, as maids in hotels and private homes or as workers on sugarcane plantations. Pam's decision to become a nurse grew out of the experience gained while looking after her younger half-sister in Guyana as well as her niece after her mother died while giving birth in Barbados. During that time too, she was saddled with looking after her two younger siblings, and all this before she was sixteen. It was from this culture of caring that her desire to be a nurse had evolved.

"Okay, this is what I will do. I will pay for you to have private tuition for one year to pass the qualifying examination to do nursing in England and then fund the cost of your travel there." This caught her by surprise. She immediately stopped what she was doing and embraced him. It was a dream come true. She was only eighteen, but when the SS Napoli left Barbados bound for England on a bright September morning in 1959, she was one of a group of girls on their way to study nursing at a hospital in Colchester, England. It broke her heart to see her mother waving her good-bye as the small boat taking them to the ocean-going vessel pulled away from the wharf on the day of departure.

Pam made a few friends on the three-week voyage, but one stood out. Jean was a young Trinidadian girl who was also on her way to the same hospital in Colchester. They were a support for each other in a country which, at that time, was very hostile to newcomers. Pam was about 5ft 7ins and of medium build but with a waist that brought her reasonably close to the hourglass. Her beautiful brown eyes and slightly curled lips made her the kind of person you would want to know about, for it was her total countenance that oozed with warmth and caring. So, it was no surprise that she had created a small group of friends around her on the three-week journey to England. But quite unknown to Dennis, that attractive young woman who had invited him to sit next to her on the train that morning, was also trying to weather the storm of a tempestuous marriage.

As young trainee nurses, Pam and Jean shopped together in the local town but the lack of entertainment in Colchester suited to their cultural tastes meant they often went to London on their week-ends off where there was a greater chance of finding entertainment with a Caribbean flavour. They frequented Brixton, Hackney, Harlesden which were already emerging as centres of concentration for people from the Caribbean. Not only were they known for their large markets where Caribbean food could be bought, they were also centres of entertainment for people from the Caribbean. It was a time when house parties were the norm. They would dance to Calypso, Reggae and Soul while stuffing themselves with curried goat and rice washed down with a helping of whiskey, rum, Bacardi, baby-champagne or lager. Such parties also afforded the opportunity to meet friends and catch up with recent gossip and the latest news from home all of which gave them a feeling of parity and security, a comfort zone in a foreign land. But it was one such occasion that proved to be the catalyst for an unwanted pregnancy followed by an unhappy marriage.

The usual Saturday night party was in full swing at Diane's. She was about seven years older than Jean or Pam and was also a close friend. She had arrived in England five years earlier. Like all black parties at that time it was well attended for such parties provided an occasion for Caribbean blacks to jam till the early hours of Sunday morning although it was not the kind of scene welcomed by their white neighbours. Pam was in a close dance with a man she had met earlier at one of Diane's parties. Like Jean, he was also Trinidadian and had taken quite a fancy to dancing with Pam whose vertical motion was often perceived as reflecting a horizontal intent. The phone in the hallway rang. "Pam, Pam it is for you" came a shout from the hallway.

"I wonder who it is calling me at this time of the night and how did they know I am here," she pondered with a puzzled look. "Kindly excuse me for a moment," she asked, reluctantly sliding out from the arms of her dancing partner. She slowly weaving her way pass couples seemingly welded together in the kind of groovy moment normally associated with the late hours of a house party in the 1960's and 70's. Couples were so engaged that they were oblivious to Pam meandering her way pass them to the telephone in the hallway. "Pam speaking," she volunteered, with an expression of sheer curiosity. Within moments she put the phone down and slowly turned with a look of utter disappointment and horror. It immediately caught the attention of her friend Jean who was at pains to find out who had called Pam at that time of the night.

"Pam, you don't look so good, is something the matter?" She was concerned that Pam's 'after midnight' sexy look was suddenly replaced by a look of sheer desperation. It was as though the blood was slowly draining from her face.

"Oh Jean, you wouldn't believe this," she replied in a choked voice.

"Believe what?" asked Jean hurriedly with probing eyes.

"The couple, with whom I was going to stay after the party, just called to say they have a family crisis and can no longer put me up for the night. What am I going to do? I don't know anyone else." A long-drawn-out groan of despair tore from her lips. Jean was much shorter with brown eyes and slightly on the chubby side and, like Pam, a great party-goer but, unlike Pam, she lacked a certain refinement as was shown in the way she dressed and spoke. But one of her strengths was the ability to manipulate others to achieve her objectives. She also knew that Saturday midnight was not the best time to start looking for some place to stay in that part of London.

"Okay, don't worry, let me see what I can do," uttered Jean looking around anxiously before disappearing quickly into an adjacent room and soon to re-appear with a friend Elton, whom she had met through her boyfriend Winston. She had explained the situation to Elton, a workmate of Winston, and asked whether he could put Pam up for the night. Elton, seeing Pam's plight, agreed to do so. He took no convincing for, although his eyes were almost half-closed from the amount of alcohol he had already consumed, he was sufficiently alert to see more than Pam's plight. She was wearing a mini-skirt which supported a low back and front arm-out top. With her hair in drop-curls at the back, she was the kind of person to whet any man's appetite and set his hormones racing especially at that time of the night. Elton jumped at the opportunity.

"Can I have a word with you in the kitchen, Jean?" requested Pam, feigning a calm.

"Of course," she replied, leading the way to the kitchen which surprisingly was free at that moment. It was usual to find guests wondering in and out in search of extra helpings of food and drink which would eventually cause the limited space to become rather cramped.

"Jean, are you sure it will be okay to put up at this man tonight?" she asked, looking somewhat apprehensive and nervous.

"You'll be alright Pam. I have known Elton for some time now and I have always found him to be a nice person. Furthermore, he is a friend of Winston, my boyfriend." Pam did not know London that well and was not aware of the bed and breakfast facilities available in, that area and, even if she did, prices would have been out of her reach anyway.

"Does he have a girlfriend? Not than I am interested, it is just that I don't want to get into a struggle verbal or otherwise with his woman," exclaimed Pam looking very concerned.

"He has a girlfriend, but I really don't think there is anything in it because he doesn't seem to be serious as he still lives on his own. According to Winston, he prefers to be one of the boys," declared Jean with an encouraging smile. Just then their eyes met. Pam gave her an anxious glare and shook her head. Elton was from Barbados and had arrived in England about four years earlier than Pam to work in the maintenance division of British Railway. He was shorter than Pam and of medium build and, like Pam, he too had only received an elementary education but, unlike Pam who was always keen to improve her socio-economic status, he was quite happy to remain in the railway job.

Elton had no desire or plans to move forward and upward. Apart from house parties, his only other interest was having a good time with his mates in the pub and the betting shop particularly on weekends. By then, the betting shop and the pub had become the focal points for young men from the Caribbean and it was not unknown for many of them to lose their weekly wage because of this addiction. But Elton was also known among his friends for being somewhat jealous of those whom he saw trying to better themselves to the point where he often became verbally aggressive. Pam was young, attractive, and impressionable and one who wanted to achieve as much as possible. Becoming a nurse was simply a visible expression of a more fundamental goal, that is, to prove to herself, her father, step-mother, half-sister, uncle and mother that she could make it despite not having a secondary education. And yet, to some extent, she was not sufficiently street-wise.

It was after midnight when they arrived at Elton's flat. "Close the door quietly behind you, we don't want to disturb the other tenants," he admonished. A gentle touch on the light switch revealed an uncarpeted-stairs which creaked under every step taken. It was a characteristic feature of many older terraced houses of that era. Elton's first-floor bed-sit in Tufnell Park, North London was modestly furnished with second-hand items: a single bed, a two-seater, one small table with one chair and a ward-robe that had seen better days. As was the norm, the floor was covered with linoleum with a rug next to his single bed and, like other young men from the Caribbean, he too had a small drinks cabinet and, of course, a small music centre. But a quick glance revealed it was not what she expected. It was harsh reality. She looked absolutely horrified and nodded momentarily unable to speak. Cold fingers of fear suddenly gripped her for she was now all alone in a room with a man about whom she knew absolutely nothing apart from what Jean had hurriedly told her about two hours before.

"But you only have one single bed," she uttered, looking very startled and uncomfortable at the very thought of sleeping in a two-seater.

"Well, it's me alone, so what's the point of having a double bed?" he said matter-of-factly and shrugging his shoulders while putting on to make a cup of tea. Pam had never lived on her own for, on arriving in England, she had gone directly into nursing quarters and therefore had no idea what it was like living in rented accommodation. "You can have the bed, I will make do with the chair," he quickly added, seeing the disappointment on her face. The alcohol in her blood from the party suddenly evaporated allowing her to get the message, his underlying agenda. It was now 1:30 a.m. and, with nowhere else to go, Pam was well and truly trapped. The stage was set for a one-night stand, a night she had not anticipated and one she came to regret. She was naïve to think that she would somehow escape the supercharged needs of a bachelor after a night of curry goat and rice, rum and whiskey.

After a few drinks and soft music, she was led like a lamb to the slaughter. It was not love at first sight. It was not love at all. She was not even infatuated with him but realized that, in the circumstances, she had to pay a price. She did, and in more ways than one for, by becoming pregnant, she had to sacrifice her nursing career in the third and final year of her studies. It was at that time when the system did not accommodate nurses who got pregnant. In her naivety, she had not prepared herself for any unforeseen circumstances and, in his selfishness, he was completely oblivious to the likely impact it would have on her career. She was now pregnant for a man who had no intention of supporting her career, a man who was interested purely in his own physical gratification and who had selfishly brought her career in nursing to an abrupt end. As a result, she found herself having to marry a man she never loved, a man who could not see pass his nose, a man without vision.

****

Pam was not working, and they were going through a rough patch brought on by the shortage of money and the tense atmosphere of a marriage that carried all the hallmarks of coming to an end. They were now living in a one-bedroom flat in Kentish town not far from the train station. The grim surroundings on the outside together with the loneliness indoors bore down on her heavily. It sometimes caused her to think of what life could have been had she been able to finish her course in nursing. She relived every second of what happened after the party that Saturday night and wished she did not find herself in the situation to seek help. A dense November fog made her more depressed forcing her to think she had to do something and thought an evening after dinner would be best to do so.

"Elton, I am going to see if I can get a job because you are not giving me enough to cover house-keeping," she uttered and waited for a response, but she knew from experience that his response would not be supportive. He finished his dinner and levelled his eyes with hers.

"Where do you expect to find work around here?" he asked bluntly.

"A friend of mine told me they are vacancies at a soft drinks factory not too far from here. I can try there."

"If that is what you want, then go ahead." It was a reply that surprised her. Never before had he responded so positively to any of her suggestions. But little did she know that he was already working out that he would contribute even less to housekeeping if she is working, leaving him more to spend on drinking and betting on the horses. Whenever asked to increase his share of the housekeeping, he would refuse vehemently. It was evident that his money was haemorrhaging through the pub and betting shop, a situation which often resulted in torrid verbal outbursts. And yet, throughout all this, Pam never lost sight of her goal and, even though her chances of becoming a nurse had now been dashed, she was determined to press on and improve her social and financial status.

Unlike Elton, Pam was not content with the monotony of factory work and was always on the lookout for an opportunity to move into a more challenging and rewarding job, one that offered career prospects. Unknown to him, she later successfully applied for a clerical job in the Ministry of Transport at their London Bridge Office. It was a stroke of luck because computers had just been introduced to the UK and Pam was recruited to be trained for work in the computer department. She knew that telling him would meet with disagreement and discouragement for he would see such a job as her wanting to rise above him. Elton was quite content to settle as a maintenance worker at British Rail and always felt that Pam should do likewise in her factory employment. It was a matter of power and control. She therefore thought it prudent to choose a suitable time to tell him but had decided that it would not be a matter of getting his permission to do so but one of information giving. That moment came one evening as they sat viewing TV. It was a commercial break when she took the opportunity to make a pot of tea.

"Elton, I wanted to tell you this long ago, but we seem not to be able to talk anymore without fighting." He seemed oblivious to what she was saying. Instead, he reached for a glass and poured himself a whiskey. Pam took an audible deep breath for she had witnessed this behaviour many times before. "I recently applied for a job in the Ministry of Transport and I got it," she uttered in a dry monotone voice and with an expressionless face as she waited for a response which again was not forth-coming. He remained glued to the last race on TV. Even the word *congratulations* had taken leave of his vocabulary. He showed no interest. It was a strung-out moment of silence eventually broken by the shuffling of a newspaper. He poured himself another whiskey, one of his props. Pam pulled back and stared at him as he settled back in his chair. After taking two sips of his liquid courage, he turned slowly to face her with an expression that mirrored what he was about to say, for he was a man consumed with jealousy.

"Tell me, how is it that you are able to move from being a factory worker at a soft-drinks factory in Tufnell Park to the clerical grade in the Ministry of Transport at London Bridge? What man did you have to pay to help you get that job and how much did you have to pay him?" He was blunt. The words ripped into her like a sword. She looked daggers at him as she reeled under his onslaught and an angry retort sprang to her lips as she literally threw the dirty dishes into the sink.

"You son of a ------, is that what you think of me?" she snapped. Just then, the doorbell rang. It was Jean her friend and it was her first visit to their apartment. There was no warm welcome, no hugging, simply, "come in Jean, sorry about that." It did not take long for Jean to realise *all was not right in the state of Denmark,* an alternative to saying *things are not going well.*

"Is anything the matter?" asked Jean, sensing that the atmosphere could be cut with an axe. But she soon assumed a look of disappointment for she did not expect Pam to be home at that time.

"Yes Jean, quite a lot," Pam replied, while quickly trying to work out why Jean had paid them an un-announced visit. Little did she know that Jean was on a mission and had hoped to find Elton home alone. Pam was to be on a late shift and was not expected home before nine. But while she was surprised to see Pam in such a foul mood, Pam had noticed the disappointment on her face when she saw it was her who opened the door.

"Oh Jean, you don't want to know. I wish I had never met or got married to that man," she blurted with a heaving bosom and spitting fire.

"Seems as though I have come at the wrong time," were the words Jean managed to muster and made a half turn to go back through the door.

"Oh no, you haven't. You have come at the right time to see the man I have for a husband," declared Pam as she hurried to the back room to continue where she had left off with Elton. "You bastard," she said, railing at him, "but the reason you can think of me like that is because of the price you made me pay for staying one night at your place. I had to give birth to a baby, not out of love but out of your selfish desire to satisfy your needs at all costs. You never cared about me or my career which I had to sacrifice because of your selfishness." A broken sob escaped from her lips. Among the dark thoughts burning indelibly on her mind was: *'I will never ever forgive you for this.'* Elton eyed her disdainfully and then slammed out. Jean looked on in astonishment with a feeling of guilt, knowing that it was she who had told Pam he could be trusted. But during such fireworks, Pam let slip a remark pertaining to the new job.

"What's this I am hearing about a job Pam, you didn't tell me you had a new job," asked Jean with an inquisitive look under a slightly furrowed brow.

"Yes Jean, and that is what this is all about. When I told him that I had applied and got a job in the Ministry of Transport at their offices near London Bridge, all he could ask me was, what man did I have to pay and how much, not congratulations." This immediately triggered a feeling of jealousy in Jean whose mind was suddenly invaded with a number of thoughts like *'Why should she be so lucky to have a job like that in the city after working at a soft-drinks factory? What is more, she will be earning a lot more than me.'* "I don't know why I didn't call off the wedding when I had the chance to do so," added Pam, now boiling with anger.

"Why, what makes you say that?" asked Jean, looking rather curious.

"I should have known the kind of man he was before we got married. You might not believe this Jean, but the week before the wedding we had a big bust-up. That week, quite unknown to me, we had received a letter stating that our electricity would be cut off if an outstanding bill was not paid by a certain date. When asked why, he replied that there was no more money. I found out later that he had spent the money in the betting shop on the horses. I then had to approach a friend of mine for help. I felt so ashamed," she uttered, and she shook her head. "Sorry Jean, I forgot to offer you a cup of tea." Jean walked quietly across the room and gazed for a moment at the street below before answering. She had sensed that a crack was developing in the relationship and was already beginning to make plans how she could capitalise on it to her advantage.

"No thanks, I will soon be leaving," she replied and, in order to reinforce her mask of sincerity, proceeded to tell Pam about her growing disillusionment with her boyfriend Winston. The idea was to make Pam believe she had her support. Steeped in jealousy and realising she had made a wasted journey since Elton was not at home alone as she had expected, she decided to curtail her visit. But she now had a good idea of what was going down between Pam and Elton although the expression of surprise and disappointment on Jean's face did not go unnoticed by Pam. Yet, she opted to put her thoughts on the back burner for the moment. She saw Jean to the door and, with a cold expression, turned away thinking of Jean's facial expression on finding she was at home. Making her way to the kitchen, her brown eyes were magnified with tears which gathered momentum and cascaded down her face. She wanted to run and keep running. She wanted to run herself out of the mess she was in. But those tears also expressed a joy to know that at last she would no longer be dependent on Elton. Standing there, she thought to herself, *'thank heavens I'll be out of that monotonous drudgery of factory work and low pay and into a job more in line with my ability.'* She saw the new job as giving her a chance to regain her confidence and salvage some respectability in the eyes of her friends and family, as well as putting her back on track towards her goal.

This was the background of the woman with whom Dennis was beginning to fall madly in love. But it was the thought of a black woman working within the city centre that took Dennis by surprise arousing his curiosity so much that he felt it warranted investigation. *'What school did she attend in Barbados? How qualified is she? How long was she in England?'* were some of the thoughts that occupied hid mind. He had the notion that, to work in The City, the centre of London and the financial hub of the world, would require a given set of qualifications. These and many more thoughts kept buzzing around in his head like flashes of lightning. *'Perhaps I can get something going here, but would she be interested? Is it possible that such an attractive woman working in the City of London would not be attached? Maybe she has her eyes on someone else.'* Such burning curiosity got the better of him. He seized the phone with the kind of haste that saw him dispatch a pile of papers in different directions on the floor. This hurricane but funny act was enough to force another question from his friend Laurey sitting opposite.

"Dennis, are you *sure* you are alright?" he inquired with a quiet chuckle, seeing the funny side.

"Oh, ah, ah, yes, I am okay," he replied, smiling rather sheepishly while quickly gathering his papers and thoughts together. With hands that trembled more out of expectation than fear, he dialled the number given and had hardly dialled the last digit when, he was greeted with, "Ministry of Transport, Pam speaking." It was as though she was waiting at the other end, it was a voice so dulcet, so refined, he could sit all day and listen to it. It was that very voice he had heard on the train - the kind of voice which, without seeing the person, would tell you she was warm and welcoming. For that moment, so different was his world, that he almost forgot to respond. A combination of surprise and excitement had gripped him. *'Oh, the number works,'* he muttered to himself quietly. This moment of silence, though only a split second, seemed as long as an hour until it was suddenly broken by his response. It was an expression of joy and astonishment that did not go un-noticed by Lawry who again merely chuckled.

"Oh, ah… hello, it is Dennis," and he apologised for his delayed response. The clock on the wall was showing 10:30 a.m., time for the mid-morning tea break but he was almost oblivious to the rattle of cups and saucers as the tea-girl did her rounds. Soon, staff were tucking into cups of tea and biscuits, while exchanging experiences from the night before or just sharing light jokes. Dennis seized the opportunity to have a brief chat.

"Hello, how are you?" These words were carried on such a wave of excitement that he could almost feel the heat it generated within her but there was neither the privacy nor the time to indulge in a long conversation on an office phone, at least not the type of conversation that people who, highly infatuated with each other, would like to have. For Dennis, making contact was enough. The rest of the morning saw him desperately trying to focus on his work so elated with joy was he, now ignited by a spark of love. It became the centre of conversation that day during his usual pub lunch with Lawry at the Square Rigger, a pub on the northern approach to London Bridge just around the corner from his workplace. It was fitted out like a schooner with decks and memorabilia from the world of boats and catered mainly to the taste of city workers from around the Bank of England, Cannon Street, Thread Needle Street, Monument and Thames Street.

6

Rendezvousing on the platform at Kings Cross Underground station as often as possible became the norm, only occasionally broken when Dennis happened to arrive too late to join her. In the ten minutes it took the train to get from Kings Cross to Bank Station on mornings, they would exchange pleasantries and interesting thoughts. But there was, however, still a shade of curiosity lingering in Dennis' mind. *'Okay, so she answered the number I dialled, but how can I be sure it was the Ministry of Transport at St. Christopher House. I have to find a way of satisfying myself without appearing to rock the boat.'* He was beginning to invest quite a lot of emotional capital in this venture therefore to allow it to run aground would be more than disastrous. In short, he was falling in love and they were beginning to write a love-story in which they were to be the leading players in a world that was fast becoming their own creation.

It was about two weeks later, and they were having a quiet chat over the usual din from the rattle of the train. Pam was also trying to finish a crossword puzzle before she reached London Bridge station where she would disembark. Dennis leaned across and glanced at the paper for a moment. "Try using the letter 'd' there," he suggested quietly hoping that, should it be correct, it would enhance his esteem in her eyes. She did, and the crossword was completed. "Thanks to you, clever boy," her impulsive smile casting a ray of Caribbean sunshine throughout an otherwise sombre carriage.

"Why not let us have coffee at Jolly's café tomorrow morning before we go into work, it would allow me to say thanks for helping me with the crossword," she suggested. "I sometimes meet some of my work colleagues there on mornings. It is only small, but it serves very nice coffee," she added while putting the paper away. Jolly's was a small café at the western end of Cannon Street. You opened the door to four tables on either side of a central walkway. A red and white checked tablecloth covered each table with its two cream-painted hard-bottom wooden chairs. Posters, showing blends of coffee and types of breakfast, broke the orange-painted walls. This was in a culture of aromas from freshly roasted coffee beans making it the ideal spot during cold winter mornings for having a coffee and a chat.

"Yes, I'd like that very much," he replied before wishing her a nice day and hurriedly leaving the train at Bank station. But he yearned to see her more and more, for each time he saw her, he was struck by how attractive she was, the way she spoke and her ability to ignite his innermost being. The next morning was not one to be missed and he knew he must not be late at Kings Cross. Within five minutes of arriving on the platform, a slight breeze emerging from the tunnel, together with an increase surge of passengers on to the platform, told him the train was approaching. As it was slowly coming to a halt, he could see her peering through the smoky window hoping that he would be the one to join her in the seat next to her. This he did. "Oh, you *do* look nice," he commented.

"Thanks," was her response with a light contagious chuckle. Less and less attention was now given to crossword puzzles and more and more to each other. It was Autumn and getting sufficiently chilly for her to wear a light autumn coat that morning. Her's was cream, an A-line style skirt with a close-fitting a broad belt of the same colour. It carried an upturned collar inside which sat a light brown scarf folded twice with both ends resting neatly on one shoulder. A light brown bonnet rested snugly on dark brown hair allowing a few curls to protrude. She looked absolutely stunning. They opted for a table in the corner at Jolly's. Assisting her to remove her coat slowly, her very presence began to ignite his physical and emotional being causing his body temperature to rise sharply and adding to

TROPICAL HEATWAVE

the conditions that caused windows to steam up on a rather chilly autumn morning in London.

"Can I help you?" It was the waitress, an experienced looking woman in her forties, who had obviously perceived they were two people stealing love on the side but who, at that moment, would welcome a hot cup of coffee on such a chilly morning.

"Two coffees please, milk, no sugar," requested Dennis. Holding hands across the table allowed their eyes to meet. It was a moment of her being that demanded admiration. Coffee never tasted so delicious, sipped as it was in a setting dominated by the woman who was beginning to fill his brain, his every self. It was a focus only occasionally interrupted by flickering neon lights in a show window on the other side of the street. They talked, they chuckled quietly, and they enjoyed the moment. Something was happening. It was like being swept along on a log in a current over which they seemed to have no control but which, they hoped, would eventually take them to a safe harbour.

"Why don't I walk you across the bridge this morning and see you safely in your office?" he suggested, catching her by surprise and causing her to raise her eyebrows.

"Thanks, but will you get to work on time?"

"Yes, I will have enough time to do so," he assured her.

"Okay, if you want to," she replied with a mild pensive look. She tidied her coat, reached for her bag and, with her hand tucked firmly under his arm, they were soon strolling hand-in-hand across London Bridge, one of the bridges linking London south of the Thames with the City. It was a little damp that morning and a light early autumn mist hovered over the Thames partly obscuring Tower Bridge in the distance over which, like London Bridge, commuters were pounding their way five abreast to the City. The mist was sometimes sufficiently thick in places to warrant the occasional blast of a horn from a river boat below. Walking together, vibrations laced with anticipation and excitement, seemed to drive every movement of their limbs. Within fifteen minutes they were at St. Christopher House where Pam worked, a 1950's building with thick walls and four floors. This was the moment he was waiting for to remove all doubt. They quickly pecked each other on the cheek before she turned with a half twirl

45

allowing the coat to show off its A-line cut and joined others making their way through the glass revolving doors and up the stairs. Mission accomplished, he was at his desk within ten minutes. He was a few minutes late but, for him, that didn't matter too much. For him, what mattered most that morning was the short but enjoyable time they had together.

They continued to have morning coffee at Jolly's until Pam suggested one morning that they could also occasionally meet on or near Southwark Bridge at lunchtime for a chat. Soon they were lunchtime spectators for the scene below: barges laden with cement, timber and other commodities making their way up and down the river, each with its bow like a giant chisel ploughing through the water, creating a stream of foam on either side. Red double-decker route-master buses, decorated on either side with multicolour posters, rumbled their way across the bridge to and from the city centre. Together they enjoyed the river-scape dominated in the background by St. Paul's Cathedral from which the clock chimes brought sweet music to their ears, for such chimes always seemed to be heralding the advent of something precious, a long-lasting love affair. It is against this background that they would often meet during lunchtime for a breath of fresh air or a stroll while reflecting on their individual lives and the journey they had made so far.

An early autumn day provided the perfect setting for an extended lunchtime stroll along Victoria Embankment adorned with a carpet of yellow, brown and bronze leaves from the beech and elm lining the embankment. The sun was at an angle creating shadows between pools of flickering sunlight that enveloped them with a kind of warmth that seemed to stimulate their hormones. Pausing for a moment to gaze at the river traffic, he looked at her and, sliding his fingers slowly around the nape of her neck, pulled her gently but firmly close to him and, as their lips met, he felt his touch acting like a slow seductive drug on her senses. With her arms around him, he could feel heat and excitement rising within her as she abandoned herself to that tantalizing sensation that was igniting her senses. In that searing moment of intimate contact, something as highly charged and as electrifying as a lightning bolt, flashed between them. She looked serenely into his eyes. "I can see my image in your eyes," she uttered softly. Just then he felt her sudden shocked reaction, and, from her quivering body, he knew she was also aware of it.

But, seeing each other every day and sometimes twice a day, did not reduce their burning desire to communicate even more and by whatever means possible. They had just emerged from London Bridge Underground station one morning and were making their way to St. Christopher House for it had now become Dennis' practice to see her safely at work. Without changing the pace of their step, she turned to him and said quietly and in a jerky voice, "Darling, I am going to write you a letter today." "Oh, that would be very nice," he replied with an affirmative nod. He could see from the sparkle in her eyes that she was serious and that she wanted to express her feelings in a manner that would, perhaps, allow them to flow through her pen on to the paper, and then to be read and inwardly digested by him as an indelible record. After lunch that day, to his amazement, the letter arrived by internal post, a system whereby government departments within a given circumference exchanged information by courier.

After lunch that day, four pages neatly folded and forced into a brown envelope showing all the signs of bursting at any time, landed on his desk. As he started to read, he could see it was meant to convey a feeling, a mood, the germ of something she hoped would develop and bind them together. It was a passion that had to be set free; a passion, though light as air, was as strong as an iron band. Many letters flowed between them and, it was with great eagerness that they would each await the arrival of the daily courier carrying good news sealed in a small brown envelope which often provided the topics for their evening conversations. They would describe the love they had for each other, the eagerness with which they looked forward to meeting each day, the passion, the moments they enjoyed together, be it on the train, in the café, on London Bridge or even taking the occasional quiet stroll along Victoria Embankment at lunchtime.

7

A mid-afternoon April shower was heavy enough to see water flowing swiftly to drains on Cannon Street but, that day, not even this could dampen Dennis' usual eagerness to see her that evening. Sitting at his desk, he could hardly contain his excitement. *'I must not be late, I must not be late this evening,'* were thoughts uppermost in his mind forcing him to glance at the clock on the wall almost every minute while tapping a pencil on his desk. *'I must not keep the woman with whom I am beginning to fall deeply in love, waiting. That would be a disaster.'* Their usual lunchtime meeting had left him buoyed up and by 4:15 he could feel himself revving up. Colleagues were already donning their light spring coats in readiness for the journey home. It was 4:30 pm when Dennis grabbed his coat, seized his brief-case and, without waiting for the lift, bolted down the stairs with the kind of speed that saw his light mackintosh spread-eagled in the air like batman. *'I mustn't be late, I mustn't be late,'* he kept saying to himself while carving a straight line through the flow of rush-hour pedestrians pounding their way to Cannon Street or Bank or London Bridge station. His sole objective was to be at Kings Cross on time.

He arrived at Bank Station with just enough time to snatch an evening paper from the newsboy and shoot down the escalator like a horse released from the starting gate. At Kings Cross, he positioned himself in what he considered the best vantage point on the platform which soon became crowded partly obscuring his vision. He was a man on a mission. *'I have to be at a point where she can see me as soon as she steps on to the platform.'* Between passing trains, he gazed at posters on the opposite wall and wished that one day he would be able to take his heart-throb to one of the shows advertised. He thought of what it would be like to escort her elegantly dressed to a theatre or a classical concert or even to a top-class restaurant offering more than just a nice meal, perhaps a dance as well. Six trains rumbled in and out at three-minute intervals each discharging and taking on its load of passengers. To the sound of *'mind the doors'* from the platform guard, each train would depart, leaving him to sweat as he gazed at the red rear lights disappearing in the distance through the tunnel. What was once a crowded platform would now be empty if only for a moment.

As he stood gazing anxiously in the direction from which the next train would appear, he was becoming overrun with worrying thoughts. Excitement was slowly giving away to anxiety, for the wait seemed interminable. *'Am I late? Have I missed her? Has she forgotten? More to the point, has she decided not to turn up?'* This onset of such thoughts ended abruptly by the usual feel of a gentle breeze on his face signalling the approach of an on-coming train. With the rumble getting louder and the breeze getting stronger, he peered into the distance anxiously awaiting its arrival. Every sinew in his body began to tighten. By now, he was surrounded by an avalanche of passengers flooding on to the platform from all directions. His added fear was that, it being rush hour, he could quite easily miss her. *'Why do they have to crowd me now?'* he thought, his eyes darting between obstructive bodies. He longed for a magic wand with which to make them disappear. Through all this he held his own and, with fingers crossed, he meticulously filtered every wave of passengers leaving the train.

'This has to be the one. She has to be on this one,' he said, casting an anxious glare in the direction of the on-coming train. Soon he spotted the High Barnett sign on the front of the approaching train. It was the train she always used because the Mill Hill branch would not take her to Kentish Town where she lived. Passengers alighted and headed for the exit or interchanging corridors. With his heart pounding almost out of control and his eyes piercing the distance, he saw first, one leg and then the other step smartly onto the platform just seconds before

the doors were about to be closed. *'I know those legs. Those are the very legs that captured my undivided attention many times before.'* A feeling of renewed excitement gripped him. Squeezing his briefcase tightly and without hardly any head movement, he quickly moved his eyes vertically upward to be rewarded with the sight he was so anxiously awaiting. *'I am not late after all, nor has she forgotten.'*

Pam looked one way and then the other and then their eyes met. What was once a crowded platform a minute ago had now become a deserted place except for two who approached each other with expressions that said it all before they even said a word. Tension in his body began to ebb away like water draining from a bathtub. With every step made toward each other, smiles got broader and broader. They were soon in each other's arms and, with their lips pressed together and eyes closed, and with words hanging in the air, they allowed their senses to sizzle hot and intoxicating. Irresistible currents of energy flashed between them. He could feel her body shivering with sensation. She was almost weightless. Desire had unfurled between them sweeping them up into a thrilling vortex making them oblivious to others around them for, in that instant, the rest of the world didn't matter. At that moment, they were a world. But suddenly, she jerked her head backward and released her grip, opened her eyes and looked around quickly and with some concern.

"We have to be careful Dennis, I just remembered," she whispered hastily, her head moving to the right and then smartly to the left. Cold fingers of fear had suddenly clutched her. Being a major change station for six lines, their favourite platform at Kings Cross was also a meeting point for other couples with similar ideas. But for Pam and Dennis, there was always some danger lurking in the background, for there was a chance that, quite unknown to them, they might be seen by someone who knew their spouses.

"Why?" he asked, gazing at her with a somewhat puzzled look but, with his arms still around her, he guided her slowly into a more secluded place where they would be less likely to be trampled on by the swift current of commuters. "Is something the matter," he asked, as another train pulled into the station.

TROPICAL HEATWAVE

"I have a friend who also works somewhere around London Bridge and who goes home around this time. She knows my husband Elton and I am sure if she sees us, she will tell him," she exclaimed glancing around nervously.

"What does she look like?" hastily releasing his arms and joining her in scrutinizing each wave of commuters.

"She is shorter and darker than me, wears glasses. She is a kind of busy-body, you know the type, so we have to be very careful."

"What makes you think she would do such a thing, after all, she is a friend of yours, isn't she?"

"Well, she has visited us on more than one occasion and I could tell from her body-language that she wanted to make a play for Elton and sometimes I could tell when he was speaking to her on the phone." Dennis could sense that Pam was very concerned and uneasy, and why not? After all, it could mean the possible end to a relationship that was about to take off. "I think I saw her in the train as it pulled out although I am not too sure, but what I can tell you is that, although we didn't see her, she probably saw us," said Pam, now more worried than ever because she felt they were too late. Dennis became immediately concerned as he felt a wave of terror washing over her. He knew then that they were crossing a dangerous barrier and that the situation would have to be handled with the greatest care.

"But how did you meet her?" he asked with a slightly furrowed forehead.

"We met on the train to Kings Cross one evening about a year ago, and it was then she told me she knew Elton and that she was divorced."

"Do you think she is on the lookout?" uttered Dennis with a chuckle.

"Of course, she is. I have seen the way she plays up to him when she comes to see us, so now you see why we must try to avoid letting her see us," she added, sounding convincing.

"Oh, I see, and what is her name?"

"Gladys," glancing over her shoulder as if afraid that someone might overhear what she was saying. Dennis narrowed his eyes and was silent for an extended moment.

"That woman has to be confronted. Her sting has to be drawn before she can poison our relationship," he declared in a rather

51

hurried but concerned voice. They moved to a more secluded location inside one of the nearby arches, moving apart on the arrival of each train and then returning to their former position as soon as the train trundled away. "I think your train is approaching," he uttered softly trying to string out the moment. With a parting kiss, he saw her on to the Northern Line before making his way to board the Piccadilly Line on another platform. After that, they not only saw each other every morning and sometimes at lunch, they now did so every evening as well.

This arrangement worked well for the next five months which was why Dennis was not prepared for what was to follow. It was Wednesday morning when he arrived at Kings Cross at the usual time and waited for her train to arrive. One, two, three, four trains arrived and disappeared in the tunnel. Several more did, leaving him dazzled as he peered at the changing red signals. He checked his watch. He knew he was early. *'I am never late. Perhaps, the train was so crowded that I missed her. Perhaps she saw me but could do nothing about it. Maybe she is not well and has decided to stay at home,'* were some of the thoughts crowding his mind as he jostled among passengers for the best position to see her in the usual carriage.

It was now 8:15 and he had to be at work by 8:30. In total disappointment he boarded the next train his eyes, like laser beams, penetrating every corner of the carriage in the hope of spotting her. *'What if she didn't manage to board the usual carriage or even get close to her usual seat? That would be enough for me to miss her during the rush. Maybe her friend saw us and told Elton forcing her to cut short what we had going.'* By Friday, what he thought was just one of those things had created a void in his daily experience leading him to conclude that she had dropped him. With each passing day, he would look for something: a letter or a phone call. There were no more meetings, no more coffee mornings at the small café in lower Cannon Street, or evening snogging on the platform. Even in the company of his work colleagues or when caught up with bustling commuters at Kings Cross, he felt alone. Gone was the thrill of travelling to and from work. It was as though he had lost his *raison d'etre* for living for she had taken a part

TROPICAL HEATWAVE

of him with her. It had all suddenly become so hollow that he felt as though his life had slipped over a cliff in a moment.

Every morning he would arrive at Kings Cross and wait to join her in the usual carriage, but alas, in vain for the more he looked, the less he saw. He no longer felt like getting a seat at Kings Cross and if he did, he always saw the person next to him as undesirable company. Every evening he would arrive on time for the rendezvous that never took place. Instead, he would be left a lonely figure gazing at the posters on the wall. Nor did the masses milling around him at rush hour do anything to reduce his pain and his loneliness. He was shattered and all alone in a maddening crowd. Weeks passed, then months as he searched desperately for answers, hoping that one day he would see her again. And often, as he stood there, he would quietly recall some of the lyrics of two popular songs: *Have you seen her? Has anybody seen my Pam? Why did she have to abandon me like this?*

Dennis no longer heard her dulcet voice on the phone or saw her sitting in the carriage on mornings awaiting his company. He no longer saw her stepping out of the carriage to join him on the platform. Gone was that radiant smile that greeted him, the look that tore his very heart out every time he saw her. He would quietly call her name, but no one would answer. His whole world had collapsed. He would look at the posters on the other side of the tracks without seeing them and then, with tears on the point of overflowing, he would make his way home, a lonely figure, his body numbed with sadness. He tried desperately not to allow it to affect his work, but it was very difficult concealing it from his friend Lawry on the other side of the desk. This became known to him one day on a lunchtime walk along Pudding Lane not far from his workplace in Cannon Street. They often took a lunch time walk around East Cheap, Cheap Side, and Lower Thames Street, including Billingsgate Fish Market. Lawry felt that, as a friend and colleague, it was his duty to introduce Dennis, who was new to the area, to some of the history within which they were working. Dennis always expressed his appreciation for what he was doing but, on this day, while reading the plaque at the foot of the monument commemorating the Great Fire of London which took place in 1666, Lawry noticed an unusual quietness in him.

"Hey Dennis, you don't seem to be as jolly as you usually are, and I noticed you didn't say much this morning during tea-break. Is everything alright with you?" He expected an answer, but Dennis remained focused on the plaque. At that moment, he was trying to envisage what life must have been like in 17th century Pudding Lane with its cobbled street, hemmed in on either side with timber framed buildings from which hanging signs told you the business within. His attention was only broken by the sound of rattling wheels on cobble stone. It was a horse-drawn dray cart delivering barrels of beer to a pub (public house) nearby.

"Well, not quite," he replied and proceeded to relate the whole story to Lawry and, as usual, the conversation soon turned to political issues or even the daily brigade of mini-skirted office girls they would observe from their fourth office window in Cannon Street, that pageantry from the fourth-floor window. It was a pageantry they never missed at tea break. But would such chats give Dennis renewed hope and would they be enough to see him safely over this hurdle?

8

Three months later, Dennis was sitting in the sweltering summer heat on the Piccadilly Line underground train on his way home. He had had a hard day and was mentally exhausted which left him dosing quietly as the train rattled its way to Turnpike Lane station. Others were either themselves sleeping or reading a book or a paper. The carriage was like any other carriage on a London Underground, quiet except for the occasional shuffle of a newspaper. Perhaps it was a dream he had, or it was a flashback to a previous conversation they had while on the train one morning. Whichever it was, he recalled Pam saying, *'Dennis, I think I might be moving from St. Christopher House.'*

'What are you talking about?' asked Dennis frantically, the expression on his face making it quite obvious that he was caught by surprise. 'Where are you going?' he added, thinking that, if she was moving to another building in London, they would still be able to see each other.

'The Ministry of Transport is moving part of its office to Hemel Hempstead and they have asked me if I would like to go. It is a new town in Hertfordshire about 40 kilometres or 25 miles north of London. They even took me to see the new office and a three-bedroom house goes with the job,' she uttered, and his face sank a few centimetres.

'Have you given them an answer yet?' He asked, knowing deep down that, for a person living in a one bedroom flat in Tufnell park, to be offered a job and a three-bedroom house in a new town, would be hard to refuse.

'Not yet,' she replied, 'but I have to let them know by the end of this month.' Dennis was not too sure whether the expression on her face was one of joy or sadness or even a combination of both, but he was stunned. It was as though he was hit with 1000 volts.

'Oh ___,' was the only word that tumbled out of his mouth. For once, he had run short of words. Drought suddenly hit the conversation. Nothing more was said for a drawn-out moment. Seconds passed. 'Well, I am pleased for you,' but inwardly he was tearing apart. Several images and thoughts galloped through his mind like, 'Would I ever see her again? Would she find someone else's shoulder on which to rest her head? Despite this, I must not be so selfish as to deny her an opportunity of bettering herself.'

This spell, be it a dream or reflection, was only broken by the screeching of brakes signalling the arrival of the train at Turnpike Lane station where he would disembark. He said goodbye to some of his commuter friends before making his way across the nearby small park. Perhaps it was the heat of the afternoon that made him sit for a short while on a park bench. From here, propping on an arm of the bench, his attention was drawn to a small group of mothers with their under-fives sitting on rugs and blankets enjoying the sunshine, but he also had time to reflect on the wonderful moments he enjoyed with Pam. Not far away minor skirmishes were breaking out among a small flock of pigeons competing for crumbs left by the group of children, some of whom found pleasure in running after them causing the birds to take to flight.

It was during this afternoon theatre that Dennis slowly convinced himself Pam had made the move to Hemel Hempstead. 'But why did she have to treat me like that?' he pondered. For almost three weeks he grappled with these thoughts trying to find an answer but without success. During the months that followed, he suffered emotional pain the likes of which he hoped he would never have to experience again. A pang of restless worry gripped him. He continued to wait and look mornings and evenings, but always, the more he looked, the less he saw. 'What would make her do such a thing? And how could she go without even leaving me a forwarding-address or telephone number? Could this be the same woman with whom I was beginning to fall passionately in love?' It was a thought that carried the possibility of sending him into orbit.

Day by day, Dennis did his best to shelve the whole experience but, again and again, the same questions kept popping up driving him to the point where he felt he had to do something about it. '*I know what I will do, I'll spend as much time as possible on my part-time job both during the week and on weekends. That way I'll have less time to think of her,*' he said to himself, and that is what he set about doing but, alas, he couldn't help thinking of her and the promise of a new life he had seen in her. It was driving him out of his mind. He had to find her whatever it took and with some urgency.

Two months later Dennis emerged from Turnpike Lane station to the sound of chirping birds in the nearby green on an early autumn afternoon. Floating leaves, brown and gold, were already beginning to settle gently on the grass beneath. He had heard this chorus many times before but this time, what came with the chorus was the thought of the usual barrage of questions and verbal explosion awaiting him on reaching home. When added to the various thoughts that careered through his mind during the day, he concluded it was better to have his dinner at a local Steak House not far from the station than try to do so at home. He had never gone to this restaurant before although it was near to where he lived and by which he had passed several times before. It was not the lap of luxury, but he had been told by a friend that it served the best steak in the area. The interior décor was simple which, together with a shaded lamp on each table and walls with soft colours and windows offering an uninterrupted view of the nearby park, made it a pleasant place to have a meal.

He selected a small table in the far corner where he sat sipping a glass of cold beer and each time he replaced the glass on the table after a sip, he would peer into it while running his forefinger several times slowly around the rim. It was a deep concentration for, not only was he trying to bring meaning to what had happened, he was also trying to find a solution. It took the wailing sound of a fire engine speeding its way to Wood Green about a kilometre away to break his concentration, causing him to raise his eyes to a horizontal position and gaze around for a moment. Had he not done so, he would not have noticed another couple sitting at a table in the opposite corner less than three meters away. They had finished their meal and were probably just having an after-dinner drink. As he watched them chatting softly and sipping on what seemed to be their second bottle of wine, his mind became overtaken with images of what might have been had he not lost Pam. Unable to take anymore, he was about to leave the restaurant without ordering a meal when he was suddenly distracted.

"Oh! Hello Dennis." It seemed to be a voice from the past causing him to turn sharply while clutching the door handle. On recognising the face, he joined their table. "Fancy meeting you here. I didn't know this was one of your favourite eating places," declared David, a chap of slightly bigger build and a bit older. They had both left Barbados around the same time and had worked together as postal sorters at the same main postal sorting office in London. They were never very close friends but respected each other and had not seen one another since Dennis had left to join the clerical service in the Finance Branch of the post office. The woman sitting opposite David slowly turned her head. She knew Dennis' voice but seemed momentarily unable to speak. Instead, she managed a side glance at him with a soft smile. It was a glance carrying a message known only to them. Dennis responded with a cautious but covert smile and, although they had only been visitors in each other's world, he felt his heart tug.

"Hello David, nice to see you again after almost six years," stuttered Dennis, finding himself in the grip of a hand shake with a broad smile. The woman's glance had brought back fleeting memories of the times they spent together at beach picnics and house parties in Barbados. They had met at a party in a beach restaurant given in honour of one of the well-known cricketers. The strengthening bond between them was only broken when Dennis had to leave the island without even letting her know and this brief encounter only served to rekindle the hurt it had caused them both: it was a hurt he saw even then in her face as she tried to feign a soft smile.

"This calls for a celebration," uttered David signalling to the waiter to bring another bottle of wine. "Oh, by the way, this is Judy my new girlfriend. We met two years ago, and she is very nice," he added with a broad grin. *'You don't have to convince me, my friend, I knew her long before you since she was one of my former girlfriends in Barbados,'* Dennis said to himself. Judy acknowledged the compliment from

David while allowing her eyes to covertly settle gently on Dennis who was quick to sense what was going on. Nor did this go unnoticed by David although the conversation that followed was mainly about their days together in the post office. But during the conversation Dennis accidentally let slip that his marriage was going through a torrid patch. Judy angled her head while staring down at the glass of red wine in her hand. What she heard had set her thinking. *'Perhaps I might be able to rekindle old flames here if I could see Dennis sometime. After all, he at least owes me a date, considering he left the island without telling me,'* she thought and sighed quietly which drew a suspicious look from David.

"Excuse me for a moment," she requested and made her way to the washroom returning ten minutes later with an enhanced makeover and Dennis could not resist giving her a compliment with his eyes rather than with words. He took a sip of wine and cleared his throat.

"David, you are a very lucky man to have such a nice girl." She was touched by Dennis' compliment and sent him a thank-you smile. David chuckled loudly, gazing into her face. Judy was very attractive, and it was then that Dennis deeply regretted what had happened in Barbados, but it also served to bring into sharp focus the gem of a girl he had lost in Pam and made him even more determined to find her. But David had noticed the subtle eye contacts and body language between them. He poured himself another glass of wine and straightened himself in his chair.

"Do you two know each other?" he asked Dennis awkwardly, his eyes darting between them suspiciously. Judy coughed lightly on a sip of wine while covertly putting one finger to her lips as though to say, *'don't say anything.'* Dennis looked and felt slightly uncomfortable. He was caught off-guard by the question, but he had got Judy's message. They both denied it almost simultaneously. It was as though they had rehearsed the response. A moment of silence followed until the phone behind the bar rang.

"It's for you David," shouted the bar-tender, "you can take it in the small back room." David asked for an excuse and made his way hastily. Dennis saw this as a small window of opportunity to have a quick chat, to catch up with old times.

"Why not let us exchange phone numbers before he gets back," suggested Judy anxiously, "and thanks for not letting David know we were an item in Barbados. He is a very jealous man and I know what it would be like if he knew."

"How have you been doing?" asked Dennis with a look of excitement fleeting though it had to be.

"I didn't think you cared after you left Barbados without letting me know," she replied with a pointed look. Dennis shook his head and gave an audible sigh.

"I am sorry," he said softly and regretfully as memories came flooding back. "After what happened in Bridgetown market five months before I left, I was forced to cool it for a while at least until the dust from that volcanic verbal explosion had settled." Unfortunately for Dennis, Susan's mother had got wind of the secret relationship between Dennis and Judy and, on meeting Judy one afternoon at the bus terminus in Bridgetown, launched a ferocious verbal attack on her who was in no position to launch a strong counter attack. So loud was the outburst, that it forced birds in nearby trees to take flight. This drama, which occurred at the hottest time of the day, attracted the attention of a small group of women, including mauby vendors as well as roasted nuts and sweet vendors, to pause and look on in amazement while voicing their opinions. It was soon after this outburst that Dennis left for England. "I found it very difficult to get away to meet you after that," added Dennis, seeing that the five intervening years had not eroded the feeling they had for each other.

"You know, I always loved you and those feelings haven't changed," she said and sighed as the memories of Saturday evenings at the Plaza cinema or a stroll together through Queen's Park or the beach picnics at Crane Beach, at Belleplaine or at Silver Sands or Mullins Beach. She recalled the times she rode pinion on his motorcycle with the air flowing freely through her dark long hair. "It really hurt when I heard you had married Susan. Why did you do such a thing and so suddenly?" Her voice trailed as she cast a beseeching look at him. He nodded, unable to speak for a short while.

"I know, because I have similar feelings and I have always regretted what I did but it was a difficult situation." He sounded depressed and

TROPICAL HEATWAVE

she reached across the table and held his fingers before levelling her eyes with his.

"Was Susan pregnant?" she asked under a furrowed forehead. Judy had heard about Susan from some of her friends and had concluded that there was no compatibility whatever between them, which is why she asked such a question. It was the only reason she could muster for such a whirlwind marriage.

"Yes, and you know quite well that, as a teacher, I was expected to marry her even though I was never in love with her," and he went on to tell her a bit more about the eventual breakdown of his marriage.

"Is that why you were sitting on your own looking so lost? I find it hard to believe that a man like you will find it difficult to find someone to comfort you." They had just promised each other to keep in touch when David suddenly returned to find them swiftly releasing their fingers. The telephone conversation seemed to have gone well because he was carrying a broad grin. But Judy, sensing that he had seen them holding hands, decided that the best way to defend was to go on the attack. "That was a very long conversation and who could that be who knows you are here at this restaurant and at this time?" David was caught off-side, he did not expect a mini-inquisition. He performed a series of mental backward flips and then shrugged his shoulders looking matter-of-factly.

"That was one of my work colleagues asking my advice on a problem he has." This drew a suspicious look from Judy whose sandy eyebrows shot up to her hairline. "Are you sure you two never met before because, from what I saw, it seems to me that you know each other," he uttered with a defiant lift of his chin. His eyes bored into Dennis' who was saved by approaching footsteps. It was a waiter.

"Can I get you all anything else?" Dennis and Judy welcomed the interruption.

"No," replied David, his face taking on a more intense look.

"Then I'll get your bill." They spent the intervening five minutes getting their things together to leave. Goodbyes exchanged, David and Judy made their way to the station. Dennis resumed his journey home but after ten paces he suddenly stopped, turned and, for a lingering moment, gazed at Judy going away in the distance. *'To think that she might have been my wife were it not for the stupidity that got me into a loveless marriage,'* he muttered quietly to himself. But, meeting Judy and David that evening, made him more determined to have a nice woman like Judy and spurred him on to do all it took to find his Venus. He shook his head and made a long, drawn-out groan before continuing his way home.

Rekindling old flames with Judy was very tempting especially in the light of his current situation. Despite this, however, he thought it better to put the whole idea on the back burner for at least six months for he was still hoping that one day, yes, just one day, Pam would return to him. That evening, as he settled down in his study to read the daily news; the mental turmoil, created by the hurt at losing Pam and the recent temptation to rekindle things with Judy, was only momentarily ameliorated by the pitter-patter of raindrops on the window pane from an evening shower. He wheeled his chair fully back while stretching his legs fully out under his desk and gazed at the wall map of London. *'Where could she be among the eight million in this city?'* In frustration, he leaned forward and, with his head between his hands, allowed his pen to drop freely to the desk. The agony was never far but, in this deep pensive mood, he recalled Pam telling him about a good friend Jean, a Trinidadian girl whom she had met on the boat to England and who was also going to the same hospital in Colchester to do nursing. *'If I could just touch base with her perhaps she might be able to tell me where to find Pam. But what if she knows and refuses to tell me? After all, being a good friend, she might have been told not to say anything. Or worst yet, what if she knows nothing? But it's still worth a try.'*

After two months of prolonged agony, he could feel himself fast disappearing into sentimental oblivion. In utter desperation he decided to contact Jean but there was one major problem, he had no contact number. It was useless using the phone directory because he did not know her surname although what he did have was the street in which she lived. Pam had given it to him one morning while having coffee in the little café. With this renewed hope, he frantically fingered through the pages of his old diary like a ferret anxiously in search of food. He could feel his body getting warmer with heightened expectation and was almost to the point of exploding

TROPICAL HEATWAVE

when suddenly, there it was, *Jean's phone number and address* on a page slightly obliterated. Without a moment to spare, he seized the phone and dialled frantically, his fingers engaging in a nervous tapping on the table as he waited anxiously to hear a woman's voice at the other end. Then, as though by divine intervention, came a voice seemingly out of the mist.

"Hello, Jean speaking." Never before was a voice more life-saving and more hope-giving. A moment of silence gripped him for he could not believe his luck. Already he could feel his misery begin to fade. He took a deep breath.

"Hello Jean, my name is Dennis," he replied with some buoyancy and with an audible exhale of air. He could feel the phone slipping slowly from his sweaty hands so elated with joy was he. "You don't know me, but I have heard a lot about you from someone whom I think is a mutual friend." Jean was as surprised with his opening statement as he was at hearing her voice at the other end of the line.

"Oh, who is that friend?" she asked hurriedly.

"Pam," he replied lingering for a second on the name.

"Oh yes, how is she? I haven't heard or seen her for some time now and I often wondered what had become of her, but I hope she told you nice things about me," and she chuckled softly. "I have only seen her a few times since she got married and I was always anxious to know how she was getting on." Dennis' excitement jumped to a new level, making it appear as though the mirror over the telephone table suddenly became partially clouded over from the steam generated by his body. *I am on the right track. All I have to do now is to handle the situation with the greatest of care. But I must also show Jean I hold her in high esteem by painting what I know about her with a broad brush. It might not work but it is a chance I have to take,'* he hastily thought.

"Oh yes, she told me about your days as nursing students at the hospital in Colchester and of the days you would go shopping together in the town centre as well as the occasional weekend in London."

"It was not easy, but we survived. We found time to enjoy ourselves. There were only a few of us from the Caribbean at this hospital so we stuck together. We would go to town mainly to window shop because, being trainee-nurses, we had very little money. We tended to use some of the leisure activities at the hospital, dancing for example. You see, there were not many black young men in Colchester and we didn't fancy what we saw. We would save our money and come to London once in every two months if we had weekends off together and we really looked forward to the house parties. My boyfriend Winston, who also lives in London, would take us around and tell us about any parties taking place on Saturday nights. In fact, that is how Pam met Elton her husband."

"Oh, really, is that so?" It was clear to Dennis that Jean was a wealth of information. He just had to play it sensibly if he was to re-connect with the girl whom he saw as offering him fulfilment of life.

"I do know that, since she got married, she was having some problems with Elton who seem to be into drinking and gambling on the horses, you know the kind of thing. But I must be careful because I don't know you. You might be one of Elton's friends and I won't want to make matters worse for her," exclaimed Jean sounding cautious.

"I understand but you don't have to worry. You are safe with me. I don't even know Elton," he said reassuringly and hoped that this would give her the green light to trust him for he had to extract as much information as possible from her.

"Well, from your voice, you seem to be a nice man. I often thought things were getting quite rough between them and she even hinted she was thinking of leaving him claiming he was often verbally and physically violent." *'Perhaps this was what I saw that morning when I first saw her on the train,'* he quickly thought. "She even mentioned in passing that she had met someone on the train one morning on her way to work, but I never pressed the issue, nor did she tell me who he was. Was it you?" There was a drawn-out silence. *'I always felt Pam was hiding certain things from me and I* was correct,' was the thought that immediately gripped Dennis but he had kept Jean waiting for a response while in this thought process.

"Are you still there Dennis?" He was suddenly overcome by the thought of what she must have been going through when they met for the first time on the train and her effort at feigning a calm during such a torrid marriage.

TROPICAL HEATWAVE

"Yes, yes, sorry about that," he blurted, and, at that moment, he knew that he would have to give something to get something.

"Yes, I am that man," he replied in a baritone voice of the type that tends to attract a certain type of girl. He had thrown a dice over which he had no control. He could only hope it would bring him a good return, for the alternative was too hurtful to think about.

"You see, she never told me your name," she said warmly as though she regretted not knowing Dennis before. From the change in the tone of her voice, Dennis sensed an eagerness in her to see him and, even though they could not see each other, he perceived a certain glow in her face.

"Perhaps that was because we had not long met each other........." he exclaimed, allowing his voice to fade away to give her maximum time to speak while he continued to doodle on his notepad.

"Pam is a very nice girl," she volunteered. "I must know because we met on the SS Napoli in 1959 on the way to England and became very good friends." Dennis' approach was successful so far. His anxiety had now subsided to the level where he felt confident enough to ask that all-important question, the answer to which would determine whether there was any chance of him ever seeing Pam again.

"When was the last time you spoke to her or saw her? I'll tell you why. I have been trying to contact her for some time now but without any success and I just wondered if you might have a number I could try." He used the kind of telephone manner that was entreating rather than demanding, so desperate was he.

"Look, I don't know if she has moved and has changed her phone number, but now that you want to get in touch with her, I think I should do so even for myself. But pardon me. I must cut this conversation soon because my boyfriend Winston will be home within the next five minutes. But why don't we meet sometime in a convenient place where we can talk?" was her hurried request. It was a request that left Dennis feeling positive but also apprehensive.

"Certainly, I'll appreciate that very much. In fact, I'll do better than that. Why don't I take you out for a meal one evening? This will give us a chance to see each other for the first time and have a quiet chat over a nice meal, how about it?" She needed no further convincing.

"Yes, why not?" lingering on the word '*not*.'

"How about that Greek restaurant near Marble Arch, you know the one?" He suggested.

"Oh yes, that's the one near to the cinema."

"Ok, shall we say, Saturday at 5 o'clock?"

"Yes, but you must remember I have to be home before 10:30 because Winston gets home around eleven on Saturdays."

"Oh, don't you worry I'll make sure you are back in time."

"Ok, Saturday it will be then," and they both chuckled. Dennis welcomed the idea and breathed a sigh of relief before replacing the receiver. He had at last made a breakthrough. That mist of misery that enshrouded him for weeks and months was at last slowly beginning to lift. Jean was known among her friends as a bit of a flirt who would stop at nothing to get hold of the man she was after, nor was she slow to seek revenge should anyone get in her way. Winston, her boyfriend, was also from Barbados and had arrived in England one year after Elton and, after a few odd jobs, he too joined the ranks of those employed by British Rail.

Although Dennis was now more hopeful about the chance of seeing Pam again, he was bombarded by several worrying thoughts putting his mind in spin-dryer mode. '*Suppose this light I see at the end of the tunnel is an approaching train, one that will run me over? Although I welcome the idea of meeting Jean, I cannot understand why she can't continue the phone conversation at a more convenient time, say, tomorrow. How do I know she doesn't have a hidden agenda? Or did my baritone voice and phone manner stimulate that seat in her emotions impelling her to want to meet me soon? What if she likes what she sees? How do I know she isn't thinking of using the moment to her advantage to out-manoeuvre her friend? Could my inquiry about Pam have triggered the idea that I am available, ready and willing to play ball? Worse of all, can I trust her not to pass this information on to Elton?*'

These were the unanswerable questions prompting Dennis to conclude that he might well be going one step forward and two steps backward. And yet, as he slowly replaced the receiver, he felt they were in some way in the same boat. She supposedly knew nothing about the whereabouts of one of her best friends and, perhaps, Pam didn't want either of them to know what was going on. She was perhaps playing it safely. But, in spite of this, Dennis felt he had at last made some positive inroads. He had made a move in the right direction.

The three days leading up to the meal felt like three months so anxious was he to meet Jean for, in her, was his only hope. Saturday finally came, and Dennis arrived at the restaurant quite early even though he had reserved a table. The popularity of the restaurant demanded that you did so. He was never late for a date nor would he allow this to be the first time. This gave him some time to mull over another worrying thought. *'Suppose she doesn't turn up? Suppose Winston returns home earlier than anticipated? How would I know?'* These and many more *'what ifs'* began to crowd his mind as he stood outside the restaurant anxiously awaiting the arrival of every bus from Kensal Rise. It was a focus only occasionally interrupted by crowds emerging from Marble Arch underground station to make their way along Edgware Road or Oxford Street to shop or simply to spend the evening dining and dancing or going to the Odeon cinema just fifty metres away. But before he could be swept away in such a wave of thoughts, she was stepping down from the bus no more than ten meters away. He knew it was her. It had to be her for she had given him a description of herself and what she would be wearing. Soft smiles of mild excitement broke out as they recognised each other from a distance.

"Hello Jean, how nice to see you," giving her a brush on the cheeks. "You look exactly as you described yourself," and she thanked him for the compliments, looking around as though she was expecting one of Winston's friends to suddenly pass by.

"You don't look too bad yourself," she replied, looking up at him with an approving smile and raising her voice to be heard above the din of traffic and the busy world along Edgware Road. Jean was short, certainly much shorter than Pam and with large brown eyes that seemed to take in an entire scene, though quite attractive. She was wearing a short grey coat, for the falling golden leaves had signalled mid-autumn and the arrival of a spell sufficiently chilly to warrant the wearing of a light coat. She had taken pains to dress in a manner that would not arouse her boyfriend's suspicion in case she was seen by him or one of his friends.

With greetings quickly exchanged they hastily made their way into the restaurant to be escorted to their table. A waiter soon appeared to pour them each a glass of red wine. After a couple of sips, they immediately commenced to indulge in the kind of exchanges normally reserved for those who have met for the first time but who share a common interest in a mutual friend. It was something like a game of chess where you played and watched the game while trying to work out your opponent's next move. It was an opening conversation only interrupted by the waiter returning to take their order. But it was something about her manner after those first sips that triggered off thoughts in Dennis' mind. Every time she reached for her glass to have a sip, she made sure that she revealed as much of her cleavage as possible making it somewhat difficult for Dennis to remain focused on why they had met. It seemed as though her body language was designed to send him a message. *'Am I in for a surprise? Could she be offering something beyond Pam's phone number and address?'* he pondered.

Whatever her hidden agenda, they were obviously anxious to meet each other, but they were playing this opening scene with a measure of caution. It took three glasses of Mateus Rose, a brand of Portuguese medium sweet frizzante wine, to bring about a meltdown in Jean to the point where she was now sufficiently at ease to verbalize her thoughts and allow her words to flow as freely as a waterfall. Dennis knew then that he wouldn't have long to await the kind of information he was seeking, for Jean was already showing she was quite talkative and good company.

She straightened herself up and looked at him with laughing eyes. "I wanted to meet you and I am glad I have because you are everything I expected you to be," she exclaimed with a teasing look to stimulate the palate of his mind.

"Oh really," he replied, allowing his gravelly voice to linger while taking note of the carrot she was dangling for it did not take too long for him to realise that Jean was probably hoping that they would slowly merge into each other's world.

9

As it was a Saturday evening the restaurant was full which was why she was extremely careful not to be seen by anyone who knew her. She was constantly scanning customers entering the restaurant because she felt it would be the kind of place some of her countrymen would frequent. "Please pour me another glass of wine," she asked, but before Dennis could do so, a waiter standing nearby, stepped in. She took a couple of sips and then she sat back with her legs crossed. "Winston and Elton were friends for a long time. They both work for British Rail and, like many men from the Caribbean, they like the betting shop, the pub, party-going and to be one of the boys. I often felt that this so-called *'going-out-with-the-boys'* scenario on weekends is just a cover up for having a fling. Pam always thought it would be a blessing in disguise if it would encourage Elton to leave and go after someone else," she volunteered. Dennis picked up on the tone of her voice when she made the final statement.

"What makes you say that?" he asked pointedly through narrowed eyes. She shrugged and then laughed softly. It was as though she felt she was about to move into dangerous territory and therefore wanted to be cautious. She sighed.

"I am not sure I ought to be telling you this because Pam is my good friend, but I know she never loved Elton. In fact, it was only by sheer chance that they met, and it is he who brought her nursing career to an abrupt end out of his sheer stupidity and selfishness," she declared, whereupon Dennis cleared his throat before topping up the glasses.

"Oh! What do you mean by she never loved him?" He was now keen to know more especially as Jean had now mellowed sufficiently to release vital information. Jean proceeded to describe in as much detail what had happened that night at the party and blamed herself for Pam's misfortune. But Dennis was quick to perceive that she was using this expression of guilt as a means of boosting her esteem in his eyes. She wanted him to see her as a nice person.

"I felt long ago there was nothing left in their marriage. I could see that, although they were together, there was no togetherness and I can even recall Pam telling me she never loved him, nor did she think she ever would and that the marriage was a mistake which she regretted." Dennis popped two olives into his mouth, took a sip of wine and sat back in his chair as Jean continued to express her thoughts about Pam's marriage. The restaurant was still full, and candles were flickering as waiters moved swiftly between tables to satisfy customers. This, together with Greek statuettes in illuminated coves bedecked with laurel leaves, helped to enhance the mood. The waiter arrived to take the order.

"I'll have a steak, medium to well-done, together with a Greek salad and French fries."

"Thank you, madam, and you, sir?"

"I'll have a similar thing but with the steak well-done."

"Thank you, sir." Within twenty minutes they were doing justice to a well prepared and presented meal. Light conversation over dinner provided Jean with a platform on which to test the waters. Comments on the interior décor of the restaurant was accompanied at times by the kind of body language aimed at revealing her underlying intent. And then Dennis recalled Pam mentioning that Jean was very flirtatious and that she would do whatever it takes to get hold of the man she is after. However, mindful that time was limited because she had to be indoors well before Winston got home, Dennis thought he had to get to the real reason for their meeting, namely, to discuss what could be done to re-establish contact with his elusive Pam. He was about half-way through his steak when he lifted his glass half-way and angled his head.

"So, it appears you and Pam are well acquainted with each other, yes?"

"Yes, we go back far," popping her large brown eyes, suggesting there was a lot more to come.

"It was a good idea for both of you to come to London together on your weekends off. At least it gave you all something to which to look forward," he added, in an effort to keep the conversation flowing in the direction in which he wanted it to flow rather than allowing her to move it in a direction more to presenting herself.

"We were young and free, and we really went partying in those days. I don't know why, but whenever we went to a party, the guys always wanted to dance with us," she exclaimed and smiled aiming a meaningful glance at him.

"Let's face it Jean, you two were bringing a Caribbean touch to English dancing in those early days of immigration from the Caribbean, and who better to do so than you two!" he exclaimed with a wry smile and she chuckled loudly.

"I can even remember Pam having a crush on a chap she met at one of those parties, but I don't think anything much came out of it," she declared looking rather coy as she paused for a few seconds expecting an immediate response. *'Could this be the man whom she has chosen instead of me?'* he pondered but remained silent, feeling that the next person to speak would lose the game. It was a concept he had brought from the insurance world and had implemented on many occasions to close a deal successfully. The idea was based on the notion that, as a sales representative, once you had made your presentation and had completed the summary and closing stage, you remained silent, because, the person who spoke next was generally the loser. In other words, if you disciplined yourself not to be tempted to speak first, then there is always the chance you will get the business.

"I think his name was Sidney and like me, was from Trinidad. I often wondered what became of him because he seemed a nice chap. Like you, he came to England to go to university but, unlike you, things didn't quite work out for him. Instead, he ended up working in a clothing factory before going to USA."

"How did you come to know all of this?" Dennis asked, squinting short-sightedly at her while trying to catch the attention of a waiter for coffee. At this point he thought it wiser to say as little as possible and listen more.

"I met him on a one-day trip to Amsterdam. In fact, Pam was also on that trip and, not only were we on the same coach, but happened to be at the same hotel. Since then, he attended a couple of my parties. I think he fancied her and I also had a crush on him but with Winston around I couldn't do much about it," she exclaimed and smiled proudly. Dennis suddenly realised he had prised open the door to what appeared to be a wealth of useful information. He looked at her under a furrowed brow. *'But why is she telling me about another man presumably in Pam's life, bearing in mind that she is a good friend of Pam in whom I am showing an interest. What game is she playing? And is betraying her friend part of her strategy to divert my interest from Pam to her? If so, she is doing a very good job of it,'* he thought quietly though not surprisingly from what he had learned about her from Pam and indeed from what he had seen of her so far. Jean had disclosed, either by chance or intentionally, a glimpse of her underlying goal at a time when Dennis was most vulnerable. All she had to do now was to follow it through.

Dennis was right. Jean was pressing on with her agenda and, in keeping with his character, he soon perceived that she had other more sinister ideas. From the trend of the dinner conversation, he felt that, bouncing around in her mind were thoughts like: *'I must make sure that, if Pam leaves Elton, she does not run into the arms of Sidney. He is one of my options not hers. I am keeping him on the back burner for myself and Pam must not be allowed to get to him. After all, I met him first at a party well before she did. I must reconnect her with Dennis at all costs even though I fancy him myself.'*

At that moment the aroma of freshly made coffee told them the waiter was on his way with theirs. Dennis reached slowly for an after-eight mint allowing his fingers to caress the one he had chosen while trying to put meaning to what he was hearing. Several thoughts ripped through his mind in quick succession. *'I think Jean is a snake in the grass. She is on a mission and this is her moment. Helping me to reconnect with Pam could have two possible outcomes for her and put her in a win-win position. If Elton finds out, it could mean that Pam may have to run to me, giving Jean a chance to make a serious play for Sidney. If Elton does not find out, Pam could continue to have a fling with me, leaving both Elton and Sidney wide open for her. What a clever move! I wonder on what burner she has placed me! The mind boggles.'* But, on hearing the name Sidney, Dennis' ears pricked up. It was the first time the name of a man, other than Winston her boyfriend, had been mentioned. *'This is worth a probe,'* he said to himself, *'but I must not appear too anxious to find out too much about him for fear she might stop the flow of what might well be a gem of information,'* he thought to himself and then signalled a waiter to bring two more coffees.

"How did you know Pam had a crush on him or that he was interested in her?" The waiter arrived with the coffee and two liqueurs. In the course of sipping their liqueur, their eyes met in a moment of message-sending stillness. Words hung in the air for a while. Dennis felt then that his thoughts were right and that she was about to entangle him into her web.

"Well, at one of my parties Sidney was dancing with a girl but he just couldn't take his eyes off Pam nor could she off him even though she was dancing with another man. It was as clear as crystal. Mind you, I often wondered if such a relationship would have got anywhere because I can also remember Sidney telling me he would like to go to America, Boston to be more precise, to live and she was still a trainee nurse at that time," she said dismissively. After spending three years in England, Sidney had left for Boston, Massachusetts to join his brother in the clothing business. But, while he was in London, his charisma was such that he had no problem attracting some of the most attractive girls at parties among whom were Jean and Pam.

"But didn't you think he might have said that just to impress you?" he asked in a quiet but searching voice while adding more milk to his coffee. Even before Jean mentioned it, he had already worked out that she too was interested in Sidney but was using the moment to see how far she could get with him.

"Oh no, he wasn't interested in me," she replied in a coy manner. "He is tall, and I am too short for him. Besides, Pam has the height and could dance much better than me. You see, Pam is endowed with a nice figure which I don't have so she flaunts it, and why not? I had no chance." From the way she spoke as well as her facial expression, Dennis detected a hint of jealousy and that she was also managing to direct proceedings in a way that would give her options.

"Oh, I see, but whatever happened after that?" asked Dennis tentatively.

"Well, we *did* catch up at one or two parties after which Sidney just disappeared, because I never saw him again. Whether Pam did, I don't know although, strangely enough, I can remember her telling me, less than two years ago, that she wouldn't mind going to America to live. I suppose she was coming to the end of the line with Elton who was continuing to treat her very badly. At the time, I just took it as one of those things. I never paid much attention to it because I didn't think she would be bold enough to leave Elton even though she would mention it to me from time to time." She paused for a long silent moment. A brain-wave had momentarily crashed on her mental shore and they stared at each other with a deep pensive look. Suddenly her eyes popped.

"Are you thinking what I am thinking?" she asked, sounding anxious and now looking rather worried.

"I don't know, but what are you thinking?" he replied curiously.

"Do you suppose she has----oh no----could she?" she asked, her face now quite ashen. The smile that lingered throughout the evening suddenly vanished.

"Quite honestly Jean, I don't know what to think but what I *do* know is that strange things can happen in life."

"Sidney did say he was thinking of going to Boston where he has an older brother who is doing quite well in the clothing business. Come to think of it, Pam had also mention Boston on the odd occasion," she added hurriedly. Dennis paused for a while. His brain was about to suffer the likes of a volcanic implosion as he struggled with all sorts of computations to arrive at why she would want to do so and yet, still lurking around in his mind, was that abiding thought: *'She has gone. She has turned her back on me. What have I done or more to the point, what is it I have not done?'* He paid the bill with his eyes fixed on a single statuette as though in a state of stupor, when he suddenly realised the conversation had come to an abrupt end. He raised himself slowly from his seat to leave the restaurant when Jean, still seated and equally perplexed, looked up at him with those large appealing eyes and held his hand.

"Dennis, Dennis, let's not jump to hasty conclusions. Pam and Elton might have moved and changed their number. Give me a chance to find out. Winston and Elton meet very often particularly on weekends in the pub for a drink or in the betting shop. Perhaps Winston might be able to help." He listened and, without saying a word, started to make his way very slowly to the door. Halfway through the door he made a half turn with an almost expressionless face.

"Jean, I want you to promise me one thing. If you find out anything, please let me know."

"I promise you I will, but do understand that, as a young attractive woman, Pam is quite capable of doing anything." Jean had to find Pam for she now saw her as an integral part of her own plan. Crossing the road to the bus stop, they could see the bus to Kensal Rise approaching. Dennis had just enough time to thank her for coming. It was now 9:30 pm and Edgware road was ablaze with show-window lights and neon signs. He held her arms and gazed into her eyes for a quiet moment before giving her a parting peck on her cheeks which she managed to manoeuvre to her lips. Sitting on the upper deck of the 'route master bus,' the then model bus used by London Transport, she had time to reflect on the evening. *'It is a pity I had to leave because I felt we were now getting tuned into each other and would have been happy to enjoy the rest of the evening together,'* she thought to herself.

A slightly chilly autumn breeze forced him to raise his collar as he stood watching the bus disappear north along Edgware road and thinking that he had at last made some substantial ground in his search for the only one he really loved. He felt hopeful that Jean would be the key to finding the missing link and, although astonished at what he had learned, he felt the evening had turned out better for both of them than they had probably expected. But, from that moment, he also had a feeling there was something more to Pam he had not yet uncovered. *'Is she the kind of person quite capable of successfully juggling three men? Or has she arrived at a set of cross-roads requiring her to make the kind of decision that would change her life forever and that therefore required her to take some time out?'* These were some of the burning thoughts that buzzed around in his brain. But, on his way home, yet other disturbing thoughts, emanating out of the chat over dinner, crashed onto his mind. Thoughts like: *'Jean would have to be very careful in the way she goes about getting any information from Winston because, if Elton or Winston did get to know what she was up to, it could mean never seeing Pam again. But what prevents her from telling Elton all we talked about and blowing the whole thing apart. Can I really trust her?'*

While admiring the illuminated shop windows from the upper deck of the bus she had time to mull over several thoughts, *'I am already beginning to see Winston as more and more undesirable, useless baggage I could dump. He is really getting in my way especially now that I have met Dennis and have had my perceptions of him confirmed. Perhaps, if I play my cards right, I might be able to get hold of him and do to Pam what she did to me.'* She now loathed everything that Winston did and was. Her main objective was to get back at Pam whom she saw as causing the breakup between herself and Sidney, a kind of revenge grail. She was just waiting for the right moment. Quite unexpectedly an opportunity had arisen out of Dennis' burning desire to find Pam. Would it be Elton or Dennis?

10

Having laid the foundation on which to develop her plot, Jean proceeded to drive home the advantage. It was 4pm on a Friday evening when she arrived home much earlier than usual. That extra time was needed to set the scene for a quiet Friday evening with Winston from whom she wanted some vital information. *Fish and chips* was the traditional Friday evening meal in England at that time. It was a dish that warmed to the palate of almost everyone. There was nothing better than having a helping of *fish and chips* straight from the shop served wrapped in white paper and then enclosed in newspaper to retain the warmth. Newcomers to the country soon caught on to it. Jean and Winston were no exceptions. However, the meal that Friday evening would be different though not so different as to arouse Winston's suspicion because he was not to question the reason for the change. Jean had prepared boiled gammon slices topped with pineapple rings and served with chips.

"That was very nice Jean but why the change from the usual meal?" asked Winston reaching for a can of lager as he settled himself in his usual chair to view TV. Jean had brought in an extra supply, a box of six which she had placed on the fridge. Horse-racing on the TV was now the focus of his attention while working out his winning chances on the next race from a folded *Racing Post*.

"By the way Winston, when last have you seen Elton?" It was a soft and entreating voice, one that would see Winston responding without asking probing questions. He topped up his glass and took three good sips through the white foam with his eyes still focused on the TV, all of which delayed his response.

"Oh, just a couple of weeks ago, why?"

"I just thought I haven't seen Pam for quite a while and it would be nice to have a little get-together over a couple of drinks and a few nibbles." Winston was now so focussed on the last race of the day on TV that he never even noticed she had placed another lager on the small side-table next to him. Realizing he had not added anything to his income from that race, he placed the *Racing Post* on the little table, opened the bottle of beer and turned to Jean with a mild look of surprise.

"Oh, I really don't see Elton as often as before. He now works at another depot, but he was in the betting shop with some of the boys last Friday. After that we went to the pub for a drink."

'Why doesn't that surprise me?' muttered Jean under her breath.

"I was thinking that, if we were to invite them for a snack next Saturday evening, Pam and I could catch up with old times. What do you think?"

"Sounds okay to me. Why not give her a call and see what they are doing Saturday," he suggested, reaching for his third bottle. His suggestion to give Pam a call caused a wave of excitement to overtake Jean. It was exactly what she wanted, the opportunity to speak to Pam or Elton.

"I would, but I think I have misplaced their number. Do you still have it?" shuffling feverishly in her bag for a number she knew she didn't have.

"Yes, I think so. Oh, by the way, I forgot to tell you that they moved to Hemel Hempstead some time ago and they have a new number. Let me see if I have it in my wallet, Elton gave it to me not long ago in the pub. Ah, here it is." This was music to Jean's ear.

"Thanks, I'll call Pam tomorrow. But I wonder why she didn't let me know she was moving," she added. It was about 5:30 pm the next day when she gave Pam a call just when Elton was at work. Greetings over, Pam proceeded to tell her about the harsh time she was having with Elton. The small telephone table was near the window adjoining the street door allowing Pam an uninterrupted view of Elton when he crossed the small green in front of the house on his way home.

"Oh Pam, why didn't you tell me?" exclaimed Jean, feigning surprise and distraughtness at what Pam had told her. It was merely a ploy to extract maximum information.

"I didn't want to bother you with my problem," replied Pam, in a voice tinged with bitterness.

"But if you decide to leave, where will you go?" It was said in a manner that forced Pam to respond the way Jean wanted her to. She had no idea that Jean was now on revenge grail.

"I am thinking of going to USA where I have two friends. One was a nurse here before she moved to Boston, but I am not too sure I can trust her because she knows Elton. The other also lives there but he worked in a clothing factory in the east end of London before he left for America. I met him at one of your parties some time ago and he assured me that I would be welcomed at any time." Jean's ears pricked up. Alarm bells started to ring. From the description given she had a very strong feeling it was Sidney, but she stopped short of revealing her knowledge of him to Pam.

"Oh really!" drawing out the word *really* in a voice betraying a slight hint of unease, "and what made him give you that open invitation?"

"I told him I was married and about the hell I am going through." The silence that followed was only broken when Jean gave a sigh of relief and regret. Relief to know that Pam was already seriously planning to leave Elton but regret that, as a loose cannon, she could end up in the arms of Sidney.

"I didn't know that you two had something going. You kept that very quiet Pam. But do you think he is still interested?" The jerkiness with which the words left her lips suggested it was not the answer she expected from Pam who continued to tell her how the friendship between her and Sidney had developed and that it was only his going to Boston that had interrupted it.

"I haven't spoken to him for a while but when last I did, he was still interested in having me over. What I *do* know is that I cannot take any more from Elton. I have had enough, and I *have* to do something about it." Jean had succeeded in drawing Pam into her grand scheme of things by getting her to release much needed information. She now had an idea of Pam's intentions. '*I must do everything to prevent her and*

Sidney from getting re-connected. It would destroy my plan and anyway, if I didn't get him, why should she?' were her immediate venomous thoughts. She knew that Sidney's business in Boston was doing well and felt that she ought to be the one to share some of his success. Pam, the long-standing friend, was now seen as a serious threat and enemy number one.

"Before you make up your mind, I have something to tell you which I am sure you will like to hear," implored Jean with some urgency. She was satisfied with some of what she had heard but suddenly realised that speed was of the essence if she was to keep her plan on course.

"Oooh! What's that?" asked Pam, settling herself comfortably in the chair next to the phone, her attention partly drawn to a small group of 'under-sevens' playing football on the small green.

"I went to dinner with a guy called Dennis who said he knows you and would like to get in touch again. You know him?" There was a drawn-out silence. She was startled. Pam would rather Jean be kept far away from Dennis because she knew Jean was like a cuckoo, a bird that evicts another small bird from its nest and then takes possession. But the mere mention of the name Dennis immediately sent her brain into fast rewind regurgitating pictures of Kings Cross, London Bridge, Waterloo Bridge, but most of all, the man who had fallen head-over-heels in love with her. Just then a feeling of guilt ripped through her paralyzing her ability to speak. She could feel every pang of hurt she had caused him by leaving him stranded every day at King's Cross.

"Pam, are you still there?" came a quiet but penetrating voice.

"Oh yes, ah… ah, yes I know him. I met him last year on the train on my way to work one morning and he is a bit of alright."

"Is that so?" in a tone that caused Pam to think she did not expect such an answer, "and did he have a crush on you?" Pam chuckled softly.

"I could tell he fancies me, but the problem is, he is married and although he said he was planning to go for a divorce, I am not too sure I can depend on that." At this point, Jean suddenly realised that, should Pam and Elton split, there was a chance she could even go for Sidney even though she met this new boy. She therefore was determined to do all it took to prevent this happening. It was now a matter of working

TROPICAL HEATWAVE

fast and discreetly to steer Pam away from Sidney and in a direction that would fit into her own grand scheme.

"Oh! I see. Look Pam, I have known you for a few years and I think I know the kind of person that would be well suited to you. I only met Dennis once. He recently took me out to dinner and, from what I saw, he is very polished and well educated. What is more, he has a very good job. Okay, so he is married, but are you going to let that hinder you from having a real go, especially if the man is considering divorcing his wife?" Seeing that Pam was determined to leave Elton, she decided to hedge her bets by encouraging her to go for Dennis. "Over dinner he was on the point of breaking down as he told me how much he loves and misses you. He also said that for days and weeks he would stand on the platform at Kings Cross waiting for you. He is really a broken man who would do anything to see you again. I think you are more certain about Dennis. He is here, Sidney is in Boston. Give the man a call if you still love him and at least let him know you are still around. What do you have to lose? Do you still have his number?" she asked forcefully, relaying the event in as much detail as possible. Pam inhaled audibly. She felt she had already released too much information to Jean who she knew was very good at manipulating others to achieve her objectives. She also wondered why Jean was so empathetic and willing to help but, by that time, she had laid it on sufficiently thick and heavy as to plunge Pam into an awful sense of guilt. She had to be sure Pam would take the bait and by-pass Sidney.

"Yes, but how did he manage to take you out to dinner?" asked Pam somewhat taken back and with a hint of jealousy in her voice.

"He sold me an insurance policy a few weeks ago and thought it a good way of saying thanks for doing business with him," replied Jean. "He seems desperate to get in touch with you. Lucky for him, he came across my number which you had given to him some time ago and thought I could help," she added. But Pam had not picked up on her underlying agenda.

"Look Jean, I can see Elton coming across the green, so we have to end the conversation, but I promise you I will give Dennis a call." *Why is she so anxious to hook me up with Dennis again? What game is she playing? What's in it for her?'* were some of the thoughts bouncing

81

around in her mind. Suddenly, she found herself having to be sure she knew where she was placing her front foot before lifting her back. She had to make up her mind whether it would be Sidney or Dennis before leaving Elton, especially since she knew Jean was quite capable of going after both.

On his way home, Elton had stopped to buy an evening paper, which he had folded to the racing-page, a sure indication that he had already visited the betting-shop. The conversation with Jean had thrown her into a spin. As she slowly replaced the receiver, she regretted having told Jean so much and now felt paralysed. She felt like an apple blossom caught in a late Spring frost. But it left her thinking. *'How could I have treated Dennis like that and to think that, after all I did, he is still interested in me who suddenly dropped him? How stupid could I get? I think I shall have to move pretty quickly because, from what she said and the way she said it, it seems to me she could be interested in him.'* During the next two weeks Pam weighed up the pros and cons between taking up the offer from a successful businessman living thousands of kilometres away in Boston and a professional living in London about to commence divorce proceedings against his wife and who loved her.

11

It was a hot Saturday afternoon in July and Dennis was about to make his way to see a prospective client. Weekends afforded him maximum time to get on with his other job as a part-time insurance representative. The sweltering heat of the day did not help him, dressed as he was in a dark suit as was customary in those days for such work. Being the kind of man who paid a lot of attention to his appearance, especially when meeting a prospective client, he was using the mirror in the hallway to fix his tie and put that final touch to his hair and moustache. He lived by a bit of philosophy which states that one does not get a second chance to show a first impression. As he turned slowly to pick up his bag, the phone rang. Normally, he would hardly answer the phone on his way out to a client for fear of arriving late but, on this occasion, hurriedly putting his bag down, he took up the receiver. Perhaps, it was meant to be, for it was once again his lucky day.

"Hello, Dennis speaking," he said in a professional tone thinking it might be one of his prospects calling to reschedule an appointment which was not unusual in such a business.

"Hello," the warm voice said, "remember me?" He knew the voice. It was that dulcet voice that had always teased the palate of his mind whenever he heard it. He quickly took the phone from his ear and momentarily gazed at it. *'Could this be……?' 'Could it really be…?'* In a split second his mind went into reverse mode recalling the entire conversation with Jean at the restaurant. *'Did she do it after all? It is almost a year since I heard this voice. But how can I forget it when it is that very voice - so smooth - that sucked me into that enchanting vortex of the caller's charm? And now once again, that same tone and telephone manner leads me to conclude it can only be one person – Pam, my Venus.'* But while in this accelerated pensive mood and before he could respond, there was that voice again, this time with a measure of astonishment racing down the phone line. *'Has Cupid released another arrow and given me a second chance?'* He muttered to himself, his heart stepping up a beat to keep pace with his expectations.

"Don't tell me you have forgotten me already. It is Pam," she said breezily and chuckled softly because she found it hard to think that he would have forgotten her voice.

"Oh…hello," he replied frantically, "ah, ah, ah, anyway, how are you keeping?" were the only words he could muster on an audible intake of breath for he was immediately drawn up into another world. His response was a kind of quivering and certainly not the kind she expected from a man desperate to find his soul-mate as Jean had explained.

"I am still here," she replied calmly, her voice carried on a sigh of relief. Dennis glanced through the little side window next to the street door as though in search of something to control his excitement. Identifications re-established, Pam gave him her new address and telephone number and began to apologize. For Dennis, this was one time any appointment with a client would have to take second place. His briefcase was soon on the floor again.

"Sweetheart, no need to apologize," he said with a sigh, the words jumping from his mouth as though he was breathless. "It is so nice to hear your voice again, I thought you had given up on me." He now sounded conversational, overwhelmed as he was with delight and an up-welling of joy at the thought that he could once again look forward to seeing that warm face again. It was evident to both that they had missed each other very much.

"I am coming to London next Saturday to get my hair done, and I'll also be seeing Jean. Perhaps you can meet me just outside Ladbroke Grove station, let us say about one o'clock."

"Of course, I would like that very much." His response was quick and positive. He was in no position to hesitate.

"Ok, see you at Ladbrook Grove station next Saturday at one." That afternoon, after putting the phone down, he stepped outside to share any passing breeze. There were hardly any clouds in the sky and the air was so still in the brilliant sunshine that you could hear the bird-song from the nearby park. Mothers with prams laden with multi-coloured balls, soft drinks, cakes and rugs were making their way with their little ones to the park to spend the afternoon. Even the local pub kept its doors open to catch the semblance of any breeze that would cool its inmates as they gently sipped pints of cold beer. But he felt assured that, whatever the reason for her temporary disappearance, re-connecting with her would give him a chance to mend the breach.

One of the things Dennis did not yet know about Pam was her dogged determination to achieve her objectives. She realised it would not be easy to get anywhere with the type of husband she had and so, seeing he was an obstacle, she concluded that, ridding herself of him was a matter of some urgency. In her current position as a member of a pool in a London office of the Ministry of Transport, there was no knowing how long she would have to wait to get promotion despite her proficiency. This was one of the reasons why the job in Hemel Hempstead appealed to her so much. It offered her an opportunity to head a small team and to move from a small one-bedroom flat in a terraced house in inner London to a three-bedroom semi-detached house in the suburbs of Hemel Hempstead with a garden. And she would also be near to her best friend Beryl who was already living there. But, in her naivety, she also saw the job in Hemel Hempstead as a way of ridding herself of Elton. She was hoping that his desire to be near his friends, the betting shop as well as near to his work, would be enough to make him turn down the chance of accompanying her to Hemel Hempstead, particularly as their marriage was showing signs of breaking down.

Just as well I decided to pick up the receiver this afternoon. Once again, luck is on my side. This time I am going to make sure she does not disappear again,' he thought. He looked in the mirror again, adjusted his tie once more and mopped his brow before seizing his bag. Excitement combined with the heat of the day had put his sweat glands into overdrive as he made his way to his first appointment. During the week that followed, a week which seemed to be the longest in his life, his mind was swamped with flashes of the past: the moments of having coffee at Jolly's, chatting on the station platform or just strolling across London Bridge or along Victoria embankment.

A few days after that critical but memorable phone conversation, Dennis suddenly remembered they agreed to meet at 1:pm on the very Saturday that he was about to change his old Ford Anglia for something a bit more modern. *'I cannot take the chance of changing my date with Pam for fear she changes her mind, but I hope I'll be able to change the car and get to Ladbrook Grove Station on time,'* was the thought uppermost in his mind. As he drove to the car dealer that Saturday, he had time to reminisce over the little Ford Anglia that had served him well. It was a two-door model with one door threatening to drop off at any moment and that was kept in place with carefully concealed twisted wire. *'It is this old car that has served me faithfully and that has taken me into every nook and cranny of North London in search of insurance business. This is the car that has enabled me to boost my financial position. It is also this little car with which she is familiar having driven in it on several occasions prior to her disappearance.'* These were some of the thoughts with which he had to grapple: thoughts which made him feel he had done an injustice to his little Ford Anglia when he saw it dangling in the air at the end of a crane, as it was hoisted onto a truck bound for the scrap yard.

But such thoughts were soon replaced by the anticipation of driving a more modern car, and the excitement of his one o'clock rendezvous. But in carrying out the car-change, he arrived late at Ladbroke Grove Station rendezvous. He waited, but in vain. *'I have missed the one chance I had of getting together again. I couldn't even keep an appointment as vital as that. What must she be thinking of me? I have fouled up the one chance lady luck gave me again.'* These were the thoughts preoccupying his mind as he drove home a very depressed man. Pam had arrived at Ladbroke Grove Station as agreed and, after some time waiting, had decided to go back to Jean's apartment. So upset and annoyed was she that it was only Jean's rational thinking and hidden agenda that saved the day for Dennis. She was determined to guide Pam away from Sidney whom she saw as her possession. It was in her interest to get Dennis and Pam re-connected.

"I'll put the kettle on. A cup of tea might help," uttered Jean who had read the situation correctly. "Something might have happened for him not to be there, why not call him and find out?" she suggested sounding concerned. These words fell on deft ears. Pam remained unmoved sitting in an armchair looking rather grim and oblivious to what was on the TV, but Jean was bent on achieving her immediate objective and, despite the disappointment, could see that Pam was still anxious to see Dennis.

"No, why should I call him?" snapped Pam, "he is the one to call me. He stood me up." There was a feeling of deep frustration in her voice. "If he knew he couldn't make it, why couldn't he call? After all, he had your number." Jean quickly realised that the heated situation needed something more than words to cool it down. A short trip to her small drinks cabinet saw her return with two small glasses of rum which they sipped against a background of light music Caribbean style. Once again Dennis was lucky because Pam was eventually persuaded to make that all-important call. Dennis had already arrived home and was having a soft drink while brooding over his lost opportunity. He glanced at his watch. It was 2:05. The phone rang. It was as though he was anticipating a call and in his desperate dash to seize the phone, he knocked over his glass of lemonade. But the fog of misery, which hung over him since missing the appointment, was already beginning to lift from his brain.

"What happened to you?" came that dulcet voice tinted this time with a slight hint of disappointment and disgust. He somehow managed to put together an acceptable excuse but avoided telling her it was because he was in the course of changing cars. He wanted it so much to be a surprise since she was accustomed to seeing him with the old Ford Anglia. '*How nice it would be to meet her in a new car!*' he thought.

"Ok, meet me at the same place at three o'clock and you better not be late this time." Even though he could hear disappointment in her voice, he could detect she was still looking forward to meeting him.

"Don't you worry about that darling, I can assure you I *will* be there and on time," and he hoped he had salvaged the situation. It was 2:20 pm when, with no time to waste, he set off in his new car in the hope that the look of the car and the smell of recently valeted upholstery alone would serve to be a good enough apology. But then he suddenly thought, *'What will she look like after almost a year? I forgot to ask her what she will be wearing. Could she, like me, be also planning a surprise? More to the point, would she spot me in my new car?'* These and other thoughts flooded his mind as he drove along Seven Sisters Road and Tufnell Park on his way to Ladbrook Grove station. Within about 100 meters of the station, he could see in the distance someone in a very distinct outfit standing just outside the station. *'That has to be her. Dressing up is in her blood. She is the kind of person who would wear a red top tucked in closely at the waist and supported with close-fitting white trousers exhibiting an irresistible outline.'* With her hair brushed back and finishing in drop-curls fronted by a pair of well-designed shades beneath which protruded those lips, the ones that brought so much delight to him in the past on Waterloo Bridge and the platform at Kings Cross, she was just stunning. Standing there, she had tremendously improved the scenery of an otherwise drab surrounding dominated by a grey railway bridge now begrimed with a thick layer of soot from passing traffic over the years. Such was the scene that gradually unfolded before his eyes.

'My word, could that really be her? Could that be the woman with whom I am falling in love? Is this what I would have missed and, perhaps lost, had I not been here on time? Maybe, this is meant to be a surprise,' he said quietly to himself, for never had he seen her dressed like that. But while savouring these moments, he suddenly realized she would be expecting him to turn up in an old Ford Anglia and that she might not spot him after all. He didn't have long to wait for, within a few metres, he could see she was focusing anxiously on the approaching car coming slowly to a halt. It was then that he knew she had spotted him for she immediately broke into a smile that would have charmed even the great Thor, the god of thunder. As though by special telepathy, the passenger door automatically opened to receive what he considered one of the most beautiful specimens of nature: his Venus.

"How are you keeping?" she asked on an audible intake of air, her eyes popping with delight, for at that very moment, they had fallen in love again.

"I'm okay, and you?" he asked, overwhelmed by what he was seeing.

"I'm still around. This is very nice," she uttered, glancing around the interior while running her fingers over the upholstery.

"Thanks, in fact, I only got it today," he said in a quiet voice and she looked at him slightly amazed.

"I expected to see you in your little Ford Anglia," she added with a chuckle, the kind he had often heard over the phone or on the platform at Kings Cross.

"This is the reason why I missed you earlier."

"What do you mean," she asked with a slight look of wonderment.

"When we agreed to meet today I had forgotten that I had also arranged to pick up this car today. I didn't want to change our date because I was afraid you might change your mind," uttered Dennis apologetically. Pam chuckled loudly. Her eyes sparkled with excitement at seeing him again and at the sight of a car more suited to the occasion. It was as though they had met for the first time for he could hardly get over how even more attractive she looked after almost one year. He thought then that, had this been the first time he had seen her, he would most certainly have fallen in love with her at first sight.

As she settled herself into the seat, the fragrance she wore was so mild and relaxing that it seemed to infuse him with emotions as seductive as the person wearing it. There were always moments of her being that demanded his admiration, and this was one of them. It was that strength of presence that can emanate from a person you love as you look at them. Slowly removing her shades to reveal a pair of brown eyes beneath well-groomed eye brows, she turned gently and looked at him. Her eyes twinkled like the star which follows the moon on a crisp clear night. He pulled up in a small car-park and, stretching out his left arm, allowed his fingers to settle gently on her right knee. It was a touch so soft, yet so electrifying, as to elicit a deep heave of her bosom as she breathed a sigh of relief. This was repeated for a few moments, a few minutes to be exact.

"You look wonderful," he said, the words leaving his lips in slow pulses, "and I am so happy that, at last, we have been re-connected." It was a joy augmented by the knowledge that, directly above those knees, was the most beautiful pair of thighs now brought into sharp focus by the tight-fitting white trousers that defined the lower part of her body. Soon they were in each other's arms once more. It was a kiss filled with passion, emotion, and all the feelings they shared. And it was one that set her pulses racing, leaving her aching for more. They were breathless when they surfaced and gazed into each other's eyes as though to say *why did we have to part?*

"You don't look so bad yourself?" she replied softly, each word seemingly truncated by a short breath telling him that the gentle touch had caused a melt-down and a collapsing at the knees. They began a conversation which they both now hoped would cement their friendship as they headed for Hampstead Heath, one of the few salubrious spots left in London, and a favourite for those wanting to spend a romantic afternoon in a natural setting rich in fauna and flora. As they strolled, they would occasionally stop and gaze into each other's eyes with words hanging in the air. Together, they meandered among clumps of ancient and recent wood. From a bench, they were entertained by jackdaws and parakeets darting around in a hawthorn near a pond all adding to the natural ambiance. Rays of sunshine filtering through the branches would settle softly on their faces infusing their bodies and emotions. When they kissed, he could sense she felt the warmth of his arm as he held her starving body clenched in a primitive craving that screamed out for the ultimate fulfilment. They talked. They laughed. They felt free sitting and watching the blazing sun hang low through the shade of a small purple wood when the sight of a small flock of deer, grazing on a nearby slope, seemed to trigger his need to eat.

"Fancy an Indian meal this evening?" he asked affectionately.

"Yes, that's okay with me, but where are you thinking of going?" she asked with a slightly furrowed forehead. She had a vague idea of the area but no in-depth knowledge of the types of restaurant to be found within close reach from the heath.

TROPICAL HEATWAVE

"I know a nice Indian restaurant in Leicester Square. I have taken one or two of my clients there before just to say, '*thank you for doing business with me.*" Pam raised her eye brows recalling Jean telling her how she had met him. But at that very moment too, she realised that Dennis had done better than she had expected. He had upgraded from an old Ford Anglia car to a more modern Rover and from Jolly's café to an up-market restaurant in Leicester Square.

"That's great," she responded, with a look of surprise tinged with delight. Heading back south slowly along Edgware Road, Cricklewood Broadway and Kilburn High Road, she had time to glance momentarily at illuminated shop windows displaying a range of attractive garments and to express her likes and dislikes of the various designs. From King's Cross station they took a cab to the restaurant where they were welcomed by a smartly dressed waiter. It appeared as though he knew they were a couple in love because he ushered them to a table for two in a secluded corner. Dim lighting provided the perfect ambiance for the occasion. It was located above a large commercial retail outlet and well positioned to attract passing trade and local trade as well as tourists. But it differed from many others in that the attendants were all in traditional Indian dress. Once seated, Pam allowed her eyes to do a quick inspection and to admire the detail paid to the interior décor in an atmosphere impregnated with spices.

"Oh, this is nice!" she exclaimed with a smile of satisfaction.

"What would you like to drink, sir?" It was the wine waiter.

"I'll have a bottle of Bordeaux red, please." Pam gave Dennis a half glance and smiled quietly. She did not expect him to be so precise.

"You seem to know your wines now, Dennis."

"You see darling, when you did your disappearing act, I threw myself whole-heartedly into my part-time job. It was a way of coping with the heart-breaking vacuum in my life. As a result, not only did I earn some useful extra cash, it also gave me an opportunity to meet a good cross section of people many of whom I would take to dinner as a way of showing my appreciation. It was then that I learned quite a bit about wine." She nodded in quiet agreement.

"I am truly amazed at the strides you have made during that time. You have gone up in the world, a far cry from the days of the Ford

Anglia. I am never going to do such a silly thing again because, as from now, I am going to make sure that I am your lady and you are my man." With hands clasped across the table, he had time to look more closely at the beautifully designed top, embroidered with lace sufficiently deep to reveal the upper surfaces of two shimmering liquid ebony balls that seemed to glow even under the dim amber lights of an Indian restaurant. And this was rounded off with an attractive necklace and a set of ear-rings through which the light shone transforming them seemingly into liquid icicles. They talked of many things: how they met, their rendezvous at Kings Cross, Southwark Bridge etc. and sometimes, they would look at each other and, without uttering a word, say how much they loved each other. Now into her second glass of wine and with her cheeks already a-glow, a chuckle signalled the advent of something either funny or interesting.

"Dennis, I am sorry for what happened, but the pace was getting too hot and I was afraid Elton was on the verge of finding out," she volunteered in an apologetic voice. Dennis sat back in his chair and gave her his undivided attention for he was anxious to learn more about what had derailed their love-train and brought it to such an abrupt halt.

"What gave you the idea that he was getting on to us?" he asked conversationally.

"I had the feeling that Gladys, the woman whom I pointed out to you at Kings Cross station that evening, might have seen us and told him," she replied, looking around anxiously as though she still expected the same woman to turn up at any time at the restaurant.

"What made you think so?" he asked, his pinched features confirming his worst fears.

"Well, I noticed he started to look at me somewhat suspiciously if I got home slightly late. In fact, from the tone of whatever he had to say, I would swear he had asked her to watch me on evenings. He even knew that I would alight at Kings Cross on evenings instead of going straight home. I am sure she would sit where I couldn't see her because the information he got was very accurate. I believe therefore he now looks at me suspiciously if he gets home before me and I arrive later than he expects me to. So, you see, I had to cool it a bit otherwise

I might not be here talking to you now." She dabbed a teardrop from her cheek which alerted him as to what was going on in her mind.

"I couldn't help thinking that, for some reason, we had suddenly drifted apart as quickly as we met. But, when you think of it, I believe we are meant to be together. It was by sheer co-incidence that we met on the train that morning at Kings Cross. You could have been sitting in any other carriage. And now, after missing our rendezvous earlier today, here we are together again. Best of all, we are re-connected at a time when you need someone to help you carry the heavy burden of a torrid marriage. So, in appreciation of the invisible powers that brought us together again and the love we share, let's have a toast," uttered Dennis, all of which brought a mild but infectious chuckle from her. "Here was I thinking you were seeing someone whom you loved more than me, a one-time secret admirer. How silly of me even to think like that!" he added, looking quite relieved when suddenly, she looked at him with a blank expression. It was as though he had just touched a sensitive nerve. Spinning around in her mind were thoughts like, '*has he heard about Sidney and, if so, I wonder who told him.*' Nor did this change of facial expression go un-noticed by Dennis.

"To be honest, there were times when I felt like getting away from it all," she exclaimed sounding rather coy and paused for a moment to get his response.

"All of what?" he asked in a gentle but subdued inquisitive manner.

"Well, things got so bad at home that I thought of going to America to join a friend I had met sometime before I met you." The mere mention of America threw his mind into fast rewind and the conversation he had with Jean. "Unfortunately, while we were at the early stages of getting to know each other, he migrated to Boston before we could even get a relationship off the ground, but he had said that I would be welcomed to join him at any time." Her lips quivered as she spoke, and Dennis observed she was a bit nervous. At that moment the conversation was broken by the arrival of the dinner. As expected, it comprised of a number of small dishes, each containing a blend of flavours demonstrating a fabulous use of herbs and spices.

Pam's outpouring was beginning to make sense in the light of what Jean had told him causing him to drift into a pensive mood throughout most of the meal only raising his head occasionally to ask a question. He soon worked out that she had been in contact with this chap Sidney whom Jean had mentioned at the restaurant in Edgware Road. He topped up the wine glasses and cleared his throat and, after two sips, continued to listen as Pam unwrapped her story while twisting a paper napkin into almost nothingness.

"Considering the stress which you were under, I can hardly blame you for being attracted by the lure of a better life in America, as you saw it?" But there was now no doubt in Dennis' mind that Pam's objective was to get away from Elton as soon as possible and by whatever means it took. She was a desperate woman.

"But why didn't you take up the offer from Sidney?" he asked, with an angled head and a slight squint in his eyes as he stirred his coffee after adding a lump of sugar. Pam lifted her shoulders and did not answer for a few moments. She was searching for the right words which came wrapped in a sigh sufficiently deep to cause the candle on the table to flicker almost to the point of being extinguished.

"I found myself really torn between three and I couldn't quite make up my mind: Sidney in Boston, Elton at home and you in London. I didn't know what to do. Things between you and me were moving very fast and I was afraid Elton might have done something stupid if he had found out and before I had time to put anything in place, so I thought the best thing to do was to cool it a bit and not to see you for a while. What is certain is that I cannot take any more of Elton and I must get away from him as soon as possible." Dennis shot her a quelling glance and accepted what he had heard for he had no intentions of getting into verbal combat with the woman he loved. He could see that she was glad to relieve herself at last of that burden.

Pam and Sidney had met at one of Jean's house parties where they had quietly managed to sow the germ of a relationship. It was a party which Elton could not attend because of his work schedule thus giving Pam the opportunity of dancing with anyone. And, being attractive as well as a good dancer, she had no shortage of takers. But it was also the moment for Sidney to advance, which he did and with enough success to stimulate a desire in Pam to want to join him sometime later. It was therefore hardly surprising to find her wanting to take up his offer

TROPICAL HEATWAVE

now that she was anxious to get out. In a strange way, Dennis began to empathize with her because, being very perceptive, he had worked out that her mind had become a battle ground of competing emotions like: *should she accept Sidney's offer? Should she wait for Dennis? Or should she remain with Elton despite a torrid marriage? Or again, 'should she just go off on her own?'* These, he could see, were some of the thoughts tearing her apart. He had to resort to this line of thinking in an effort to bring meaning to what she had done and the dilemma in which she found herself. He hoped that getting to know how she was thinking and the fact that they were now re-connected, would help them to build on that foundation they had made prior to her flight. He had never stopped loving her. In fact, he loved her even more in her absence. Dennis therefore decided it was prudent not to pursue the Sidney matter any further for fear it might create the kind of pressure that would probably force her to make a quick get-away to Boston.

"But when did you move to Hemel Hempstead?" he asked to change the trend of the conversation.

"Oh, I moved there about six months ago," she replied apologetically and with a feeling of relief seeing that Dennis had not shown any signs of being annoyed at her temporary disappearance.

"And how is it I didn't see you on the train in the three weeks before you left?" He had a rather confused look as he asked that question, know that he always stood in the correct spot to join her carriage.

"I was on the same train but in a different carriage. I would see you on the platform at Kings Cross, but you couldn't see me." Guilt and remorse enveloped her face as she bit back a sob. "It really hurt to see you standing on the platform as the train pulled away every morning and evening." There was a lump in her throat as tears slid down her cheeks. "You see, I thought that, by taking the job and the house in Hemel Hempstead, Elton would not want to come, and you would eventually forget me, but I can see I was wrong because it was I who could not forget you." Dennis handed her his hanky and, holding her fingers across the table, he could feel fond memories seeping through their veins. He listened attentively, taking care not to say anything that would make her want to disappear a second time. He knew Hemel Hempstead, a small town about thirty miles north of London to which some government offices were migrating in the 'sixties.' It was here that the Ministry of Transport had relocated some of its offices. Pam's story sounded reasonable, perhaps not unlike that experienced by others in the ministry. He poured her another glass of wine.

"In many ways, I feel rather sorry that you had to go through all this to find out that we were really made for each other. You see Pam, we have absolutely no control over the pace at which things move in a situation like ours. Whoever does when love, like a rushing-torrent, sweeps two lovers along?" Her eyebrows shot up to her hairline on hearing what he said. It was about 9:45 when they left the restaurant. Dennis drove slowly in search of a convenient place to park within reasonable distance from Jean's flat. It was almost 10:30 when he pulled into a cul-de-sac bounded on one side by a small park. It was a privacy only disturbed by the occasional passer-by. Allowing their lips to touch softly under closed eyes, they savoured the moment that made them feel they were welded together once more.

The attraction between them had now become so intense that it seemed as though they were transported beyond the ordinary world to one that appeared magical and enchanted. She teased him with a tired smile and he could see that everything she felt for him was in her eyes, for her attraction displayed the kind of traits that made her irresistible. She had certainly seized the moment to respond creatively and with a certain naturalness that contained the mystery and allure to spark romance again. It was another moment in her being that demanded his attention. After re-affirming their love for each other and with a slight peck on the cheek, he saw her safely indoors. That night, Dennis drove away in high spirits knowing that he had succeeded in rescuing a very precarious situation. He had retrieved a jewel and vowed never again to allow her to elude him. The evening ended in a manner that would send them off feeling it was worth it and that they would be looking forward to seeing each other very soon again.

12

Like Dennis, Pam paid quite a lot of attention to her appearance which is why she visited her hairdresser's every three weeks in Kentish Town in London not far from where she previously lived. Dennis usually collected her at Kentish Town station where, after a ten-minute wait, she would step down from the over-ground train onto the platform with a head-scarf tied neatly in a bow under her chin. It was customary in those days for women to wear head scarfs, probably a legacy from the Second World War and before. Over a coffee in a nearby café, the conversation was usually centred around what happened since they last met and how much they missed each. After that, he would see her safely to the hairdresser's usually for a 2 o'clock appointment. They would meet again for a *fish and chips* meal and a chat about 5 pm and, since she had to be indoors by 8:30 the latest, there was hardly ever any time left to do anything else. It was on such a Saturday evening at their usual cafe that Dennis, with furrowed brow, gazed pensively at her across the table.

"You know Pam, I've been thinking that seeing each other every three weeks is good but, if our relationship is to really grow and develop, we will have to come up with a plan that would allow us to spend more quality time together." She raised her eye brow with a slightly angled head and a soft smile because she had a similar thought.

"How do you plan to do that because, if I come to London more often, Elton will get even more suspicious and wreck everything," sounding a bit depressed as she spoke, knowing this was yet another obstacle they would have to overcome, a hurdle they would have to jump over together.

"I have no idea yet, but we have to work on it and come up with a plan very soon." Summer arrived bringing with it that smell of radiant heat from tarmac and brick infused with that from any nearby vegetation. It was Saturday, and England was locked in a thrilling cricket test match against the West Indies at Lords, the home of cricket. Elton had settled down with a few beers and a copy of the *Racing Post* to watch the match on TV before leaving for work at 7:30 pm. After tidying up the kitchen, Pam joined him to watch the game, cricket being a passion among both men and women in and from the Caribbean. The doorbell rang. It was Diane whom they both knew and who was also a mutual friend of Jean and Pam since they would sometimes go partying together. Diane was about the same height and build as Jean but, being much older, she had the kind of experience and street sense which they sometimes lacked. At forty-two she had already gone through two marriages and, since her last divorce, had not yet found a suitable man. Living in a two-bedroom flat in Camden not far from Jean, meant that Diane became friendlier with Jean than with Pam.

"Hello Pam, how are you keeping?" Pam was surprised to see her. She had never visited before.

"Oh hello, do come in, it's nice to see you again after such a long time." Pam followed this with her usual enchanting smile and a hug.

"Sorry about dropping in on you like this but I came to Hemel Hempstead to see a relative of mine and I thought I would pop in to see how you all are getting on," she said with apologetically.

"How very nice of you! Elton has just gone to the betting-shop to place a bet," Pam replied warmly and hurried away to put the kettle on. It was customary and probably still is, to welcome a visitor with a cup of tea.

"I won't be long because I promised my daughter to be back home by five o'clock the latest. I haven't heard from you for some time now and I wondered if both of you would like to come down next Saturday afternoon for a few drinks and snacks. Jean may be there as well. She told me she caught up with you." Pam received this invitation with

TROPICAL HEATWAVE

excitement carried on a broad smile. It was the chance for which she was looking. Her brain moved up a gear. She was already beginning to see how it could help to solve the problem faced by herself and Dennis.

"I am sure Elton would like that very much if he is not working that night. I'll get back to you very soon to let you know the position." After a chat over a cup of tea, Diane made her way hurriedly back to the train station. Pam closed the door and turned slowly. She was beginning to hope that Elton would be working that evening. *'This could just be what Dennis and I are looking for to remove this obstacle. If handled* carefully, *this could provide a reason for going to London on the occasional extra Saturday but first, I must get Elton to accept Diane's invitation to visit her next Saturday evening.'* These were some of the thoughts that suddenly flooded her mind. Within ten minutes Elton returned from the betting shop.

"By the way, while you were out, Diane dropped in. She said she was in Hemel visiting a relative and thought she would pay us a brief visit. You remember her? We were introduced to her at one of Jean's house-parties a while ago," Pam declared, sounding cheerful.

"What did she want?" he asked, settling himself in his chair.

"She has invited us for a drink and snacks next Saturday evening. What do you think?" uttered Pam and she remained silent with fingers crossed.

"Yes, I remember her. It will depend on how I am working. Let me check." He put the paper on the floor beside him to search through his workbag for his roster. For Pam, the fact that he wanted to look at his duty roster was a good sign. "Oh! damn it, I am working late next Saturday so that's no good for me. Anyway, you all haven't seen each other for a long time so why don't you go. If I can get away early I might still be able to drop in although it might be a bit late." Pam's eyes lit up at the suggestion but, in spite of this, Elton failed to read the situation. Perhaps he was too focused on the next race from the dog track. But his suggestion to visit Diane was music to Pam's ears who was determined to exploit every opportunity to see Dennis more often than on every third weekend. But, to do so, she also knew she had to convince Elton that staying over at Diane on the odd Saturday night would be nice for her and Diane.

99

"I have had a fairly heavy day at work, so I am going to have a bath and go to bed," he said, sounding weary. This gave Pam an opportunity to put the first stage of her plot in place. Satisfied that Elton was asleep, she reached for the phone.

"Hello Diane, about next Saturday evening, I will be coming but I am not too sure about Elton since he is working late," she uttered, full of excitement. She did not expect Elton to agree so easily. That was not his style.

"Okay Pam, I'll see you Saturday evening," replied Diane equally excited. Next morning Elton's breakfast was increased by an extra egg and two rashes of bacon. It was her way of saying thanks to Elton and preparing him for the next stage. She had just arrived at Diane's that Saturday evening when the phone rang. It was Elton calling to say he could not make it. Pam made no delay in alerting Dennis to the situation, suggesting that he could join her at Diane's. They had a wonderful evening. These occasional Saturday afternoon visits to Diane's worked well for a time until, during their daily rendezvous at Kings Cross one evening, he drew her closely to him.

"Sweetheart, I think we have now reached the point where we are yearning to spend even more quality time together," he exclaimed, and she nodded in quiet approval. "I don't think that, for two lovers sharing Cupid's arrow, seeing each other on the occasional Saturday afternoon is good enough," he added, and waited for her response. She lifted her head from his chest and levelled with Dennis' eyes. A gentle breeze flowing down the track slightly ruffled a few curls in her hair.

"I have an idea," she said calmly, and Dennis looked at her with a shallow smile. "What if I can persuade Elton to allow me to stay over at Diane's on those Saturday nights when he is working, then you will be able to join me there," she suggested, looking very hopeful. Dennis looked at her apprehensively. *What plan would she be able to hatch that would convince Elton it was okay for her to stay over at Diane's on the occasional Saturday night?* he wondered.

"You sure you can do that. What reason will you give him?" But before she could respond, the slow movement of people from the waiting room together with a rattling on the rails, caused them to quickly look south, it was her train approaching. He gave her a peck

TROPICAL HEATWAVE

on the cheeks and saw her safely aboard. On his way home, Dennis couldn't help wondering what stroke she would have to pull to jump through this hoop. On the train, she had time to mull over a few thoughts. *'If I can get Elton to pay a couple of short visits to Diane with me, he might see her as a good family friend and allow me to spend more time with her. I feel this will work provided it is timed well and is handled carefully.'* She hit on the idea of raising the topic on one of those rare occasions when they were having dinner at the same table. This was one of those obstacles she alone had to deal with. She knew he liked apple crumble as a dessert and made one for dinner the next day. This he enjoyed very much. Pam cleared the table and joined him in the lounge to watch a popular soap opera.

"Elton, I tend to feel a bit lonely on those Saturday nights when you are working and, even although we don't say much when you are here because you are usually glued to the TV, at least you are here," she exclaimed, and awaited a response. He raised his eye brows. It was as though he never expected her to make such a statement. It had always been his attitude to take her for granted. Everything about him screamed suspicion.

"Yes, and what are you saying?"

"Well, I just thought it would be nice to spend some of those Saturday nights at Diane's and come home the next day. She is also on her own and we would be good company for each other. It would be better than staying here alone," she replied rather awkwardly and managed a wobbly smile as she waited with baited breath for an answer she hoped would be favourable, for a lot depended on it. Much to her surprise, he agreed it was a good idea. Pam showed her appreciation by pouring him a whiskey on the rocks which he thoroughly enjoyed since it was poured by her. She had accomplished the second stage of her plan. Even then, Elton had failed to recognize that his mental and physical abuse was gradually ostracizing his wife. He did not read the situation. He was driving her straight into the arms of a man who had fallen deeply in love with her, someone who was already recognizing and appreciating her good qualities. Next day, she conveyed the good news to Dennis who was equally elated with joy.

101

"What a stroke of genius! I always thought it is better to leave such plans to the woman," he declared in a tone suggesting he was really looking forward to their occasional Saturday night together although, at the back of his mind, he wondered whether Diane could be trusted. The plan worked well for a while until one week-end they found themselves sailing too close to the wind and in danger of wrecking the boat. Dennis had just completed a week's course in 'motivation' at a hotel near Heathrow Airport and had arranged to meet Pam at Diane's as usual. It was 3:30 that afternoon when he pressed the doorbell which immediately opened to disclose his Venus.

"Did you see or hear me coming?" he asked, closing the door quietly behind him. He turned and, before another word could be spoken, found himself embraced with the kind of passion only felt when two lovers have not seen each other for a long time. It was an embrace that slid slowly into a prolonged kiss. Holding her for a strung-out moment in his arms against his charcoal grey suit, he could feel two hearts beating as one and hoped that the passage of time would never blot out the memory. For them, at that moment the world stood still. Deciding she must have a breather, she threw her shoulders back and, with his arms still around her waist, fixed her eyes on his with that usual seductive charm.

"You look very nice, how are you and how was the course?"

"Phew, thanks, I am fine although a bit mentally exhausted. The course was very interesting and informative, but I'll tell you about it later because right now I will do with a drink." They made their way slowly up the stairs to the sitting room on the first floor. It was a two bedroom flat in a terraced house opposite a small park in Camden, north London. In the far corner of the sitting room was a standing lamp with tassels hanging from the shade. A small coffee table adorned the centre on which was a vase of artificial chrysanthemums around which Diane displayed family photos. There was also the TV and, of course, the music centre. Off-white net curtains were framed on either side by drapes reaching down to the floor. Dennis slowly removed his jacket and Pam removed his tie. Together they sat on the twin settee and proceeded to say how much they had missed each other. He also

TROPICAL HEATWAVE

spoke in more detail about the course adding that it had given him a much-needed boost.

"I am so glad to see you and I want you to know how very proud I am with you," she said softly. "It seems so long since we last met. I thought this afternoon would never arrive." The rattling of teacups and the whistling sound of a kettle told them that Diane was preparing a welcoming cup of tea. But Pam made sure he got that whiskey first.

"Thanks very much and oh, by the way darling, I hope you brought along an evening outfit," he uttered breezily. She looked at him with a teasing smile.

"Don't you worry darling, I am always ready for any occasion," she replied, "you know I always pack something just in case. But what is it in aid of this afternoon?" She was already feeling touched by his kindness when Diane entered the room with a tray of tea and Madeira cake all of which enhanced the ambiance of the afternoon.

"I fancy a night out on the town. I want us to celebrate a successful course and your skill at finding a way around our problem." It brought chuckles from everyone in a room already charged with the evening expectations. "We could go to a nice restaurant or to a nice show or both. How about it? After all, you are not going home until tomorrow afternoon," he added. He knew what the answer would be because her eyes lit up with excitement reminiscent of those of a child who was suddenly told it was going to a fun fair. His idea was to enjoy every moment because they never knew when they would have such an opportunity again even though she had obtained Elton's consent to spend the occasional weekend with Diane.

"Yes, why not? That will be great. Give me about forty minutes to get ready." She placed her cup on the tray and disappeared into the box room next door. Dennis occupied himself watching one of his favourite Saturday evening TV programs, professional wrestling, only to be occasionally interrupted by Diane's effort to strike up a conversation just when his mind was totally engaged with the woman in the next room. But even then, the same thought kept bugging him: *'can we really trust her any more than we can trust Jean, and what does she have to gain by helping us?'* Within twenty minutes Pam emerged

103

wearing a dress that not only moulded every inch of her fabulous figure but had a touch of subtle sex-appeal. Dennis' eyes popped.

"Oh, you look absolutely gorgeous," he commented with a sigh.

"Thanks," she said as she made a half turn as though modelling an evening gown.

"She really does," echoed Diane slowly but with an expressionless face which did not go un-noticed by Dennis. He had also detected a lack of zest in her voice, her expression and in her compliments, that told him she was feigning sincerity. But she had not done a very good job at masking her sudden gut-tearing jealousy which immediately hardened suspicious thoughts in Dennis' mind. Within ten minutes, they were making their way to Euston from where they would take a taxi to Victoria Embankment. On the way, they glanced at her at every available opportunity.

"By the way, did you notice that Diane didn't break a smile when she agreed with me that you looked very nice?"

"No, why?" she asked, casting an anxious glance.

"I think we have to be very careful here because it seems to me that a certain amount of jealousy has suddenly developed."

"Pay her no mind, Dennis," and she shrugged her shoulders. Within twenty minutes, they were strolling through the romantic gardens of Victoria Embankment, a little oasis amidst the hurly burly of the tourist land of Westminster. On the boulevard they paused for a few minutes to read the plaque at the foot of Cleopatra's Needle, an Egyptian obelisk brought from Alexandria and erected on Thames Embankment in 1878. It was a warm, balmy evening and there was hardly a breeze as golden rays of early sunset were beginning to settle gently on the Thames. It was the kind of evening that saw several couples taking advantage of such lovely strolling weather. They talked and laughed as they walked together soaking up the riverside atmosphere. After about forty minutes they were about to turn into The Strand when she made a half-turn gazed at him with a look that reflected her personality.

"Oh Dennis, how nice it is to be able to walk along here and enjoy each other's company in such beautiful surroundings!" He looked at

TROPICAL HEATWAVE

her and nodded in total agreement touching her gently on her fingers protruding from under his arm.

"Darling, I think we ought to find a nice place to eat. What do you think?" he asked, and she agreed.

"It is amazing what a walk beside the river can do for you," she exclaimed squeezing his arm with a chuckle.

"Some time ago, someone told me there was a nice French restaurant in Soho. Fancy trying it?"

"I don't mind since you seem to be good with your surprises." It was now 8:30 and the lights along the embankment were providing a water dance by reproducing themselves in glorious shimmering reflections on the river. He hailed a taxi and within fifteen minutes they were in Soho, predominantly a small, fashionable multicultural area of central London. With its clubs, public houses, bars, upmarket restaurants and a few sex shops scattered amongst them as well as late-night coffee shops, the streets have an *open-all-night* feel at the weekend. About ten meters from where they alighted, he could see a man dressed in the uniform of a commissionaire very akin to the French style.

"Look Pam, I'll bet you anything he is associated with the restaurant we are looking for because the hat he is wearing is French," remarked Dennis, keeping his eyes firmly focused in the direction of the uniformed character. This was confirmed by a neon sign flashing above his head, *La Boulogne*. "There you are," said Dennis, feeling very pleased with himself.

"Who is a clever boy then?" she commented with a soft smile.

"Looking for a nice place to dine, Sir?" asked the commissionaire in a polite old English manner.

"Yes," responded Dennis, fascinated by the uniform.

"Well, you need look no further. Would you like to follow me, Sir?" They gladly accepted his invitation and, after exchanging a few pleasantries with him, were directed to the entrance. They had arrived at possibly the only French restaurant in London Soho at the time.

"How exciting!" she thought, as they were welcomed into the restaurant and helped by an attendant to remove their coats.

"Table for two, sir?" inquired the waiter with as smooth a voice you could ever hear.

"Yes, thank you" Dennis replied. The waiter ushered them to what was in fact the only vacant table on which stood a candle. Once comfortably seated, a waiter lit the candle and handed them the menu.

"Just let me know when you are ready, Sir."

"Okay, we will and thank you so much."

It was a small restaurant tucked away in the middle of Soho but one that could boast its interior décor and cuisine. Directly ahead of them was a mural depicting the Champs Elysees spreading out from the Arc de Triomphe. On the right was the Eifel Tower and on the left, was the Seine adorned with brightly illuminated pleasure boats carrying those who prefer to see Paris from the river by night.

"How nice it would be to visit Paris one day and see all those places and to dine at a lovely restaurant on the Champs Elysees!" commented Pam, thrilled by her surroundings. Dennis agreed with a gentle nod of the head. Dennis ordered a bottle of Bordeaux red, his usual, to start off a truly romantic evening. As they sat slowly sipping their wine and admiring the surroundings, he could not resist extending a small sincere compliment to the lady in blue sitting directly opposite him. She wore a long blue evening dress reaching to her ankles, elevated on a pair silver heels. It was low-cut revealing her two precious gifts on which gently sat a silver necklace complimented with a set of silver ear-rings. She radiated sheer charm. And all this against a background of light music coming from a piano in a corner.

"You look so beautiful, tonight," he commented. "I am glad we decided to come here. It is nice, isn't it?" he added.

"Yes, it's very nice indeed," she replied, allowing her eyes to move slowing around, surveying the scene in general and the picturesque murals in particular. It was her first glimpse of what Paris had to offer. Dennis signalled to the waiter that they were ready to order and, twenty minutes later, they were tucking into a tasty meal: prawn-cocktail as a starter was followed by roast beef, parsnips, roast potatoes, and then a small cheese-board followed by pears in wine and strawberry ice cream and finishing with coffee and after-eights. And as they indulged, they couldn't help but reflect.

"This is a far cry from the restaurant in Kentish Town at which we often had a quick meal, isn't it?" he murmured, and Pam chuckled as she remembered some of the evenings they sat eating sausage, beans and mashed potato before she was forced to rush for the train home. A sudden flickering of the candle forced them to look around. A light breeze from the door signalled the arrival of a group of four musicians that had just entered suggesting that they were going to be treated to an evening of music.

"That's nice, I didn't expect that, did you?" she commented, her eyes reflecting the lit candle on the table.

"No" he replied, now taken in by the French setting as much as she was. It wasn't long before they were treated to a medley of songs. But there was one tune *You've Got A Friend* sung by the lead singer, one that they heard for the first time and that always remained fresh in their memories. Maybe it was because it added that something to the ambiance that evening. It was a song that ever after was to bring back memories of that lovely evening in a French restaurant in the middle of London Soho, an evening they would never forget. It was not quite dance music for there was no room in such a small restaurant to dance. Instead, it was music more suited to easy listening: one that blended nicely with the décor, the food and the company. By then, there was a glow in Pam's cheeks suggesting she had mellowed into the evening. It was approaching midnight when Dennis hailed a cab to take them back to Euston to pick up the car. At Diane's, they had a cup of tea to round off the night before retiring to a single bed in a small box room.

"How cosy can you get?" he exclaimed observing that, once in bed, there would be no room to move. She looked at him and, before turning the light off, whispered easily.

"Who cares, as long as we are snugly sharing the same single bed," she declared, pulling the blanket over her. Sunday morning arrived with its usual tranquillity and the kind of atmosphere indicative of such a day. Nothing stirred but a newsboy on his bike darting in and out of small gates on his paper-round and the rattle of milk bottles as the milkman made his deliveries. Then suddenly, this all-pervading stillness was smashed by three loud blasts on the door bell sufficiently loud and long as to awaken the immediate neighbours. It was about

6:15 a.m. Someone was on a mission, a mission of some urgency or impending danger. Curtains in neighbouring houses on both sides of the street stirred. Dennis and Pam stared at each other with nerves as taut as violin strings for, at the back of their minds, was that abiding thought that something could go wrong when you are stealing love on the side. Nothing was said for a moment. It was an expression of fear. Dennis sat up with an anxious look.

"I wonder who it is ringing the bell like that at this time of the morning, a Sunday morning at that, waking up the entire street?" he mumbled sounding a bit disoriented. In this state of uncertainty, Pam quickly manoeuvred her way with some difficulty to reach the window and peered through a corner to see who it was so determined to gain entrance so early. Dennis waited anxiously, his eyes focused on Pam as a worried frown crept swiftly across his face. Pam released the corner of the curtain. Words were hard to find as she drifted between disbelief and despair while feeling almost paralysed.

"Who is it Pam?" snapped Dennis, observing that she looked deathly pale and frozen as she stared at him in panic. "Who is it?" he asked again this time with greater urgency. She was speechless. Her mouth tightened into a harsh and bitter line. A long drawn out groan of despair tore from her lips. Terrifying thoughts suddenly gripped Dennis: '*suppose it is Elton, what will we do and how will I escape? But most of all, what will he do with her?*' It was a visitor they did not expect. Dennis knew then that he was about to realise his worst fear. Pam was hardly able to release the words but, when she did, they shot out from her mouth like bullets. With eyes popping, everything about her screamed fear as she looked at him with terror in her eyes.

"Oh, my god, it is Elton. What the hell is he doing here now?" A few seconds passed. Then the would-be intruder made his intention quite clear with a second and even more persistent blast of the bell. This time it was a blast loud enough to set dogs barking and cause a small flock of birds in the small park on the opposite side of the street to hastily take flight.

"We only have a few seconds to decide what to do in the time it will take Diane to go down the stairs and let him in," blurted Dennis. It had to be a snapped decision and one that will work.

"Let's hope that Diane takes her time getting down the stairs to the door or, better still, it being so early, refuses to let him in," said Pam. With their hearts pounded away in harmony, they could only hope that, by some telepathic method, their thoughts would reach Diane. However, they were not about to wager on what she would do. Pam grabbed her dressing gown and took three deep breaths to calm down. "I can't let him see me agitated and full of fear, it would blow the whole thing. I must appear cool and collected. I'll go to the sitting room. You keep still," she urged, and slipped into the sitting room where she sat quietly reading the Sunday paper to feign a calm in the midst of impending doom. They could hear Diane making her way slowly down the stairs which creaked with every step she took. *How can she expect me to remain still in the face of an on-coming almighty explosion? I hate to think what could happen if he decides to come to this room first?'*

Dennis could hear Diane remove the chain from the door and the click of the lock. There was no exchange of greetings between them. Within a split second, Elton was pounding his way ahead of Diane up the stairs like a charging bull. There was certainly no doubt about his intention. In the small box room Dennis kept his fingers and all parts of him crossed. Beads of sweat, seemingly as large as golf balls, crashed to the floor from his face as he waited for the likes of a battering-ram to burst through the door at any moment. Instead, he heard the door to the sitting room open with a loud bang. He had visited Diane before and had a good idea of the layout of the flat. Pam was sitting in an armchair reading the Sunday paper or pretending to do so while waiting for the gladiatorial clash. Elton's decision to by-pass the box room, caught Dennis by surprise but it allowed him a split-second breathing space to come up with an escape, even though there was only one way out. Short of jumping through a first-floor window, the only other option was the very stairs his opponent had just come bounding up. He was trapped. Metaphorically speaking, he was caught with his trousers down.

'What if he is carrying a dangerous weapon?' he thought, as he began to mentally write his epitaph in fast forward mode. *'Those wonderful moments they spent together; the joy she brought into his life now to come*

to an abrupt end again. What would become of her? What would become of so nice a woman that illuminates every room she enters, that has a smile so enchanting as to soften the heart of the most ferocious ogre?' The persistent loud blasts on the door-bell, followed by the hammering of his footsteps up the stairs, had brought the tenants in the building, some wearing their night clothes, into the hallway to find out what the commotion was about.

Elton's entrance to the sitting-room was immediately heralded by an avalanche of obscene language so heavy, that it appeared to make the glasses in the nearby cabinet rattle. Diane, who had retreated to the safety of her bedroom, briefly re-appeared to close an upper vent to the window to contain the racket. Pam was now standing with her arms folded next to the window with the curtains closed. She stood next to a standing lamp. *'I am going to let him have it with the base of this lamp if he attacks me,'* she said quietly to herself while remaining as calm as possible as he blew like a whale, snarled like a dog and bellowed like a raging bull. Only intermittently would she make a short response to defend herself as best she could. It was hopeless.

But this sustained loud outburst fortuitously provided Dennis with a way out. *'Perhaps if he keeps up that level of barking, I might be able to make a speedy escape and make a dash for it. But my next move has to be quickly and quietly executed for the slightest rustle could bring him charging into this room like a bull in a china shop. To fail, could quite likely mean sudden death. But the longer he keeps bellowing to the top of his voice the better it is for me to escape.'* These were some of the thoughts flashing around in his mind like lightning in a thundercloud. Dennis was not a man seeking the thrill of a daring escape. Instead, it was a matter of survival. It was something he had to do and quickly.

But just then it appeared as though a psychic power had suddenly intervened for he detected an effort on Pam's part to keep Elton bellowing to give him time to get away. He slipped on his trousers (no time for underpants), and jacket (no shirt) with a speed he never thought possible and waited for the moment when Elton was at his highest. With thoughts whizzing around in his head at what could be the possible outcome if he failed, he grabbed his bag and, moving with the stealth of a panther, tip-toed shoeless down the stairs taking care to avoid the creaking spots. It was like picking his way through a mine-field but with some urgency, Opening and closing the street door without so much as a click from the Yale lock, he hastily made his way to the car parked just below the very window against which Pam was standing in readiness for armed combat. It must have taken less than ninety seconds. As he did so, he suddenly realised that the other tenants and the neighbours, having been aroused by the blasts on the doorbell and the commotion in the room, would now be seeing him, less than half-dressed and bare foot, making a mad dash for his car to make a speedy getaway. And all this on what, until then, was a quiet Sunday morning. They were treated to a piece of drama made even more entertaining because it was live, free and unexpected. Dennis opened and closed the car door with a most feathery touch and hoped that it would respond to the first turn of the key. It did, and he was away in a flash.

At that moment there was a sudden pause in Elton's thunderous tirade. He looked at Pam with an intense aggressive glare which she returned the glare, but with real fear gripping at her heart. And then he suddenly thought he heard a car started and made a dash for the window just in time to see two red lights rapidly disappearing in the distance. He turned with an expression that reflected dreadful wrath and resumed his verbal onslaught bordering very closely to a physical battering. Pam believed it was only the presence of Diane that stopped him. Once out of reach, Dennis had time to fast rewind the scene. '*Either he didn't know I had a car or, if he did, didn't know what type and what colour, otherwise he would have seen it parked just below the window but then, the whole thing would have taken a different turn, one I hate to think about. But I feel guilty at leaving her alone to face the music. I am sure she might be thinking that I bailed out in her hour of greatest need. But, to confront Elton at that stage, would have been premature since we are not yet ready to come clean. Phew, that was a close call, too close for comfort.*' He was now more than five kilometres away and out of immediate danger.

Back at the apartment, and even under such an attack, Pam still had time to think about what would have happened had Elton made the box room his first port of call. But the whole scenario triggered several other worrying thoughts in Dennis' mind as he drove homeward along Tufnell Park Road and Seven Sisters Road. Thoughts like: *'How did Elton know to call at six in the morning? How did he get from Hemel Hempstead more than thirty miles away to Camden so early on a Sunday morning when there was hardly any public transport? He had no car and indeed no driver's license. Could he have been lying in wait at a friend nearby? More to the point, could it be that we were set up by Diane, and if so, why? Who could be so heartless to add further pressure to a woman already suffering so much at the hands of a brutal husband?'* He was so engrossed in these and other thoughts that, at traffic lights, he constantly had to be reminded by a quick toot of a horn from behind that it was time to go.

It was at one such traffic light that he suddenly realised he was not fully dressed. His immediate concern now was to find a convenient place to get himself presentable before arriving home. This problem was solved on reaching Finsbury Park, a large park located in North London adjacent to Seven Sisters Road. He pulled into what was an almost deserted park to address the situation. As he did so, he thought of the Venus he had left behind and was overcome with guilt. He could hardly wait to learn how the unfortunate episode ended. The next twenty-four hours were perhaps the most stressful he had ever lived through. Until he heard from Pam he would be ripped apart with emotional agony for he was well aware that the outburst at Diane's would continue for a long time.

13

It appeared to Dennis as though Monday would never come, so anxious was he to hear what had happened. It was 8:30 and Pam had just signed in to her work-place when Dennis called. She had just enough time to put her bag away before reaching for the phone but, although she knew he would be anxious to learn what had happened after his swift getaway, she was also aware it was neither the time nor place to have such a conversation. Already Dennis felt better that he had heard her voice and they agreed to talk about it after work that day. It was 6:20 pm when his phone rang, and he knew who it was so there was no need for identification.

"Are you okay?" popped out of his mouth anxiously.

"Let us say, I am still alive," she replied, sounding distressed. "Anyway, sorry about this morning, but I couldn't speak in front of my work mates." But, flashing up on Dennis' mental screen, were images of what might have taken place after his great escape.

"Don't worry, I understand. I just wanted to hear your voice," he declared, and sounded concern.

"I must be quick because Elton could be here any moment now." But, before she could tell him the story, the bus was pulling up at the bus-stop on the other side of the green which she knew he would soon be crossing armed with his bible, the *Racing Post*.

"Listen, if Elton is working Saturday, I will come up to Hemel Hempstead about 12:30 and we will go for a drive," he hurriedly suggested.

"Great, I'll like that very much, 12:30 it is then in the town centre in the usual place. See you there. Bye darling." The click of the phone as she replaced the receiver and the rattle of keys at the door almost coincided. During the following four days, he called her at work very briefly just to hear how she was for any extended conversation was out of the question. It was mid-June and temperatures were in the mid-twenties that Saturday afternoon when, as he was about to park in the town, his attention was drawn to two mallards taking off from the surface of a small pond, their watery runway. And, not far away, there she was sitting on a bench feeding other mallards competing for every morsel of bread she threw into the pond on the Gade, a small stream flowing through the town. Here, part of the stream was converted into small ponds making it a haven for wild fowl. Less than two hundred meters away was the weekly outdoor Saturday market always well attended by folk meandering between the many varied and colourful stalls. But it was also the very market frequented by Pam and one of her colleagues during lunch on Tuesdays. In fact, they were so well known to the stall-holders that they were often referred to as sisters, since they seemed inseparable. This made it even more imperative for Dennis and Pam to leave the area before they were spotted. Now settled, she placed her bag on the back seat and glanced at him.

"I am glad you came slightly early because I was beginning to get worried that someone might see me sitting there dressed like this and tell Elton." They both breathed a sigh of relief.

"Nor would we want anyone to see you getting into the car because that would be a disaster. Do you have any particular place in mind you would like to visit?" he asked driving along the high street as Pam's eyes darted right and left in search of any likely danger.

"No, but I only want is to get out of here before we are seen," she replied, getting herself ready to take evasive action beneath the dashboard should she see any one known to Elton.

"Ok, let's go to Ashridge Estate where I know it will be okay in the safety of the quiet countryside. There we can have afternoon tea and a quiet walk through the woods. Have you ever been there before?" he asked with a quick glance.

"No, but I have heard quite a lot about it from a couple of my friends at work who said it is worth a visit."

"Yes, that is true. With its ancient woods, rolling chalk hills and lush meadows, it is considered an area of outstanding natural beauty in the Chilterns. It covers about twenty square kilometres, much of which is woodland straddling Hertfordshire, Buckinghamshire and bordering Bedfordshire," he exclaimed, drawing on his geographical knowledge of the region and it drew a smile of appreciation from her.

"Can we stop at the first convenience shop on our way, I just want to get a packet of minty sweets?" she requested.

"No problem." Looking at her, going to and returning from the shop, made him realise how lucky he was to have such an attractive woman, dressed as she was in her mini-skirted pale green suit with a large white collar sitting gracefully on the jacket. When combined with her heels, she was eye-catching. To say that Pam was always meticulous about her appearance would be an under-statement. But, driving along that kilometre of the A41, lined on both sides with elm, beech and silver birch, she was unusually quiet and responding to any question as briefly as possible. Not even the leaves shimmering in the afternoon sunshine seemed capable of bringing her back to her usual self. Except for the noise of wrapping paper as she opened a sweet to pop it into his mouth, the silence was so deafening, he could hardly stand it. And yet, he sensed she would have much to say when she was ready but that she was only waiting for the right moment. Although he was at pains to know what had happened since that eventful Sunday morning, he thought it better not to press it too soon. However, this did not stop his mind from wondering. *'Has Elton broken her? Is she about to give up, to surrender herself to him? Is she going to tell me that this is our last meeting?'* These were some of his worrying thoughts. Any ensuing conversation during the drive from Hemel Hempstead to Ashridge Common was fairly low key. It therefore came as a relief when they were eventually pulling into the car park dominated by an obelisk.

"That looks impressive," she commented, gazing at the obelisk, a Bridgewater Monument built in 1832 to commemorate the Duke of Bridgewater as a pioneer of canal building. It was now about 1:30 pm, just the time for a light lunch at the visitor's centre. Having changed into more comfortable walking shoes she got hold of a footpath guide and they set off on a walk, her hand securely clutched under his arm as per usual.

"Isn't it a beautiful afternoon?" he commented looking into her eyes.

"Yes," she replied, tossing her head back to inhale as much of the fresh country air as possible as they strolled through a part of the wood dominated by the sweet chestnut, ash, maple and straight trees all reaching up for the sun.

"Do you know that Ashridge common is nearer to you than it is to me in London. How come you two never visited it?" he asked, in order to get conversation going.

"We have no car and he can't drive and, even if he could, this is not the kind of thing in which he would be interested anyway," This topic was interrupted by an unusual sound high up in the branches.

"There it is," said Dennis, pointing to a little bird chirping high up on an overhanging branch.

"What is it?" she asked, peering through the flickering beams of sunlight.

"I think it is a bullfinch. Can you see its grey back, red breast and white rump?"

"Yes, what a beautiful little bird! This reminds me very much of that afternoon we spent on Hampstead Heath, only this is larger." She then tried to divide her attention between the bullfinch, a green woodpecker and a variety of shrubs like blackthorn, hawthorn, elder and hazel, all providing nesting sites for the blackcap, the sparrow and other birds whose chorus seemed to provide the theme tune to this unfolding drama.

"If you look over yonder, you will see two fallow deer. Probably theirs were the footprints we saw back there on the footpath," he said, pointing in the direction of a clump of sweet chestnut,

"And what kind of butterflies are those darting around on that hawthorn hedge? she asked, now looking very interested.

"They are the Speckle Wood, one of the main types found in this woodland." As they ambled along, rays of sunshine penetrating the branches fell gently on their faces in a series of flickers and, as if to add to the theatre, squirrels performed a series of gymnastics in branches above. Perhaps it was the ethos of such natural surroundings that eventually caused a change in her mood, for she now seemed ready to chat. "I always feel that, the closer you are to nature, the greater its therapeutic effect," he said affectionately, which drew a soft chuckle from her. It was as though this oneness with nature had prompted her into giving vent to some of her innermost thoughts. Standing for a few minutes admiring fauna and flora, she made a half-turn forcing their eyes to meet.

"I wonder how it would feel just to be like those birds: free and without a care and to be in a different world, one in which you were not constantly hammered by someone. Wouldn't that be nice!" He looked at her and nodded in quiet agreement, but he could see there was something other than or in addition to the Sunday morning saga of a week before, causing her great distress. Her temporary relief brought about by the walk seemed tinged with bitterness. She wanted to exit her mind, her thoughts and her sentiments. It was as though she was carrying a bundle of thorns under her arm which inflicted pain every time she moved her arm and which she was anxious to release. He held her closely and, standing there wrapped in their world against an oak and a background of colour and song, he saw themselves as the only players in a theatrical scene wishing that, for them, the course of true love would one day run smooth.

"Let's find somewhere to sit and drink in the atmosphere," he suggested. They didn't have to look too far for, in the near distance, was a large log, the trunk of a beech uprooted in the storm to hit the southeast of England a couple of years before. It was lying horizontally beside a small pond on which a couple of water fowl moved gracefully among water lilies and bulrush. Here they sat, an eloquent silence prevailing for a while, their attention now focused on the pond and its resident players of ducks, frogs, newts and dragonflies. Diverse hues and shades of light pulsed in the atmosphere around them. It was a silence only broken by the stomping feet of two horses and the jangling of harness as two horsemen came riding by.

"Good afternoon" said the riders, passing less than three meters away.

"Good afternoon," they replied almost in harmony, as they watched a 'true symbol of the English countryside' disappear slowly in the distance. She wished her agony would disappear in a similar manner. They talked about several things and yet she seemed reluctant to relive her experience of a week before. *'I can't hold it back any longer. The suspense is killing me. I have to know what is going in her mind: how she feels and what she wants to do,'* was the thought uppermost in Dennis' mind. He drew her close to him and rested her head on his chest. One duck leapt from the water with a splash, then the other and together they flew away into the distance leaving the world momentarily to silence and to them. Dennis closed his eyes for he was already feeling immense agony from her unspoken words.

"Darling, you promised to tell me what happened following my hasty getaway. Are you ready to tell me now?" he asked affectionately looking at her with a slow smile. She took some time to reply. It was as though she was stringing out the moment and he could see she was quietly rewinding a scene that hurt as she did so, an experience that induced anguish and immeasurable pain. It was a scene she never wanted to relive. She raised her head slowly.

"Oh Dennis, Elton was so loud that morning that I didn't even hear your car when it moved off. He carried on for quite a while after you left until Diane had to ask him to quiet down because he was disturbing the neighbours and the other tenants." As she spoke, he could feel her whole body even then vibrating with fear. "I kept wondering if you had managed to creep out while he was at the top of his voice. You have no idea how relieved I was when I returned to the box-room to find you had gone. How did you do it?" she asked with an expression of amazement against a background of silent tears already coursing down her cheeks.

"All I can say is that I am glad I had the new car because the little old Ford Anglia might not have started as quickly, and the result might have been different. Anyway, I will tell you more later, all I want to know is how you got on that evening, especially when you got back home."

"You might not believe this, but that man carried on even on the train. I felt so embarrassed and he was even worse when we got home."

She paused and hit back a sob. Dennis' heart sank in anticipation of what he was about to hear bearing in mind she was rather silent until then. Not even the king-fisher, poised on an overhanging branch on the far side of the pond baiting its next meal, could hold his attention.

"When we got in, I went straight to the kitchen to prepare a meal. It being late I thought I would cook some rice and chicken, because rice would not take too long to be cooked. He was sitting in his usual place. Not even the TV was on. There was an eerie silence. Then I heard him go to the drinks cabinet and pour himself a large drink, a signal I could expect the worse. The very sound of the whiskey entering the glass sent shock waves throughout me and I could feel my body quivering with fear." Her voice trailed off as a broken sob escaped from her now trembling lips. Suddenly, the floodgates opened. Sobs from deep within crashed onto Dennis' pillow-like chest. He held her in his arms as she closed her eyes. Then suddenly, a sweet sense of security started to well up inside her. A penetrating sweetness was gently breaking through her pain.

"Let it come out my dear," were some of the words he managed to muster in his effort to console her. She took a couple of tissues from her handbag and blew her nose while trying to speak over the rustling of leaves and a murmuring breeze.

"He then burst into the kitchen with eyes like steel and, before I could think, he started punching me around most of the blows landing firmly on my head and belly. I knew I was no match for him, but I did the best I could to defend myself." She paused, and Dennis dabbed her eyes. Even then he could feel every blow that landed on her body. "There was a small pot of water just on the boil on the back burner. I grabbed it and threw it at him most of which caught his arm. He screamed, he swore, and he roared but, before he could get his act together again, I rushed pass him up the stairs and locked myself in the bedroom and then drew the bed against the door for more protection. I kept wondering if I had done him in but within minutes he was banging on the door with the force of a kicking horse. I thought he was going to get in at any moment and finish me off. I saw my end flash before me. Suddenly, he stopped. I could hear him go down the stairs and through the street-door. I waited for a while before coming out. He had gone. I concluded he was on his way to the hospital," she explained, her throat tightening with unshed tears. Dennis could hear the terror in her voice at having to relive such a moment and, as he listened in awe, in wonder and in pain, an icy blast of horror ripped into him as fierce and painful as a dagger.

"What happened after that?" he interjected quietly, and she let out an audible sigh.

"When he came back about one hour later he kept his distance, but I could read what was going on in his mind and they were not nice thoughts. I believe he didn't know what next I had up my sleeves. He spent the remainder of the evening doing what he is good at: drinking, watching the TV and studying the racing form. I didn't think I ought to chance it sleeping there that night, so I went to my sister Maria who lives in Birch Green about thirty-five minutes-walk away. He had calmed down by the time she brought me back next day. Nevertheless, I decided never again to sleep in the same bed or in the same room with him for there was no knowing what he would do next."

"That was a good idea," uttered Dennis gazing at her in sheer astonishment. The thought that she might not have been there talking to him threw his body into a kind of mild shivering convulsion. He held her in his arms again and did what he knew they would both enjoy. It was a long and drawn-out kiss that said she had his full support. But this unfortunate incident had brought them even closer together. They re-affirmed their love for each other and agreed that nobody, not even Elton, was going to change that.

On their return to the visitors' centre, they settled for a cream tea: a pot of tea served in china ware, hot scones, clotted cream and strawberry jam, her favourite. Not far away were shelves packed with information: maps of the common showing the various walks, the history of Ashridge House and estate, pamphlets on the flora and fauna, lists of guided tours in the House and around the common, and many other useful snippets of information. And all within a culture of soft classical music like *Pacabel by the Sea*, a piece of music that not only served to assuage her aching heart but one that became part of their collection. Perhaps, it was the sound of waves lapping on the beach and the rattling of pebbles carried back to sea in the tune, that helped to steady her nerves. She placed her cup neatly on the saucer and sat up.

"How do you think Elton knew you were at Diane's that Sunday morning and how did he know to call so early in the morning and not Saturday evening when we weren't there?" she asked, looking rather puzzled. The question set his mind racing.

"Sweetheart, your guess is as good as mine," he replied under a furrowed brow while adding some extra clotted cream to his scone.

"The only person who knew what we were doing was Diane," she exclaimed. This remark immediately set Dennis thinking because he always held the notion she ought not to be trusted any more than Jean her friend. He felt that, as they were both from Trinidad, they would have a lot in common some of which he had observed at a couple of Jean's house parties.

"Yes, but why would she want to do a thing like that to you a friend?" he asked, "and what about Jean, can you remember letting it slip to her about our plans for that week-end?" he added, gazing at her meaningfully.

"No, I haven't spoken to Jean for quite a while." He could see her brain was working overtime to come up with an answer.

"Suppose someone saw us Saturday evening and phoned Elton," piped up Dennis matter-of-factly. Pam topped up the cups allowing the tea to leave the pot very slowly and looking very pensive as she did so.

"I know he has a friend who lives on the same road as Diane although he doesn't say much about him." This drew an anxious glare from Dennis who thought it would be extremely difficult for Elton to get from Hemel Hempstead to Kensal Rise by train so early on a Sunday morning. He always felt whoever alerted Elton would have had to be nearby.

"But, if it was Diane, why would she want to do such a thing to me?" she added, her eyes narrowing in sheer disgust and rising disappointment.

"Have you ever stopped to think she might be jealous?" declared Dennis, biting into another scone in a manner that forced some of the cream to escape on either side of his mouth, much to her amusement. It was her first smile for more than an hour.

"Jealous about what Dennis?" she asked with a stern countenance. "Every time we go there, I always make sure I buy groceries for her, so she would not have to use hers to prepare a snack or meal for us."

"That's odd, because what you don't know is that I would also give her money as well and, if I forgot, she would ask for it," added Dennis with an uneasy look.

"What?" she snapped sharply, anger roiling in her stomach and in her eyes, the kind of anger you would not want to test. "That cow," was her blunt retort, holding on to the word 'cow' as long as possible, as if to indicate that was the end of the line, the end of their friendship.

"Stop, think for a moment Pam. Look at the way you dress and the places we go," he urged.

"Yes, but she always tells me how nice I look and……," Dennis cleared his throat and interjected.

"Do you *really* think she feels happy you are having such a nice time at least once every month and she doesn't go anywhere, not even once every six months?" he asked pointedly.

"Nobody stops her from doing what she likes so why should she want to rain on my parade?" was her angry retort with a loud animal-like howl ripping from her throat.

"I noticed something in the tone of her voice and in the expression on her face when she told you how nice you looked that Saturday evening and I can tell you that what she said was not supported by her facial expression and perhaps feeling," declared Dennis.

"Well, I don't stop her from buying her clothes or going where she likes, so why should she be so stupid to think and feel like that?" came shooting back to Dennis in a voice of utter fury.

"Perhaps she feels left out Pam," he replied in a sage-like manner. "Let's face it, you are very attractive, you dress well, and you make friends easily. If you add to that the fact that you are a very good dancer, because dancing is in your blood, you can see why she might be a bit jealous. She might even be thinking: why should you be so lucky to have a boyfriend who loves you and takes you out often, while she finds it difficult to find a similar man with whom she can have a similar relationship and experience."

TROPICAL HEATWAVE

"But are you telling me that is why she would blow the whistle on me?" Pam was now so worked up that he could see steam of hatred gushing from her very ears. It was only the soft strings of Mantovani piped around the visitors' centre that quelled the situation if only temporarily.

"Life is full of surprises my dear, but there is something else which I haven't mentioned because I didn't think it was worth even thinking about at that time." Pam immediately stopped putting more jam and cream on half of a scone and looked at him with an inquiring frown, her eyes boring into his as she held the scone aloft.

"Come on then, what is it? Did she ask you to make love to her?" she asked with a fearsome pout. Dennis gulped, squirting tea from his mouth across the table.

"Don't be ridiculous. You know she is not my type. Furthermore, do you see any similarities between you and her?" Dennis was a well-educated and very charismatic chap, the kind of man to whom many girls would gravitate. Pam knew that Diane was not the type Dennis would fancy but also thought there was no harm in seeing if she could be wrong.

"Well, what is it then?" her brow becoming more furrowed with anticipation. Dennis took a deep breath, sat upright in his chair and looked around to make sure no one was hearing.

"I had the feeling for some time now that she wanted me to play the game with her."

"What game? Don't make me laugh. What do you mean? Anyway, how did you know that?"

"Come, come my dear, a man gets to know these things. From the way she always wanted to talk to me whenever you were not in the same room, I sensed she wanted to join in the fun. But I think she was also sensible enough to realize she couldn't compete with you. However, it didn't stop her from having a go. Of course, I never responded, nor did I have any intention of doing so." He felt the inquisition only came to an abrupt end because Pam was more concerned with getting hold of her and, if possible, squeezing the life out of her. She was seething with anger.

"Well, if she did not succeed then, she has no chance now because that's the end of it with us. I am never going back there again." He saw a killing rage like a fountain of fire rising within her. Resentment and hatred were now roiling deep within her causing more and more heat to rise her cheeks.

"Come on now, there is no need to resort to physical violence," Dennis admonished quietly.

"Why didn't I see this before? I should have known something was up because I noticed something in her face when she made out she was complimenting me on the way I looked, but I just dismissed it. Thinking of it, I have to admit there was a tone of envy in her voice." Dennis glanced at his watch. It was 4:20 and time to get her back to Hemel Hempstead town centre where she would take a bus or taxi home. Walking hand in hand together back to the car, they paused for a moment and embraced each other and then he levelled his eyes with hers.

"I feel as though we have been ship-wrecked and that we are holding on to each other for dear life. All we can hope is that we reach a safe harbour very soon. Sometimes my dear, we have to weather the storm together. Such a time is now." Altogether, they had had a wonderful afternoon. On their way back using a slightly different route, they couldn't help but reminisce on the experiences of the week. But the afternoon on Ashridge Common had brought them even closer together. They were soon in the town centre where, with a touch of the lips and a brush on each cheek, he saw her safely into a taxi for home. As for him, he made his way merrily back to London, satisfied that they had become even stronger in the face of adversity.

14

As the months rolled on Dennis and Pam tried to meet as best they could. This was very infrequently with long periods of up to four weeks between meetings. They had decided no longer to visit Diane and therefore now depended very much on the phone to remain in contact. What was certain was that they had no intention of breaking off the relationship although Dennis was a bit taken back by what she said on her way to take the train at Kentish town one Saturday evening. They were just pecking each other on the cheeks when she looked at him with a soft smile, "Dennis darling, I think we ought to take it easy for a little while. We don't want anything to happen again that would force us to declare our hands before we are ready. Until then, we must play it very carefully."

"Ok, whatever you say," he replied, agreeing very reluctantly. His eyes were instantly concerned. Losing her last time had marked him severely and he also knew from experience that her *'cooling off a bit'* meant not seeing each other for almost a year. On his way home, he kept pondering, *'Is she about to do this again? How can she expect us to go for such long periods without having the occasional longing for what we share?'* Yet he knew she was right. It meant no more staying over on Saturday nights at Diane or, for that matter, at any one else for a couple of months.

It was now November three months later and Dennis was expected to attend an award ceremony hosted by the head office of the insurance brokerage for which he worked on a part-time basis. He had done very well and was expected to receive an award. All sales representatives and their partners were invited but he was not about to attend any function without having the company of Pam. *'I really don't like the idea of attending this function without having someone to accompany me. I wonder if Pam will do me the favour,'* he thought to himself. It was early autumn and golden leaves floating through the air were settling softly on the pavement below as he stood by the window gazing at two youngsters making their way home from school. But the question uppermost in his mind was, *'how is she going to get away with spending more than half the night away? There is only one way to find out,'* he thought. He sat as his desk for a few moments in a pensive mood before dialling and he was lucky in that Elton had not yet got in from work.

"Hello, my dear, are you free to speak?" he whispered.

"Yes, nice to hear from you after six weeks and how have you been keeping?"

"Very well indeed. I want to ask a favour of you and I do hope it is possible."

"You know I'll do anything for you my love especially now it seems things have settled down again." He could hear the excitement in her voice as she spoke against a background of one of her favourite tunes.

"I have been invited to the annual awards ceremony given by the head office of the insurance brokers for which I work. I believe I'll be given an award for top sales twice in one year beating even the full-timers and I wondered if you would like to accompany me that evening. It will be held at a country estate deep in the heart of Surrey and it is highly likely that you will get back home after midnight. Take some time to think it over." He could hear anticipation and excitement in her voice when she replied.

"Of course. I will do whatever it takes to be there. Just give me the date and I will work out something with Elton. Just leave that to me," was her response in that dulcet tone with which he was so familiar.

The day arrived. That Saturday evening Elton left for work at 5:30 for the night shift with the understanding that Pam would be having *a girls' night out* with some of her workmates from her office. How wrong could he be! Instead, Dennis picked her up at six and headed down the M1 motorway and across London into the heart of

Surrey. Once out of London they ran into a thin autumn fog which reduced their speed, but they eventually arrived at a country house in the village of Ewhurst, a beautiful village in the Weald District of southern England. Even though it was night, Pam was bowled over by the beauty of the village with its winding leafy lanes. It was here in a ten-bedroom Tudor style country mansion that the function would be held.

Dennis seized every opportunity to show her off and she had never disappointed him. For him, the highlight of the evening was not so much the receiving of an award; for him, it was more the expression on her face when, after receiving a solid gold clock, he turned slowly and looked at her. She was wearing a smile second only to the glow of the rising sun on a tropical island. There was something indescribably sexy about her that filled the entire room. To him she was elegance personified. Walking slowly back to join her, he said to himself, *'How lucky I am to have someone here like her to share this moment with me. What a moment to experience with the person you love!'* And, from the look on her face, he felt sure she was saying the same thing. Soon he was back to a warm embrace. Her arms still around him, she pushed her shoulders back and with that enchanting look, said: "Oh Dennis, I am so pleased for you. You make me feel very proud," and they both chuckled softly.

The reception that followed was her stage. She was a people's person and it was here that her dynamic personality came through. Dressed in a sleek, black evening dress that moulded every inch of her figure, she mingled with colleagues who seemed to gravitate toward her as she shared and enjoyed the jokes between the exchanges of introductions. Dennis would often be caught up with small groups sharing experiences of work. But when they were together dancing, Pam would put her hands around his neck and allow her body to glide like an eel smoothly and rhythmically to the beat of the music, while the touch of his arm around her seemed to make her glow inside and tremble with yearning.

"Oh darling, you look truly wonderful tonight. I believe I am the luckiest man in this room. You have really made my day." She said nothing, but simply pulled him closer to her and shed a tear-drop of joy. With the party now over and everyone saying their good-byes, they set out for Hemel Hempstead. It was about one in the morning when, on stepping out, they suddenly realized it had snowed.

"Oh Dennis, perhaps we should have reserved a room at the house after all. You think we will make it home before morning?" she asked looking somewhat terrified, for not to be seen at home before Elton's return from work would certainly have meant disaster. They were along a narrow winding country road bedecked on either side with overhanging branches of conifers on which freshly fallen snow had settled when nothing was said for a short while. He was searching for something to say. Something that would re-assure her they would make it.

"Of course, my dear, we'll make it, don't you worry." He didn't want her to think he was of a similar opinion.

"I hope so," she replied but with some concern. Less than thirty minutes into the journey they came to a moderately steep incline, a characteristic of the Weald where they got stuck halfway up. The Weald is unique, for with its vast expanses of beech, oak, hazel and sweet chestnut woodland, it is the most forested part of England. But here too where hills and valleys dominate the landscape, roads connecting villages are narrow and sometimes steep in places. The snow was about ten centimeters deep by then and, after minutes trying in vain to free themselves, she turned to him with a worried look.

"What are we going to do, Dennis?" she asked, with terror in her eyes. Dennis leaned on the steering wheel for a moment. He knew he had to think of something.

"I am not too sure yet," he replied, trying desperately to come up with an idea. It was the kind of situation which would require help, but it was also that time of the morning when there was nothing else on the road. Suddenly an idea sprang to his mind dating back from his boyhood days in Barbados. He sat up.

"I'll tell you what I am going to do. I am going to try reversing down to the bottom of the hill, turn around and then reverse up." She gazed at him in horror. She had never seen it done before.

"How are you going to do that without skidding? Do you think it will work?" she asked, "because I can't see that working."

TROPICAL HEATWAVE

"I don't know but I have to do something otherwise we could be stuck here till morning."

"What a disturbing thought! I am not even dressed to walk," she mumbled. Without further delay he put the car into reverse and allowed it to make its way slowly to the bottom of the hill where he turned and proceeded to reverse up the hill. Having completed this manoeuvre successfully, they were on their way again. A glow came back to her face with a smile of delight. Once again Dennis had come up trumps in her perception of him.

"That was a clever move, where did you learn that?" she asked with a slight giggle.

"Oh, I learned that as a boy back home in Barbados. If a truck loaded with sugar cane got stuck going up a hill on a wet muddy road, the driver would roll back down the hill, turn the truck around and then reverse up the hill."

"Really, but I am from Barbados too and I have never seen that before," she exclaimed, gazing at him with a searching look as though to say, '*ah…yeah, right.*'

"That is because in St. Phillip where you lived there were no un-surfaced roads. Even the side roads are covered with tarmac or a rough surface of ground-in limestone. In St. Andrew where I lived, many side roads were merely un-surfaced clay tracks, dry weather roads you may call them. Also, while there are no hills in St. Phillip, there are many in St. Andrew which is the hilliest parish in the island and, what is more, we get a lot more rain in St. Andrew than anywhere else on the island," he said, expounding the virtues of his parish.

"Oh, I see" nodding in agreement while saying quietly to herself, '*that shows my parish was more developed than yours anyway.*' It was the first time they had shared a joke in thirty minutes. They continued their journey passing the time reflecting on the evening. Pam fastened the first three buttons on her coat and once again settled herself in the seat. "Oh Dennis, I really felt very proud seeing you receive that award for top sales twice in one year, even beating the full-timers, and a solid gold clock at that." He acknowledged the compliment with a look that said it all.

"Oh, my dear, when I turned with the award in my hand and looked at you emanating such beauty, I could only think it was courageous and nice of you to take the risk to be with me on such an occasion. I really felt on top of the world." As they crossed Westminster Bridge and made their way across north London, they were surprised to find there was not even a flake of snow to be seen. This left Pam puzzled but Dennis was able to explain the situation using his meteorological knowledge gained from his degree in geography. She just listened in amazement at how knowledgeable he was. The night had not been without its surprises but, on a whole, they felt it was very enjoyable and one they would remember for a long, long time. In the absence of any snow, Dennis was able to make good progress and within another thirty minutes Pam broke a moment of silence.

"Junction 7 coming up, Dennis." It was said in a voice that suggested an aching sadness to know that their night was fast coming to an end.

"Oh yes," he replied quietly, sharing her sentiment for he too had hoped that such a moment would never come. They both yearned for just one more night. Within a few minutes, they were leaving the M1 for the road leading to Bennetts End in the suburbs of Hemel Hempstead when it dawned on him that they ought to stop in a convenient place and say goodnight or good morning, depending on how you looked at it, in the proper manner. Without even discussing the matter, he pulled into a minor road which was a kind of cul-de-sac at the end of which, about one kilometre away, was an oil depot in the midst of acres of open land. They were also now about four kilometres away from her house. Such were her feelings that she yearned to surrender herself to him willingly, voluptuously and wantonly. They were soon in the back of the car indulging in what parting-lovers would do. After all, who was going to be around at 2 a.m. on a chilly morning in late autumn, he thought to himself. But, within fifteen minutes, this assumption was dashed, when he saw the lights of a vehicle slowing approaching. It was as though they were lying in wait. It was to be one more of the un-expected.

TROPICAL HEATWAVE

"I think there is a car coming," he said, in a voice that suggested alarm and surprise.

"What car at this time of the morning and out here?" she snapped, a long-drawn-out groan of despair tearing from her lips.

"It's the police," he hurriedly replied seeing the car coming slowly to a halt less than ten meters away. There was no doubt in his mind that soon they would be knocking on his steamed-up car window. They had less than three minutes to develop a strategy. He made sure the car blanket was securely fixed over them as they sat up.

"Now you let me do the talking," he strongly admonished.

"You have to because I wouldn't know what to say anyway," her voice slightly muted with fear and engulfed with panic. Dennis could feel his heart pounding away and his mouth getting dry as he awaited that dreaded knock on the window. Within a couple of seconds, there it was. He lowered the window.

"Are you both okay, sir," the officer asked politely, lingering on the word 'sir' in a quiet but authoritarian manner. Dennis cleared his throat.

"Yes, officer" he replied, having a fairly good idea of the next question.

"Only, is there any particular reason why you stopped here?" Dennis quite rightly felt it had something to do with the fact that they were within easy reach of an oil depot. It was unusual to see a vehicle parked within such a distance from the oil depot during the day hence the reason for the police to investigate the night parking.

"Yes. You see officer, we are just returning from a function that was held deep in the heart of Surrey but there was some snow on the ground when we left which delayed our journey back and made me a bit tired, so I thought we ought to stop and have a short break." This brought a wry smile from the officer who nodded as though to say, *I understand*.

"Very sensible too," he replied. "Ok, have a rest and be careful how you go."

"Thanks officer." Dennis could feel the tension in his body gradually ebbing away like ripples retreating to the sea. Having the window down to speak with the officer had made the car somewhat cold, a situation which Dennis quickly addressed.

"Phew, that was close," said Pam with a deep breath to release the tension built up over the last five-minutes. This was of course followed by fits of laughter causing the car to steam up once again.

"I bet you they are having a good laugh too. Do you really think that he, for one moment, believed what I told him?" remarked Dennis. The answer was in the expression on her face.

"Anyway, what matters is that he accepted our story," Pam replied smiling back while quickly changing into her usual office clothes which she had taken with her in a small bag. "I know we would both like the night to go on for ever, but I think it's time to get you home." In less than fifteen minutes, he was parked within fifty meters of her house. This he considered a safe distance from any prying eyes even at that time of the morning. With a quick peck on the cheek, he saw her safely indoors. But, the moment she entered the door, she knew immediately she would have a torrid time.

"That's odd, I didn't leave that radio on," she said quickly to herself as she hit the switch in the hallway to reveal Elton descending the stairs with squeezed features. He was a man boiling with hatred and wrath. Red dilating eyes and the smell of alcohol permeating the room signalled a man capable of doing anything. She walked across the room and closed the curtains. She turned and there he was standing before her breathing heavily. It was like a dragon spitting fire. His chest and shoulders rose and fell with every breath, the intensity of his eyes revealing the depth of his anger. Pam kept her cool knowing she was caught out.

"I saw you getting out of your man's car. You didn't go out with any girls, you......" he growled, "you went out with your man, but you didn't think I would be home, did you?" He continued in this explosive manner but stopped short of physical violence. Perhaps it was the memory of what he had suffered on the last explosive encounter, together with the effect of excessive drink, that made him slump on to an arm chair and thwarted another massive midnight blow-up. Pam held her calm knowing that, to do otherwise, would certainly have led to physical violence. But from the amount of alcohol he had consumed, she worked out that he had spent the evening in the pub with his friends instead of going to work that night.

132

15

Pam and Dennis continued to meet although less frequently for it became more and more difficult now that Elton was aware that something was going on. It was a period that threatened to rock the relationship. There was however, an event to which Pam, like most Caribbean folk, always looked forward. It was now August and the Notting Hill Street Carnival was one week away. It was an annual festival started by the local Caribbean Community in Notting Hill, London in 1965. As a cultural event, it aimed at binding the various islanders together in a form of identity and strength in a country that was not always too welcoming. The festival, which attracted more than two million people, was deemed the largest street party in Europe. For two days, you are entertained by Steel bands and floats, each expecting to be judged the best. Flamboyant Soca and Calypso dancers move to the beat of sound systems bellowing out Reggae, Soul, Dub, Soca, and Calypso all filling the air. Street stalls laden with a variety of Caribbean and other cuisines invite you to engage your taste buds and feast.

Jean and Pam had always attended the festival, and this was to be no exception. But this one was to be a bit different. For Jean, it was more than a festival. For her, it would be the perfect setting for her next move, another twist of the dagger. They were contemplating which float to follow when Jean had an idea. "Let's see who will be the first to spot one of our mutual friends," she suggested. They chuckled together and continued to comment on the various costumes on passing floats. But Pam was completely unaware of Jean's sinister thoughts. Thoughts like, *'I am not telling her that Sidney might be here, she may want to pick up where she left off.'*

It was a bright, sunny day with very few clouds in the sky, the kind of weather that suited the flimsy outfits worn by revellers demonstrating their interpretations of the music in a variety of gyratory movements. And, carried along in this stream of colour, music and dance were Pam and Jean with skirts sufficiently high and tops sufficiently low to reveal beads of perspiration like crystals in the sunlight, trickling down their ebony skin which, as though polished, shone under the strong summer sun. Suddenly, Jean pulled up. Unknown to Pam, her eyes had fallen on the back of a familiar head among a group of men having a drink at a near-by drinks stall. It didn't take her long to work it out and, at a convenient moment, she gave Pam the slip and made a bolt for the stall. Sidney, her boyfriend, was having a thirst-quenching beer with a couple of friends from Boston when someone on a passing float shouted, "Sidney, Sidney, how are you keeping?" In turning to say hello to a long-standing friend from Barbados, and with his hand still held high in the air, he was obstructed by an advancing pair of bouncing breasts threatening to free themselves from their harness at any moment. Sidney and Jean embraced with the kind of fervour that left his shirt wet with moisture from her heaving body. This close embrace triggered a thought. "I must use this opportunity to press whom my advantage over Pam." She was now on fire with passion and eagerness.

"Oh Sidney, you have no idea how much seeing you here today means to me. You've made my day by coming. I missed you so much," she uttered, gazing up at him while still in his arms. She had to make sure his attention was focused on her. To allow him to see Pam at that moment would not have served her purpose and yet, at the same time, she wanted Pam to see her in Sidney's arms and lubricating the conversion with the occasional kiss. But Sidney kept looking around as though he was expecting to see someone else. He felt strongly Pam was not far away because he knew they always attended the event together. This sideshow at the drinks stall attracted the attention of other folk who enriched the occasion with comments in true Caribbean style and flavour.

"No Pam?" he asked her. "That's rather strange because you two always go around together," he added, looking disappointed, his eyes anxiously penetrating every wave of passing revellers. Seeing his persistence to see Pam, Jean spoke up.

"Yes, she is here but we got split up somewhere along the way," she said in a loud voice to make herself heard over the din of a passing calypso band. Sidney was much taller than Jean and, as he held her, he used his height to continue surveying the crowd. Pam's absence had thrust him into thoughts like: *'Where is she? Perhaps she and Jean are no longer friends. You are ok Jean, but I am really interested in Pam.'* It was some time before Pam, realizing Jean had given her the slip, began peering frantically through the hot, sweaty, gyrating bodies. Suddenly her eyes landed on a small group of five sharing jokes over large helpings of fishcakes and cold beer. She shook her head as her lips twisted into a snarl. She could hardly believe what she was seeing for there was Jean in the arms of Sidney and caught up in a passionate kiss. For a moment, she found it difficult to come to grips with the scene. *'Is that really Jean I see over there wrapped up in Sidney's arms?'* she asked herself under a frowned forehead while walking slowly but meaningfully over to the stall.

Sidney eventually emerged from the kiss to find Pam slowly approaching. They were no bouncing breasts this time, but Jean had successfully put the next stage of her grand plan in place, namely, to ensure Pam had seen her wrapped in Sidney's arms. Embarrassment, surprise and regret were written all over his face. His eyes popped as he tried to free himself from Jean's grip which was now growing ever stronger as Pam approached. It was as though Jean was saying, *'I was here first.'* It was her first shot across Pam's bow. Pam kept her poise, the kind of upright deportment acquired during her days in nursing. She tried to conceal her emotions as best she could but, by then, beads of sweat generated by the heat of the day and the anger roiling in her stomach, were channelling themselves into her cleavage, immediately attracting Sidney's attention.

"Hello Sidney, I didn't know you were coming this year. When did you arrive?" she asked in an icy voice. At first, she avoided Jean's eyes but now horrified and shocked, her eyes darted between hers and Sidney's with various thoughts zipping through her mind. *How did she know where to find him? Was she expecting him? Was it pre-arranged? And why didn't she tell me?'* With great difficulty, Sidney eventually managed to free himself from Jean's clutches and started to make his way toward Pam with outstretched arms, but she would have none of it. Instead, she turned her face and took two steps backward. This did not go unnoticed by his friends one of whom shouted, "You are a lucky man Sidney. You have one woman crawling over you for your attention while you are targeting another one to gain her attention." This brought a round of laughter from the others. It was the kind of joke they would share for a long time especially after a few drinks at their local pub.

"I came in Friday and was trying to get hold of you since then but without any luck. Jean didn't seem to know where you were." As he spoke, an apologetic look crept across his face. Pam shot Jean a venomous stare which threw Sidney into some confusion. *'Why did Jean not tell Pam I was coming?'* he pondered, as Jean tried masking her guilt with a sheepish grin. She took two sips from Sidney's cold bottle of beer, drew closer to him and again clutched his arm, this time even more closely, leaving Pam in no doubt about the message she was sending. Pam, who now seemed oblivious to the music and colour around her, took a deep breath.

"To tell you the truth Pam, I wasn't too sure he was coming so I thought it best not to raise your spirits," she replied matter-of-factly. Sidney gave her a suspicious look. He was beginning to unravel the plot.

"Oh, I see," retorted Pam, her eyes now moving slowly between them, "I didn't know there was something between you two. Anyway, from the looks of things you both seem to be doing alright. Sorry, don't let me disturb you." With revulsion gripping her, Pam turned her attention to passing floats with their stunning dancers and bands booming out music so loud that it was almost difficult for them to hear themselves speak. But for Pam, neither the music nor the colour any longer appealed to her. Jean's stab had cut deeply into her pride.

"I wanted to tell you this long-ago Pam, but I never had the chance," shouted Jean. "Sidney and I knew each other well before he met you. The reason I didn't make it too obvious at the party is because of course Winston was around. You see Pam, he is my man and I am his woman." Her whole demeanour was designed to let Pam know who was in charge. Pam glared at her and shivered convulsively with anger. Sidney, already broiling in the afternoon heat, was now hot under the collar by this steamy verbal confrontation. He was speechless. It was an embarrassing moment for him. Jean was laying claim to him and was telling Pam to 'shove off.' Again, he tried to embrace Pam who again would have none of it. He looked at her blankly with no idea what to say. She scorned him and couldn't imagine ever kissing him again, so disappointed and enraged was she. Jean, a so-called good friend, had closed one of her escape valves for, like Jean, she had regarded Sidney as an option, a possible escape valve from Elton if necessary. Jean however had a different agenda. She was playing the *'first come, first served'* card. Sidney, who was definitely not prepared for such drama, called for a 'rum and coke' and downed it in one go. He was failing to tighten his grip on Pam and was therefore now losing the woman who was his real reason for coming to the Carnival that year. *'What can I do to retrieve the situation or is it too late?'* he pondered, seeing he had lost control of the situation. Pam's love for him was waning fast. Jean shot him a quelling glance on an appealing look before a double intake of breath.

"Look Sidney, I am sure you know that Pam is married and anyway, she has her eyes on somebody else, so you see she already has her hands full with her husband and a fellow. I don't really think she has any time left for you. Don't you see she wouldn't even let you touch her?" she uttered with a hard grin and Pam gave Sidney a cold look. Buzzing around in her mind was the thought that she was made to look a fool and that, *'if Jean could do this to a good friend, then she is quite capable of doing anything.'* She was just about to leave the scene when she turned and looked at Jean with utter contempt and scorn in a manner only seen among Caribbean women.

Dejected and disappointed, Pam was about to re-join the mainstream when her attention was suddenly drawn to Jean's boyfriend Winston in the distance with three friends. This took her by surprise because Jean had told her he was not attending the festival that year.

He too was a Trinidadian who, like Elton, had arrived in England during the mid-fifties and had found work with British Rail and had also taken a liking to Saturday nights in the pub. Pam felt that his decision to attend the festival after all might have spawned from a growing lack of confidence in Jean whom he suspected was playing away. May be, it was a burning desire to satisfy his curiosity that made him change his mind and attend. After a few drinks, he had started to meander his way against the flow of revellers, stopping from time to time to say hello to other friends. This casual meandering was brought to an abrupt halt when he spotted Jean and Sidney standing together with a few friends like a little whirlpool at the side of a moving stream but, on seeing there was no Pam, he immediately decided to make himself less conspicuous and observe from a safe distance. *'I wonder what's going on over there, looks like some kind of drama unfolding. And where is Pam? She and Jean always attend carnival together. Why don't I remain out of sight for a while? Who knows, I might learn something,'* he muttered while gazing steadfastly at the sideshow. He observed the way Jean looked at Sidney and the way she cuddled up to him giving him the occasional peck on the cheek and had time to read her body language. Having had his suspicions confirmed, he decided to make an appearance which impelled Pam to return and witness the outcome. No pleasantries were exchanged nor was there any preamble for Winston resembled a storm cloud ready to burst as he made his way slowly but purposefully to the group. Jean was stunned and shocked to see Winston and attempted a wobbly smile. He paused glancing from one face to the other.

"Who is this man. Do you know him Jean?" asked Sidney, casting an anxious glare and looking very uneasy. Winston stood motionless, his eyes boring into Jean's and seething with anger on finding out he had been taken for a ride. Jean slowly released her grip on Sidney and oddly enough, soon became unmoved by the unexpected arrival of Winston. He gave her a penetrating look and then launched into a vicious verbal onslaught that seemed to drive up the temperature of an already superheated festival.

"You know Jean, I have always had my suspicions about you. Now I know I was right. For some time, I felt we were drifting apart, but I couldn't put my fingers on it until now. It is quite clear to me you have made your choice and that all you were doing is stringing me along until you find another idiot into whom you could sink your venomous claws. You, are free to go with him because, as from now, there is nothing more between us. I don't want to see or speak to you ever again. I will collect my things from your place and go." Jean said nothing. Instead she merely listened while looking at Sidney for support which did not forthcoming. That said, Winston proceeded to re-join his mates in the adjacent bar, one of many selling rice and curry goat, ackee and saltfish, codfish cakes, to mention but a few. Pam remained aloof, anxious to see Jean's reaction for, although she appeared to be slightly shocked, she didn't look too worried. Over time, she had come to see Winston as a bore and was glad to see him go and now he had played right into her hands. She could now focus her attention on Sidney.

"Actually, you can do whatever you like Winston, because you are a waste of time and space anyway." She bellowed, her voice rising above the din of music blasting from passing heavy sound systems. Jean showed no remorse, had no soul and was cruel beyond measure. She was now confident in her claim to Sidney who, on the other hand, was very surprised at the way she had treated Winston in public. Winston had seen Sidney at one of Jean's house-parties but had no idea something was going on although he had a feeling she was playing out but no idea with whom. He did not express any surprise just disappointment. Sidney, now more aware of Jean's agenda, expressed his disgust with Jean and, seeing that he was fast losing his grip on Pam, got himself another rum and coke and squared up to her.

"Jean, I think you ought to know that my primary reason for coming here was to see Pam but, because of you, I have messed things up. In any case, what makes you think I would want to carry on with you after the way you treated Winston in public? How do I know you wouldn't do the same thing to me? Consider our relationship finished as from now." Everything about him screamed regret. This caught Jean by surprise, sending shock waves throughout her entire body for she was sure she had him within her grip. Things had suddenly backfired and she was not ready for it. Sidney had dropped Jean, but he had lost Pam. Jean had lost Sidney, her boyfriend Winston, as well as a good friend in Pam. Large beads of perspiration tumbled from her face on to her heaving breasts. This combination of regret, disappointment, anger, hatred and intrigue rose into the atmosphere like Indian smoke rings in a western movie.

This supercharged moment of verbal exchanges set Pam's thoughts racing. She removed her shades slowly and dabbed her eyes for, whirling around in her mind, were thoughts like: *'How can I trust a man who comes to Carnival without letting me know, a man I find out has been carrying on with my best friend despite his promises to me. And how can I ever trust Jean again? At least I now know the man I want.'* She thought of the wonderful times she had spent with Dennis and the future they had planned together. Suddenly, Jean found herself completely isolated. Things had not quite gone the way she had planned but she had another card up her sleeve, another hammer blow to strike. Seeing Pam as causing the break-up between herself and Sidney as well as Winston, she now set out more doggedly on revenge grail.

Winston soon found himself a flat and moved away from Jean. Sidney was so distraught at missing out on Pam that he returned to Boston two days later. But, in the week that followed, worrying thoughts invaded Pam's mind. Thoughts like: *'What will she do next? Will she tell Elton that there was something between Sidney and me or even about Dennis?'* At home, she panicked whenever the phone rang. *"Could it be Jean about to spill the beans to Elton?"* Every time she saw Elton making his way home across the green from work, she expected a sudden outburst. Such thoughts kept her on edge for many days.

16

It was a cool evening in early November and, in the little wood beyond the green, the elm and beach were already signalling the onset of autumn. Children were already trailing their feet through small mounds of red and brown autumn leaves and squirrels were busy gathering acorns and hazel nuts. In the foreground, another group of under-fives was kicking a ball around assisted by a black and white poodle whose barks added to the jolly atmosphere. That evening, Elton had decided against going to the pub for his usual pint before going home which unsettled Pam. She was loading the washing machine while taking in a ringside view of the under-fives theatre on the green when the phone rang just as Elton entered the door. Her nerves tightened with despair. Her breathing shortened as Elton took up the receiver.

"Hello and how are you keeping?" The person asked. It was a voice he knew. She knew from the expression on his face.

"I am okay," he replied a little surprised.

"Are you free to speak?" asked the caller.

"Yes, but give me a moment," he whispered hurriedly, while partially closing the door between the hall and the kitchen but, by chance, leaving just enough of a gap to allow Pam to get the gist of the conversation above the din of the washing machine. An inner feeling told Pam it was Jean seeing that he opted to close the door. Her heart stepped up a beat. She could only think of Jean becoming revengeful and spilling the beans.

"Are you doing anything special next Friday evening after work?" inquired Jean in a persuasive voice at which point the washing machine stopped.

"No, why?" he asked easily, drawing out the "o" for a few seconds while making himself comfortable on the seat next to the small telephone table.

"Can you pop around after work? I want to discuss a few things with you. I don't want to say much at this time, but I think you ought to know that Winston and I have broken up. There is a lot more but let's leave that for when you come." She hoped that releasing this piece of information would be enough to make him take the bait and spur him into making the visit a priority. The hushed tone of the conversation suggested Pam was not to know. Elton slowly replaced the receiver and turned with a pensive look mixed with wonderment while placing the *Racing Post* quietly on the phone table. *'What is so important that she couldn't tell me on the phone? And why the secrecy? I suppose the only way to find out is to go,'* he said quietly to himself while entering the kitchen.

The series of contours across Pam's forehead as he did so, suggested she was curious, but she refrained from asking who it was or what it was about. She had overheard enough however to conclude that he was not coming home straight from work on Friday which to her was nothing unusual. She had seen that many times when, after collecting his wages, he would often remain in London with his mates for the weekend. But this Friday evening would be slightly different and there was also something in Elton's expression that told Pam something sinister was brewing. Elton was surprised at what he had just heard but Jean had said enough to convince him the visit would be worthwhile. Her objective now was to kill two birds with one stone.

Jean lived in a one bedroom flat on the first floor of a terrace house in Kensal Rise less than thirty minutes from Diane who was also one of her good friends. It overlooked a small urban open space used by pedestrians as a short cut from one road to another. Apart from a few swings and benches, and the odd beech, there was nothing too attractive about this small park. In her front room, a large bay window provided a suitable framework on which to hang a set of floor-length pale blue drapes, an appropriate backdrop to her three-piece suite, TV and stereo. On a small rug in the centre stood a coffee table on which was mounted a spherical glass vase with an assortment of artificial flowers. It was the kind of furnishing seen in most flats rented by folk from the Caribbean at that time. She had two days to prepare for Elton's visit. '*I will take half day off from work on Friday to make sure I have everything prepared because I really don't want anything to go wrong. I want his visit to be such that he will want to visit me again and again,*' she thought to herself as she went about making the necessary preparations. She was bent on giving the dagger that final twist, so the setting had to be right if Elton was to be lured into her grand scheme. The meal would be curried lamb with rice and peas together with all the trimmings to bring about a truly Caribbean flavour. On her way to the butcher's that afternoon, she met Diane.

"You are in a bit of a hurry," exclaimed Diane, looking somewhat curious.

"I am rushing to the butcher's before he closes to buy some lamb for dinner."

"What's the special occasion because you don't normally have lamb on a Friday evening?" she asked, and Jean chuckled half-sheepishly.

"As a matter of fact, I am having Elton over for a meal this evening. I might as well tell you because you will get to know anyway."

"Is Pam coming?"

"No, I want to discuss a few things with Elton in private and I don't want Pam to know yet," she replied, avoiding Diane's eyes. Diane raised her eyebrows and gave her an angled look before wishing her 'good luck' and resuming her journey. That evening, on the dinner table were two glasses and a bottle of Barbados rum which she knew Elton adored. From her collection of music, she selected tunes she thought most suitable for the occasion. The stereo was set to fill the room with something Caribbean within five minutes of his expected arrival, something she knew would set the mood. She slipped into her bedroom to dress, an exercise which did not take her very long as she had planned to leave very little to the imagination. She had just put the final touches to her eyelashes when the door-bell rang. It was Elton. After a final check on her hair and make-up, she gingerly made her way down the stairs and greeted him with an enchanting look enhanced by her large brown eyes.

"Hello Elton, come in." They brushed each other's cheeks and he handed her a small bouquet of flowers and a bottle of white wine. He had rightly worked out that dinner would be on the menu. "Thanks for the flowers, but why the bag?" she asked breezily. *'I wonder if he is planning to stay the night and hence some extra clothes. If that is so, it is fine by me.'*

"Oh, I have my usual clothes in here. I plan to change before I set out for home. I had a feeling it would be an evening that would include one of your nice meals, so I thought I would dress accordingly," he replied with a broad grin. She was slightly disappointed with the answer. She was expecting him to say something like 'just in case I have to stay the night.' However, she wasn't too bothered because she was confident she would succeed at her plan which started the moment he entered.

"That's rather nice of you," and this time she hugged him. He had visited the flat on a few occasions as one of the guests at her parties but this time it felt and looked different. On his previous visits, he would always be welcomed by one of the party-goers some of whom would have been dancing to calypso or reggae while others would simply be chatting on the landing and enjoying curried goat and rice or Jamaican patties and much more. This time he was greeted by one woman boasting an attractive Afro hair-style. He knew her for some time, but never before was he privileged to such a visible feast. It was more than he expected. *'I suppose this is all part of the first course,'* he thought to himself. She wore a kind of loose fitting kaftan imprinted with Caribbean scenes of coconut palm, sandy beaches and rum cocktails. With baggy sleeves and a wide low-fitting neck, the whole outfit came to an abrupt halt about eight inches above her knees. It was the first glimpse of the kind of evening she had in store for him.

Elton closed the door quietly behind him before spending a few moments in awe and wonder at what he was seeing, all of which, of course, he liked. But it also set his thoughts racing. *'I wonder what whirlwind is she walking me into? Is this the same Jean I always knew? If so, why would Winston want to walk out on such a woman?'* But, before he could set the house ablaze with such burning curiosity, he was making his way up the stairs three steps behind her. Jean was keenly aware that every step she took would give him a miniature panoramic view, enough to whet his appetite and send his pulses racing. The room he entered exuded an ambiance quite different to that to which he had been accustomed. The laid table with a bottle of rum, the light Caribbean music, the smell of Caribbean cuisine, and a woman dressed to attract the attention of the most resistant stud, were enough to satisfy his curiosity and fondle his desires. He deposited himself on the double settee. Jean walked over to the stereo and changed the tune to something more seductive. "Can I get you a drink?" she asked, with an expression of confidence that her next move would be successful. She wanted the scene to stimulate the palate of his mind and fondle his desires.

"Yes, of course," replied Elton, gazing at a photo of the West Indies cricket team hanging on the wall opposite. He was just about to glance at a photo of Jean and Pam as nursing students on a weekend trip to Amsterdam when he suddenly remembered he had not specified what type of drink he preferred. "Oh, I'll have a whiskey please," he shouted while slowly removing his jacket and hanging it over a chair next to him. Jean went to a small cabinet which, when opened, revealed a partly mirrored interior presenting an image of double its content. From her collection of alcoholic drinks, she took a bottle of whiskey and disappeared, allowing Elton's eyes to roam around the room and his thought processes to move up a gear which they did. *'What if this is a set-up? But why would she want to do that to me? After all, we get on well.'* Jean soon returned with two whiskies on the rocks. Elton took his and sat back in anticipation of her joining him on the settee. He was not disappointed. After a sip of whiskey which seemed to have an immediate mellowing affect, he placed his glass on a small side table and cleared his throat.

"I am sorry to hear about Winston. What caused it? By the way, I didn't tell Pam what the phone conversation was about, and I made sure she didn't overhear." He was unaware that Pam had already worked out it was Jean to whom he was speaking although she wasn't bothered because she had hoped that he would find someone and just buzz off.

"Thanks, I would hate to know that she knew it was I on the other end of the phone that evening." After a quiet opening chat about this and that, it was time for dinner. Elton was still held in suspense as Jean poured another whiskey before leading the way to the small dining table in the adjoining room.

"By the way Elton, can you remember a chap called Sidney?" bending across the table to serve him some rice and peas. It was a stance that allowed her to display two of her most attractive endowments which compelled Elton to linger for a moment on this *sidedish*, a kind of, let us say, starter. Jean was fully aware of this and did not hasten. She was a woman on a mission and Elton was falling for the bait.

"No, I can't say I do," the words stumbling from his mouth in a slow jerky manner, so absorbed was he in the side show.

"I believe you met him at one of my parties. He is a Trinidadian like me, tall chap," she added. This brought furrows to Elton's brow as he tried desperately to remember Sidney while trying to cope with the dishes appearing before his eyes.

"Why, what about him?" he asked pointedly, anxious to know more. Jean sighed heavily and aimed a meaningful glance at him.

"Well the showdown occurred at Carnival because of him," she declared as they touched glasses.

"What showdown, what happened?" he asked smartly, helping himself to fried plantain.

"I was having a drink with Sidney at one of the stalls. We got a bit close, you know the kind of thing that can happen after a few drinks and the sound of calypso music. He was holding me closely when Pam, who was doing her thing behind a float, saw us and came over. For some reason, it was as though she did not expect to see us together." She paused momentarily and waited for his facial expression, but he simply nodded his head and wanted to believe her.

"Yes, I know Pam and the way she does her thing when there is music. But why would she be annoyed at seeing you and this fellow together?" he asked, and Jean smiled casually.

TROPICAL HEATWAVE

"The way she looked at us told me she was not at all pleased. In fact, even when Sidney tried to say hello to her, she shrugged him off. It was as though she didn't expect to see Sidney and me like that. I had to tell her I knew Sidney long before she did because I could clearly see she was very annoyed." Elton squinted short-sightedly into her face with a tight-lipped expression and paused for a few seconds in pensive mood. He was replaying a scene. *'Perhaps that was the man who brought her home that night,'* he pondered while helping himself to more curried lamb.

"So, what happened after that?"

"Well, I didn't know that Winston was at the Carnival. He had told me he wasn't coming but suddenly he turned up with two of his friends. And you know what he did?"

"No, but you are going to tell me," he replied in an undertone that said, *'I am all ears.'*

"He positioned himself in a place where he could not be seen by us but from where he could hear and see what was going on between Sidney, Pam and me. Having had his belly full of it, he appeared and accused me of having a relationship with Sidney and ended our relationship there and then. But quite honestly Elton, it doesn't bother me the slightest bit because I was getting fed up with him anyway." As she spoke, she could sense that Elton empathised with her especially when he placed a tentative hand on her shoulder.

"You mean he ended it just like that?" he blurted, looking horrified.

"Yes, just like that," she replied matter of factly and shrugged her shoulders.

"But, what was all of that to do with Pam. How does she fit into it?" He had an idea, but he was trying to build a bigger picture of the scene and now had his ears tuned into every word Jean said. Most of the delicious meal had by now disappeared leaving unsightly dirty dishes. She asked for an excuse and started to take them to the kitchen leaving Elton to return to the sitting room where he enjoyed one of his favourite tunes while gazing at the photo of Pam and Jean. But between the clatter of dishes, Jean declared in a voice loud enough to reach him in the sitting room.

147

"But Elton, something happened that day which took me by surprise."

"Oh, what was that," asked Dennis, now looking more curious while trying to squeeze as much information as possible out of her.

"Well, as soon as Pam came over to where we were drinking, and I told her I knew Sidney before she did, her face took a plunge. She looked very surprised and you could see she was very jealous and didn't like what she was seeing. I hate to tell you this, but it did leave me thinking that there might be something going on between the two of them, because they both appeared unhappy and disappointed. Seemed as though my presence had prevented them from getting closer together that day.

"But do you know who had a crush on whom?" he asked with a hardened look. By now Jean had joined him on the settee again.

"Come on Elton," she said with a light chuckle, "if you are standing close to a man and another woman comes up and appears to be jealous, what would you think? It set me thinking, for it was not too long ago she told me she was thinking of going to Boston to visit a friend and that's where Sidney lives. You don't have to be a rocket scientist to work that one out." Their eyes met and as he sat there for a long silent moment, the music seemed no longer to penetrate his ears. An expressionless look gripped his face. He had another drink, this time a large one because this was an experience for which he was not quite prepared.

It was 6:30 in the evening and the amber glow of the street lights was penetrating the window. Jean strolled across the room like a Miss World contestant, closed the curtains and switched on the standing light in the corner next to the stereo. She selected a CD more in keeping with the moment before settling snugly next to Elton. The scene was now set. Elton levelled his eyes with hers.

"But is there something really going on between you and this Sidney fellow?" he asked, because he was aware that she was quite capable of playing the field with more than one man at the same time. He had gleaned this information from the occasional light conversations he would have with Pam about their days as young trainee nurses in Colchester. It was this which made him decide to take along a change of clothing that Friday evening.

"At one of my parties Sidney *did* make a play for me but nothing came out of it because Winston was around which made it very difficult for me to respond. By then, he was already becoming a bore anyway, so it doesn't bother me that he has gone," Jean uttered breezily and with a feeling of confidence that her plan was working. Elton, now feeling satisfied that it wasn't a set-up, made his way to the cabinet and poured them both a gin and tonic water. He leaned forward to hand her the drink in the process of which he found her very receptive to a gentle kiss on the lips. She sighed heavily which lead him to conclude that, if he played her game, he would drag more information out of her. Or was it because, having had his appetite whet, he was beginning to find her more entertaining?

"But when did Winston move out?" he asked quietly, his mind now becoming invaded with thoughts like: *'You know, I feel she is making a serious play for me and why not? After all, Winston has walked out on her.'*

"Last Thursday," she replied without any hint of regret which convinced Elton it was safe to play the game.

"Do you know where he is staying?"

"Someone told me they saw him shopping in Cricklewood Broadway not far from here. I believe he probably has a flat or perhaps a woman somewhere in that area. Anyway, I don't care." Elton reached for a hanky from his jacket pocket and mopped his brow several times. Perhaps it was the highly seasoned food and the alcoholic drink together with a rather warm room or, may be, his anticipation of what was coming, that caused his body to overheat.

"But, I thought you two were getting on well."

"Quite honestly, I don't think I ever cared much about him. I certainly was not in love with him, but he contributed to the upkeep of the flat. Apart from that, he seems to have no ambition. I know that it will be difficult to keep this flat, but I am hoping that I will soon find someone better to join me." Her voice trailed off as she cast a beseeching look at Elton who nodded and tried to manoeuvre the conversation in a different direction. *'Is this meant to be an invitation?'* he thought, *'and is she trying to sink her claws into me because she is infatuated with me or because she finds me a likely contributor to the upkeep of her flat.'* What he did not realise was that, while financial assistance was the obvious, her underlying aim was a burning desire to revenge Pam. He had misread the plot.

"Let's dance," she suggested, "this is one of my favourite tunes." They danced quietly to the tune of *Stealing love on the side* during which time they held each other closely and moved rhythmically and seductively, while sipping from each other's glass. At that time, there was nothing telling them they would ever be together. The moment was interrupted when the chimes of Big Ben on TV signalled the beginning of the ten o'clock news.

"Oh dear, I have to go very soon because it is getting late and I have a long journey and the buses at the other end aren't too reliable," he declared, releasing her reluctantly.

"Don't you think you ought to stay over because you are not quite fit to travel, not even on public transport," she admonished. It was an offer he could not refuse. The following morning, he would wake up next to Jean who was satisfied with the way the evening had gone. *'I think I have succeeded so far because, from what I told him about Pam, he will no longer trust her,'* she said to herself. *'Now all I have to do is to make sure Dennis hears about Pam's performance at the carnival and, who knows, he might even drop her as well leaving the way clear for me on two fronts.'* She had succeeded in driving a wedge between Elton and Pam, and probably between Pam and Dennis. Not only would this have given her revenge on Pam but provided her with options.

Elton left Jean after lunch next day and arrived home by mid-afternoon. On the train, he had time to reflect on what Jean had told him and the night they had together. There was now no doubt in his mind that she was making a play for him. Jean had obviously managed to stimulate him into having an interest in her, but he was now more consumed with the idea that Pam had found two other men, Sidney and Dennis, whom she obviously thought more desirable than him. As he alighted from the bus and made his way through the little wood and across the green, he was already pumped up to the point of exploding.

Pam was preparing the evening meal when she happened to glance through the kitchen window and saw him approaching. The hard look on his face, as he approached the door, once again told her the next few hours would be torrid. She feared the worse had happened for she was suddenly hit with the thought that Jean had pulled the plug on her. She didn't have long to wait. The street door was opened and closed with such ferocity that two small pictures, dislodged from the wall in the hallway, ended in a mixture of broken glass, paper and wood on the floor. The *Racing Post* was ejected from his hand with such force that it flew like a missile and landed firmly on a chair. There was the usual sound from the opening and closing of the drinks cabinet. He had done what he was accustomed doing, namely, to reach for the bottle and a glass. This time, there was no sipping of this drink. Instead, it was dispatched in one go. Fully charged up, he burst open the kitchen door with such force that it rebounded, dealing a heavy blow to his face. This did not help. The bull was now let loose in the china shop once again. She immediately concluded that whatever Jean had given him had worked.

"I know all about you and your men," he uttered with a pinched face. "I know about you and Dennis and about you and Sidney. You are nothing but a ----------, and you can't deny it because I got it from one of your best friends," he bellowed, his eyes blazing into hers. The sound waves generated by this thunderous outburst seemed to cause glasses in the kitchen cabinet to vibrate with resonance. Pots and pans, like flying-saucers, were soon whizzing around the kitchen, some crashing into walls while others narrowly missed their intended target by her quick footwork and swaying movement of her upper body. Such was the onslaught, that she grabbed the only means of protection at hand, a rolling pin, to defend herself and, surprisingly, she mustered an unusual level of courage to respond with steel in her voice.

"That's rich coming from you. Where did you sleep last night, not that I care? Don't tell me, I'll tell you. You slept with that b------ Jean. You suit each other. Why don't you leave my house and go and live with her," she snapped, now pumped up and ready for action. The house was of course in her name since she had signed for it as part of the package offered by the Ministry of Transport to move from London to Hemel Hempstead.

"I now know what you were doing when you made out you were spending Saturday nights at Diane," he snarled, spitting fire. Armed with the rolling pin, she held her ground. This explosion of sustained torrid language reverberated across the green entering neighbouring homes, causing dogs to bark and disturb the tranquillity of an otherwise peaceful Saturday afternoon in a quiet suburban neighbourhood. Suddenly, and in the midst of this violent explosion, the doorbell rang. Elton answered the door. "Yes, what do you want?" he snapped, with a pointed look and an intense aggressive glare.

"I am sorry to bother you, but you all are disturbing me and the rest of the neighbours," exclaimed the old lady with quivering lips while pointing to the surrounding houses as she spoke. "If it doesn't stop, I will have to call the police," she added before taking two steps backward and beating a hasty retreat. Just as well she did, because Elton might have responded with a punch in the face for intruding, he was the kind of man who believed in physical force to solve differences. But it was her intervention that eventually brought about a simmering down of this boiling cauldron. For Pam, what had started as a love-affair between her and Dennis, had now become a spawning ground for a matter of some urgency. *"I must get out of this place as soon as possible, whatever it takes. I just cannot take any more of this. Jean has spilled the beans on me, that b...'* were thoughts buzzing around in her mind. She had to find a safe haven quickly. Jean had succeeded in lighting the fuse. The question was, who would now be consumed in this inferno?

17

Pam and Dennis continued to meet every third Saturday afternoon when she went to the hairdresser's in London. But during that period too, Elton had kept up his tortuous behaviour on Pam while at the same visiting Jean every other Friday evening under the cover that he was doing overtime. It was on such a visit that Jean thought she would test the waters just to see if her plan was still on track. They were viewing TV when she used a commercial break to make a pot of tea. She added milk to both cups and turned to Elton with a frowned look.

"By the way Elton, how are you getting on with Pam these days? I don't hear you say much about things at home," and she waited anxiously for his reply.

"We don't say much to each other, but I noticed she has been attending a number of courses to do with her work and I often wondered what she is up to," he uttered. He had never told Jean about the explosion they had a few weeks before.

"I can tell you now that she is a very ambitious girl and will not stop until she has risen further up the ranking order. For instance, look what she did when you were living in London. Quite unknown to you, she applied and got a job in the Ministry of Transport computer department. So, what makes you think she might not be doing a similar thing now?" Elton's brain immediately went into rewind mode recalling what happened less than two years before when she secretly applied and was offered the job.

"What do you think she's going to do if she gets promotion? I'll tell you. She will look for a man higher up than you, a man like Dennis who is well educated and doing well in his profession and whom she is already seeing. She wouldn't want you anymore," added Jean with a contented look for she was satisfied with the way things had gone so far. Elton simply nodded, finding himself momentarily unable to speak. He had always failed to recognise Pam's goal in life. Instead, he had seen her only as a working woman put there to satisfy his physical needs and to carry out the daily domestic chores as a housewife as well as contributing more than her fair share to housekeeping. He had found it difficult to accept that, although they had come from similar backgrounds and with the same level of primary education, Pam would want to improve her economic and, indeed, social status. One of the main ways in which she differed from him was in their philosophy of life. She had a determination and burning desire to achieve a better quality of life. He was quite happy with the status quo, working as a labourer at British Rail and having fun with his mates.

"Sometimes she invites some of her work colleagues for a meal, but they are not my type and she knows that," he grunted.

"What do you mean?"

"Well, they are always white, and I don't like the food she prepares for them and they don't like my music. Also, they don't talk about things I like to talk about. It becomes very boring," he declared. In his comfort zone with his other Caribbean friends, he was more at home talking about their cricket stars or the odds in horse or dog racing or even the latest records to be released by favourite black singers.

"And what do you do?"

"Often, I try not to be there or if I am, I soon go out leaving her to it," he said, and she aimed a meaningful glance at him. Pam was an excellent cook who was always looking for an opportunity to demonstrate some of the culinary skills she had acquired in Guyana and Barbados. This is one of the reasons why she would occasionally invite a couple of her senior colleagues for a light meal or drinks. Covertly however, she always hoped it would help to pave the way to promotion. But it was on such an occasion that Elton showed his true colours. It was Friday evening and it was seven when the door-bell rang. She knew it was her guests because they were never late.

"Elton, please see to the door for me," she asked while putting finishing touches to the table.

"They are not my guests," he growled and remained glued to the TV. She welcomed the guests but had to make a special effort to conceal her anger. She could therefore hardly wait to give vent to her feelings about his behaviour before and during the dinner party. The dinner would have been better but for the bitter ingredient of Elton's presence. With the guests on their way home, he returned to his TV, having said very little at the table. It was an embarrassing moment for her. He had obviously set out to hurt her by damaging her credibility.

"Why are you always so rude and unwelcoming to my guests? I could see they were uncomfortable in your presence. Seems to me you are determined to ruin my present career like you did when I was in nursing. Why do you dislike my friends so much?" she snapped, anger roiling in her stomach and tears flowing down her cheeks. He remained focused to the TV, his pinched features confirming his emotions. His was a kind of jealousy and obsession that often spilled over into the occasional house party they would attend. She was not expected to dance with anyone else but him although, for a man from the Caribbean, he was very bad at it. If she did, it would often end in a brawl much to her shame. What made her endure such treatment over so long a period left Dennis baffled until one day in mid-summer. It was half-term break from school and Dennis was enjoying a refreshing cup of tea before settling down to catch up with news on the TV when the phone rang. '*I could really do without any disturbance now,*' he said to himself while reaching for the phone. It being mid-week, Dennis did not expect a call from Pam. Nor did he anticipate that things would take the kind of turn that would demand immediate action by him.

"Please Dennis, you have to get me out of here. I can't take it anymore," came a quivering voice choked back with tears. "There is no let up from the kind of treatment I am receiving from this man. Last week he punched me about my head so badly that I had to wear dark glasses to work to hide the bruises and swelling around my eyes," she tried to explain, her voice sometimes hardly audible. Tired as he was, he snapped to attention the moment he heard the first words. It tore him apart to hear such an unusual penetrating tone in her voice. She was clearly a woman in distress and in need of urgent help.

"Okay, listen, don't say any more," he said calmly, trying to settle her down. "Meet me in the town tomorrow around lunch-time and let's see what we can do."

"I'll have to take some time off, but that should be okay." Her speech was interrupted by the occasional sob indicative of one trying to hold back tears. He always felt that there are times when a person should follow their instincts and that hers was saying it was time to make a break. He often sensed a feeling of determination in her to get away from beneath the pain and humiliation she was suffering.

"Okay I'll see you tomorrow at about one o'clock by the shoe shop next to the market square. But do remember it is market-day tomorrow in Hemel Hempstead and the town will be very busy so we will have to be very careful not to be seen by one of Elton's friends," she implored. Dennis put the phone down slowly and made his way upstairs to his study. Clasping his hands behind his head, he leaned back in his chair and toyed with a few ideas. *'I have to do something quickly. What is certain is that I must come up with something that will work, one that will solve several problems in one stroke. I am still waiting divorce proceedings, but a desperate situation like this requires desperate action.'* He doodled on his notepad, his brain working to full capacity to come up with an answer. After a while, he dropped everything and went for a quiet stroll in the nearby park hoping that the air and the openness would clear his brain allowing him to come up with an appropriate response, one that would satisfy her. *'Perhaps we could rent a flat, but where? Should it be in Hemel Hempstead or Watford just ten kilometres south? It has to be within easy reach of her workplace. Maybe we can join and buy a house. I have enough to cover a deposit. But what if Susan should find out? How would it affect my side of the divorce? What I cannot do is to let Pam stay there and suffer such physical and emotional pain and distress.'* He returned home in time to answer the phone.

"Hello, it's me again. I was just looking through one of the local papers and I have come across a few two-bedroom flats to let just on the other side of Hemel Hempstead. Should I call the agent and make arrangements for us to see them tomorrow. What do you think?" It was a tone of desperation and determination and he detected from her voice she was expecting him to take action, to come up with something that would provide an escape from hell, and quickly.

"Yes. Why not? I'll see you tomorrow my love." He could feel the pressure bearing down on his shoulders as he returned the receiver to its position, and yet, in a strange way, she had made the decision for him. The fact that she made the effort to think of an idea and was prepared to move on it so quickly was enough to convince him that he had to go one better. '*I have to show her that I not only love her but care for her. I think I will settle for a house rather than a flat. To me, it is the better option,*' he thought to himself. They met as arranged outside the shoe shop. Approaching the rendezvous slowly, he could see her looking at the display of shoes in the shop window and he wondered what was really going through her mind at that time. He supposed it was just a way of reducing the chances of her face being spotted by an un-welcomed passer-by who might pass information on to Elton. Without the usual greeting, they hurried to a nearby café off the main street for coffee.

"Oh boy, am I glad to see you!" she exclaimed, taking an audible intake of breath before proceeding to give him a blow-by-blow description of her recent sordid experience. As she spoke, he could see there was an echo of the recent past making her tremble. It was a piercing blow of despair. He held her hand across the table and felt her body still vibrating with fear. It was one backed up by what he saw when she removed her sun glasses. The bruises and the look in her eyes rooted him to the spot. Anger within him reached boiling point as grief sat like a knot in her throat. There was no doubt in Dennis' mind that things had got worse during the intervening weeks. It being lunch-time and market day, the café was reasonably full forcing Pam to replace her shades as quickly as possible. Dennis said very little giving her the time to get it off her chest. He caught the attention of the waiter and asked for another coffee. This time it was an espresso to which he added a little milk and took two sips.

"One night last week, he was so violent that I had to run out in my dressing gown across the green and stay at a neighbour's house."

Dennis gritted his teeth in agony and anger for, even as she spoke, tears welling up in her eyes cascaded down her cheeks. '*Why should such a woman be subjected to such treatment?*' he thought to himself, but he also knew Elton wasn't going to let her go without a fight. After all, why should he when she was the main bread-winner. But there were times too when Dennis even saw Elton as an intruder doing all he could to frustrate the growth of that special something that was developing between Pam and himself. And then it dawned on him that he himself could lose her to Sidney if he could not come up with a workable solution to her plight. Dennis took another sip of coffee and levelled his eyes with hers with a pensive look.

"I think that, since we both have reliable incomes, we ought to join and go for a house instead of a flat. If you agree, we can start looking today," he suggested, all of which immediately brought her a feeling of relief and she managed a weary smile.

"What a good idea! But I don't think we ought to buy one in Hemel because it would be too easy for him to find me."

"Oh yes, you are right. Then let's go to Watford and see what we can find there." In less than twenty minutes they were on their way along the A41 to Watford, about ten kilometres south of Hemel Hempstead. As a gap town in the Chilterns, it benefited from national road and rail routes through the natural gap and witnessed a faster industrial growth than Hemel Hempstead. It was small wonder that it became a magnet for those seeking a pleasant suburban life with convenient commuter facilities. Neither of them had visited Watford before which was why the theatre, a listed Edwardian building in the town centre, attracted their attention.

"Dennis, look over there just opposite the theatre is an estate agent. Why not let us try him?"

"Okay," he responded. It was the first agent they came across after leaving the car park. Very soon her eyes were gliding meticulously from side to side across the prices in the display window. Once seated, they were greeted from the other side of the desk by a dark-suited, bespectacled figure who threw his shoulders back to give them his full attention. Pleasantries quickly exchanged it was time to get down to business.

TROPICAL HEATWAVE

"I could see from the attention you were paying to the architecture of the Watford Theatre that you are new to these parts, so how can I help you?" came that polite salesman like invitation carried on a welcoming smile.

"We are looking for a house somewhere in north Watford," said Dennis.

"I don't have any thing on my books in that area at the moment." It was a reply that sent a chill down Dennis' spine and he thought *'Is there a touch of racism here or does he genuinely not have anything on his books in a sought-after area in suburban Watford for people like us?'* The phone rang and the agent asked for an excuse to have a brief conversation after which he put the phone down swiftly and looked at them with a smile. "Today is your lucky day. That call came from someone asking me to see their property in North Watford, Garston to be more precise. If you have a car, you can meet me there and we could look at it together right now." This dispelled the worrying thoughts Dennis had and brought broad smiles of hope to all. Within fifteen minutes, they were pulling into a cul-de-sac of 20 semi-detached three-bedroom houses all built between the first and second World Wars. Each had its green hedge and small white wicket gate. For folks like Dennis coming from inner city terraced housing, this semi-detached suburban in a residential cul-de-sac was a step up. At the end of the close was a circus dominated by a large mature willow. They immediately fell in love with the area. At the end of this tree lined cul-de-sac was the property. Dorothy the owner, was soon giving them a guided tour starting with the garden which immediately captured Dennis with its vastness. When combined with the allotments at the back, it had a feeling of wide open space not experienced in inner city living. It was a three-bedroom semi-detached sited in such a way to receive the morning and the afternoon sun.

"As you can see, it is a well-kept property in a pleasant well sought-after area of suburban North Watford," exclaimed the agent, satisfied he had found us a property that suited our needs. It was more than what they expected. "Within fifteen minutes one could be in the town centre and it also has the added advantage of being within easy reach of Watford over ground and underground rail stations, as well as the M1 motorway and other roads to London and other regions," he added. Dennis and Pam nodded in agreement. After taking all the necessary measurements and with the price agreed, the agent made his way back to his office leaving them to have a chat with Dorothy. Dennis wondered why she was selling the property located as it was in such a nice area, but before he could ask the question and, as though they were of similar thoughts, Pam piped up.

"But why do you want to sell such a nice property?" she asked, for although excited at having found a suitable house, she was curious to know why a person would want to sell such a property in a well sought-after area.

"Well, you see, I am a physical education teacher at a local school nearby and I plan to retire very soon, in fact, as soon as the house is sold. Wally here (pointing to a fairly corpulent figure sitting on a folding chair next to her) was a butcher with his own business but has now retired. We both plan to sell and move to the south coast, perhaps near to Brighton," explained Dorothy. Located on the south coast of England, it is considered to be one of the more salubrious part of England and favoured by the retired who could afford to purchase a property or afford the rent for senior citizen accommodation. Dorothy was in her early sixties and, being a PE instructor, very agile and alert. "Wally owns an even larger four-bedroom house in another well sought-after suburban area less than ten minutes-drive away," she added. "Would you like to join us for afternoon tea?" It was a perfect setting for such refreshments: a large lawn with wide borders of wild flowers and dwarf apple trees. It was a true rustic setting that offered a tranquillity only occasionally broken by a variety of birds that seemed to regard the garden as one of their favourite spots to burst into song while foraging for succulent worms.

"Oh, I do like this house and its location," declared Pam, lingering on the word 'do.' "This is even more than we expected."

"I think this calls for a celebration," declared Wally, slipping into the house and soon returning with four glasses and a bottle of chilled white wine. It was as though he had anticipated the outcome and had got the wine ready. Smiles of expectation moved quickly among the group of four seated on white wrought-iron garden furniture around a white table on which stood a bottle of chilled white wine, tea for four and slices of Victoria Sponge. Dorothy and Wally had a buyer while Dennis and Pam could see their dream coming to realization.

"I am so glad we have been able to reach an agreement so soon because I can see my dream beginning to unfold," commented Dorothy. For Pam, it would be the entrance to a new world, one which she hoped would bring her satisfaction and pleasure. After agreeing a price for the furniture, they said their good-byes and made their way back to the estate agent to complete the necessary documentation. On the way, Dennis could see Pam was elated with joy. Her spirit rose to new heights.

"Oh Dennis, I do hope we can get that house. You think we can?" she asked. Dennis side-glanced her with a gentle nod in a manner that suggested he knew they could. He was doing very well as a part-time insurance broker and, unknown to Pam, had managed to set aside a tidy sum. He was more concerned as to how they would be received in a close dominated by middle-class whites although he felt this was a hurdle which they would get over together.

"Oh, but how are we going to get a mortgage?" she exclaimed with a rising wave of concern. She was unmindful of his connections with two building societies in Watford for which he marketed a variety of products. This afforded him easier access to mortgage facilities than was normal for immigrants.

"I wouldn't worry about that too much. I am sure someone out there will give us a mortgage. After all, as I said before, we both have reliable incomes and work in well-grounded establishments: I, for the Department of Education and Science and you, for the Ministry of Transport." This he said with an air of confidence and unshakeable calm.

"Okay, whatever you say," she replied. Soon they were again sitting opposite the agent who peered over the rim of his wire-framed glasses and asked that all important question.

"Have you any arrangements for obtaining a mortgage?" looking Dennis straight in his eyes with a look that said, if you don't, I can point you in the right direction.

"No," replied Dennis, "but I will be doing so as soon as possible within the next two days." Having been told the amount of deposit required and by what date, they left the office with the kind of excitement shown by children as Christmas approaches. But there was to be one more important question on this matter. As soon as they got into the car, she turned to him once again with a rather worried look.

"Oh, wait a minute, where are we going to get the deposit from because I don't have a lot?" He knew she didn't have too much money. How could she, when she had to make the major contribution to the running of the house in Hemel? If she had any, it would probably have been difficult for her to access it without Elton getting to know. Besides, Dennis felt that he had to demonstrate the depth of his caring for the one person he really loved. He had to come up to the table.

"I think I have a little bit put by that can take care of that." With this assurance, she settled in her seat to be driven back to Hemel Hempstead. It was then that Dennis realised everything rested on his shoulders but that, although she had heightened expectations, he could sense she still had an underlying feeling that there was still a small chance he might not pull it off. At the same time, he knew he could not afford to lose face and lose her confidence. He had to do it. It was now imperative that he did so and with some urgency.

18

It was early March and Japanese Cherry trees along the banks of the gently flowing River Gade were already heralding the arrival of spring with their pink and white flowers. On the gentle slopes of the stream a carpet of blue bells, daffodils and tulips joined in this celebration of colour. And not to be left out of this celebration of a new season, waterfowl were giving their young ones their first swim across the pond partly shaded by a weeping willow. This was the view Pam and Beryl shared from a large window in the riverside café while having lunch one day in early Spring. Beryl was white, short and fairly attractive who, like Lesley her husband, was a chain smoker. Pam and Beryl became known to each other when they were both living and working together in London. Pam had taught her the rudiments of punch-card operating back in the early sixties when computers were first introduced. They often went shopping together or walking around the Friday market in Hemel during their lunchtime and, like Pam, she too liked to dress well. They shared each other's secrets but, as Beryl and Lesley were both known to Elton, Pam suddenly became apprehensive about telling Beryl about her plans to leave. *'Can I trust her with this one?'* she asked herself. That day at lunch the conversation followed the usual trend until Pam cleared her throat and smiled with a soft chuckle which did not go un-noticed by Beryl.

"What are you smiling about? Come on share the joke," she urged with a soft smile and an entreating voice stealing its way through a plume of smoke rising from her face.

"Okay Beryl, I have something to tell you, but you must promise not to tell anyone, not even Lesley because the remainder of my life depends on it." Beryl's eyes became larger and brighter as she looked at Pam with great expectation. Pam glanced over her shoulder to make sure no one else could hear her in what was fast becoming a crowded café.

"This must be good news because you are smiling," muttered Beryl, her ears like antennae ready to receive the news above the lunch-time buzz. Pam ordered a pot of tea for two and, for an extended moment, listened to the gurgle of the tea as she poured the first cup for Beryl. She took an audible intake of air and straightened herself in the chair.

"I met someone a little while ago on the train. He works in the City and he seems to be very nice indeed." Her body language was telling the story far more accurately than she was. Beryl took two deep draws on the cigarette and knocked the ash in the saucer before slowly levelling her eyes with Pam's and with a slightly more serious look.

"How long ago was this?" she asked, with the voice and look of a mother. She was thinking what could be the outcome should Elton get to know because she was aware of how violent he could be. It was a testament to how much she cared for Pam who stared down at the cup and saucer clutched in her hands.

"About a year now. He is from Barbados and somewhat polished."

"And you mean you didn't tell me?" replied Beryl, with a mixture of surprise and deep concern.

"I wanted to get to know him better before I said anything." Beryl blinked about five times in one second before taking two more quick draws on the cigarette, followed by an exhale of smoke in a manner reminiscent of someone in deep thought. She was thinking like any woman would before asking the question most women would. She pulled herself up in her chair and looked Pam fully in the eyes.

"Is he married?" she asked with an expressionless face. Pam hesitated for a moment, searching for the correct words to say.

TROPICAL HEATWAVE

"Yes, but he is currently going through a divorce," she hastily added. Beryl dropped her shoulders and now looked more relaxed. But, being also a friend of Elton's, she realised that from that moment she was caught up in a situation requiring split loyalties and sworn confidence. She spent a few seconds gazing at the Gade flowing smoothly by. "And by the way, before you ask, the divorce proceedings started well before I came on the scene," added Pam in a hushed but hurried voice. Already she was realising this was another hurdle over which she would have to jump in the pursuit of her goal which was to rid herself of Elton and have Dennis.

"Thank God for that," piped up Beryl, taking a few more puffs on the cig this time knocking the ash off briskly in the ash tray. But soon the smile which had begun to float across her pink face was overridden by a frown. "But Pam, are you telling me you are really thinking of leaving Elton, and are you sure you are doing the right thing? I know quite a bit about the cruel treatment you are getting from him and, although it doesn't surprise me to learn you are seeing someone else, I am not convinced that, leaving Elton, is the best thing to do." Beryl was a person who believed strongly that everything ought to be done to avoid a marriage break-up. It was an opinion rooted in her Catholic upbringing which differed from Pam's, which was Anglican.

"Yes, because I am not prepared to put up with any more of his treatment. I know your thoughts on marriage but Beryl, you are not the one getting the punches from a man you don't love. I feel if I don't get out I will end up dead or in some hospital. All he seems to want me for is to clean and provide his meals and make a major contribution to the house keeping while he blows out his money on gambling and in the pub with his mates. Whenever I ask for more housekeeping money, it always ends up in a massive quarrel and sometimes a battering. You don't know what it is like to have to run to a neighbour in the middle of the night or to be punched around by a man?" Her throat tightened with unshed tears. Beryl's mind drifted between despair and disbelief as Pam continued to tell her the sordid details.

"I don't know why you don't go to the police about it," exclaimed Beryl who was hoping that, if the police intervened, it might cause Elton to stop his brutal treatment and force her to change her mind

165

about walking out. Pam glared at her with squinted eyes under a furrowed brow.

"And what will the Police do?" she snapped. "They are never keen to get involved in domestic matters. Besides, going to the police might even make matters worse for me. I can see that, for my safety, I will have to leave. I know it means giving up a house which came with my job but if it means that, then so let it be. Anyway, if things work out the way Dennis and I planned, I want to move out very soon." By now the tone of the conversation had risen to a level to attract the attention of those sitting at adjacent tables. Beryl put her finger to her lips suggesting to Pam that she should speak more quietly.

"Yes, but sometimes it is better the devil you know than the devil you don't know. And what does your new boyfriend think about it?" declared Beryl,

"Oh, he is all for it. He is planning to move out anyway as he has to sell his house as part of the divorce settlement and, by the way, his name is Dennis." From the tone of her voice, Beryl concluded she was fighting a losing battle and that Pam and Dennis were determined to move out and live together.

"How do you manage to see each other?" asked Beryl with an inquisitive look while sending more smoke rings into the air.

"When I was in London, we saw each other almost every day and most times twice each day. Now we meet whenever I go to London every two or three weeks to the hairdresser. The reason I didn't tell you before is because I wanted some time to satisfy myself that he was serious."

"And is he?" asked Beryl with an angled head.

"Oh yes. The only thing holding us back now is somewhere to go."

"But, what about Elton, suppose he finds out?" Beryl asked, looking very concerned.

"Who is going to tell him, you? You are the only person I have told because I know I can trust you." Pam thought that the best way to earn her confidence on this one was to nail her to the spot by adding the words, '*I know I can trust you.*'

"Well, if that is what you want, but I am just a bit worried that you may be leaving certain for uncertain, that's all," she added with a rather cautious expression. Pam took another sip of tea and levelled her eyes with Beryl's.

"Look Beryl, the only thing certain about Elton is the horrible way he treats me, and I can do without that. Do you know that we even had a fight the night before our wedding? This is a chance I am prepared to take. And by the way, please, please don't even tell Les because men tend to think similarly and stick together."

"That's alright, your secret is safe with me. You know I care a lot for you, but I am only concerned that you might be exchanging one bad situation for another. I feel that, given time, Elton could change. But, as your best friend, I am prepared to accept your wishes and decision." Pam attempted a smile and then glanced at her watch.

"Oh dear, look at the time. I think we better get back to work Beryl," she uttered while hastily getting her things together. What Pam did not tell Beryl was Dennis' plans to buy a house. She wanted to be sure it would take place first. She did not have long to wait for within two weeks after applying for a mortgage, Dennis received news that it had been granted and he could hardly wait to call her at her office. It was just before tea-break that day when the phone on her desk rang.

"Oh, hello Dennis," was her greeting conveyed on nerves as taut as violin strings. She was aware of the difficulties black immigrants faced when approaching a bank or building society for any type of loan and therefore fully expected a negative response to Dennis' application for a mortgage.

"Hello Pam, how are you keeping?" He deliberately responded in a slow and somewhat muted voice. He knew how she would be thinking and therefore wanted to tease her if only for a moment. He could hear tension in her voice as she sweated with anticipation.

"I am okay, but you don't sound your usual self," she said, muffling the receiver, "I bet you haven't got the mortgage." Dennis paused for a few seconds and then chuckled quietly.

"Of course, we've got it," his voice reaching a crescendo and, before he could say more, she put the receiver on the desk and rushed over to her best friend, and in a subdued shout said, "Beryl, Beryl…

you wouldn't believe this, we've got it, we've got it." Beryl took a deep pull on her cigarette and coughed twice.

"What are you talking about Pam, you've got what?" looking somewhat baffled.

"The mortgage, of course," she replied, bursting with excitement. Beryl looked more dazzled. The news had caught her by surprise, but she was also pleased when she heard it.

"Oh, great news and I am so happy for you," exclaimed Beryl. But as they embraced each other with a shared excitement, a more puzzled look crept across Beryl's face. "You didn't tell me you were going for a house." The words flowed slowly with a mixture of joy tinged with disbelief in her facial expression which set Pam thinking. *Doesn't she think that I am good enough to move from a rented terraced council house to own a semi-detached in the suburbs of Watford?* she pondered quietly. Nor was Beryl unique in her thoughts because it was in the seventies when black immigrants were not expected to own a semi-detached house. It was a thinking that often tested the friendship between blacks and the host community.

"No, because I wanted to be sure the purchase was taking place," she said, still unable to contain herself. It was a moment of exuberance abruptly interrupted when she suddenly remembered she had left Dennis hanging on the phone. Surprisingly, he was still waiting.

"All we need to do now is get the deposit to the solicitor as soon as possible." he continued. She was hardly able to contain herself, but they managed to end the conversation with a promise to talk all about it at their next rendezvous. Such excitement caught the attention of other colleagues in the room, including the boss.

"What's all the excitement about, Pam?" he inquired, his eyes protruding above his glasses. When told, he offered his congratulations which did not go down too well with some of the others at a time when most of them were still in rented accommodation. Not only was she the only black in the entire building, she had only recently joined the staff. The whispering which followed was centred on, *'how did she do it?'*

"Can I have fifteen minutes before tea-break, I have to do something urgently?" she asked the boss with an appealing look.

TROPICAL HEATWAVE

"Of course, you can," he replied. She returned at the start of the morning tea-break with an assortment of cakes for everyone. This went down well. But Pam's delay in telling Beryl about the house purchase left her thinking. '*She was late telling me about Dennis and now she tells me about the house after the purchase. What's going on? I'll say one thing for her though, she knows how to conduct her love affair in private,*' were some of the thoughts invading her mind. Beryl and Pam were so close that they referred to by most of the market traders as '*two peas in a pod.*' They would share and enjoy the same jokes over a pub lunch, a coffee in the cafe or having a lunchtime stroll through the market or even on the banks of the Gade.

So thrilled was she, that she changed her next appointment with the hairdresser for a week earlier, the Saturday of the current week. Sitting on the train that Saturday morning to London, she had time to have a meaningful gaze at gardens of semi-detached houses backing on to the rail tracts as the train passed Bushey and Harrow, two large districts on the outskirts of Watford. Pam was already creating images of what hers would look like. '*I would like a garden with a vibrant splash of colourful bedding plants against a background of roses, fuchsias and azaleas, as well as a small pond with goldfish gliding smoothly between the drops from a small fountain. And if I can keep the lawn well-manicured, I really think the whole garden will look very nice indeed. I always wanted a house with a large garden.*'

They met after her visit to the hairdresser as usual and went for a celebratory meal in a nearby restaurant in Kentish Town: nothing too fancy because she could not stay out late, nor did she want to ruin everything at this stage. In fact, she had to be home no later than nine, just before Elton was due to arrive from work that day. Nevertheless, they had enough time to enjoy the moment and savour the taste of success together.

"Oh Dennis, thank you very much. I feel so happy. I can hardly believe it. Imagine, my own house with a large garden, and semi-detached as well." As she said that, she leaned over the table and gave him a good hug. Seated once more, she stretched her hands across the table and holding his, she gazed firmly into his eyes with a look of pure sincerity. "Thank you very, very much. I am on my way." As she spoke, he could feel joy and excitement with every heart beat that drove the blood through her fingers. What is more, she was already beginning to look the woman to adorn such a house. From there on, things moved very quickly. Within two weeks Dennis received notice that the completion date was set for August 25th, four days after her birthday. Arrangements would now have to be made to get her moved without Elton getting to know. They knew that the longer it dragged on the greater the chance of him getting wind of it, so it was now a matter of combining speed with caution. It was lunchtime when Dennis called three days later, and she knew it was he before he spoke.

"Hello Dennis, how are you, are you okay?" There was a distinct up-beat in her voice for she was a woman elated with joy.

"I am okay. Just to let you know that completion date has been set for 25th August, just one week away," he replied, sounding equally excited.

"Oh good, great," she said. "I now have to get someone to move my things because we only have a few days left before we take possession." She winked at Beryl who worked out from her expression that it could only be Dennis to whom she was speaking for she seemed on top of the world.

"Say hello to him for me and tell him, I haven't met him yet, but he seems to be a very nice man," interjected Beryl on a whisper loud enough for Pam to hear.

"Did you hear that Dennis?"

"Oh yes, I did," and they both chuckled.

"But we have to be very careful here because we don't want Elton to spoil things," he admonished in a quiet voice.

"You leave that to me, I know a small removal company that will do the job," she added, confident that she was able to pull this off secretly.

"Okay, I will leave that to you, but you must keep me informed of the arrangements because we don't want anything to go wrong now." Pam shared this information with Beryl who immediately set out to come up with an action plan. After two days Pam called Dennis to say everything was in place to move on the Saturday morning, the 26[th,] He wondered how she would do it with Elton around. It was clear he was unaware of her ability to come up with a strategy to overcome such a hurdle. That night he could hardly sleep. '*This is the second time*

TROPICAL HEATWAVE

that Elton has become a bit of an obstruction. 'I hate to think what could happen if Pam is caught in the act of moving. I think I will go up to Hemel as early as possible to give her a hand and my protection,' he mumbled to himself. He was getting ready on the Saturday morning to go to her place in Hemel Hempstead when, on checking the post just before he left, the phone rang. Dennis hurried to pick up the receiver tripping over his bag for he was anticipating the worse. *'Perhaps Elton has got wind of the move and is abusing her physically, and I am so far away...,'* raced through his mind.

"Hello Dennis, how are you?" was the greeting from the other end wrapped in excitement which left him rather confused. It was not what he was expecting. However, as she didn't sound distressed but instead, rather cool and collective, his anxiety began to ebb away quickly.

"I am okay. I am just getting ready to come to you. Is everything going as planned?"

"Yes, everything went as planned," she replied with a slight chuckle.

"What do you mean by 'everything went as planned?' Where are you?" he asked anxiously.

"I am in the house," came back the reply, sounding very cool and composed.

"What are you talking about? What house?" he hurriedly asked.

"We only have one house together and it is in Watford." It was not the answer he was expecting. He expected the call to summon him for help or that something had gone disastrously wrong.

"What!" he replied briskly, "the removal van must have got to you very early and where was Elton when you were doing this?" expecting her to answer this barrage of questions simultaneously. She took a deep breath and chuckled softly,

"I moved last night." It was a reply that added more confusion to his already baffled mind.

"What did you say? What do you mean you moved last night? How did you do that? I thought the removal van was due to get there this morning." He was unable to wrap his brain around what he was hearing.

"Well, it was like this," and she sighed heavily.

"Hold on a minute," he said, drawing up a chair, so intent was he to give her his full and undivided attention. *'What did she do to pull off*

171

such a daring exercise during the night? How did she persuade the removal company to come at night instead of this morning? And where was Elton?' These were some of the thoughts that suddenly flashed around his brain in the time it took him to draw up a chair.

"After I spoke to you about the removals company, I had a better idea. I remembered a friend of mine, Enid, telling me that a man with a van had moved her for a reasonable price."

"Who is Enid," he interjected.

"She is the girl we visited one Saturday evening in Kennington near Brixton. She told me he was the cheapest she had found and that he would come whenever I wanted him. I contacted him, and he agreed to do the job during the night which was better since Elton was working night," she explained. Standing next to the patio door as she spoke, she could feel the August morning sunshine stealing its way through the glass doors and settling gently on her back forcing the stress and heartache of recent times to ebb away. She breathed a sigh of relief for she sensed her life was about to take a new turn, one she hoped she would spend with the one she really loved and the one who also showered her with love.

"But how did you get the keys to the house?" piped up Dennis.

"My boss allowed me to leave work early, so I was able to collect them from the estate agent."

"And how did you get all those things packed in readiness for the move before Elton left for work?"

"I didn't do a thing until he had left for work which was about eight. I then moved as fast as I could to pack those things I needed in boxes I had hidden in the shed. Also, Beryl and Lesley came and gave me a hand. The van arrived about eleven and the driver and Lesley helped me to get two beds and wardrobes as well as a dressing table down the stairs."

"But what if Elton had come back or what if someone had seen what you were doing and got in touch with him?"

"Well, he didn't," she replied, with a feeling of great satisfaction. Dennis breathed a loud sigh of relief. "I'll tell you what, I'll be there within the next hour and you can tell me all about it then." Without any further delay, he got ready and set off for Watford. As he drove

TROPICAL HEATWAVE

north up the motorway, his mind boggled to think what would have been the outcome had Elton returned home when she was loading the van. He could see nothing less than World War III breaking out. But Dennis' thoughts went beyond this second great escape. '*This is one hell of a woman I have. Who else would be prepared to undertake such a daring and hazardous move all on their own? She has demonstrated grit, determination and drive, qualities I welcome in a woman destined one day to become my wife,*' he thought quietly to himself. He felt happy that he had rescued her from the clutches of one whom she never loved and one at whose hands she had suffered so much physical and emotional distress and pain.

His indulgence with such thoughts was soon broken by the oncoming sign for junction 5. Leaving the motorway for the A41 leading to Watford, he began to anticipate the kind of reception awaiting him. It was an imagination overflowing with a variety of images. The last leg of his journey took him along that stretch of the A41 which resembled a French boulevard with elm and beech swaying their branches gently in the summer breeze as though welcoming him to Watford. It was 9:30 that morning when he pulled into the cul-de-sac to park in front of number 25.

"Oh Dennis, it is so nice to see you," she said softly with a kiss he thought would never end. Opening his eyes, he realised that, standing before him in his arms, was one of the cleverest and courageous women he had ever met, a woman who had proved to be strong and capable in a terrifying situation. This is the woman with whom he would soon be spending the rest of his life. Hand in hand they walked around as she gave him a tour of her new house.

"Did you do all of this?" he asked, in sheer amazement, seeing that everything was in place as though she was living there for some time.

"Yes," she replied with sheer delight. Dennis could hardly find words.

"But how did you get the bedroom furniture up the stairs?" he asked with a furrowed brow.

"Oh, the driver helped me again," she hastily replied, looking very pleased with herself.

"That was very nice of him," exclaimed Dennis, still struggling to come to grips with what Pam had done. After a mid-morning coffee, they spent much of the time going around the garden admiring the splendour of wild flowers they had seen on their first visit when they had gone there with the estate agent. They paused for a moment next to a dwarf apple tree and she turned to him with a regal look.

"I have some ideas for the garden. I got some of them while on the train to London two Saturdays ago," she declared, and proceeded to describe the plan she had for what she wanted the garden to look like. He nodded in agreement, for one thing was sure, she was already expressing her interest in gardening, much to his delight.

"Perhaps we could put a small pond over there," she said, pointing to a matured rhododendron, "and if we added some asters and godetias on the borders in front of delphiniums and roses, the whole garden should look splendid indeed." It was the kind of picture Pam had often seen at least once per month on the train from Hemel Hempstead to her hair-dresser in Kentish Town, London.

"We could also have a glasshouse in the corner near that Lilac," added Dennis, pointing to the shrub overrun with a variety of butterflies.

"And, from the number of apples on those four dwarf trees, it seems we will have a good crop in November," she exclaimed. But it was the sheer space and size of the garden which fanned out at the back that took their breath away. It gave them a feeling of openness and space. On his way back to London that evening, he couldn't help thinking how lucky he was to have such a courageous woman. *'What a move! What a welcome! What a woman!'* he said to himself.

19

Elton had spent that weekend with his mates in London. It was dark as he emerged from the nearby grove to cross the green and approach the door. *'Why is the house so dark and why is there no light?'* It puzzled him, for it was about 7:30 pm and Pam would normally be up viewing television. There would also be at least one light in the hallway and the curtains would be closed. He was oblivious to the neighbour's cat which knew him well and which came running to him as though to deliver a message. A feeling of despair suddenly gripped him. His heart began to swell with dreadful fear as he quickened his pace. *'This is rather strange! She couldn't have gone to bed already. It's only about 7:30. Maybe she has gone to visit her friend Beryl,'* he pondered with his eyes now firmly focused on the street door. Every step felt like a step too far. He frantically opened the door to total darkness and hastily hit the switches to the hall, the kitchen and the lounge almost at the same time. Standing at the foot of the stairs, he looked up. "Pam, Pam… Pam are you there?" but no one answered when he called her name. He suddenly had that feeling, it was an eerie feeling.

He charged up the stairs and hastily swung open the door to each room, but to no avail. If there was any alcohol remaining in his blood it quickly evaporated in the heat of the moment as he made his way slowly down the stairs. In this state of hateful emotion, he had left the street door open allowing the cat to follow him up and then slowly down the stairs. At that moment, he felt it was the only friend he had. In total confusion and despair, he had not seen the letter Pam had left on the worktop in the kitchen. Most of the lounge furniture was still there but, on rushing upstairs again to have a closer look, he was speechless. The dressing table, one bed and one wardrobe were taken, and her clothes were no longer there. Reality now struck him like a thunderbolt released from mighty Olympus. The wife he had always expected to be there had fled. Yes, vanished without trace. Overcome by a soundless look of sharp pain, a loud animal-like howl ripped from his throat as he did what he was always good at doing when faced with a crisis. He reached for the whisky bottle, poured himself a large one and then ambled his way to the kitchen where he came across. Frantically, he opened it like a student opening an envelope bearing the results of an examination.

Dear Elton:

By the time you read this letter I shall be far away. I wanted to do this long ago but the time was not yet suitable. I have had enough of your mental and physical brutality and I am not prepared to put up with it any longer. I held on because I thought you would change, but it is now quite obvious you never wanted to. Think of the times you kicked and punched me about like a punch-bag all because I asked you for more housekeeping money. Instead, you would prefer to go to London on weekends with your mates leaving nothing for the housekeeping. And when you come home you were always bursting with alcohol. Think of the time you put me in hospital because, not only did you kick me under my belly, but you kicked me down the stairs as well, ending in my having to have a full hysterectomy. You paid so much attention to me that you didn't even know I was pregnant. Or think of the times I had to run out in the middle of the night in my dressing gown and seek help from a neighbour across the green, or the times you disgraced me at parties. I knew you were probably having an affair with someone in London and that you would see her when you say you were with your mates. To tell you the truth, I wished you had gone off with her because there was nothing left of our marriage for years now, not that there was anything in the beginning anyway. It was over before it even started. Think of the weekends you left me at home wishing I had the comfort of a man. All you really wanted me for was to be a general slave and to keep a roof over your head. I have left half of everything for you. You can have the suite in the lounge because I never did like it anyway. The house is in my name, but I am sure you will know what to do about that. Yes, you can go to the housing authority and get the rent changed over to you. By the way, don't even bother trying to find me because I never want to see or hear from you ever again. She loathed everything he was and did.

As he read the letter, the past came roaring back. It was the moment of truth. He was devastated and wished he could put back the hands of the clock. It was perhaps the first time he was made to understand what an unworthy husband he was. '*I hate my mates for encouraging me to stay out so often on weekends gambling and drinking,*' he said to himself. It was always easy for him to blame others for his mistakes. He hated the times he would get home drunk and take it out of Pam. A hideous shame came rolling over him as he suddenly realized what he had lost and felt alone and vulnerable. He realized he had lost a woman who, despite the cruel treatment he meted out to her, never flinched from her role as a wife. His meals were always ready, his clothes were always washed and most of all, she always contributed the major share of the housekeeping. He had lost a good companion. There was no longer Pam on whom to lean. There was an eerie silence as he sat stunned and shocked. With half a bottle of Scotch finished, he fell into a deep sleep, the kind that brought on a dream, a revelation more like it.

'*I know I am at fault but if you give me a chance, I will do everything to make sure it does not happen again.*' *He could feel every punch he gave her, he could hear her cries for help and her pleas to him to stop. He could hear her say coldly across his words. 'Let me say something bluntly to you Elton. An unfortunate situation and your selfishness brought us together, but I never loved you nor have I ever forgiven you for what you did to me to satisfy your physical desire. And even if there was any way of love developing you never gave it a chance. You made sure of that. I am sorry, but it's too late. You didn't want a wife you wanted a slave and a punch-bag.'* He was only awakened by the chimes of Big Ben on TV signalling the ten o'clock news. The realization of all he had lost clawed at him with a deep agony of regret. Pam had eventually rustled up the courage to make that all-important life-saving and definitive leap.

The following day Dennis turned up at Pam's new residence, as promised, carrying flowers and a bottle of red wine. She was preparing Sunday lunch but took time out to greet him in the only way she knew before he stepped out onto the patio at the back to drink in the view. It was another sunny day and bees, their black and golden bodies glistening in the summer sunshine, were foraging for pollen and sweet nectar among the wild flowers while filling the air with their orchestral buzz. Birds in the nearby oak and holly, not wanting to be outdone, were contributing their sweet sounds to what was perhaps nature's way of welcoming Pam and Dennis to their new home. Just as she joined him on the patio, a green woodpecker dropped in on the lawn and, unmindful of their presence, was enjoying the local fayre of succulent worms. With hands around each other's waist, they moved slowly to the fence at the back to have a look across the allotments where holders were busy carrying out summer chores. Dennis took a deep and audible inhale of breath.

"You can see they are enjoying what they are doing. It reminds me very much of those mornings on my way to school as a young lad in Barbados. I would pass men and women working in the fields of young sugar cane on the sugar plantation. Under the tropical sun, their broad straw hats and colourful scarfs flopping in a gentle breeze, they would be having their daily chit-chat or singing familiar songs as they toiled all day," he exclaimed.

"Yes, that was the usual scene throughout most of the island. Those people really worked hard in those days. You had to feel sorry for them making their way home on evenings with their clothes saturated with perspiration. But look at the size of the cabbage and lettuce and the tomatoes over there already turning red," she said, drawing his attention to two senior citizens adding water to the thirsty crop. "It must give them a good feeling to be out in the open air growing some of their food. I know it does take some work but look at the exercise they are getting, and the food does taste nice and fresh." She too was recalling life in the Caribbean where, in the absence of refrigeration, most fruit and vegetables were grown locally and consumed fresh.

Dennis sent her a soft side glance behind squinted eyes as though to say, '*my word, you are well informed.*'

"Do I detect you are hinting at something here?" commented Dennis quietly, "because if you are thinking what I think you are thinking, please understand that I am not cut out for that kind of work, relaxing though it may be." and they chuckled. "But what I also like is how they sometimes sit outside their little sheds having a cup of tea while chatting or just admiring their crop," he added. In the midst of all this, he found time to gaze at the person who had defined everything he had always wanted in a woman and who, like crops in the neighbouring allotments, only needed tender loving care. His only regret was that they didn't meet earlier. "Umm, something smells nice inside," he commented, turning his head in the direction of the kitchen.

"That's my roast beef." Pam was well known among her friends for her culinary skills and she wasn't going to miss an opportunity to show them off to Dennis. It was soon time for lunch, the first they would have together. Sitting opposite each other at a small circular table, they toasted with red wine. This was followed by two sundae glasses of melon balls flavoured with a drizzle of sugar cane cordial and a sprinkle of powdered ginger and finished with a glazed cherry on top.

"Where did you learn all this?"

"I learned how to prepare melon balls in Guyana and so I thought it would be nice to have it at our first Sunday lunch together in our house," she responded with a smile of sheer content. The main dish of roast beef, roast potatoes and Yorkshire pudding was followed with home-made apple crumble and custard. It was a meal that was to be talked about for a long time to come. After lunch, they sat on the lawn under a mid-afternoon sun only occasionally broken by a passing thin cirrus cloud. Sitting there, they yearned for a season of everlasting summer that would allow them to enjoy the kindly radiance of the sun. It being Sunday, folk in the nearby allotments had gone home and, except for the distant hum of a lawn-mower, all was relaxingly quiet. Reflecting on the many rivers they had to cross to reach this port,

Dennis turned and looked at her blankly with no idea how to say what he wanted to say. And yet he felt it was the right setting to disclose a significant piece of information which he hoped would be favourably received. He carefully put a spoon of ice-cream into her mouth. As though wanting to join the audience, a couple of robins settled themselves on the back fence. It was a tranquillity only momentarily broken by the flapping wings of four wood pigeons taking to the air from the large oak in the neighbour's garden. This convinced him it was the perfect setting for what he had to say.

"Pam my love, I have something to tell you and I hope you will take it in the spirit in which it is given." Pam remained on her back, her attention drawn to swallows above using the rising thermals over the allotments to feed on the wing. A few seconds passed before her eyes moved slowly from the sky to Dennis.

"Oooh,….. what is it, good news or bad news?" she asked with baited breath, her eyes fixed on his. Dennis cleared his throat twice.

"I suppose you know that things have moved faster than we expected and that I am not yet in a position to join you." He paused, feverishly awaiting her response. She hesitated for a moment searching for the correct words to say for she realised that, having done so much, it would be unwise to rush things by insisting that he should join her immediately.

"Yes, I know that. So, what are you trying to say because I am fully aware of the situation and I am happy to wait? All I ask is that you spend weekends with me."

"Thank God for that," he uttered quietly before breathing a sigh of relief. It was the response he was hoping she would give. It was as though she could read his mind and knew what he was about to say.

"Well, you have to give me two years."

"Two years, why two years?" she asked, looking a bit disappointed that he had not planned to join her sooner. Dennis took two sips from the cup of coffee he had with him.

"You see, you have just left your husband after ten years of marriage and it is not unknown for some people to run back to their partners after a cooling off period." She didn't respond for a few moments. Instead, an expression of utter disgust swiftly invaded her face at the idea he could even think like that. But things were now moving fast and, bearing in mind what he had gone through in his previous marriage, he wanted to be sure his front foot was safe before lifting the back. In other words, he wanted to be sure this was what they both wanted because he had no intention of having a repeat performance.

"What do you think I am?" she snapped, "and what makes you think like that after what I went through with him? Why would I want to go back to a man who was so brutal to me?" she declared vehemently and looking somewhat horrified. "Look Dennis, you have given me something I never thought I would have. You have given me another chance and you have put me in a house I can call my own but most of all you have given me the kind of love and affection I always wanted." For a silent moment, she looked at her clutched fingers resting on her knees and he could sense that, in her mind she was reliving with horror and debilitating grief, every punch, every kick. He could feel the brutality knotting her stomach. Pain was running through every nerve, every vein and every muscle. Grief and hate had overtaken her body like an invading army leaving carnage in its wake. As her mind retreated, she cringed in agony and Dennis regretted having made the statement. Holding her close to his chest, he apologised profusely and, as though placed to stifle the kind of emotion that had just infiltrated their company, their attention was suddenly drawn to a small flower growing near the edge of the patio. It was a pansy displaying its colours of gold and black and, like the pansy, there she was once again, glowing in the afternoon sunshine. But he also sensed she had discovered another side to herself. She had broken free from the shackles of a life that had restricted and condemned her to an almost feeble subservience but that she was touched by his kindness. "Fancy a cup of tea?" she asked. The sparkle that had deserted her a while ago had returned and she sent him a contagious smile as she sprang to her feet.

"Yes, I really would do with a cuppa," he replied. Perhaps the excitement of the moment had brought on a thirst. Making their way toward the patio door, they stopped to share the thrill of the little pansy. "There is more to that little pansy than just its beauty," declared Dennis, "I feel at one with it. To me, it embodies the kind of affinity and common bond emerging between us." He held her in his arm for a few moments and, were it not for her shallow breath against his chest, he would not have known she was alive. While standing there lost in their own world, the 4 o'clock sun burst through from a small bank of grey clouds, its golden beams streaming into the room ahead of them. Some settled on her cheek while the remainder, like a cataract of brilliant light, filled almost every corner of the room.

"But I want to return to what I mentioned a few moments ago. I suggested two years because I thought it would allow you enough time to decide what exactly you want. I don't want you to feel under any pressure to have me living with you because of the house. It will also give you time to get accustomed to making your own decisions about what you want and to stamp your character on the house. I will pay the mortgage and the taxes. All you have to take care of are the services: electricity, gas and the housekeeping. Of course, if at any time you find yourself short, please don't hesitate to ask," he said calmly smiling down at her both and with their hearts caught in love's glare.

"I'll be alright once you promise me you'll be here every week-end," she exclaimed in a hushed voice and then her eyes met his.

"Of course, I will sweetheart," replied Dennis affectionately and they were soon settling down to tea and Madeira cake. Perhaps it was the gurgling sound of that first cup being poured and the bronze colour of the tea itself that set a trend of thought in motion causing her to reflect momentarily on what she had suffered and where Dennis had brought her.

"Thank you for giving me the chance for the first time in my life to make major decisions and not have them dismissed by a man who never even gave them serious consideration. For the first time, I will be making my own decisions that will not end in confrontation involving verbal abuse and sometimes a barrage of blows from him," she uttered. Everything about her screamed regret about her past life and Dennis let out a stifled groan.

"I often wondered why you endured such treatment for so long until I remembered the reasons you gave me for moving to Hemel Hempstead. It was really a bit naïve of you to think that making such a move would get rid of him," he added with a wry smile. "Of course, the difference now is that you have someone who is deeply in love with you and is here to take good care of you," and he could see she shared his passion.

"Elton loved London and his mates so much that I thought he would be unwilling to leave them, especially since the marriage was already on the rocks, but I was wrong," she exclaimed, suppressing a shudder as she gazed at Dennis. "This time, I hope I am rid of him for ever. Thanks to you my darling."

"Let's hope that he sees sense and leaves you alone because you never know how he may react to a man taking away his wife from under his very eyes," declared Dennis with some measure of concern. That evening, driving back to London, he was suddenly overcome by some slightly worrying thoughts. *I wonder how she will feel living there alone during the week. Will he find her and pressurise her into going back to him and will she do so after the novelty has worn off?'* Dennis saw it as a challenge they would have to face together. On evenings, she was now taking the bus to Garston in the suburbs of Watford instead of to Bennetts End in the suburbs of Hemel Hempstead but there was always time for a chat with work colleagues before her bus arrived. About two months later she was having a chat with Beryl who was also awaiting her bus to Leverstock Green.

"You look more relaxed these days Pam. Let's hope it was the right decision you made to break free after all," remarked Beryl puffing away at her cigarette. "And how are you managing on your own?" She was obviously worried as it was the first time Pam was on her own and that she was taking on a great responsibility.

"I am managing quite well even though I see Dennis only on weekends."

"Well, that's not too much of a price to pay considering what you have: a house of your own and peace of mind," uttered Beryl. At that moment, Pam's eyes popped. A long-drawn-out feeling of despair tore from her lips and an unflinching stare gripped her face. "What is it Pam?" asked Beryl hastily, now looking in the same direction as Pam. It was Elton making a swift approach, a man on a mission. It was the moment they were dreading as they stood hoping that the buses would soon arrive. There was no preamble.

"I know you are living on your own because he has a wife. What makes you think he is going to leave his wife for you? How does it feel to be lonely?" he growled at her with a terrifying expression. Pam eyed him disdainfully while steeling herself for his words. Just then her bus turned up in the nick of time to rescue her from an evening of severe verbal bombardment. But it had left her thinking. Elton was determined to launch his counter attach just at the time when she was feeling vulnerable. Some of the thoughts running through her mind were, '*I am there alone all week and I wonder why Dennis has to wait two years to join me. Is he not courageous enough to make a clean break from his wife and join me after all?*' and she wondered if it wasn't a glimpse of the future. Her mind became a battleground for conflicting thoughts causing her to momentarily lose confidence in herself. But would she stick with it or would she return to her former place in Elton's life?

20

Every week-end saw Dennis in Watford as promised. Driving along the tree-lined A41, he was always reminded of that first Saturday he did the journey to find the woman he loved safely in residence. To lay down by her side and to wake up with her, made it a week-end treat for which he could hardly wait. He would usually arrive on Friday evening and return to London on Sunday evening after tea. But it was a Sunday evening in early September that was going to be different. He was about to roll out the second stage of his grand plan. Tea was over, and they were enjoying each other's company while viewing TV when she turned to him with sorrow in her eyes. She was wishing he wouldn't have to go.

"Dennis darling, it is 7:30 and almost time for you to go because you have to go to work tomorrow and it's a long drive back." Floating though her mind at that moment and, indeed every Sunday evening, would be words from a well-known song, *good night my sweetheart, for it's time to go* and, with tears slowly welling up in her eyes, she would wonder when she would hold him again. This would soon be followed by a parting kiss on which they would have to survive for another week. Standing in the doorway and watching the car turn out of the close into the main road every Sunday evening made her feel as though he was taking a piece of her with him.

"Thanks for reminding me," avoiding her eyes while he continued to sit glued to one of his favourite Sunday evening TV dramas. Soon, it was eight o'clock and a concerned expression emerged on her face.

Not that she wanted him to go for she always wished the weekend would never end. They would usually have a parting cup of tea before he set out on his return journey. This she prepared and as she was about to make herself comfortable and enjoy the drink, she gazed at him with a slight frown.

"Dennis, aren't you going down because it's getting a bit late darling?" she asked, looking slightly concerned. He folded his arms and continued sitting for a long silent moment. Then, without saying anything, he rose quietly, made his way through the patio door and on to the lawn which by now was slightly brown from the summer sun. He beckoned her to join him. Just over the back fence, a scattering of allotment holders was gathering their tools signalling the approaching end of the day. Lengthening shadows heralded the onset of twilight. Wood pigeons and black birds were retiring to their nests in the neighbour's oak while the twittering song of the sparrow was turning still in the holly overlooking the garden, and the robin had already taken up residence in the branches of the rhododendron. He pulled her gently to him, held her in his arms and gazed into her eyes in which he could see a bottomless pool of love.

"Do you know what year and what month it is?" he asked easily. She stared at him in wonderment.

"Of course, I do. Today is Sunday and it is 1975 but what's that to do with anything?" she asked, under a curious frown. He looked at her and smiled with a soft chuckle. He found it hard to believe she did not immediately recall the promise he made her.

"You really don't remember?" his chuckle breaking into a controlled laugh.

"Remember what?" looking even more puzzled as she stared deeply into his eyes through the descending evening shadows.

"Well, let me help you. Can you recall me telling you, two years ago, that I would give you two years to be absolutely sure you would not want to run back to your husband? Does that ring a bell?" A smile crept slowly across his face as he waited for the response which was slow in coming. Her mind went into rewind. Perhaps it was the wine that slowed her down. Very soon that puzzled look was fast giving way to one of satisfaction and delight.

"Oh that," she said, raising her eyebrow with heightened excitement. "Phew, is it two years already?" The whole thing was now beginning to make more sense to her for it was two years almost to the day that she had made that life-saving leap.

"Well my dear Pam, the second stage of our grand plan begins here and now because, short of getting the police to get me out, I don't intend to go anywhere. As you may recall my dear, both our names are the documents for this house which gives me the right to join you as an occupant. You have a problem?" This he uttered with tongue in cheek while trying desperately to hold back laughter. But before he could do so, he found himself caught up in a kiss that said more than words could ever say. It was a kiss through which they shared one breath, one heartbeat and one moment: a wordless intimate communion wrapped in a silence that was very eloquent. When they at last surfaced, she expressed her joy at the realization that he had joined her and that they were now ready to declare their intention to be a couple doing things together, going shopping together, visiting friends together and planning together. They were now an item.

He returned to the car to fetch his suitcase because next day, and for the first time, he would be leaving from Watford for work. He would be joining the commuter traffic to do his daily twenty-mile journey to London. His arrival home on evenings would now be greeted by a woman gently moving her slick body to the soft beat of a reggae or soul tune while preparing the evening meal. At the dinner table, they would talk about the kind of day they each had but Dennis would always insist that she tells him about her day for he saw himself as the person on whom she should unload any stress from work. He hardly ever spoke about his day. But it was a Wednesday evening when he came in from school. Things didn't feel right. That home-coming atmosphere did not grab him. They greeted each other with the usual brush of the cheeks but there was no soft music in the background and not much to say. Her response was damp. He could sense something was wrong, that *things weren't alright in the state of Denmark* as the Brits would say.

"Are you okay?" he asked gently, noticing that she was not her usual perky self. She even seemed unmindful of the single packaged red rose he had brought her that evening. She was just about to cut a tomato when he slowly took the knife away and placed it on the work-top. They were now facing each other, his arms around her waist. "Okay, what's bothering you my dear?" he asked in an appealing voice. As she looked at him, tears settling in her eyes combined to form miniature rivulets flowing down her ebony cheeks. *'This is serious,'* he concluded quickly to himself while taking a tissue from a box nearby and gently dabbing her eyes.

"Oh Dennis, I am so sorry," and she paused for a moment choking back a sob while wiping the tears from her eyes between sobs.

"Sorry about what my love?" he asked, sounding worried and suffering unbearable suspense as his eyes sought hers for a long moment.

"I didn't tell you because.......... I didn't want to bother you. I thought I could handle it myself."

"Handle what, darling?" he asked sympathetically, his heart beginning to beat faster and throb with palpitating fear. He started to become overheated. The palms of his hands got clammy. His expression got stiff. "Let's sit," he suggested. "Now take your time and tell me all about it, sweetheart."

"About a week ago, Elton came to my office and started saying things to put me down in the eyes of my work colleagues as well as being very abusive. My boss walked in and immediately told him not to come back on the premises again. But he also told me to deal with it as soon as possible and that it was not nice having my domestic problems aired in the office and that, if I fail to do so, he will have to take disciplinary action. Oh Dennis, as if it wasn't enough to have him harassing me every evening at the bus stop, I now have my boss after me. I don't know how much more of this I can take." Her brown eyes were magnified with tears and her lips trembled. Dennis reached out and held her close to him for a lingering moment. Anger roiled in his stomach.

"What did you say to your boss?"

"I told him I'll do my best to deal with it. Beryl witnessed all that went on that morning and came over to my desk to give me some

TROPICAL HEATWAVE

support. She saw it was a horrifying experience and suggested we have our packed lunch by the river that day as she could see I was distressed. We opted for a bench as close to the river as possible to have our lunch. I always liked feeding the ducks and it gave her a chance to blow her smoke rings into the air without disturbing anybody,"

"And what did Beryl have to say?"

"I could see she was beginning to have doubts about whether I did the right thing."

"What made you think like that?"

"She always said Elton would not take it lying down and that he was likely to do something stupid since he was still my husband and that I am not sure if I will ever be your wife." Dennis was of course surprised to find that Beryl was losing confidence in him. "And she wanted to know what I was going to do about it because it could cost me my job," she added.

"And what did you say?"

"I told her I wasn't sure what I was going to do but that I hadn't spoken to you yet," and a broken sob escaped from her lips, "but I was surprised by what she said," she added.

"What did she say?"

"She said, *call me old-fashioned but I always believe a wife's place is with her husband.*"

"And how did you take that?" asked Dennis, sounding shocked.

"I gave her a hard look and asked her if she would prefer me to go on enduring that kind of treatment because of an old-fashioned belief, and she simply shrugged her shoulders. It was only because we had to return to work that the conversation came to an end."

"And have you seen Elton since your boss spoke to him that morning?"

"Yes, but he now comes to the bus stop when I am waiting for the bus on evenings and carries on in front of the other people waiting. I don't know what to do Dennis." The waterworks were now in full flow. It set Dennis' mind racing and bringing to the forefront a great British saying: *when the going gets tough, the tough gets going.* With that in mind, he took a deep breath and rose to his feet with a defiant lift of his chin.

"Something has to be done because Elton is intent on revenge. He is now using a strategy designed to force you to return to him. I think you ought to seek legal advice as soon as possible. What about leaving work a little early tomorrow and going to one of the solicitors in town?" he admonished. With this action-plan in place, he poured themselves a white martini and added a white grape to each glass. She was eventually able to resume preparation of the evening meal and soon they were tucking into it against the kind of soft musical background designed to cheer her up. She followed his advice which quickly resulted in an injunction preventing Elton from coming near her work-place or harassing her on the street or coming within a given distance of her. She was just about to serve the desert when he observed that the unfortunate saga had taken a lot out of her for she was looking extremely stressed. Dennis enveloped her in a hug.

"Do you fancy a night out?" he asked in an upbeat manner to lift her spirit and she managed a watery smile.

"I don't mind. I think it is just the thing I could do with at this time." It brought back a sparkle in her eyes. "Why not let us find somewhere in London where we can have a nice dinner and dance tomorrow night, somewhere we can have a relaxing evening. You know, one where you have to wear formal dress etc. I fancy that kind of evening out," she added breezily but already with an air of excitement. It was the kind of thing they did from time-to-time. It gave them something to which they could look forward especially at times like these. It was also an opportunity for her to display some of her dancing skills and to fashion one of her evening gowns. For Dennis, it was merely a chance to showcase the woman he loved.

"Yes, why not? What a good idea!" he replied. They were soon fingering through the phone book to find a suitable venue which turned out to be an up-market place in Baker Street - *The Barracuda* - offering a four-course dinner and dance. Here, formal dress was expected, and a reservation made. That Saturday evening, he had finished dressing and had gone downstairs to wait for her in the hallway. This gave him time to observe some of the interior décor they had added to the house, especially the cork tiles on the wall going up the stairs. He had added a coat of clear vanish to give them a mild glossy finish. Not only did they look attractive, they also helped to keep the house warm in winter. He was very proud of what he had done since it was his first attempt at such a thing. He also had time to fondle the pink and white flowers of a fully-grown *Impatiens (busy Lizzie)* in the hall. At about three feet tall, its array of small pink flowers sometimes fell onto the small mahogany telephone table above which was a large wall-mounted mirror. The bannister was brilliant white with glossy black wrought-iron s-shaped mouldings running along the stairs which was covered with a fawn coloured thick carpet, a reflection of Pam's taste.

His focus was only broken when footsteps on the landing compelled him to look up and, just about to descend the stairs, was an attractive specimen of nature. "Oh, I do like the dress you are wearing, it makes you look even more beautiful," he commented, giving her a saucy wink. She thanked him for the compliment and proceeded to descend the stairs. It was a dark maroon long dress with long sleeves and a close-fitting tunic collar trimmed with strips of silver embroidery. In her right hand, she carried a clutch bag with sequins to match the embroidery around the tunic collar. Her hair, swept back to finish in dropped curls, revealed subtly shadowed eyelids and manicured eyebrows. Pam looked utterly stunning as she carefully descended the stairs and slipped her feet in her heels. He greeted her at the foot with a gentle kiss, enough to say how beautiful she looked, but careful not to disturb her make-up. As he hugged her, she could feel his desire for her. He glanced at his watch and then back at her, but she looked at him as though to say, '*Come on, this is neither the time nor the place*,' and he responded with a broad smile. It was a moment of her being that demanded his admiration.

Soon they were on their way in the kind of car that complimented the kind of woman and the way she looked that evening. It was a Jag: white, with red interior, an expression of his success as a part-time insurance broker. As they pulled away and headed for the motorway, several thoughts filled his mind and he went silent.

"What are you thinking about now, you are very quiet, and that's not like you?" she asked giving him a side glance.

"I am just thinking how lucky I am to have sitting beside me one of the most attractive women I have ever met, a woman who is not backward in flaunting her shapely figure whenever the opportunity arises. What a pleasure to have such a woman grace my car!" She acknowledged the compliment and smiled softly. It all helped to set the tone for the evening. Within an hour, they were pulling up outside the club where they were met by an attendant who politely requested the keys to park the car in a subterranean secured parking bay. Another attendant took their coats and ushered them to their table where they enjoyed a lavish five-course meal to the strings of a small five-piece band playing dinner music from Mantovani, that master of melody. After dinner, Pam took a sip of brandy and reached for an after-eight mint chocolate.

"I am really looking forward to some after dinner dance music," she remarked, and she did not have too long to wait. Dinner over, they were treated to a good helping of dance-music suited to the waltz, three-step and jive. It was her chance to demonstrate one of her skills which she did admirably. Dancing was in her blood.

"By the way, I always wanted to ask you where you learned to dance ball-room because it is not the thing normally learned in Barbados. I did mine at the London Institute of Education when I was qualifying for the post-graduate certificate in education."

"I learned mine at the hospital in Colchester as a trainee nurse. It was one of the major past-time activities arranged for the hospital staff and since we never had money to go out, we made use of what activities they had," she replied. She was better at it than Dennis and where she thought he was a bit weak, she would say, "I will lead this one, young fellow," much to his amusement. They left the club that morning about 1 a.m. It became one of their regular nights out for a few years. It was 2 a.m. when they got in. Pam quickly slipped off her shoes and made her way up the stairs. With coats safely tucked away in the closet, Dennis checked the phone for any messages. There were a few, but one in particular warranted a replay. *'Hello Pam, it is Diane. I haven't heard from you or seen you for a long time now and I was wondering if everything is alright. Please give me a call when you get the chance. I would like to have a chat with you about something.'* Dennis could hardly believe what he was hearing. He raised the volume on

TROPICAL HEATWAVE

the machine to its fullest in the hope that Pam would hear it from the shower room.

"Did you hear that Pam," he shouted, aware that the noise from the shower could make it difficult for her to hear.

"No, but who was it?" her voice making its way through partly closed doors down the stairs to Dennis.

"That was Diane," he shouted, making sure his voice reached her up the stairs. Pam poked her head through the sliding shower doors.

"What does she want now?" came the sharp retort, dispatched on a brow-puckered frown.

"She wants to know why she hasn't heard from you and has asked if you would like to give her a call sometime to have a chat."

"What? Does she want to make more trouble? I really don't think I want to talk to her after what she did." The very thought of talking to Diane raised her body temperature, accelerating evaporation of water on her ebony skin.

"Never mind, I think it is polite to do so and there is no harm in giving her a call. Who knows, she might want to apologize and be friends again," exclaimed Dennis wisely and with a slight chuckle. Pam emerged from the bathroom in her full length grey satin dressing gown in readiness to join him for a cup of hot chocolate.

"I am really not too keen to call or speak to her. I am only doing it because you want me to do so." Her voice was now impregnated with fury. After lunch the next day and under duress she reluctantly called. They had not seen or heard from each other since the *great escape* that Sunday morning because Pam had deduced it had to be Diane who had blown the whistle on them.

"Oh, hello Pam, how are you keeping? I haven't heard from you since that dreadful Sunday morning fiasco and I wondered if everything was okay with you," said Diane sounding nervous and feeling rather awkward. The immediate expression on Pam's face suggested she wanted to tell her in no uncertain terms what she thought of her there and then. It was only Dennis' gesticulations in the background that prevented it. He quickly topped up their wine glasses and encouraged her to take a few sips to calm herself down.

"I am okay Diane and, in spite of everything, I am still here," she said bluntly and sounded very unhappy. The fine hair in the nape of her neck was becoming stirred. The memories, like a storm wave, came surging back together with remembered fear. Dennis could sense that, without saying anything more, Diane had got the message. Pam was not interested, and she was certainly not in any mood to speak to her. For a moment there was an uneasy silence.

"Look Pam, I know you probably think I told Elton that Dennis was here with you that Sunday morning and I cannot blame you for thinking like that which is why I would like to talk to you." It was a plea from a person who wanted to be heard. Pam looked irate and immediately interrupted her.

"Talk and say what, Diane?" she snapped, the temperature rising in her face and voice. The atmosphere became so charged that it was only the smooth fragrance she was wearing that seemingly told Dennis she was not caught up in a whirlwind of evil thoughts.

"I would like you to hear me out, please. Look, is it okay if I come up by you next Saturday?" Pam covered the receiver and again there was a long, drawn-out silence this time followed with a deep sigh.

"Dennis, what are we doing next Saturday afternoon?" She had hoped that he would say they had a previous engagement, but it turned out they would be free much to her regret and disappointment. In fact, they had planned to have a quiet Saturday evening listening to music over a bottle of wine and nibbles.

"Yes, that will be alright but make it after two. That would give us enough time to get our shopping done." The response was short, sharp and terse. In the meantime, Dennis put some nice music on the stereo in the hope it would help to calm her down.

"Thanks, I'll see you then." With Saturday shopping out of the way that day, Dennis was in the glasshouse adding plant food to his plants. He was a very keen gardener, the kind that paid meticulous attention to his plants. His glass-house, though small, was equipped to ensure plants received the correct amount of water, light, heat and air-flow. Pam soon joined him, her face plastered with mixed emotions over the pending visit of Diane who was due to arrive in less than an hour.

TROPICAL HEATWAVE

"I wonder what she is going to say because I don't think she can say anything that will convince me she was not the culprit. And she ought to be ashamed to call and ask to come to my house." An animal-like howl ripped from her throat. Dennis sent her a quelling glance and she managed a weary smile but, by this time, he too was becoming rather perplexed as to why Diane would want to meet Pam to talk about what had happened. Gliding through his mind were thoughts like: *'What is she up to? Whose side is she on?'* Amidst these thoughts and ponderings that filled the glasshouse, the door-bell rang. It was Diane's first visit to their house and September still held enough sunshine and warmth to enable them to have afternoon tea on the patio. She immediately fell in love with the house but was overwhelmed by the garden, its size and the variety of flowering plants: godetias, clarkias, simplicity, begonias and geraniums aligning the borders with a variety of traditional and hybrid roses in the background.

"What a beautiful garden!" declared Diane, hovering over the word *beautiful* for a while, as she stepped through the sliding door onto the patio. Dennis had added an extension to the back of the house and thought that a patio looking onto the garden was quite fitting and it was sufficiently large to accommodate lunch or dinner. "And you are so lucky too not to have any houses directly behind you, only allotments," she continued, allowing her eyes to feast on the variety of fruit and vegetables grown in the allotments behind. "How did you find this house?" she asked with wonderment creeping across her face but quietly sensing that she was not altogether welcomed by Pam. Dennis started to explain when Pam asked to be excused. It was as though she couldn't stand the company of Diane and she was not doing a very good job of concealing it, nor indeed, did she want to. But under no account would she let her husband down. She soon returned with all the ingredients for a refreshing afternoon tea served in bone china accompanied with mouth-watering salmon and cucumber sandwiches and chocolate cake. After a glass of chilled white wine which seemed to relax all present, Diane now felt sufficiently comfortable to take centre stage. She took a deep intake of breath and levelled her eyes with Pam's.

"I want to let you hear my side of the story because I felt you might have blamed me for what happened that morning." It was said in an apologetic voice, expecting an interruption at the end of every word she uttered. Instead, it drew a deep silence from Dennis and Pam so intent were they to hear what she had to say, but it was a silence that was eloquent. '*What can she say to convince us she is not guilty?*' was the shared thought. Pam drew her chair nearer to the table and replaced the cup slowly in the saucer with an expressionless under look. Her's and Dennis' eyes met and held for a moment. "I hope she doesn't launch an all-out attack on Diane at this point. To do so could destroy any chances of finding out who spilt the beans on us that Sunday morning," he said quietly to himself, hoping that Pam would be thinking likewise.

"The truth is I don't know what to think any more Diane, because I don't know who to trust," she blurted with a side glance that failed to conceal the tightness around her eyes and mouth. Dennis sent her a quelling look hoping she would stay calm, for he so much wanted to hear what Diane had to say. Diane gave Pam a blank look and then continued.

"That evening when you told me you were coming to spend the weekend, I thought knowing you and Jean are good friends from your nursing days, it was a good opportunity to see her as well, so I told her. She *did* ask whether Dennis would be coming along but I said I wasn't sure. Believe me Pam, I was as surprised as you to see Elton that Sunday morning." Her face looked, and her voice sounded utterly sincere. Pam looked at her with a fearsome pout and a hint of disbelief. There was a drawn-out silence broken only when Dennis' friends, the two robins, joined them on the patio to feed on crumbs from the table. They were the robins that often darted between his legs in search of succulent worms whenever he was turning the soil for new plants.

"I don't know what to say, but what I *do* know is that Elton has a friend who lives about six houses along the street from me. Do you think that whoever told Elton knew it would have been better if he turned up on the Sunday morning rather than the Saturday night? And that they would have worked out you would probably be out the Saturday night and it would therefore be better to turn up on the Sunday morning?" added Diane gazing into Pam's face for any visible sign of approval. For a moment, Pam played with her silver bangles before turning to Dennis with an expectant glare. She wanted to believe Diane. "If that was so, then Elton could easily have stayed overnight at his friend. This would have made it easy for him to pounce on you," continued Diane as Dennis topped up the wine glasses.

Pam's eyes popped. She gave Dennis a serious but pensive look. Her brain had suddenly slipped into fast rewind. *'What if she is right? Jean lives not far from Diane. It is one thing to claim possession of a man whom we both know, Sidney, but another to sink so low as to betray a friend like me whom she knew for so long, except......,'* Pam pondered quietly for a moment, the fog in her mind parting like drapes, allowing her to read the situation for the first time. She started to relive the scene at the Carnival. Her expression suggested deep thought and a possible answer. For her, the penny had dropped but Dennis was still in the dark. Pam left the table momentarily to return with a fresh pot of tea. She plunked herself down in the chair with such force that they were surprised it hadn't given way. She refilled the cups and threw herself back in her seat.

"From what you are saying Diane, it doesn't at all surprise me if Jean is the culprit after what happened at the Carnival," said Pam, looking rather coy. Dennis sat up, he was anxious to learn what had gone on at the Carnival to bring about the Sunday morning debacle. A pang of restless worry suddenly overtook Pam as a horrible feeling of dread gripped her gut. She wasn't too sure how Dennis would take what she had to say and went painfully silent for an extended moment before clearing her throat. Diane now found herself in the position where she was anxious to hear what Pam had to say.

"Look Dennis, I was going to tell you, but I never expected it to come out like this. What happened took place well before you came on the scene." The fact that whatever happened took place before he was on the scene made him no less eager to hear about it. He always felt there was something she was hiding which is why it immediately drew his undivided attention. They both felt it was the kind of gossip likely to set the brain tingling. "It happened at one of Jean's parties. A chap called Sidney made a move for me. I noticed he was looking at me regardless of whom I was dancing with. Eventually he asked me for a dance and one thing lead to another. I saw him a few times after but, before we could really get anything going, he went off to America, Boston to be more exact. However, he *did* say if I wanted to, I could join him at any time. I never bothered although I did hear from him frequently." Dennis and Diane sent each other an intense glare.

"So, what's that to do with anything?" asked Dennis, still rather perplexed and as focused on Pam's words as a dog awaiting something to drop from a dinner table.

"Two years ago, he was back on holiday in time to attend the Notting Hill Carnival, but I had no idea they had something going nor did I know he was planning to attend." Dennis and Diane continued to listen with baited breath.

"But how did you come to know they had something going?" piped up Diane, now as equally perplexed as Dennis.

"Well, she and I were dancing behind a float. Suddenly and without any warning there was no Jean. She had vanished. Minutes later I spotted her caught up in Sidney's arms kissing passionately. I told myself it was not happening because I was refusing to accept what my eyes were showing me. Until then, I had no idea they were an item although I had the feeling she wanted me to see them wrapped up in each other. She was surely making a statement that she was laying claim to a man on whom she thought I had a crush or who had a crush on me. The truth is that, we fancied each other." Pam paused for a moment to assess Dennis' reaction from his facial expression.

"What did you do when you saw them?" asked Diane, now very anxious to get to the bottom of it, seeing it as a piece of gossip that could help to vindicate her.

"I decided I would say hello to Sidney anyway but, as I approached, she continued to reinforce her position by tucking her arm securely under his. He tried to break lose but was restrained by Jean carrying a grin so wide that it almost split her snub-nosed features in half. *"Sorry I had to leave you like that Pam,"* she said, *"but I couldn't resist joining Sidney as soon as I saw him. You see, we were an item before you came on the scene."* I could sense that Sidney felt uneasy and, to some extent, embarrassed while she trumpeted on about how long they knew each other and that they kept in touch after he had left for Boston. And she had the audacity to tell Sidney in front of me that there was no use chasing after me as I was already seeing someone." Dennis and Diane gazed at Pam in sheer astonishment, nodding almost simultaneously.

"I see, so by putting Sidney off you and perhaps, you off Sidney, she was making sure she had unimpeded access to him. How clever! I didn't think she was like that," declared Diane. Dennis topped up the cups, but it was evident from his facial expression that his brain had moved up a gear.

"What happened after that?" he asked, his eyes dilating with unbounded eagerness to know.

"The whole thing exploded right there."

"What do you mean?" asked Diane, "and what thing?"

"Sidney dropped a bombshell," replied Pam with a quiet smirk of contentment on her face. "He made it clear to Jean that his reason for being at the Carnival was in the hope of meeting me not her. But I sensed he was worried that he was losing me. He tried again to get close by buttering me up with his smooth words, but I was no longer interested in him. He blamed her for destroying any chance he had of ever getting close to me and dropped her there and then."

"What do you mean by he dropped her there and then, Pam?" piped up Dennis now wrapped in undivided attention.

"Well, he just told her it was over, finished and that he never wanted to hear or see her again." He said that while keeping his eyes partly focused on me.

"How did she take it?" interjected Diane.

"Well, before she could respond, and as if that wasn't enough drama for the day, her boyfriend Winston unexpectedly turned up. He had by chance spotted us near the drinks-stall in heated exchange which, I suppose, together with the body language, must have told him something was up. He had hidden himself away and observed the drama from a good vantage point."

"How did you know that?" asked Dennis with narrowed eyes and angled head.

"As he approached us, his face was grim. There was no mistaking that he was on a mission. He didn't like what he was seeing or hearing, nor did he have to hear any more. In this atmosphere of betrayal and disappointment, Winston told her in no uncertain terms what he thought of her and ended the relationship." Dennis just nodded and shrugged his shoulders, but he was also thinking that if Sidney dropped Jean, he could still be pursuing Pam. It was a thought shared by both him and Diane. Minds were beginning to boggle.

"From what you have just said Pam and from Diane's thoughts on the matter, there is no doubt in my mind that Jean is the culprit, after all, she had a motive and a goal. She had invited you to her party to find that she was in danger of losing her boyfriend to you, a close friend. From then on, she saw you as an intruder and was on revenge grail by spilling the beans on you," exclaimed Dennis. It was a thought that found favour with Pam and Diane.

"I have to agree with you, but I am very surprised she would behave like that. You knew her from your nursing days at the hospital in Colchester and you were good friends and I also knew her almost as long as you Pam, which is why I am appalled at what she did," declared Diane after a deep inhale of breath.

"But that's not all. Listen to this." Pam drew up her chair and they all had their elbows on the table. Dennis again gave her his undivided attention for, by then, he had learned that when Pam prefixes a statement with '*listen to this,*' it is serious and worthy of close attention. "I think she is now sticking her claws deeply into Elton," she added, feeling somewhat relieved that everything was now out in the open and that she had nothing else hidden from Dennis.

"What are you talking about, Pam," piped up Diane, now even more confused, "and what makes you think so?" This brought a smirk to Pam's face.

"Well, she invited him for dinner one Friday evening supposedly to talk over a few things very soon after she and Winston had broken up. They must have had a lot to talk about because it turned out he spent the night and came back home next day to crucify me. He said he knew all about my relationship with Dennis and Sidney, and that he had got it from one of my good friends." Diane looked horrified and shook her head. That evening she left more confused than when she arrived. Despite this, she felt she had cleared the air and regained Pam's friendship. Dennis saw the whole fiasco as something to forget for it had occurred before he was the new boy on the block. At the same time, there was no doubt in his mind that Pam felt somewhat uneasy about the whole shebang, but he reassured her it would take a lot more than that to derail their love train.

21

Tulips and daffodils in the garden and bluebells beneath the oak in the neighbour's, were heralding the arrival of young spring with its flowery garland. Apple trees in nearby allotments were showing off their white flowers that merged into shades of crystal as they absorbed the watery sunlight of early spring. The Japanese cherry in the neighbour's garden was boasting its pink flowers. Dennis' two friends, the robins, were perched on the fence gazing at them in what seemed to be sheer curiosity as he and Pam strolled around, taken in, as they were, by bird-song and the various shades of spring foliage. Black birds, sparrows and magpies were paying their usual mid-morning visit to the lawn in search of succulent worms which gave away their positions by the scattering of worm-mould.

"I think I'll get my sun glasses, do you want yours as well?" she asked, the mid-morning sun sufficiently bright to bring a squint to their eyes. It was within this natural setting that Dennis and Pam were having mid-morning coffee on the patio. The neighbour on the right, a kind of matured bachelor in his late sixties,' was already quenching the thirst of his tomato seedlings with a generous helping of water from a watering can that had seen better days when he observed the couple.

"Hello Dennis, you better take these before they all go," requested Alex, handing him a tray of young fuchsias from his glasshouse. He was a retired policeman who, since retiring, he had plunged himself totally into the breeding and cultivation of a variety of fuchsias most of which were meant for local garden centres.

TROPICAL HEATWAVE

"Thanks Alex and what a gorgeous day!" declared Dennis, taking the trays of young plants. Alex always paid meticulous attention to the cultivation of his fuchsias making sure each variety was carefully labelled. Young seedlings were set out geometrically in trays and placed on raised benches in his glasshouse which was automatically ventilated by a roof window and watered by a timed water spray.

"It certainly is," replied Alex at which point two wood pigeons in the oak tree burst into song and a green woodpecker touched down on the lawn to forage for food between the border plants. Even the allotments at the back were already buzzing with life. Dennis and Pam had now been living together quite happily for about three years, but he felt that, like any other woman, she would want to be married and therefore might be wondering when he would make the proposal. Perhaps it was the ambiance produced by the combined effect of flowers, bird-song and spring sunshine that inspired him to think that the right moment had arrived. He felt the natural setting provided was the moment. He was into his second cup when he placed it on the gently table and pushed his chair slightly back.

"Please excuse me for a moment darling, I'll soon be back." As he rose, she looked up at him and was a bit baffled.

"Why, where are you going?" There was no answer and it was not the kind of thing he would normally do. Making his way through the patio door, he could feel her eyes boring into his back. Various thoughts were running through her mind: '*he didn't say he was going to the bathroom, I didn't hear the phone ring and there was no knock at the door.*' Dennis returned about five minutes later carrying two glasses and a bottle of chilled champagne. He didn't quite know why he had kept the two bottles on the fridge and for so long. Perhaps it was because he was subconsciously thinking of such a moment as this. She looked at him under a frown and, as he placed them on the table, she wondered what was about to take place at 10:30 in the morning.

"What is all this in aid of Dennis?" she asked with a searching voice and slightly squinted eyes while he did his best to mask his emotions. "My birthday has gone and so has yours, so what are we about to celebrate?" she added, gazing at him with one of her soft contagious smiles. There was still no response. He sat quietly, filled the two glasses with a degree of panache and, holding her hand, he slowly pushed a beautifully designed engagement ring onto her finger. Raising his head slowly, he looked her firmly in her eyes which by now displayed the kind of brilliance only seen in a star on a cloudless night. They were now holding each other's hands across the table with his eyes searching hers. He was about to do something that would bring her the kind of instant relief and enjoyment she could not have imagined.

"Darling, will you marry me?" For a moment, her world stood still, she was unable to speak. There were two heart-beats of silence, hers and his. And as though understanding what was happening, the two robins dived from the fence onto the garden and, with a few hops, made their way onto the patio where they proceeded to serenade them with their song. She looked at him softly but with a kind of radiance that could only be experienced in a spring-morning sunshine. She eventually found her voice.

"Of course, I'll be happy to marry you, darling." Her sweet contagious chuckle caressed the mid-morning air and her gentle voice and charming smile which always stirred him, did so even more at that moment. Sitting quietly for a few moments, Dennis had time to let significant thoughts rise to the surface. *'I can see in her everything I want in a woman. I can see her upbringing suits her perfectly to become my wife, something she has already proved during the last three years. She is perfect in every way.'* They rose together, took a sip from each other's glass and hugged in an embracing kiss, made all the more pleasant by the warm sunshine invigorating their backs. He kissed her with the full measure of his desire. Wrapped as they were in the peaceful breezes that caressed the flowers, it felt like a season of everlasting spring. With her heartbeat eventually returning to norm she gazed at the ring.

"Oh Dennis, it is very beautiful. I didn't expect this so soon after you moved in. You really caught me there again. I wondered why you kept that champagne so long on the fridge because it is not like you to keep wine that long. By the way, when did you buy the ring and how did you know I would like it?" This brought a chuckle and a slightly raised eye-brow from Dennis.

TROPICAL HEATWAVE

"I always knew the type of ring you would prefer; the rest was easy." She looked at it again and again while sipping her wine.

"Oh Dennis, it's really, *really* beautiful," she said affectionately, the flow of words interrupted by each breath she took as her dark brown eyes filled with tears of joy. Pulling him even closer to her, she expressed her thanks and joy with an extended full-blooded kiss before settling back in her chair with a feeling of contentment engraved on her face. It was an expression that said more than words could ever do. "But what brought this on today and at this time of the morning?" she asked softly. With glasses topped up they reclined in their chairs: she to listen and he to explain.

"Well, I thought to myself we have got the house and I have got promotion all in the same year. Also, you have proved yourself to be strong, courageous, loving and caring during the last three years. The only thing stopping us from getting married is the question of divorce, but I also felt that any woman would like to be proposed to in the proper manner, you know, a moment she can savour and remember. Why this morning? Well, here we have a beautiful garden, a beautiful spring morning and we are even serenaded by our friends, the robins, a perfect setting for an occasion like this." She nodded in approval, replenished the glasses and, throwing her shoulders back, laughed heartily. She was touched by his kindness.

"Since you put it like that, I have to agree."

"I think both divorces ought to be completed within the next four to six months. That being the case, we might probably be able to get married sometime next year. What do you think?" She took some time to pluck the words from the midst of her thoughts. Excitement and love had now lifted her to a new height.

"Next year would be fine, say around August. The weather ought to be nice and we could have the reception here in the garden which ought to be in full bloom by then," she replied before dashing off to make fresh percolated coffee. With every sip and with the spring sunshine falling gently on her now glowing cheeks, she floated away slowly into a sea of contentment and Dennis had a moment to reflect.

"Darling, isn't it strange?" he remarked.

"What? You have another surprise?" she asked with a slight chuckle.

"Well it seems not too long ago that we met on the Northern Line and now here we are in our garden making our wedding plans. You are certainly a dream come true." He gazed into the distance without seeing or saying anything for a moment. Memories were seeping through his veins. He was recalling the moment when she danced in and out of his love beam and of the times he thought he had seen her on the platform or in the shadows of a smoke-filled carriage. Pam gently touched his fingers, causing him to snap out of his temporary trance.

"Why have you suddenly gone so quiet?"

"Oh, I was just reflecting on the tempestuous seas we had to navigate together before reaching this port. Anyway, I don't fancy too big a wedding. After all we have both been through this before when neither of us was in love with our partners. This one is special because I see you as the sun in my sky and the wind beneath my wings and that is also why I want you to be my wife and me to be my wife's husband." Pam just looked at him in sheer amazement.

"Oh no, it doesn't have to be large. In fact, I was thinking of having immediate family and a few very close friends, just the number we can easily cater for and accommodate in the garden," she exclaimed, and Dennis fully supported the idea before allowing his eyes to roam in the direction of the glasshouse.

"I think those plants in the glasshouse need some water and extra ventilation," suggested Dennis. On their way across the lawn, they were greeted with a chorus from buzzing bees sampling early flowers and by the whisper of leaves ruffled by a gentle mid-morning breeze. Here in the glasshouse, healthy scents given off by different plants seemed to add to an ambiance suitable for making wedding plans.

"These seedlings are really doing well, aren't they Dennis," she commented, "and look how the tomatoes seem to be dominating the space. Oh, and I like the way you have these seedlings geometrically set out in trays like Alex's." She plucked a leaf from a tomato plant and rubbed it between her fingers. "I do like the fragrance of a tomato plant," she added before turning to him with sheer excitement and an expression as soft as the tender leaves she caressed between her fingers. "Oh Dennis, isn't this lovely? Our first go at growing plants from seeds in a glasshouse looks a winner. It feels like Kew Gardens in here no wonder the plants are doing so well," she remarked. Just over the back fence in the allotments came the clanging of forks and spades indicating a busy morning for the holders, some turning the soil in preparation for the planting of cabbages, leeks, onions, potatoes and much more while others were adding needed compost to the soil. Rising above the clatter of garden tools was the exchange of yesterday's experiences infused with the usual helping of jokes. Dennis took a miniature hand-fork and gently turned the soil around his young seedlings.

"But about the wedding, we have to hope that all divorce proceedings are completed as soon as possible because we cannot set a date until that is done," he said quietly, as she squeezed passed him with a small watering can on her way to quench the thirst of young lettuce. They were both awaiting a divorce 'absolute' which they had estimated would be in their hands by May or June. It was during this matrimonial mood that the doorbell rang. His eyes met hers with wonderment before they looked in the direction of the street door.

"I wonder who it is. I don't expect anybody, do you?" he exclaimed with a furrowed brow as he peered into the distance. "I am not dressed to receive visitors," he said, "so this interruption better be worth it," he muttered.

"No," she replied, "but we'll soon find out," as Dennis made his way hastily across the lawn to the door, Pam returned to her chair on the patio to anxiously await him. On his way to the door he recognised the silhouetted figures through the glass panels. In their excitement and matrimonial planning, they had forgotten they had invited the Taylors (Les and Beryl) over for morning coffee. They would often exchange visits particularly on Saturday evenings when they would indulge in light humour over snacks, a drink and soft music. On other times, they would visit garden centres together and, among other things, have lunch or afternoon tea at one of them.

"Oh, do come in, it's nice to see you again," said Dennis with his usual broad smile. "Go straight through, Pam is on the patio. Please believe me when I tell you that we were so involved in what we were talking about that we completely forgot we had asked you over for morning coffee," uttered Dennis in an apologetic tone triggering a round of laughter.

"Oh, that *must* be something very interesting they were discussing Les," piped up Beryl with an inquiring look that managed to break through a cloud of smoke emitted from her cigarette. It was a thought echoed by Les who, on seeing the glasses and empty champagne bottle, felt it warranted further investigation. He was the kind of chap always on the look-out for something about which to make a joke and this was to be no exception.

"By the looks of things Beryl, it must be something very interesting or worth celebrating," he blurted. "I mean look, an empty champagne bottle and two glasses. We obviously got here too late or probably just in time, Beryl," remarked Lesley with a loud laugh. But before Beryl could respond, they were already doing their usual stroll around the garden. It was the first thing they would do when visiting each other for they were all keen gardeners. "This garden really does look nice but, if I were you Dennis, I would move those two flowering shrubs and put them more in a corner because they tend to grow fairly tall," suggested Les, pointing to two lobelias growing too near to the patio. He always welcomed an opportunity to demonstrate his knowledge of gardening by suggesting what plants could go in what spaces and why.

Once seated, they were soon enjoying coffee and biscuits and they too were forced to don their sunglasses. For a while, the fountain in the corner, displaying a prism of light in the sunshine, became the centre of attention. It was a feeling made more pleasant by the trickle of the nearby waterfall emptying itself into a small pool in which small goldfish darted around in their own world between small water lilies. Now into their second cup of coffee, Beryl adjusted her chair and her glasses and took a couple of long draws on her cigarette. Dennis and Pam knew from experience it signalled the onset of an inquisition.

"Come on then you two, what is this all about? Champagne so early in the morning! What's going on?" she asked, determined to get an answer. This brought a faint ripple of laughter from Pam flashing her eye lashes. She knew Beryl well enough to know she had no

TROPICAL HEATWAVE

intention of giving up her probe. Pam's and Dennis' eyes met and held for a few seconds as they glared at each other.

"Well, we have something to tell you." Lesley adjusted his sunglasses, his ears pricking up like those of a dog whose sleep is suddenly disturbed by an otherwise inaudible sound in the distance. Beryl, the chain smoker, took three more draws on the cigarette before releasing smoke rings slowly into the mid-morning air.

"Come on then, don't keep us in suspense any longer. Is it good news or bad news?" she asked in a state of breath-held anticipation. It was a suspense she could hardly stand especially seeing that Pam was deliberately keeping her waiting for a long-extended moment. Dennis asked to be excused and dashed off to prepare fresh percolated coffee, but he was a bit apprehensive about letting them know their plans so soon.

"It is good news," replied Pam and then dashed off to join Dennis in the kitchen where the decision was reluctantly made to tell them. Since that Sunday morning event at Diane's, they had agreed not to trust anyone, not even Beryl. Carrying a percolator and four cups and saucers, they soon re-joined the others on the patio.

"Oh, by the way Pam, did you ever get to find out who it was that squealed on you that Sunday morning?"

"Yes, we have it on good authority that it was Jean." This immediately triggered off a coughing by Beryl, spilling some of her coffee across the table. With her face now red with excess blood, she looked at Pam.

"But I thought she was your friend," she croaked.

"That's what I thought as well," retorted Pam with a look of disgust and Beryl sensed it would hurt to relive the whole sordid saga by talking about it. "Any way, the reason we forgot you were coming this morning is because Dennis proposed to me this morning and I accepted, and we were making preliminary plans for the wedding." Beryl's eyes popped. A sudden outburst of coughing, together with a fine spray of coffee from her mouth, interrupted her attempt to speak. It was the kind of response Beryl never expected. With a rush of blood to her cheeks making them almost totally red with excitement, she turned to Les and, as though he was not sitting at the same table, shouted at the top of her voice,

"You hear that Les," and she took two long drawn-out draws on her cigarette, "there is going to be a wedding," tumbled from her lips. This audible expression of excitement was loud enough to attract the attention of the immediate neighbours working in their glasshouses on either side, forcing them to look around in wonderment. Pam and Beryl embraced each other and, in all the mini-drama that was going on, Dennis thought it a good moment to slip away again, this time to get things in place for a toast.

"And about time too!" shouted Lesley. "That will give me a reason for a good booze-up. Congratulations mate," he added, before hugging Dennis and giving Pam a peck on both cheeks. Another bottle of champagne and this time four glasses were soon on the table. It was now clear that their visitors would be there longer than anyone had anticipated.

"Why not stay for a spot of lunch?" suggested Dennis, slowly placing his half-empty glass on the table while throwing a side glance of satisfaction at Pam. Lunch was a Pam's special: on each plate was a layer of lettuce followed by a thinly sliced ham. Then came a layer of thinly sliced cucumber and beef tomato followed with thinly sliced hardboiled egg, finely chopped onion and a sprinkling of parmesan cheese with a drizzle of olive oil. It was the first dish prepared for Dennis when they were stealing love on the side. The difference was that, in keeping with the occasion that Saturday, it was lubricated with champagne and it afforded an opportunity to add some detail to the plans in which Les agreed to give Pam away and Beryl volunteered to allow Pam dress at their house.

"By the way, do you get any more hassle from Elton?" asked Beryl, showing concern.

"No, not since he was issued with the injunction."

"Thank heavens for that," added Beryl with a sigh of relief. With preliminary plans made for the wedding, Beryl glanced at her watch. It had just gone four. "Isn't it strange how time flies when you are having fun!" she declared with a look of joy tinged with regret that they had to go. Within another fifteen minutes they were on their way home, but it was the afternoon spent with Dennis and Pam that filled their minds all the way. As anticipated, the divorce papers arrived in May allowing them enough time to put the finishing touches to plans for an August wedding. They were having breakfast next day when Pam added extra butter to her toast and gave Dennis a pensive look with a slightly angled head.

"What about having the ceremony at the Registry in Watford Town Centre?" she suggested quietly. She had previously attended wedding ceremonies there and liked the way they were conducted. Little did she know she would be one day in the queue.

"Sounds okay to me. It is centrally located and well served with public transport, so folk shouldn't have problems reaching it," he replied, while enjoying his Sunday morning British breakfast. "I will ask Frank to drive me in my Jag to the town-hall. You, of course, will have the pleasure of a silver-shadow Rolls Royce which will then take us both to the wedding lunch at the hotel where we can also remind all about the reception at our house starting in the late afternoon." They looked pleased with how things had developed so far.

"Let us hope that the weather is nice and that the garden is in full bloom with a splash of colour," added Pam beaming with delight.

22

The day arrived, and Dennis' brother Frank arrived from Brixton quite early that morning to make sure Dennis was well groomed and to be at the registry on time. It being a hot summer, Dennis decided to move away from the traditional dark suit to something cooler and more tropical, beige. After some final touches, they were soon on their way. It was 10:30 as they set out into a beautiful summer morning. Some of the neighbours who knew about it made a point of being in their front gardens behind their white wicket gates to cheer him on his way. Frank gave him a quick side glance.

"How are you feeling brother?" he asked with a wry smile while trying to detect any sign of nerves. Dennis cleared his throat and gently mopped his brow.

"I am okay, but I was just thinking that here I am being driven by my younger brother along a route I frequently use and often passing a building I have never entered." *C'est la vie* sometimes commented Frank with a chuckle. Within a few minutes, they were approaching their destination, an old Victorian municipal building not far from the town centre. Apart from an elm and two beech trees, there was nothing outside that would grip your attention. They arrived at 10:45 to find almost all the guests already there. *'Although I feel confident she will be on time, there is still this nagging feeling that something could go wrong to delay her,'* thought Dennis quietly to himself. He was conscious of the next wedding in the queue after theirs and was becoming somewhat anxious, for to lose your slot, would be almost total disaster. But, before he could be submerged any further in such thoughts, there was a slight movement among the guests standing outside who were all now looking in the same direction with an expression of eager anticipation. Smoke rings started to rise from a member in the group. It was Beryl. "Here comes the bride, "she shouted disturbing a small flock of pigeons in the nearby beech and causing all eyes to focus on a silver shadow Rolls Royce slowly approaching.

"Come on brother, I think we better take our seats," suggested Frank, his best man. Standing beside Pam, Dennis seemed to be listening but not hearing, so overwhelmed by the occasion was he. *'I feel as though I am in a different world: contented, satisfied and at peace with myself and, from the look in her eyes, I sense she is sharing the moment,'* he thought quietly to himself, *'nor do I have to be alarmed about two men dressed in black or wonder who bought my suit. This time, I am fully aware and in total control, for the woman standing beside me who has filled my mind for a long time, is holding pole position in my heart. Some women have beautiful eyes, some have a pleasant form and yet others, a beautifully sculptured face but, for me, she has it all.'* These were some of the thoughts occupying Dennis' mind rather than what the registrar was saying.

In less than forty-five minutes, they were on their way for a wedding lunch at a beautiful hotel set in spacious grounds midway between Watford and St. Albans. Its well-kept buildings and grounds added credence to their choice of venue. With the red carpet in place they made their way slowly up the steps. As they paused for that all-important photo call, he turned. Their eyes met. "Darling, I feel I am in a unique position to have such a person as you standing beside me radiating happiness." She acknowledged the compliment and followed it with one of her soft contagious chuckles. Her dress, bordering on off-white, had a high neck and a long slender skirt beautifully embroidered around the neck. A silver necklace sat below a pair of matching earrings that turned to crystal waterfalls in the dazzling light of the summer sun.

Frank was just about to begin the best man's speech when Lesley leaned over to Dennis with an apologetic grin. "Sorry mate for bringing her slightly late. It was all my fault. I secretly instructed the driver to take the longer route through Hemel Hempstead town centre. I thought this would allow her the chance to wave gracefully at passers-by and some of her friends who could not attend but were on the lookout for her." Dennis smiled and thanked him for being so thoughtful. In the meantime, the three-tier wedding cake was beginning to suffer in the noonday heat and had started to list slowly on one side like the leaning tower of Pisa. Fortunately, the lunch was short thus minimising any embarrassment of the cake collapsing in a heap on the table. It would have brought great embarrassment not only to the newly married, but also to one member in particular, the cake-maker who was among the guests. It wasn't long before guests were extending their best wishes and making their way home with the understanding to be back in the evening at Dennis' for a small reception.

"I like the chessboard pattern on the lawn," commented Frank on his arrival at the house with the newly wed. It was something he had failed to see when he came to collect Dennis a few hours before. "And I like the way you have arranged the seating. Whose idea was this?" he asked. Dennis had placed eight large white pots standing on short pedestals in appropriate locations on the lawn. With each pot filled with Begonias and Geraniums around a small central conifer, they added to the ambiance as well as providing focal points around which small groups could seat on rugs and cushions to enjoy the afternoon/evening. Guests were treated to the delights of a combined Caribbean, Malaysian and English cuisine, held together with rum cocktails, rum punch, and pinna colada but to name a few, and all this against a background of quiet Calypso, Reggae and Soul music. It had to be quiet music because neighbours would not have taken too kindly to loud music although Dennis had made sure of avoiding this by inviting those nearest to him to the reception.

It was into this setting that the gorgeous lady, wearing a Caribbean/Malaysian style gown made by one of her Malaysian friends, stepped onto the lawn to the applause of all but one member of a group of three sitting near a lilac tree in the far corner. It was one of the two shrubs Lesley had advised Dennis to move to that site about two years before. This gesture of contempt did not go un-noticed by Pam who did not know the person and therefore simply dismissed it with a shrug of her shoulders. "I think it is unfair that she should reap the sweets now that

TROPICAL HEATWAVE

he is rising high up the ladder in his profession. His first wife Susan should have been the one," exclaimed Shirley with a stern expression that immediately drew the attention of others in her group, causing one of them to probe further.

"What made you say that, Shirley?" It was a question that required them to come closer together to hear Shirley's response for she was at pains not to let other guests hear. Shirley had attended the same school as Dennis' first wife Susan with whom she had become very good friends. What is more, she also discreetly had a crush on Dennis although this was quite unknown to him at the time. Her hidden reason for attending the reception was to see the woman Dennis had married. But unknown to Shirley, her initial comment was overheard by Beryl serving drinks to the group nearby. Horrified at what she had just heard, she wasted no time in making her way to make it known to Pam who was helping her sister in the kitchen.

"Pam, can I have a quick word," requested Beryl, looking stunned and shocked and with a face which seemed as though the blood had been drained from it.

"Of course, Beryl, you look pale, is anything the matter?" Asked Pam, looking rather concerned.

"I don't know yet, but there is someone in the group near the lilac tree stripping you to bits." This immediately gained Pam's undivided attention.

"What do you mean by *stripping* me to bits and who is it?" responded Pam, her eyes hastily scanning the lawn. She immediately ceased helping her sister with the curried goat and rice and to give Beryl her full attention. Beryl discreetly pointed out the offender and returned to serving the drinks. Pam beckoned to Dennis who quickly made his way to the kitchen. With anger roiling in her stomach and fire flashing from her eyes, she related the story pointing out the culprit.

"That cow, and to think that she wasn't even invited. Who the hell is she anyway and who brought her?" she snapped. Just then, it seemed as though a small swarm of butterflies darting around in the Lilac, sensed something close to a volcanic explosion was imminent and took to hasty flight.

215

"I believe she came with Frank," replied Dennis placidly, and with a quelling glance in an effort to calm her down. But Pam was in no mood to be pacified. Instead, she was about to burst through the patio door to launch a brutal attack on Shirley, the offender. It was with the greatest difficulty that he managed to stifle an ensuing explosion by persuading her that, to do so, would not be in keeping with the spirit of the occasion. "I will deal with it at the appropriate time and in my way," he admonished. Moments later, he happened to catch Frank on his own.

"Can I have a moment, Frank," he requested in an unruffled manner. They moved to a more private place. "Beryl was serving rum punch to that little group next to the group of over there by the Lilac when she heard Shirley slagging off Pam. Of course, she told Pam and I have had great difficulty restraining her from blasting Shirley to pieces even at her own reception."

"My wife invited her quite unknown to me," explained Frank awkwardly and looking rather embarrassed for, although she was quite known to him, he did not invite her. He knew what would have been the likely outcome and she did not disappoint him. "Please do not bring her back here ever again because I cannot guarantee how it may end if Pam gets hold of her," implored Dennis in a very cool manner.

"Okay, I will speak to my wife about it. Don't you worry brother," replied Frank with a mild smile before continuing to mingle among guests who were unaware of what had taken place. In the meantime, the ambiance of the late afternoon setting was beginning to change. The sky, almost colourless during the day as if the heat had burnt out its pigment, was now undergoing a remarkable transformation. The blue was invaded by the yellowing refraction of the setting sun allowing it to be awash with an astonishing luminous green that was beginning to darken to violet in the east where night was falling and reddened in the west where it was yet to come. Dennis turned on the garden lights and, as shades of twilight began to touch the warm earth and the pungent smell of roses, honey-suckle and jasmine began to permeate the warm summer air that settled over the garden, the stage was now set for a truly enjoyable evening. A good time was enjoyed by all, the last guest leaving around 1:30 a.m.

23

They did not plan to have a honeymoon or, at least, that is what Pam thought, but Dennis had other ideas. He was always thinking of ways of giving her pleasant surprises and, since she did not have the pleasure of a honeymoon in her previous marriage, he thought it would be nice to give her such an experience this time round. *'Why don't I make this honeymoon a bit different, a bit of a surprise, though not like the one I had in my first marriage in which I played no part in the planning? It would be just the thing to put the icing on the cake.'* With that in mind, he had quietly booked a package holiday for two to Barbados staying at the Coral Beach Resort on the beautiful west coast.

It was Sunday and the morning after the wedding. As he would normally do on weekends, he brought up a tray of tea, but that morning the tray would be different. Not only would it be carrying a single red rose but an envelope. He placed the tray carefully on the small bedside table. Pam had opened the curtains fully and was standing at the window looking over the garden. The morning sun falling on her full length grey satin robe shimmered like when falling on the still waters of a pond. Floating up the stairs was the soft music from *Till the End of Time*, a collection of the world's most beautiful melodies.

"Darling, is this what a bride looks like the morning after?" he asked lovingly and with a sparkle in his eyes. She gave him a soft side glance and he joined her at the window. With his arms around her waist, they looked down at the garden where a variety of birds were competing for crumbs from the evening before. They stood there for a while drawn in by the blaze of colour provided by floribunda roses of different hues, as well as simplicity, polyanthus, nasturtiums, godetias and aquilegias, but to mention a few, for by now, Dennis had become a fairly accomplished gardener. Dennis opened the window fully allowing them to fill their lungs with air coming directly across the allotments at the rear.

"It was very nice of our guests to share such special moments with us yesterday, but what will always remain indelible on my mind is how beautiful you looked standing beside me during the ceremony. And how can I ever forget the woman who stepped onto the lawn dressed in an outfit perfectly suited to the evening," he declared. She responded with a quiet sigh and straightened her shoulders allowing a beam of sunlight to gently caress her ebony cheeks. They turned, faced each other and sealed the moment with a close embrace. It was a scene captured in a full-length mirror on the opposite wall, a scene for which they regretted not having a remote-controlled camera. But glancing over his shoulder, her eyes suddenly touched down on something unusual-something that immediately grabbed her attention and curiosity.

"What is that envelope doing on the tray Dennis?" she asked with a frowned forehead and narrowing eyes. As she turned, her robe suddenly came apart to reveal a perfect outline. The effect on him was impressive and instant for it was a visual feast to savour.

"Oh, that, ah, ah, ah......., perhaps it might be a card from one of the neighbours telling us what a nice evening they had. Why don't you open it and see," he suggested, now more pre-occupied by what he was seeing than by what she was saying. Completely overtaken with curiosity, she quickly opened the envelope. The frown of curiosity suddenly changed to a smile of surprise and delight engulfing her face and culminating in a shriek with the words, "Oh Dennissssss," drawing out the second syllable, "we shall be honeymooning at the Coral Beach Resort. Oh Dennis, that's wonderful." But, in their effort to embrace each other again, they lost their balance and fell on the bed with such force that their uncontrollable dangling legs took hold of the tea tray and all its contents dispatching them to the far corners of the bedroom. But not even that was enough to cause a cease-fire so excited was she to learn that they were going to honeymoon in Barbados. Now lying on her back, she breathed deeply but calmly behind an expression that said it all.

"Imagine honeymooning in Barbados for two weeks," she said with a muted shout, staring at the tickets which, by a stroke of luck, had escaped the deluge from the tea pot. She levelled with his eyes. "But when and how did you manage to do all of this unknown to me?" She asked anxiously, her face now as aglow as the Sunday morning sun beaming through the window.

"Well, I thought that, since you never had the experience of a honeymoon before, it would be nice to have a honeymoon cum holiday. I wanted it to be another surprise," he replied with an element of panache in his voice. She went to the window, took a few deep breaths and allowed a very light morning summer breeze to creep over her face.

"What a surprise! Our relatives and friends will be glad to see us, and when are we leaving?" In her excitement, she had failed to see the date.

"Next Saturday."

"But where will we be staying?" She had also failed to notice it was a package-holiday.

"We'll be staying at the Coral Beach Resort on the west coast, you know, it is beyond Spring Gardens when you are coming from the city. All the apartments look out onto the calm blue waters of the Caribbean." Even the mere mention of the *'blue waters of the Caribbean'* was enough to send her into a momentary trance.

"Isn't it strange how some of us have to go away for a while to appreciate the beauty of your homeland," she declared.

"Perhaps it's because we tend to take things for granted before we travel," added Dennis, feeling very pleased with himself.

"But my younger sister might not be too pleased when she finds out we are not staying at her," she added looking slightly concerned.

"Look my darling, since it is *our* honeymoon, I thought it would be better to be able to do *what* we want, *when* we want, *how* we want and *where* we want, and not to have our style cramped by relatives or friends or, for that matter us cramping their style," he admonished.

"I see what you mean. I suppose, put like that you are right," she said nodding in complete agreement. "Anyway, we could always visit them when we want to. I don't think they will mind, after all, it *is our* honeymoon," she added.

"But here is something else you don't know," he uttered with the expression of one with an inflated ego, letting the exquisite torment of her anticipation linger.

"What?" she asked in joyous expectation, awaiting yet another surprise.

"We are traveling club class," he continued, deliberately keeping his face straight this time and awaiting her response.

"Wh-a-a-a-t? club class?" her voice flowing over the words as it rose to a crescendo.

"Well I thought that, as it is our honeymoon, I wanted it to be a special flight, one that we will always remember. I wasn't prepared to do that seven-hour flight in any way less than comfort. You don't have the bother and frustration you can sometimes have when flying economy class. But you must promise me you will not tell anyone in Barbados about our honeymoon arrangements. I would like it to be a surprise for them as well," he suggested.

"But what about our good friends Grantly and Evelyn? They might not be too pleased either."

"Okay, since they are our best friends from the time they were here in England, yes, but no one else must know." They had met Grantly and Evelyn in London where Grantly and Dennis worked as sorters in one of the main postal sorting offices in London near to St. Paul's Cathedral. Evelyn was a qualified nurse working at a London hospital. They had moved back to Barbados within twelve years of arriving in England, she to work at the Queen Elizabeth hospital and he to join a leading accounting firm. Dennis was still in his maroon robe and she in her shimmering grey satin when they eventually managed to make their way downstairs to have a late breakfast. The remainder of the day saw her moving around with a hop and a skip not unlike a new-born lamb in a spring meadow.

"I can hardly believe this, us honeymooning in Barbados. Who would believe it! Me, this little girl that left the island fourteen years ago, in search

of a career and a better life, now returning to honeymoon in Barbados," she said quietly to herself as she grappled with coming to grips with the idea. This mental buzz would be accompanied by a calypso floating through the air on a beautiful singing voice, one of her major assets and a relic from her days in the Saint Martin's Church choir in Barbados. "We must make sure we have everything for the trip including morsels of wedding cake," she uttered with growing excitement.

Saturday seemed a long way off to Pam until it arrived and found them sitting in the club class lounge at Gatwick airport anticipating what they will meet on arrival in Barbados. Here, they had time to part-take of some of the light snacks and drinks provided. As the aircraft levelled off at 39,000 feet, Dennis removed his shoes loosened his tie and reclined his chair. It was a mood further enhanced by the arrival of a bottle of chilled champagne and two glasses and a card. Pam's brown eyebrows shot up to her hairline.

"How did they know we are on our honeymoon?" she asked, "you have done it again, haven't you?" sounding overwhelmed Dennis looked at her rather coy. Quite unknown to her, he had informed the airline that they were honeymooners. It certainly set the tone for the trip. Dennis held her hand with a side glance as she too put her seat in the relaxing position. He took two sips of champagne and levelled his eyes with hers.

"Less than fifteen years ago, we were two individuals traveling to England either by boat or by air in search of a better life. Today, here we are traveling club class back to Barbados on our honeymoon," he declared, and the delight on her face expressed total agreement. Flight attendants passing by would stop to wish them a pleasant honeymoon. After lunch, which had a hint of the Caribbean, they settled down to a game of scrabble, to read, to do a crossword or just have a quiet snooze. Touch-down was at 3:30 pm. Stepping onto the steps of the aircraft, they were slammed with a blast of hot tropical air only slightly made bearable by the cooling effect of trade winds blowing directly off the sea. On leaving the airport Pam donned her sunglasses hoping not to be spotted.

"We are lucky not to be seen by anyone of our relatives who might be here to say *bon voyage* to a friend or even to meet someone. Are you sure you didn't arrange this as well?" she uttered with a quiet chuckle.

Dennis merely looked at her as their luggage was placed aboard the hotel minibus.

"Excuse me driver, but it would be appreciated if you could take the route through St. George," he requested and was granted the pleasure of the more scenic route through the parish of St. George allowing them time to take in the scenery as well as the smell of tropical vegetation sweltering in the heat of a mid-afternoon sun. This was music to the ears of the cab driver who could see his takings increasing.

"Oh, Dennis, look, you remember that?" He turned and found himself as amazed as she was. Not far ahead and moving at literally walking-pace was a donkey-drawn cart. Seated precariously on a corner of the cart was an elderly man weary from his day's work and almost asleep while being taken home by the donkey which obviously knew the way. "Not only does that donkey know the way, but if he is sleeping, it also stops at every rum-shop at which the old fellow stops for a drink on his way home, nor will it move until someone gives it some kind of drink," declared the taxi driver. Dennis laughed loudly because he had a similar story.

"That does not surprise me. My grandfather often found himself in a similar position on his way home from Bridgetown on his horse-drawn cart loaded with his monthly consignment of groceries. Not only did the horse stop but it would refuse to move until given a helping of oats. All this was often completely unknown to the old man who by then would have taken a little too much alcohol on board and would be fast asleep. On arriving home, my uncles not only had to unload the groceries but grandfather as well. Now I know we *are* in Barbados," exclaimed Dennis who always considered the sight of an old man sitting on his donkey-drawn cart as part of the institution of Barbados. It was this kind of transport that often took the harvest from the country districts into the town to be sold in the street market. Such a cart would be carrying things like breadfruit, potatoes, yams, cassava, green and yellow bananas and much more according to the season. "I can well remember when, as small boys, how much fun it was to listen on evenings for my neighbour's horse-drawn cart. As it approached from about three hundred yards away, we would quickly jump aboard for a ride. It was by no means a smooth ride, but it was

TROPICAL HEATWAVE

the rattle and rumble of the wheels as the cart swayed from side to side over an uneven road, that made it such a delight and such fun."

In another forty minutes, they were at Coral Beach Resort with its white exterior walls beneath a roof of red clay tiles, all forming a suitable backdrop for red bougainvillea and green lawns dotted with the occasional dwarf coconut-palm. With the azure waters of the Caribbean gently caressing the white sands, it was a perfect setting for their honeymoon. After a quick shower, Pam emerged wearing a very short loose Caribbean style kaftan to join Dennis on the balcony. They were soon enjoying a cold coconut punch as they sat watching small fishing boats returning home with their catch. After what seemed to be a seven-hour flight, they were glad to settle into reclining chairs to enjoy the grandeur and changing colours of a Caribbean sunset.

"Oh, Dennis darling, thank you so much. I really didn't expect this. Here we are like tourists in our own country. I agree with what you said some time back: that it is strange how we had to leave home to really appreciate how beautiful this island is?"

"Well, very often that happens. But at the same time, don't forget why we left the island. It was because we wanted a better life style which is demonstrated by our very presence here."

"Oh yes," she replied nodding in quiet agreement.

"By the way, have you any idea what you would like to do this evening," he asked, "after all, it is Saturday evening which is the time for maximum entertainment here. Remember we are here for two weeks only and we have to make sure we enjoy every moment." This was Dennis' first visit to the island since leaving and it had taken him thirteen years to do so. Pam had done it twice before with a group for the annual carnival festival.

"Can you get me a large rum-punch, Dennis?" It was not long before a knock on the door indicated the drink had arrived. They continued to gaze out to sea which by now was changing into various shades of green and gold with the sun hanging low in the sky.

"Why don't we call John and Bernadette and let them know we are here," suggested Pam. John and Dennis were at one time teaching at the same school in North London where they were heads of department until John opted to return to Barbados to join Bernadette,

223

a former girlfriend whom he first met at a training college in Trinidad about two years before he left for England. At an opportune time, he re-joined her in Barbados where she had become the managing director of a beach resort in St. Lawrence Gap in the south west corner of the island.

"What a jolly good idea! Today being Saturday, there is bound to be something on at the resort," and, without any further delay, he extracted the number from a small note book.

"Hello John. Do you know who it is?"

"No, who is it?" he asked, a bit puzzled.

"Oh John, how could you forget this voice?" Pam chuckled loudly prompting John to ask who it was in the background.

"Oh, Dennis, are you on the island?" He had at last worked out that such a corruption of Barbadian and English accent could only come from one person and he was right.

"Yes, we came in this afternoon and we are thinking about making you and Bernadette our first port of call."

"That's great because we have a calypso evening one night every week and tonight is the night. Why don't you all come along?"

"We'll love to, but when does it start?"

"About seven, but don't wait till seven, come between 6:00 and 6:30 p.m. so we can catch up with old times. I'll let Bernadette know," replied John.

"It should be very good because it is carnival week and we are expecting an increase in the number of guests particularly from the UK," shouted Bernadette in the background.

"Okay, see you later." The stage was now set for the evening and, he hoped, for the remainder of their stay on the island. They were starting their honeymoon with a Caribbean bang and hoped that it would end with a bang. That evening as they emerged from the taxi to follow a short path lined with red, orange and white hibiscus to reception, in the distance they could see John's eyes popping with excitement as he approached them with open arms. "So nice to see you two again, it has been quite a while," he said hugging them together, "how are you all keeping?" Bernadette was busy making sure that all the outdoor furniture was in place for the evening. She stopped to chat with two guests when she happened to look around and see John, Dennis and Pam in what seemed to be an exuberant exchange of greetings.

"Excuse me, I have just seen two very good friends of ours from UK and I must say hello to them," and hurriedly made her way to join the group.

"Bernadette, this is Dennis and Pam about whom I often speak," he uttered and embraced them with a warm welcome.

"Hello, nice to meet you at last. John often speaks about how well you both got on when teaching at Hampstead School in London and the nice time he had when he was invited one year for Christmas dinner. He described your house as English on the outside but Caribbean on the inside." Bernadette was a pleasant, very attractive woman, highly intelligent and of good pedigree. Her eyes sparkled like a pair of diamonds beneath long dark hair that relaxed on her shoulders. From the outset, she and Pam developed a bond of friendship like John and Dennis.

"Come on Pam, let them get on with their jokes perhaps dating back from the days when they were boys together," she suggested as they set off together on a grand tour of the grounds. "One of the things I do is to make sure that the man-made and natural environments of the grounds blend. For instance, that furniture mingled picturesquely with flowering plants and shrubs and that all tables are decoratively prepared for the next meal," she explained, as she repositioned a vase of red hibiscus on a table. But floating around in Pam's mind were thoughts like: *I have to tell them we are married, but I must wait for the right moment.*

"Pam, Pam," came a shout from a table next to a dwarf coconut tree in the far corner where a group of four was sitting. She broke her pensive mood and jerked her head around to see a hand beckoning to her from a short distance. It was her cousin Linda who was in Barbados on holiday from New York.

"Seems as though someone over there knows you Pam," declared Bernadette.

"Yes, I think it is my cousin from New York whom I haven't seen for years," replied Pam with her eyes still focused on the corner.

"Why don't you spend some time with her, I am sure you have a lot of catching up to do. I will finish what I am doing and then join you for a drink later," suggested Bernadette. Pam made her way to join Linda at the pool bar where they chatted over a cold drink. They had both attended the same primary school in Barbados and were more than cousins, they had become very close friends even though Linda was slightly older.

"Fancy meeting you here after fifteen years. What happened after I left for New York Pam?" she asked, anxious to know how her favourite cousin had got on.

"I went to England and did nursing for a while. My first marriage collapsed after four years, but I met this chap from Barbados and we got married just last week which is why I am here on my honeymoon," she uttered, bursting with excitement.

"Congratulations," said Linda as they embraced each other. "But what is his name and where is he?" she asked, looking at a pocket size photo of the married couple Pam had with her by chance. "He resembles someone who attended a few of our parties in New York and strange enough, he has the same second name as your husband. My husband knew him from boyhood days in Barbados," she added. This brought a thoughtful smile from Pam wondering if it was Dennis' older brother.

"You might be right because he does have an older brother living there," declared Pam, her brow becoming more and more furrowed as she gazed at Linda.

"I usually invite him to any party held at the embassy and, from my many conversations with him, he is from a well-educated family in Barbados. If you have married into such a family, you have done very well for yourself, Pam," exclaimed Linda with a look of surprise, for it seemed as though Linda did not expect her to marry into a family of academics. It was not the kind of social leap she thought Pam was capable of making, a judgement based on background knowledge. Although they had both attended the same primary school and had done very well, the lack of funds meant Pam could not attend a secondary school at a time when secondary education had to be paid for. Linda, on the other hand, was able to acquire both secondary and tertiary education culminating as a qualified paediatrician from a New York university.

This recognition of Pam's progress and success by Linda served as a boost to her confidence and made her feel she was doing the right thing by marrying Dennis. Until then, she had certain abiding misgivings, thoughts in need of further clarification. She also knew that one of the main reasons for the breakup of Dennis' first marriage was intellectual incompatibility between him and his wife, the effect of which had spread like a cancer throughout all areas of their lives. She therefore wondered if she herself would be able to succeed where his first wife had failed. Having established that the two men were brothers from a respected family, Linda went on to describe how she became the wife of an ambassador while Pam related her life history from her arrival in England up to that moment. But it was what Linda said that left Pam more re-assured in the knowledge that her decision to marry Dennis was supported by her favourite cousin and good friend.

It was now 5:30, and a very light evening breeze gently ruffled the leaves and flowers of the bougainvillea, the hibiscus and the dwarf palm. Crickets were beginning to strike up a chorus signalling the end of the day. Sunset had already given way to the glow of garden and pool lights and the earth was radiating its intake of heat back into the atmosphere creating a desire to have a cooling splash in the pool before the barbeque that accompanied the Saturday calypso evening. Perhaps it was the cooling effect of the water together with the stimulation of frequently served rum punches by the pool that eventually gave Pam the courage to open up. Pam had chatted with Bernadette on several occasions on the phone and had struck up a long-distance friendship, which is why she felt a bit guilty not having told them about the wedding. She took three sips of her pinna-colada and cleared her throat with a smile as bright as the pool lights reflecting on her face.

"We have something to tell you," she said, sounding awkward and smiling casually.

"What, has Dennis been a naughty boy?" blurted John, who was always seeking someway of pulling Dennis' leg, a legacy from their teaching-days in London.

"Oh no, it's nothing like that." But before Pam could continue, Bernadette, like any very observant woman, caught sight of what looked to her like a new wedding ring on Pam's finger. She was somewhat hesitant to raise the matter for like Pam, she too was waiting for the appropriate moment until Linda made a passing glance at the sparkling band on Pam's finger which did not go un-noticed by Bernadette.

"John, I'll bet you anything they have got married," she declared in a quiet, confident voice, her eyes popping and expecting an affirmative answer.

"Yes, as a matter of fact," replied Pam with a loud sigh of relief.

"But when did all this happen?" asked Bernadette hastily.

"In fact, only last Saturday." This caused arms to go up with such excitement as to produce a series of miniature waves to crash against the side of the pool like waves crashing against a rocky coast. This dramatic theatre within the setting of pool lights attracted the immediate attention of others in and around the pool.

"But how come you didn't let us know Dennis?" asked John with a squint in his eyes. He found it difficult to understand how Dennis could get married without inviting him. "I am sure one of us would have come up to England for the wedding?" Pam simply shrugged her shoulders matter-of-factly and glanced at Dennis for support.

"We wanted to keep it very small and spend the money on a good honeymoon instead," interjected Dennis, with an apologetic grin while sipping on his second rum and coke.

"So, that's why you are here. What a good idea, after all, you have both been married before, so it was nothing new," added Bernadette, beckoning to one of the wine waiters to bring her two bottles of the best champagne in an ice bucket. Within minutes everyone in and around the pool were toasting them. "We wish you both the best of everything," uttered John and Bernadette, hugging them while others plucked flowers from surrounding plants and scattered them in the pool. They were soon enjoying the food and dance of a calypso evening.

"There is nothing like dancing calypso with a warm tropical breeze gently massaging your back and the sparkling eyes of an attractive partner in front of you," said Dennis with a voice loud enough to rise above the din of the steel pans while demonstrating their interpretation of the music. It was in the early hours of the morning when they got back to the apartment probably having lost almost one pound from the profuse perspiring resulting from the combined effect of tropical heat and dancing. It was an evening they had hoped would never end. But Pam went awfully pensive within a few minutes of their arrival. It appeared as though she was reliving an awful experience and that the cold fingers of fear had suddenly clutched her heart. Dennis, perceptive as he always was, spotted this, but thought it better to probe the cause after he had taken a quick shower.

"Is something the matter sweetheart because you have gone awfully quiet?" he inquired lovingly but with some concern.

"It is something that Bernadette said that is a bit worrying."

"Want to talk about it?"

"Do you recall Bernadette saying that she expected some guests from the UK to check in tomorrow?"

"Yes, and what about it?"

"I came here twice with a group to attend carnival and I am thinking that most or all of the group could be here again this year. I wouldn't be surprised to find that some of them could be among those checking in to the Casuarina Resort tomorrow."

"But why is that bothering you, my dear?"

"I am really not too keen on seeing any of them at the moment, because I don't trust them," she replied with a steely look.

"Okay, why don't you tell me all about it tomorrow but right now I think we ought to get a cold drink and go to bed if we are to be fit and ready for the next day," suggested Dennis.

24

Dennis had planned to spare no expense on this honeymoon and had requested all meals to be sent to his balcony on the second floor. It was over breakfast two days later when they were commenting on the sea-view from their balcony. Pam was enjoying a mango when she paused.

"Oh Dennis, we mustn't forget we have a lunch engagement today with Grantly and Evelyn at Neil's plantation," she said quietly, and turned her attention to a glass of golden apple juice, one of the favourite drinks on the island. Grantly and Evelyn were the only two friends in Barbados who knew about their arrival. Grantly had built a large house at Neil's which demonstrated a combination of Caribbean and Western European architecture set in spacious grounds. This was no surprise since they had both lived in England for some time before returning to Barbados as professionals.

"Thanks for reminding me but first, let's go for a stroll along the beach, it is only eight o'clock and Grantly won't be picking us up until twelve." After a short swim in the shallow waters of the Caribbean, they set out on their walk stopping occasionally to collect a seashell or throw smooth pebbles out to sea. They were reflecting on the splendid evening with John, Bernadette and Linda at the Casuarina when a beautiful shell caught her attention forcing her to investigate and probably add to her collection. Dennis gazed at her in her bikini with the mid-morning sun setting her ebony skin aglow and then turned her gently around to face him.

"There is something about you this morning that is indescribably sexy," where upon he drew her closer to him and looked into her dark brown eyes for an extended moment as they shared each other's passion. The sound of ripples taking small shells back to sea provided an appropriate backdrop with temperatures already soaring into the mid-twenties forcing them to take advantage of two lounge chairs with umbrellas by the pool.

"I do like Bernadette. She seems to be a very nice person," exclaimed Pam while Dennis made sure she was adequately covered in sun tan lotion as she laid face down on the chair. He suddenly paused. Something had caught his attention. Pam raised her head slightly and glanced at him to find out the reason for the sudden pause.

"What are you looking at?"

"There are three black chaps standing at the bar over there and, from their accent, I am sure two are from England and one from USA. And from the way they are chatting, they seem to know each other quite well," he replied, his eyes still focussed on the group of three. Unknown to Pam, Sidney was in Barbados on a business trip which he had planned to coincide with carnival week. He was on his way to Speightstown with two colleagues when he decided to pull into the Coral Reef Resort for a cold beer. Pam returned to her former position but suddenly, butterflies were in her stomach. She knew that Sidney never missed carnival and wondered if the American accent could by chance be his.

"I am really looking forward to lunch with Grantley and Bernadette today," she uttered to divert the conversation. '*If it is Sidney, I don't want him to see me now. This is neither the time nor place,*' she thought. But mentioning Grantly's name again, jogged Dennis' memory. He rose hastily from his chair with a pensive look while tapping his forehead.

"Oh dear, I just remembered. I wonder if I have that document for Grantly. You know the one," he uttered, looking slightly anxious. "I think I better quickly run back to the apartment and check. I won't be long. You'll be okay." He placed his drink on the table beside Pam and was on his way when the mixture of English, American and Barbadian accents at the bar caused him to pause for a moment for further investigation.

"Hello chaps, here for carnival?" was Dennis' opening line delivered with something between a grin and a smile. But the way the bar-tender poured the beer into three glasses with his eyes roaming suggested to Dennis he knew Sidney and the kind of man he was.

"These two are, but I am here on business," piped up the American who glanced covertly over Dennis' shoulder and allowed his eyes to settle on the woman on the lounger by the pool. The woman in the bikini by the pool had suddenly gripped his attention. This became evident to the others, including Dennis, when Sidney found it difficult to remain focused on the conversation going on at the time. Greetings over, Dennis was soon on his way to the apartment. Sidney was not the kind of man who would miss an opportunity to get closer to an attractive woman, especially as he was beginning to make a name in clothing. It was therefore no surprise to his friends when they saw he wanted to investigate further.

"That face looks familiar. Can it be ...?" he muttered, causing his two colleagues to look in the same direction for a little while.

"If it is the woman in the recliner near the pool wearing a light floppy straw hat with a pair of designer shades, she is a real stunner and worthy of further investigation," remarked one of his friends quietly while gazing at Sidney with a goading smile. That was enough to trigger him into action. '*If this is who I think it is, it might be my lucky day and to think that, had I not pulled in for a cool drink, I would have missed her,*' he thought, while making his approach with the stealth of a panther. Even before seeing her face, he knew it was Pam, but he also knew that he had very little time to make an impact.

"Hello Pam, fancy meeting you here. Are you on your own?" tumbled anxiously and speedily out of his mouth. His voice was a combination of surprise and seduction particularly as this was his first glance of her in a bikini. She put her fruit cocktail on the table and slowly removed her sunglasses. It was as though she had seen a ghost for he had reappeared again. Sidney adjusted the umbrella to shade her face and pulled up a chair. She knew it had to be a brief encounter for Dennis could be back at any time.

"No, I am on my honeymoon," she snapped. "What do you want now? Have you not caused enough trouble? I had a feeling you might be on the island because you never miss carnival. Anyway, what the hell are you doing here at this hotel? Are you stalking me?" The muted words left her lips hastily and with anxiety for she knew Dennis would be back any moment. Sidney looked briefly toward the bar to find his friends were enjoying the show which they knew had all the hallmarks of ending with a bang if he was caught.

"Did you say honeymoon? You mean to say you got married since I last saw you?" he asked in an undertone and with a look of surprise.

"What is it to do with you after the way you treated me at the Notting Hill Carnival?" was the sharp retort from her lips. "Did you expect me to wait around for you while you were carry on with Jean and whoever else? Why don't you go to Jean, she is the one that has the *hots* for you? But it would take more than you with your deceit and Jean consumed with jealousy and revenge, to prevent me from getting what I wanted," she replied, her eyes blazing at him as she spoke. He nodded momentarily unable to respond. But his mere presence had thrown her off guard and destabilised her.

"And where is your husband?" he asked hastily while scanning movement in and around the pool.

"He just popped back to the apartment to check on something. Anyway, you better go because my husband will be back any moment now." She looked very anxious and uneasy but, lucky for them, Dennis had met another old friend from England on his way to the apartment and was delayed for some time.

"Look Pam," he said anxiously and hoping that Dennis' brief departure would never end, "I am here just for a few days on business. Since last I saw you, I started a new clothing line in Boston and it's doing quite well. My offer still stands. Why don't you join me?" He implored. He had promised he would be willing to have her in America at any time. Pam sat up, replaced her sunglasses and took a few more sips of fruit punch.

"What? You expect me to give up my job and my husband to go with you?" She looked horrified and shocked, but Sidney saw this as a chance to use his financial success as a lever to take up where they had left off.

"What does it matter? You can make a lot more than you are paid in your job at the moment and you'll be working for yourself. So how about it?" He hoped that, by dangling such a carrot, she would be lured into joining him and others in his den. This set her brain in motion. *'This sounds very appealing, but how do I know it will work?'* she began to think. It was the sound of a jet-ski that broke her concentration to see a waiter arriving with a fruit punch for her. Sidney had signalled him to do so. But Sidney's words were beginning to have a destabilising effect on the marriage in its infancy.

"I just got married and you expect me to leave my husband just like that and go off with you? I think you better go before he comes back," she said, railing at him. And yet there was something telling her it might not be a bad idea to take up his offer. She was now totally confused. It was not the kind of thing you would expect of a woman who had just got married.

"I'll tell you what, think about it and let me know soon." He gave her his card and hurriedly made his way back to the bar and was able to have another but closer look at Dennis as he returned to Pam by the pool. *'He doesn't look like the kind of person to compete with me. Married or not, I can get her,'* he said to himself, and he convinced himself that he could. Pam and Dennis had been together for three years prior to their marriage, and their bond to each other had strengthened with every passing moment. Nevertheless, Sidney had sown an idea in her mind and he had fired a shot across the bow of the nuptial ship. His sole aim now was to wreck it.

Grantley picked them up at noon as promised that day. The idea was to have some time before lunch to walk around the grounds and view his garden. They strolled around admiring the plants, pausing occasionally to focus on a rose or ginger lily. Pam plucked a hibiscus, twirled it between her fingers and looked at Dennis longingly. Something told him the homeland was beckoning to her.

"You know Dennis, we ought to think of getting some kind of property here," she said matter-of-factly, and Dennis cast a surprising glance at her because he also had a similar idea but had not yet found chance to air it.

"What brought that on now my dear?" his eyes focused on yellow and red ripe mangoes hanging in a tree not too far away. Pam plucked another flower, this time a wild flower from the hedge and stuck it in her hair. It seemed as though Sidney's suggestion was buzzing around in her head causing a degree of mental conflict.

"I just think we could buy or build something and put it in the hands of an agent for the tourist industry. That way we could come here when it is not occupied," she said, levelling her eyes with his. She thought it was a way of diverting her thoughts from Sidney.

"I think that's a good idea, but we'll have to give it a lot of thought." She knew that, with an answer like that, there was a good chance of realizing her dreams though not too soon. The conversation was only broken when they were called to lunch by Evelyn.

25

After breakfast next morning as usual, they strolled together on the beach allowing the water to wash over their bare feet.

"I don't mind spending some time in town tomorrow, what do you think?" she uttered, looking up at him. Dennis gathered five smooth pebbles and threw them as far as possible out to sea. He said nothing for a few moments. He had again noticed something was bothering Pam since he met that group of three two days ago. It was as though she was again holding back something.

"That's a good idea so I'll order a cab," he replied, feigning all was well. Within 40 minutes they were alighting at the upper end of Broad Street not far from parliament building.

"Oh, I've forgotten my sun hat in the apartment," she cried. It was a necessity in the hot tropical noon-day sun. "I'll just nip into one of these shops and get one." She soon emerged a few minutes later wearing a new broad-rimed straw hat which, with her sun glasses, red boob-tube, A-line floral Caribbean skirt and white sandals, presented a picture strong enough to create a vortex of desire in any man, including Dennis. It was a picture enhanced by a background of small yachts and boats rising and falling gently in the marina as though to the chimes of the big clock on the parliament building nearby.

"Let's take a quiet walk along Broad Street, we might see something we want to take back or even run into someone we know," he suggested, while ensuring that his sun-hat was well positioned. They knew it was customary among locals to meet friends on the pavement in front of

Harrison's or Cave Shepherd, two major department stores in Bridgetown at that time. They would stop occasionally to say 'hello' to any face which seemed slightly familiar to them or to seek shade beneath any shop awning that provided a modicum of relief from a mid-morning sun beating down mercilessly on animate and inanimate objects alike.

"Isn't it amazing how, although we were born here, this tropical heat still forces us to make the occasional dash for the nearest cold drinks outlet," exclaimed Dennis and Pam agreed with a giggle.

"But have you also noticed how, like tourists, we too find it enjoyable meandering in and out of shops that beckon with their assortment of colourful Caribbean garments and locally produced handcrafts all aimed at tourists?" added Pam with a measure of excitement. Soon it was lunchtime and an occasion to settle down to a light lunch in a restaurant on the second floor of one of the large department stores on Broad Street. Sitting by a window overlooking the street to take advantage of any cooling breeze, they indulged themselves with fried flying fish, rice and peas and pumpkin fritters washed down with a cold lemonade. It was the kind of dish they had not tasted for years. From here, they had a commanding view of the drama played out below amidst the jostle and jumble of cars, cyclists and pedestrians all competing for every available space, and all this to the accompaniment of tooting-horns and ringing-bells as each one signalled their approach. But, in spite of the busy hubbub below, Dennis' mind soared well above the din below. He wanted to do something which he hoped would pay off.

'Now that I am here, I wonder if I can see Reeta my old girlfriend. I don't mind introducing her to Pam,' he thought quietly to himself, as he made his way through his second fried flying fish. Dennis and Reeta had both attended the same secondary school at the same time. Dennis and Reeta had not seen each other for more than ten years and he was anxious to see how she was doing. He had learned that she was working in the Ministry of Health in a building not from where they were having lunch. Amidst the thoughts that played on his mind, one stood out. *'Should I take Pam to meet Reeta in her office or should I ask Reeta to meet us somewhere? More to the point, should I really*

get them to meet each other?' He had a sip of his chilled beer and looked appealingly into her eyes.

"Pam, I have a good friend whom I knew from school days. I understand she works for the Ministry of Health in a building not far from here. Would you mind very much if I just pop over to her office and say hello. She has been a good friend from school days?" He stopped short of telling her she was his first girlfriend. Nothing was said for a little while because Pam was also taken in by what was going on in the street below. Till then, she had never had the opportunity of such a view from above.

"Ooooh (drawing the word out for some time), is she one of your old girlfriends?" she asked, gazing firmly in his eyes for any expression that would give him away. It was a look that eventually developed into a kind of 'permission-granted' chuckle. "Of course, and I wouldn't mind seeing her myself if only to weigh up my likely competitor, so why not bring here and let me see her or are you scared?" she suggested, teasing him with a tired smile. By now, the beer in his glass was reduced by half in his build up to the request. At that moment, her head made a ninety degree turn to the left to reveal a look tinted with a hint of suspicion. She leaned back fully in her chair while shaking the ice in her glass producing a tingly sound all of which took place throughout one of her seductive smiles.

"Ok, I will find out what she prefers. In the meantime, have whatever you want to drink, I'll soon be back." Dennis was relieved that Pam had seen the whole thing matter-of-factly. She moved to another spot on the balcony to get a better view of him meandering his way through the pedestrians and traffic below before disappearing in the distance. This gave her time for her brain to meander as well. *'I wonder if he will be lured back to his school-days sweetheart. I have never heard him say anything about her. Oh, come on Pam, stop being so stupid.'* Dennis quickly rushed up three flights of stairs to Reeta's office. Reeta was petite but highly intelligent. She was also very docile and preferred to display her feelings through actions rather than words. Her personality was such that you would want her to be your friend which meant she had a large friendship group of similar thinking. It was as though she was expecting him for his entrance saw her seemingly catapulted in his direction to greet him with a hug and a kiss. It was the kind that drew the immediate attention and astonishment of all her other colleagues on the floor and would certainly have elicited a modicum of jealousy from Pam had she been present.

"Oh Dennis, so nice to see you again after so many years, how long is it?" exclaimed Reeta, looking up at him with a smile enhanced by her dark eyebrows on a very light-coloured skin.

"About twelve years, I would say. Anyway, how are you? You look well…still the same beautiful Reeta," he declared, allowing his eyes to roam over her body aimlessly but with a measure of subtlety. The intervening years had made no visible impact on her body nor had the passage of time minimised that gravitational pull in her looks. A ripple of wonderment crept slowly across the faces of the six girls whom she supervised accompanied by a wave of whispering sweeping across the floor.

"Oh, I have never seen her do that before to anyone else, and we know she already has a boyfriend," whispered one of the girls causing a muted giggle to sweep across the floor like a soft breeze stealing its way through a slightly opened window. "Who is this chap that has suddenly brought her so much excitement," asked another who had concluded that, from his accent, he had to be living in England. Reeta was completely oblivious to this for, as she and Dennis gazed into each other's eyes, memories of their school-day friendship came flooding back.

"When did you arrive?"

"Last Saturday," with a slight expression of guilt.

"And you waited until now to come and see me?" she said with narrowed eyes. "By the way, I heard that you broke up with your wife. What was her name again?"

"Susan."

"But is it true that you have divorced?"

"Yes. Sometimes these things do happen," he replied, now seated in a chair next to her desk and responding to the occasional 'hello' from her colleagues still anxious to find out who he was and what was going on.

"So, who is on the scene now?" asked Reeta quietly but with an inquisitive voice. Dennis looked at her with the kind of expression that answered her question.

"Well in fact, apart from wanting to see you, that is another reason I am here. I have met someone since and I would………" He looked coy as he said it but, before he could finish, Reeta hastily interrupted.

"Is she here with you?"

"Yes."

"Why haven't you brought her along? Where have you left here?" and she looked rather annoyed as she spoke.

"She is in a restaurant in lower Broad Street. I had to be sure you would want to meet her. I didn't want to take any chances."

"Don't be silly, just bring the woman and let me see her. I want to see if you still have good taste. Better still, I am going to lunch in the next fifteen minutes, why don't you all meet me at the head of the High Street near the square in about twenty minutes."

"I am sorry, but we just had lunch," Dennis pointed out regretfully.

"Then meet me there tomorrow, I will take you both to lunch."

"Okay, we'll be there." Dennis quickly returned to find Pam finishing a second glass of coconut punch. Her eyes shone as she jerked her head back to hear the news.

"Well, how did it go?" she inquired anxiously with a searching tone.

"It was alright. She was glad to see me and was rather annoyed that I didn't bring you along. In fact, she wants to take us to lunch tomorrow but we must meet her near the square not far from where we got out of the taxi this morning at the head of Broad Street."

"That's nice of her," remarked Pam as they made their way down the stairs. Next day, they strolled leisurely up the other side of Broad Street which offered greater protection from the noon-day sun, arriving at the agreed meeting point a few minutes early. Pam's roaming eyes came to a sudden stop and her brow became furrowed.

"Is that Reeta over there in the near distance coming to us Dennis?" pointing to a young woman crossing Trafalgar Square and coming in their direction with a smile made more pronounced by her large brown eyes and dangling silver ear-rings, the kind of characteristics she knew would satisfy Dennis' taste.

TROPICAL HEATWAVE

"Where," he asked, looking around frantically and wondering how she could have spotted Reeta before him. "Yes, but how did you know it was Reeta?"

"Dennis, I know your taste," and they both chuckled. "She is looking in this direction and she fitted the image of the kind of girl I thought you would have as a girl-friend," replied Pam, feeling very satisfied that she was so perceptive. But before Dennis could go any further into the investigation over Pam's observation, Reeta was extending her hands to greet Pam. They exchanged greetings, salutations and pleasantries without Dennis having to say a word. It was as though he was not there, so elated with joy were the two women to see each other. A look of satisfaction and relief crept across Dennis' face, a reflection of his delight. Then, as though they had suddenly remembered Dennis was there, Reeta turned and glared at him.

"But Dennis, you are a joker. How could you leave this young woman in a restaurant instead of bringing her to see me straight away?" Reeta was petite but spoke with a lot of authority. Perhaps it was a spin-off from her management role. Perhaps it dated back to her days at secondary school where she was always well organised: hair well-groomed and uniform in top shape. In fact, even books in her school bag were positioned in an orderly manner. Dennis just shrugged his shoulders matter-of-factly with an awkward grin.

"I wasn't too sure how you would have taken it," said Dennis breezily but feeling awkward. This triggered Pam into one of her contagious giggles suggesting she had seen the funny side of things.

"What do you mean by 'how I would have taken it' Dennis?" exclaimed Reeta with narrowing eyes before making a forty-five degree turn to face Pam. "Listen Pam, we were friends from schooldays. Okay, he was my first boyfriend and I believe I was his first girlfriend and I loved him. In fact, I believe I still do," she declared with a soft chuckle, "but that was a long time ago and lots have happened since then. For instance, he got married, divorced and has now found you. I was never married, but I too have a boyfriend and I hope to be married very soon." *'Thank heavens for that. Nice to know she has a boyfriend. That will set Pam's heart at rest, I hope,'* thought Dennis quietly to himself.

241

"Oh, he didn't tell me you were his first girlfriend," piped up Pam, bursting out in laughter and joined by Reeta who obviously had also seen the funny side of things. Dennis sensed, from Reeta's words and body language, that she was happy he had found someone more in tune with him than his previous wife whom she knew and always believed the marriage would never have lasted.

"Anyway, you have done well here my boy," uttered Reeta and, after a few more pleasant digs at Dennis, leaving him feeling they were ganging up on him, she invited them to her house for supper the next day. Introductions and conversation finished, the little group of three was about to break up when Pam spotted a hand waving at them from the other side of the street. It was a wave that Dennis had already seen but was quietly trying to ignore. He had an idea of the likely outcome should the person be asked to join them.

"Who is that woman over there waving at us, Dennis?" asked Pam, forcing Reeta to turn and look, and on seeing who it was, let out a stifled groan between clenched teeth.

"Oh, it is that silly woman Violet. How did she know you all were here Dennis?" asked Reeta whose expression immediately changed to steel. But before he could answer, Violet had crossed the street and joined the group of three. He knew who it was all along but was very reluctant to have her company at that present time. They both knew she was always a trouble maker. Reeta's face suddenly hardened and her eyes looked like bottomless pits of regret. Violet was the last of four girls, two of whom were going out with Dennis' two older brothers and always thought she, rather than Reeta, had the right to have Dennis as her boyfriend from the time they were all at school together. Violet therefore did everything to disrupt the friendship between Reeta and Dennis at school. Violet was short and chubby and was fast becoming more rotund. She too was highly intelligent, although very pugnacious, one who thought her way was always the correct one and would go out of her way to prove it. In short, she had a large ego.

Dennis was a high achiever throughout school and had become head prefect, the kind of position that attracted some of the more attractive girls. Violet had the notion that she could compete with Reeta for Dennis and was quite prepared to do everything it took

TROPICAL HEATWAVE

to gain his friendship, even physical combat if it came to that. Unfortunately, he was never interested, and she never forgave him for that. As a result, she was always in search of revenge and, seeing Reeta in Dennis' company again even after twelve years, rekindled that revenge.

Violet hurriedly introduced herself to Pam and, completely ignoring Reeta, she allowed her eyes to dart quickly between Pam and Dennis before taking a deep inhale of air heaving her well-endowed bosom to its maximum. Beads of perspiration popping out on her dark skin forced her to mop her brow before directing her attention to Pam.

"Are you married to this man?" she asked, looking at Dennis and Reeta with contempt, anger and revenge burning in her eyes. Pam read the situation quickly and correctly and held an unshakeable calm. Without any preamble, Violet immediately launched a vicious verbal attack on Dennis with the sole purpose of discrediting him in the presence of Pam.

"Don't you know....?" she said, followed by a pause and an audible intake of breath as she focused her eyes on Pam.

"Don't I know what?" interjected Pam in a calm and dignified manner.

"This one here," pointing to Reeta with contempt, "thought she owned him at school. She even had the guts to take him away from one of her own cousins. He never thought me good enough because of her," she exclaimed, pointing to Reeta again. She wanted to be the one to have the head prefect as her boyfriend.

"And what's that to do with me," asked Pam, looking more and more horrified at such behaviour.

"What is it to do with you?" asked Violet rhetorically. "This man is no good. He played around with others even with his first wife and I know some of those who were stupid enough to fall for him. He almost broke Judy's heart when he left for England without telling her and this was a girl from Lakes village with whom he was going out well before he was married and continued to see her after he was married. And as for this one here," pointing disdainfully at Reeta, "she thought she owned him," she bellowed, her voice rising a couple of decibels.

"Really, why are you telling me this? Is it because you were jealous and still are?" retorted Pam with a kind of under-look.

"If I were you, I would be very careful because he could do a similar thing to you even though you are married to him," she replied. Pam's eyes moved quickly between those of Reeta and Dennis before settling firmly on Violet's with an intensive aggressive glare.

"Listen to me woman. I don't know who you are nor do I want to know, but this is my husband and I am my husband's wife. What went on before is nothing whatever to do with me, so why don't you find someone else on whom to vent your stupidity or better still, find a pool of hot tar and sit in it." This she said inclining her head regally. This boiling cauldron of heated emotions was beginning to attract the attention of a group of passers-by who stopped to have a jaw-dropping look at what was going on. The group of four was now making it rather difficult for others to pass on the narrow side-walk until they were asked to move by a shopkeeper who felt they were blocking the entrance to his shop. Reeta looked at Pam apologetically and gave Violet a scathing look, anger now roiling in her stomach.

"Pay no attention to this silly woman. She was always like that: nasty, jealous and vindictive. It wouldn't surprise you to know that, after the headmaster got her a transfer from our school to Queen's College, she came up to me one day and said she will make sure the he does not get me a similar transfer. I often wondered why she could say that. She is just a b….," declared Reeta, now steamed up.

"As for you," snapped Violet glaring at Reeta, "you always thought you were the queen and did all you could to keep me away from him and you are still doing it even now." Eventually, Reeta broke her silence.

"Why don't you shove off and look for your own kind," she retorted railing at her. Pam tried to remain as calm as possible throughout this, preferring not to be drawn into what appeared to be an outburst by a rather frustrated woman who was still engulfed in a revenge grail started in her schooldays. Pam was in no mood for a street brawl. She had worked out that Violet was a jealous woman who had not only made it difficult in the past for Reeta but was now bent on derailing their marriage to get back at Dennis. Reeta refocused her eyes on Violet.

"I really thought you had grown up by now, but I was wrong. You were always a disgrace and you still are." The heat of the day, when combined with the heat of this verbal explosion, seemed to drive the temperature up forcing Reeta, Pam and Dennis to seek shade and leave the scene to Violet who continued to shout at the top of her voice.

The situation was made even worse when, two days later, Pam and Violet met by chance at the same hairdresser's where she continued to press home the matter in a less explosive but pugnacious manner. And even though Dennis later put his side of the story to Pam who wanted to believe him, Violet had somehow succeeded in sowing seeds of doubt in her mind. '*What if she is true and how do I know he wouldn't one day do a similar thing to me even though we are now married. I wish I could do something to put it to the test. Perhaps I am more confused now than ever,*' she pondered while her head was under the drier. But would all this, combined with a future in USA, be enough to tip the balance in favour of joining Sidney in Boston?

26

It was just after ten the following night when Pam and Dennis headed for *After Dark,* a nightclub in St. Lawrence Gap and a favourite haunt for visitors to Barbados. Here, you danced all night under dim lights to a variety of music. They were in close embrace, cheek to cheek, muscles moving in harmony to the rhythm of late-night music when Pam suddenly lifted her head from his chest. '*No, it can't be,*' she said to herself, wanting to disbelieve what her eyes were telling her. Over Dennis' shoulder, and through the dim lights, she had spotted in the distance something, someone. An eerily silence gripped her. She looked at Dennis with glazed eyes. Tension flashed between them like lightning between positive and negative charges in a thunder cloud. They continued dancing, but Pam seemed suddenly to be on auto-pilot. She knew it was that re-appearing Sidney.

"Darling, are you okay?" and he sounded concerned. Through the revellers in the dim light was a figure snaking its way slowly but purposefully in their direction. Recognising something had changed, Dennis made a swift ninety degrees turn. His eyes immediately pierced the dark to focus on someone he had seen somewhere before, someone he had seen in the bar at Coral Reef Resort one mid-morning. He could feel her grip loosening. Her hands got clammy. She started to sweat. Her breathing got shorter.

"Yes, I am alright," she replied, but seemingly overwhelmed with panic, and he could feel the tension building up in her to the point where she could bear it no longer. She avoided Dennis' eyes. "Could you excuse me for a moment Dennis, I wouldn't be long." There was terror in her voice. He allowed his arms to drop loosely from around her waist seeing that she was determined to go in the direction of the approaching object. Now out of Dennis' vision, Sidney and Pam hurried to a table in a more secluded part of the dance hall. Realising he had limited time, Sidney quickly ordered a couple of drinks.

"Hello Pam, so we meet again," he said with a broad grin expressing a feeling of superiority and, as he saw it, victory. He had met Dennis in the bar at the Coral Reef Resort and was convinced he could depose him easily. Such was his ego.

"What the hell are you doing here?" She snapped with fear gripping at her heart, "are you still stalking me? You seem determined to break up my marriage even on my honeymoon. I thought we agreed to speak on the phone only." Her voice was hardly audible above the din. She looked very surprised and on edge as her penetrating eyes hurriedly scanned the dimly lit room in search of Dennis who had also allowed his eyes to meander between sweaty gyrating bodies and settle on them. Dennis was not a confrontational person although it must have taken quite a lot to see the woman he had just married wonder off to another man before his very eyes. Being optimistic, he assumed she wanted to lay a re-appearing ghost to rest once and for all. Of course, only time would tell.

"But Pam, this is a joint frequented by almost everyone visiting Barbados. What makes you think I would be different? And by the way, have you given any thought to my proposition, because it still stands?" He obviously had reason to believe that, if she was bold enough to break off a dance with her husband to come to him, he was on a winning roll.

"You seem bent on getting me into trouble. Can't you understand I am married?" This she said in a raw voice while looking in the direction where she thought Dennis would be. He was not there. He had vanished. To what part of the dance hall she knew not. Her heart stepped up a beat amidst rising waves of panic. *'I wonder if he has moved to a place where he can more easily see us and, perhaps, hear what we are saying,'* she pondered now getting extremely anxious. She was late. Dennis had already seen them but had opted to trust her and instead go to the bar.

"So, what? Because you are now married, that doesn't mean I love you any less," retorted Sidney, stretching across the table to fondle her fingers which she quickly withdrew.

"Look, I must go back now before Dennis suspects anything. I'll get in touch." Pam made her way hurriedly through the tightly packed dancers to find Dennis at the bar in deep conversation with a woman, an attractive young dame from Trinidad. Their facial expressions and body language sent an uneasy message to Pam as she approached to find Dennis making a serious move on the woman who was keen to play the game. Dennis had concluded that, since Pam had the guts to flirt in his presence even on their honeymoon, then he could do likewise. Pam's mind was now plunged into deeper confusion. It became a battleground for thoughts on which the rest of her life could depend. *'Should I go for a man whom I am still not too sure loves me but has offered me a chance to join him in his business or should I stick with Dennis whom I know I love, a man who has already shown he loves me but one in whom I now have some doubts.'* These were some of the thoughts burning deeply on her mind while making her way to the bar. But, as she replayed a mental vision of scenes associated with the above thoughts, one thought superseded all others. It was the re-assurance and encouragement her cousin Linda had given her at the Casuarina Resort.

"I can see you are enjoying yourself, Dennis," she said in a rather sarcastic manner, her eyes boring into the young woman's. Dennis detected a hint of jealousy in her voice, for the girl was as attractive as she and the positions had now changed. Dennis was now the one openly pursued in the presence of his wife. After appearing not to notice her, he eventually turned with a half-empty bottle of beer in his hand while sitting on a high stool with one leg touching the floor.

"Oh, it's you, fancy seeing you here. This is a very nice young woman I saw sitting alone at the bar, so I joined her. We were just having a chat over a couple of beers until we were rudely interrupted. After all, you were otherwise engaged, weren't you?" He topped up his glass with the remainder of his beer and Pam managed a wobbly smile. *'Am I under threat from a rank outside or am I being sent a message?'* she asked herself.

"Don't talk wet. Come on let's go back to the apartment," she suggested, now having had her feathers ruffled and, there was no doubt in her mind that, from the looks of the girl, she could be a serious competitor.

"Begging your pardon, but I must finish my drink with this attractive young lady. You see, I didn't interrupt you, did I?" They were now goading each other like wildcats. The young woman at the bar turned and levelled her eyes with Pam's.

"Why should he? We are having a great time and we were just about to have a dance." Pam sent her a blazing look with penetrating eyes.

"If I were you, I would shut up and go away while you are still ahead because, should this go any further, neither of us know how it may end," admonished Pam, with eyes like steel. The situation had all the ingredients of a violent outburst of words if not physical combat. Dennis finished his beer, thanked the woman for her company and slammed out with Pam in tow. They reached the apartment about 1:30 am. Not much was said. This worried Pam. *'Why is he taking it so calmly? Why hasn't he questioned me about Sidney?'* was the thought dominating her mind all night. Next morning, he joined some of the locals for an early morning jog on the beach and, after a shower, sat quietly in pensive mood looking out to sea. It was a scene reminiscent of that experienced on the honeymoon in Bathsheba with his first wife, when the marriage was already on the rocks before it had even started.

"How about breakfast in the open-air beach restaurant this morning?" he asked and was met with approval. The sea had already given up its turquoise look and adopted the colour of the blue sky. Sparkling under a bright sun, miniature waves were lapping softly against the stone foundation of the restaurant. In the distance four small anchored yachts swayed gently with the rise and fall of passing waves. Pam saw this calming surrounding as a perfect setting to explain the happenings of the night before. She tried to convince Dennis that she was merely trying to get Sidney from off her back from following her around and pestering her. Dennis did not respond for a long moment, preferring to listen.

"Who is this Sidney fellow anyway? Is he the Sidney you met at one of Jean's parties, the same one that caused the break-up between you and her?" asked Dennis with an under look.

"Yes," she replied looking rather sheepishly and avoiding his eyes as she said it.

"What was he doing there last night and how did he know you would be there? He glared at her and looked rather disappointed and hurt as he sliced a piece of water melon. But just then his brain went into fast rewind and a set of recent images came flashing back to him. '*I am sure he was one of those men I spoke to at the bar that morning on my way up to the apartment to check on something for Grantly*', he said to himself. Now putting two and two together he concluded that he was gone long enough to allow this Sidney fellow to make a move on his wife that morning. "Did he approach you when I went back to the apartment that morning?"

"Yes." Pam's eyes looked glazed. Her hand was shaking as she held the cup.

"Didn't you tell him that you are married and that I am your husband?" A sharp side glance with a squint suggested he didn't believe a word she was saying.

"Yes, I told him all of that, but he still seemed determined to make himself a damn nuisance."

"Yes, but that does not answer how he knew you were going to be at *After Dark*, does it?"

"Please believe me Dennis when I say it was sheer coincidence. People go where ever they want when they come to this island," she declared in a rather beseeching manner. Dennis looked at her as though to say, '*Whom do you think you are kidding?*' He was not amused but, once again, he was prepared to accept her story with great misgivings for, at the back of his mind, was the nagging thought that they had made prior arrangements.

"I think this Sidney fellow is determined to get hold of you and, in so doing, is making it as torrid as possible for me," he declared, sounding very unhappy. Perhaps it was the gentle lapping of the waves on the beach, in conjunction with an excellent breakfast, that eventually calmed everything down allowing Pam to breathe a sigh of relief for a while at least. But could she be trusted any longer?

27

Dennis decided to play things cool for the rest of the honeymoon. He had concluded that, if she wanted to run off with Sidney, there was nothing he could do. The day before they were about to return to England, the resort mini-bus had not long brought them back from some last-minute shopping and they were having tea on the balcony.

"Is there anyone else we have to see before we leave tomorrow?" he asked, topping up both cups.

"Only my sister with whom I had promised to spend one night before we go. She lives in Bank Hall." Except for small waves lapping gently on the beach below, there was a meditating silence. With both feet on the rail and crossed at the ankles, Dennis, in a pensive mood, gazed out to sea at the disappearing west-coast sunset with its golden rays dancing on relatively calm sea. It was probably the kind of thing he needed to help him conceal the pain he was going through. Within seconds, pool lights and those around the grounds were contributing to this calming effect. Without changing his focus, he broke the silence.

"Since we are leaving tomorrow, why don't each of us spend the last night with a friend or relative of our choice, you can go to your sister's and I will go to Grantly's. How about that?" This was music to Pam's ear. She was looking for a way of seeing Sidney for her own reasons.

"Sounds okay with me," replied Pam with a kind of feigned calmness to conceal her inner mood. "I will take my suitcase with me and meet you at the airport at 1:30 pm, if that is okay with you," she added. That met with Dennis' approval, although with a degree of concern which he was at pains to conceal. *'Why is she taking her suitcase. Why can't she come back to the resort for it tomorrow morning like me? It is a 3:30 flight and she has plenty time to do so,'* he said to himself quietly but with a kind of storm spawning in his brain.

"I will go to Grantly's, but I will come back tomorrow after lunch to pay the bill and collect my suitcase and then take the resort mini-bus to the airport. Please make sure you are at the airport, no later than 1:30." Pam immediately asked for an excuse and returned to the room to get her things together. Dennis remained seated and continued to watch the sun about to dip below the horizon, but he had noticed how Pam had raised her eyebrow, seemingly with delight, when he suggested how they could spend the last night on the island. Perhaps it was that, plus knowing that they would not be with each other for the last night, that sparked off a trail of thoughts in Dennis' mind. *'Maybe, that man I saw at the bar that morning and at After Dark night club, is the one Jean told me about at the dinner in Marble Arch. He spoke with an American accent at the bar and he said he was a businessman. Maybe he is the one with the clothing line in Boston who wants Pam to join him.'* Suddenly he felt very alone.

With arrangements in place, a cab took Pam first to her sister's in Bank Hall around 8 pm and then Dennis on to his friend at Neil's Plantation but his brain was still bombarded with worrying thoughts. *'After all I have done, including rescuing her from total disaster at the hands of Elton and putting her in house she could call her own and marrying her, would she do this to me? How can I compete with a man who, according to what Jean told me, is obviously financially better off than me and who seems bent at taking her away, even on our honeymoon?'* These were some of the thoughts burning his mind until he arrived at his friend where they were put to rest, if only momentarily with a rum and coke and coconut water. Meanwhile, on the other side of town, and within twenty minutes of Pam arriving at her sister's, the phone rang.

"It's for you Pam," her sister called out. Pam was putting some finishing touches to her make-up. It was a call she expected.

TROPICAL HEATWAVE

"I wonder who that is calling me!" she said, in a tone pretending she was not expecting a call. It was quite clear to her sister however that the caller knew the number, nor did she ever hear that voice before. This aroused her curiosity.

"How did that person know you were going to be here at this time?" she asked with a rather suspicious look. Pam merely grinned and shrugged her shoulders matter-of-factly. Her sister thought it wise not to probe any further and returned to her TV viewing.

"Hello. Pam speaking," she said softly, while her sister left the room. Pam made sure the bedroom door was closed.

"Look Pam, since it is the last night for both of us on the island, how about going to a club for a few hours? This will give us a chance to discuss our plans a bit more. What do you say?" It was a final attempt to bag the bird.

"Okay, pick me up at 9:00." As she replaced the receiver, she was again bombarded by thoughts similar to those she had before, except that she now wondered if Dennis would trust her any longer. At the club, they danced, drank and continued from where they had left off at *After Dark* that night. Plans for her move to Boston with him the next day were discussed in greater detail. Sidney sounded quite convincing and sincere.

"There is a lot more money to be earned in my business than you can ever earn working for the Ministry of Transport in England. What is more, you'll be free to travel whenever you want to. You like to dress up and you have a good eye for fashion which means you will be able to help me with that side of the business," he explained. This was enough to plunge Pam into mental turmoil. The temptation was great. The rewards looked attractive. *'I like what he is saying but can I trust him? After all, this is the man that made me shame at the carnival and who returned to England without letting me know, and now here he is again trying to convince me to leave my husband and go with him. What do I do? Perhaps if I spend the evening with him I might get the answer. It might give me a chance to find out how I really feel about him.'*

Back at his apartment Sidney convinced himself that she was ready to join him on the flight back to Boston which was due to depart that day two hours after Dennis' flight to London. "I plan to expand the business and would welcome any ideas you have. I am so glad you have seen sense in what I said and have agreed to come back with me. You wouldn't regret it. Taking your suitcase with you to your sister's this evening, was a good idea because you have no reason to go back to the resort," he exclaimed with a pompous look and a feeling of confidence. That night, he took her back to her sister's. "I'll pick you up tomorrow at 1:30 for the airport." Pam had agreed with Dennis to be at the airport no later than 1:30.

"Okay, see you tomorrow."

Next day, just before boarding the minibus, Dennis had time to look back at the hotel with its manicured lawns and dwarf coconut palm dotted here and there and the waves lapping gently on the white sands. He thought of the many wonderful hours they had spent together by the pool, in the bar or just sitting on the balcony admiring the Caribbean sunset with the golden rays shimmering on the water. As the minibus made its way along a slightly curving road up the terraces to the Grantly Adams Highway, he was able to capture, if only for a fleeting moment, the chattel houses and bungalows lining both sides of the route. He also had time to glance at the variety of fruit ripening on trees in small gardens: golden-red mangoes, breadfruit, golden apples high up in the trees as well as sugar-apples, bananas, and pawpaw but to mention a few. The highway took him along harvested cane fields, now bare of sugarcane and brown except where green shoots were bursting forth from recently planted cuttings. Coconut palm, towering high above houses, seemed to wave their branches to the rhythm of a gentle easterly breeze as though to say, *'It was nice having you, have a pleasant flight, please come back soon.'*

But abiding on his mind was that lingering thought: *'I wonder where exactly she is right now. How can I be sure she hasn't been won over by this Sidney fellow and is now planning to disappear for good with him? After all, she has disappeared before so what makes me think she wouldn't do it again?'* It had just gone 12:30 and some city workers were making their way home for lunch, thus increasing traffic on the highway. The reduced speed allowed Dennis a chance to be a moving spectator looking in on a cricket match played in a nearby school grounds. He marvelled at the enthusiasm of the young players each trying to

TROPICAL HEATWAVE

imitate and emulate his favourite star player on the island or West Indies team. Apart from Dennis, a small group of about five senior citizens were the only other spectators was sitting under a tamarind tree shouting instructions while having a cold drink and a smoke. Alas, this snapshot of a living pageantry of history faded out as quickly as it faded in.

And yet, popping up within this theatre of what helped to make Barbados what it is, were disturbing thoughts biting deeply into his mind. He was grappling with the agonizing thought that his love-boat could be wrecked on submerged flat rocks: rocks lying just beneath the surface and known to bring havoc to the unwary or untrained eye. He recalled noticing a slight jumpiness in Pam's actions quite recently, in fact, after the night-club debacle. Although he tried to dismiss it as no cause for great alarm, it was now a matter of great concern. *'I wonder what took place around the pool that morning or what was the real core of the conversation at the nightclub?'* His mind had now become a torrid zone as the minibus eventually speeded up to arrive at the airport within ten minutes. Dennis arrived at the airport with time to spare. While dragging his bag from the car park he accidentally bumped into someone. In the course of offering an apology and with their hands still clasped in the shaking position, a bulb suddenly went on in Dennis' memory store causing him to adopt a more curious look.

"Excuse me, but have I seen you somewhere before?" he asked conversationally.

"Yes, at one of the annual presentation ceremonies given by the Insurance Brokers Association in London. It was there you received one of the highest accolades in insurance," came the reply from a man equally excited to see him after so many years.

"Oh yes, of course. You were the only other black face in the crowd, ah, ah," replied Dennis.

"The name is Denzel and how are you doing?" Dennis apologised for his lapse of memory and Denzel saw the funny side. They deposited themselves on a bench at the entrance to take advantage of the cooling sea-breeze and Dennis thought it a good way to while away the time

255

waiting for Pam. It would also help to ease the concerns he had about Pam, if only momentarily.

"And what are you doing here, Denzel?"

"I came down with a group for carnival and we are going back today. Perhaps you may know some of them because, as an insurance representative, you get to know a lot of people." Dennis nodded his head in quiet approval.

"I am awaiting my wife who is due to be here in the next ten minutes, having spent last night at her sister's."

"Hope you don't mind me asking, but what is her name?" asked Denzel, thinking that he might know her.

"Pam," replied Dennis, hoping that his response might throw some light on the situation.

"The name rings a bell. Is she about five feet eight and can dance well?"

"Yes, how do you know that?"

"I think I was introduced to her last night at a night-club by a friend of mine. His name is Sidney whom I met two years ago on one of my visits to Boston. Do you know him?" he asked feeling rather awkward and suddenly realising he might have unexpectedly put his foot into something.

"Vaguely," replied Dennis, looking coy. A soundless look of sharp pain suddenly gripped him, leaving Denzel feeling uneasy and looking for a way out.

"I can see my group gathering over yonder so I better join them before they think I am not turning up." Dennis remained seated and was reflecting over a cold beer while gazing at departing passengers dragging their luggage to check-in when he suddenly realized it was 1:15 but there was no Pam. Soon it was 1:30 and still no Pam. Anxiety was beginning to step in. Alarm bells started to ring and loudly. *'I wonder if she has decided to take up Sidney's offer and swan off with him after all. I can't believe she is willing to give up that lovely house and a good career for the unknown. And there is a flight leaving for Boston two hours after mine which means there is very little chance of my seeing her again.'*

It was now 1:45 and ten passengers left in the queue. He got himself another cold beer which was in danger of shattering at any moment so tight was his grip on the bottle. He was tense and felt that, by the way some in the group were gazing at him, they knew what was going on. As he paced up and down gritting his teeth in sheer desperation looking for answers, his mind was bombarded with thoughts that whizzed around at the speed of a spin-dryer. Thoughts like: *'Has she been lured away by what Sidney might have dangled before her eyes that morning at the pool or that night in the night-club? After all, he is a successful business man with a line of clothing in Boston, and it would seem, unmarried. A man who travels to Barbados and London at least twice a year as compared with me, a mere teacher and part-time insurance broker. She has disappeared before, how do I know she wouldn't do the same thing again, married or not married?'* These were some of the thoughts that steamrolled his brain. He could only think there was something more to the stories than she had told him. *'How do I know that, while appearing calm on the surface, she was not busy engaging her brain as to the best way of disappearing a second time? How stupid could I get and what a fool to think that Sidney was out of her system?'* He sighed and loudly.

Just then two passengers alighted from a taxi. *'I am sure that is Jean, and the man with her, has to be Elton,'* he muttered. This was quickly followed by three other cabs carrying other members of the group, including Diane. *'Pam was correct because it seems as though the entire group came down again, and it looks as though they are all going back to England today. What a coincidence!'* he thought to himself. Jean quickly disembarked and looked around as though she was in search of someone in particular. Her search was not in vain for, less than forty meters away, was Dennis who was more conspicuous because he was standing on his own. There was no Pam. She had not yet arrived. This did not surprise Jean.

"Why don't I go over and say hello to Dennis, he looks rather lonely over there," Jean suggested to Elton. As she was about to start on her way, Elton gazed at her.

"Now you be careful, I don't want him taking you away from me as well," he growled and then watched Jean make her way across the car park to join Dennis on the forecourt.

"Hello Dennis, I can see you are about to leave, but where is Pam?" she asked with tongue in cheek, her eyes darting here and there in search of a one-time friend. '*I know there is a good chance Sidney is here because he never misses carnival. I think I will hang around a while because, if my thinking is correct, I must see what is going to happen when she arrives, because I am sure the reason she is not here yet is because she is probably with him,*' she thought quietly.

"I am waiting for her. She should have been here already, but I don't know what is holding her up," he said, sounding very dejected, his eyes scanning the entire car park.

"Wasn't she with you last night?" Jean asked cautiously with narrowed eyes. She had learned from a member of the group and a reliable source that Pam was seen dancing with another man at a night club last night. She knew that Pam and Dennis always partied together and thought it strange that Pam should be on her own. Her contact also pointed out that she seemed uneasy, as though not wanting any one from the group to see her.

"No, she spent last night at her sister's and promised to be here no later than 1.30." His eyes moved quickly left and right in search of Pam and Jean joined him in the search, so anxious was she to witness the outcome. '*I believe my thinking is correct. I think Sidney caught up with her last night. The mind boggles,*' she said to herself, seeing it as a good opportunity to give the dagger another twist. She had never forgiven Dennis for not taking her bait when offered at the restaurant in Marble Arch.

"Are you sure she is going back with you Dennis?" she asked slowly, "and how do you know she hasn't met someone here? Where did you say she was last night?" she asked with an angled head and in a tone of voice that was meant to hurt, and it did. '*I am sure she is with him. Now this is something I must see,*' she thought. She was determined to get her own back on Dennis. And, as the rising thermals of tropical heat were causing a mid-afternoon rain cloud in the east to billow higher and higher signalling the onset of a thunder storm, Jean was busy lighting Dennis' fuse for a battle which she was sure would soon take place, if Pam arrived with Sidney. She herself had already lost Sidney and had failed to seize Dennis who was perceptive enough to see through the game she was playing. This short conversion with Jean only served to rev up Dennis' already overheated mind. He was becoming increasingly anxious and, as his brain became flooded with an avalanche of mind-boggling thoughts, rising waves of panic began to show in his eyes as Jean kept up the pressure.

As promised, Sidney collected Pam from her sister's at 1:30. On their way to the airport, Sidney gazed at Pam for an extended moment. His mind was blown for he could not believe that, sitting beside him was the one attractive woman he always wanted, his biggest prize. He was now confident he had netted yet another fish for his tank but, this time, the gold one. He cleared his throat behind a broad grin. Pam remained silent. Not only was she having a last look at that part of the island, there was also a serious conflict of factors and experiences going on in her mind as to the choice she should make.

"You are awfully quiet Pam, you ought to be excited because soon we will be on our way to Boston and a good life," he commented, and she managed a wobbly smile. "I can hardly wait to see your husband's face when we tell him what we are doing. Don't get me wrong, believe me when I say he has my sympathy, for it must be horrifying becoming an ex-husband while on your honeymoon. But of course, some you win and some you lose. This time I would say I am on the winning side, wouldn't you say so Pam?" Pam shrugged her shoulders and kept her cool. She did not want to reveal her feelings. Instead, she threw him a side glance with a half grin.

It was a busy afternoon at the airport for it seemed as though airlines had laid on an extra flight to cope with an increase in the number of tourists returning to the USA and UK from Carnival week in Barbados. In another five minutes, the taxi was pulling into the car park. With thirty minutes now left before the check-in desk was closed, Dennis' heart was thudding. Blood rushed through his veins at the speed of a Japanese bullet train as he continued to scan the car park for any signs of her arrival. Suddenly, the strong afternoon sun from the west bounced off the windscreen of an arriving vehicle forcing him to look in that direction. His eyes, like laser beams, pierced the sunlight to focus on a scene that was his greatest fear. It was a scene for which he was not prepared. The vehicle pulled up. It was a taxi from which first emerged Sidney followed by Pam. '*Oh, no. It isn't – it can't be…*' he quickly said to himself, drifting between disbelief and despair. It rocked him to the core. A sharp pain engulfed his face. It was a scene that sent one thousand volts of shock through his body triggering a speedy mental rewind. *'Did she really go to her sister's or did she spend the night with him? It seems clear to me that, wherever she spent the night, they have planned to leave Barbados together on the same flight, and most certainly not for London, but for Boston which is due to leave two hours after my flight.'*

Jean wished him good luck and quietly retreated into the arms of Elton. She wanted to witness this gladiatorial clash from a safe distance.

Just then, a sharp flash of lightning followed by a heavy clap of thunder, signalled a cloudburst that dumped heavy rain on southern Barbados, including the airport, causing those arriving in the car park to make a mad dash for the forecourt. One could not be blamed for thinking it was a sign of what was about to take place. The cloudburst ended as quickly as it had started, a regular phenomenon in Barbados. Emerging from this cloudburst were Sidney and Pam slowly meandering their way through the crowd on the forecourt toward Dennis. Strangely enough, every sinew in Dennis' body that was once tightened, now seemed to relax slowly. The blood, once racing through his veins at high speed, now sank to a pace suggesting he had already given up. He felt all was now lost and that he would be returning to UK without his newly wedded wife. Or was this the calm before the storm. *'What will my friends and professional colleagues think of me having a marriage that lasted only two weeks, and a wife who was taken from me before my very eyes on our so-called honeymoon? What a good scoop for the newspapers!'* were some of the thoughts racing through his mind? As Sidney and Pam got closer, Dennis kept his calm but already, a group was beginning to form. Word had obviously got around. With his luggage held closely beside him, he was ready to go to the check-in desk when Sidney approached with a grin sufficiently wide as almost to split his broad-nosed features. He was in buoyant mood and full of confidence.

"Hello Dennis, I don't know if you know me, but I think you ought to know that Pam has made up her mind." The words from his mouth were as fierce and painful as the thrust of a dagger. Pam sighed inwardly and remained silent avoiding her eyes meeting Dennis.' She occasionally adopted a blank expression while staring into the distance. The raging thunderstorm though short, had left in its wake an ever-decreasing flow of water to the drains. Perhaps, it was the sound of the water entering such drains that helped to calm Dennis' nerves a bit allowing him to scan the crowd which seemed thirsty for blood. After all, what better than a piece of drama to see you off! He felt very much alone until he saw Reeta, John and Bernadette approaching. They had come to see them off when they spotted Dennis standing like a lonely figure in the centre of a commotion. But their very presence served to enhance courage. He looked at Sidney.

"Made up her mind about what?" he asked, sounding passive and in a polite manner in keeping with his character.

"About you and me," replied Sidney with his head held high. "You see Dennis, Pam has decided to go back to Boston with me this evening. I am sorry you will probably be the only one I know to become an ex-husband on their honeymoon. It is sad you won't be able to see her leave because your flight is two hours before ours. In fact, if you hurry," and he glanced at his watch, "you might still be able to check in on time." Dennis allowed his eyes to wander momentarily among the group which had now grown larger by onlookers who sensed that something was about to or was happening. It was a bit of unexpected free drama that could form a topic of conversation for many days to come.

"Serves you right. You are now getting a taste of what you dished out to me. You never thought I was good enough for you," came a loud shout from the back of the small crowd.

It was aimed at Dennis and came from Violet who was at the airport to receive a relative, but on seeing the commotion thought she would investigate. He knew he was fully supported by Reeta and his other friends but that, given a chance in the current explosive situation, Violet would add to his hurt by continuing where she had left off in upper Broad Street that day. *Right now, I would rather have a repeat of the last thunderstorm than have her join the fray,*' he thought quickly to himself before being interrupted by Sidney.

"I believe Pam wanted to tell you for a long time but probably didn't have the courage to do so. I want you to know that we always felt something for each other and she was always prepared to take up the offer I made. You must have known I was on the scene before you and that it was only a matter of time. It's a pity you had to get married to find that out," and he laughed loudly which signalled to onlookers that the battle had commenced. His words unglued Dennis, the full agony causing him immeasurable pain. And as Sidney spoke, he tilted his chin displaying an element of superiority and arrogance for he was now very confident he was the victor and Dennis the vanquished. Dennis was stunned and remained transfixed to the spot. A storm swirled in his eyes causing him to suddenly pull himself up. Just then, looking at Reeta, he recalled a popular British saying: *when the going gets tough, the tough gets going.* With this in mind, he made two steps forward and looked Sidney firmly in his eyes glare for glare.

"There is a word for people like you which I wouldn't use in the presence of a woman. You destroyed the relationship between Winston and Jean, but you weren't satisfied, oh no, you had to kill our marriage even before it got off the ground. I suppose it's an ego you have to feed, but one day Sidney, yes, one day, someone will also destroy you to satisfy their ego. You see Sidney, things on pedestals have a tendency to wobble and fall." Sidney just grinned sheepishly while Pam stood beside him with a rather blank look, not even an expression of guilt. It was now fifteen minutes before the check-in desk would be closed. Dennis looked at his watch and turned to Pam, his eyes boring into hers.

"And you, this is the way you treat me after all I have done for you. That morning by the pool, that night at the *After Dark* night club, and then staying with him last night under the cover that you were staying at your sister's, were all parts of your grand plan to hurt and destroy me. Why Pam? It wasn't Jean alone who was using the dagger, it was you as well, ably assisted by lover-boy here. But if you want to join his harem, feel free. You suit each other." He delivered this short but hard-hitting speech in a dignified manner even in the face of adversity and he could sense it was well received by all except Elton, Violet, Jean and Sidney. As for Pam, if she did not know before, she knew now that her husband had grit.

"I'm glad you have seen sense, I always thought you would," remarked Sidney with his head now in the clouds and grinning ear-

TROPICAL HEATWAVE

to-ear. Elton, who was merely four meters away overhearing the verbal combat, decided it was time to join the fray, this time with Jean in tow. He looked at Dennis with an intense aggressive glare. It was the first time they had met, and they stared at each other like snarling dogs although not saying a word. For a moment, electrical charges of opposing emotions flashed between them like that from the recent thunderstorm.

"So, you are the Dennis, the man who broke up my marriage," uttered Elton, venom spitting from his tongue, "and you are the man who brought her home late that night, about four years ago. I never *did* believe it when she said she came home by a taxi because I saw her getting out of the car and I am sure it wasn't a taxi. It is clear she thought I was not good enough for her, but I wonder what she thinks of you now, old chap," he blurted trying to finish a bottle of beer before checking in.

"Yes, I am the man that rescued her from the hands of a brute, a monster, and from a fate worse than hell," replied Dennis, now fired up. "But what you don't know is that she would have left you anyway, it was just a matter of time. Lucky for her, I was there to save her at an opportune moment. Unlike you Elton, who took pleasure in serving her a diet of verbal abuse and physical battering, I was able to offer her what you didn't: love, affection, care, understanding and support. And while I am on it, it was because you kicked her under her belly and down the stairs that made her unable to bear a child for me. Why didn't you pick on your kind instead of a defenceless woman whom you supposedly called your wife? You ought to be ashamed and, if I were you, I would look for a dark hole and burry myself in it." He paused, glancing from one face to another. Elton scoffed and let out an exasperating groan.

"What good has it done you," retorted Elton with a chuckle. "Don't you see she has done to you what she did to me? What goes around comes around," he added, this time laughing loudly and looking in search of sympathy from others which he never found. But, seeing that Dennis was now under severe attack from three sides: Elton, Violet and Sidney, Pam gazed directly into Elton's eyes. Perhaps it was Dennis' counter-attack on him that served as a reminder of how

263

much Dennis meant to her and how her life had changed for the better since she met him. But it had also served to make the decision making more complex.

"What I do now is nothing to do with you because, thank heavens, you are no longer in my life, and Dennis is one hundred times the man you can ever be," she declared bluntly, suggesting there was still room in her heart for Dennis, despite what was going on around her. Dennis acknowledged the compliment and nodded but, seeing it was coming perilously close to a physical skirmish, he merely glowered at Elton and dismissed him with a wave of the hand. With all parties now glaring steadfastly at each other, Jean thought it a good time to intervene with her final thrust.

"You see Dennis, I told you so that night at the restaurant. I told you she was quite capable of doing anything, something you found hard to believe," she exclaimed with a kind of *'I told you so'* grin. This statement ruffled Pam's feathers and lit her fuse. She turned slowly, levelled her eyes with Jean's and launched into her with a ferocious verbal onslaught. She exploded.

"That's rich coming from you, bearing in mind you are the person who blew the whistle on Dennis and me, supposedly your good friend, that Sunday morning at Diane's," shouted Pam with a raw voice. Jean immediately glared at Diane who assumed a blank expression. Jean was hoping for her support, but it never came. Instead, Diane avoided her eyes meeting Jean's. "You wanted Sidney who dropped you like a hot cake when he found out what a b....h you are. And when you realised that Dennis didn't care a damn about you, you then stuck your claws into Elton, and you know what, I think you suit each other, so why don't you get out of my life." Jean's jaws dropped like a fast-moving landslide. She was stunned but she was convinced that Diane had squealed on her. The ferocity of this verbal onslaught attracted the attention not only of the rest of the group, but of others, including two patrolling police officers who attempted to dampen the heat coming from this now supercharged boiling cauldron of emotions. Jean's large eyes popped, and she took a large intake of breath expanding her bosom to its fullest. She broke away from Elton and took a few steps closer to Pam who stood her ground.

"You think that, because you now have a job in the Civil Service and can buy better clothes and wear more jewellery, you are better than me. You even boasted to Diane that you can attract a better type of man, and you even managed to break up what Sidney and I had going," she blurted and made a ninety-degree turn to face Dennis standing next to his suitcase. "What you may not know Dennis, is that she was corresponding with Sidney while going out with you. Do you think you can still trust her?" she added, breathing heavily and thinking, *'here you are at the start of a second marriage and I can't even be that lucky to be married once. What do you have that I don't?'* This counter attack destabilised Pam who shot her a scathing look and then went painfully silent. Jean had delivered a very heavy blow, perhaps her heaviest and, consumed by jealousy and revenge, her sole intention now was to hurt and destroy Pam in any way she could.

Jean's remarks triggered a wave of disbelief and mistrust that washed over Dennis. He could feel his blood running cold and, for the second time, he felt alone until he was joined by Reeta, Bernadette and John who admired the manner in which he handled himself in the face of such an onslaught. On the other hand, Sidney saw Jean's counter-attack on Pam as working in his own favour. He was hoping that what Jean said would make Dennis less inclined to put up a fight for Pam, even though she was now his wife. *'This should make my final thrust easier,'* Sidney thought within himself. With this in mind, he intervened in an effort to support Pam but, in doing so, he too found himself at the acid end of Pam's tongue which lashed out like the fangs of a snake.

The air was impregnated with the kind of freshness which follows a tropical torrential downpour but, what was going on around Dennis, paled the recent thunderstorm into insignificance. *'I just want to get aboard that plane and get home even though it means doing so without a wife,'* he muttered to himself. But the very thought of losing Pam was already marking him severely. For him, life without her would be like living in a wasteland. Now deeply hurt and looking vulnerable and sad, Dennis bid his friends goodbye, reached for his luggage and turned to make his way to the check-in desk.

"Not so fast Dennis, just hold on a bit," came a sharp call from behind. Dennis paused and slowly made a one-hundred and eighty degrees turn to find himself looking directly into Pam's face.

"Wait for what Pam, because quite frankly, I don't give a damn anymore what you do. I have a plane to catch," and with a look of hurt and anger, he again turned to make his way toward the check-in desk. This time, Pam quickly freed herself from Sidney's arm and, with very little time left, grabbed her luggage, and hurriedly crossed over to join Dennis who was now caught by surprise. He gazed at her with a terrified expression. This move on the part of Pam caught everyone by surprise. A hush quickly swept throughout the waiting group now very anxious to see how the whole thing would really end. The final call for the flight came over the public-address system, but the group remained unmoved.

"Just wait a few moments, don't be too fast, it's not all over yet," she implored with a beseeching look and an apologetic smile that even then touched his heart. As she held his arm, she could feel pain and hurt radiating from his body. He himself now found it difficult to understand what was going on. The blank expression on his face suggested he was not prepared to listen to what Pam had to say. But with only ten minutes left, Pam put her hand firmly under Dennis' arm and levelled her eyes in Sidney's. Then suddenly, as though charges from the recent lightning had powered her up, the fire inside her came ablaze. She was now super-charged. They both turned and faced Sidney and the others.

"Sidney, do you really think after all you have done, I would be so *stupid* as to leave my husband to go to Boston or anywhere else with you? What do you think I am?" Sidney was stunned. He was hit with a sledge. He stood dumfounded and bewildered by her scorching opening remarks. His ability to speak had suddenly taken leave of him. There was a great divide between his brain and his mouth as he suddenly realised his dashed expectations and tried to feign a calm he did not have. He furrowed his forehead over a pinched face.

"But I thought......" tumbled from his lips, when Pam interjected sharply.

TROPICAL HEATWAVE

"But you thought what?" looking at him with revulsion and fury, her eyes blazing into his. In all those promises you made, you only rang me twice. You know why, because all the time you had Jean in the background. You were just taking me for a ride, building up my hopes. You even had the guts to make me look like a fool in front of Jean at the Notting Hill Carnival and now you seem to think that because you have made it good, you have the power to lure me away from my husband who loves and cares for me, one in whom I can have confidence. How can I trust you Sidney after all you have done? What makes you think you have the right to drag me into your harem? You see Sidney I am not prepared to become one of your chorus girls, or to cheapen myself for you. You wanted me to be a whore just like all the other girls you sleep with, yes, to be one of your bimbos. Take a good look at my husband, he might not have the money you have, but I'll tell you what, he has what you don't have and probably never will: dignity, honesty and he knows how to love and care for a woman and he is sincere, things you find difficult to understand and cope with. You ought to try taking some of those qualities on board some time Sidney. I just wish I had strangled our seeming relationship at birth and ended it even before it started."

The heat, generated by this tug-of-war of love, hate, deceit, betrayal, intrigue and revenge, was enough to provide the aircraft standing on the tarmac with the power to lift off. Sidney was caught off-guard in a cross-fire. An icy blast of horror descended upon him as his confidence tumbled into his boots. Shame engulfed him. He had toppled from his pedestal. A calmness fell slowly on Dennis whose face became twisted in an expression of disgust, as he turned to Sidney with a wry smile.

"Did you hear that, Sidney? The woman has spoken and, as you so rightly said not too long ago, she has made her mind up. It appears one of us has lost, Sidney, and it doesn't seem to be me. Is it you Sidney? You see Sidney, she does not intend to be one of your chorus girls. If I were you, I would keep well away from tropical heat-waves because such heat seems to reduce you to cinders, especially after a tropical thunder storm. You must always remember Sidney that *nothing is over until the fat lady sings.* Try to find out what that means and follow it closely."

It was a jaw-dropping experience for those onlookers who enjoyed the final stages of this drama. Pam grabbed her bag and, with her hand now even more firmly placed under Dennis' arm, said goodbye to Reeta, John, Bernadette and Grantly who had come to see them off. They turned and made their way to the check-in desk with less than six minutes to go and to the last call over the public-address system. Violet, who had initiated the heated episode in upper Broad Street that morning, was there wishing she could lay her hands on Dennis. Within thirty minutes, Dennis and Pam were up and away into the tropical sunset.

As Sidney stood gazing at the plane, his confidence completely dashed, he could only think of what might have been. He really thought he had caught that special fish for his harem fish-tank. Now comfortably settled and on their way, Pam and Dennis had time to reflect on a honeymoon that was bitter-sweet and that resembled nothing less than a tropical heat-wave. It was a honeymoon which had started and ended with a bang. Soon after the in-flight meal, Pam ended one of her responses to Dennis by asking sluggishly while yawning, "why can't the course of true love ever run smoothly. By the way, who was it that said that Dennis? I can't quite remember.........," she asked, and as the words trailed off, she yawned again and drifted into a deep in-flight sleep of sheer exhaustion.

CPSIA information can be obtained
at www.ICGtesting.com
Printed in the USA
LVHW111754140619
621280LV00001B/4/P